I0634138

My War

Norman Friedgut

122,000 words

ISBN 978-0-9841603-0-3

Preface

When my father died at age 86, they said it was from "natural causes." Technically, this meant they couldn't find any specific organ—liver, heart, kidney, to pin his death on. My own opinion is that as time passed and his arthritis grew more severe, he got tired of spending life confined to a wheel chair or propped up in bed with his hands near useless.

Perhaps, too, he was tired of living alone. Not that he ever actually did, there were plenty of grandchildren by the time my mother died, and my sisters were constantly in and out of his house fixing things for him to eat. "Food he barely touched," they confided.

I know he missed my mother, his life-long companion since the war. But she'd been dead for ten years by the time he died, her heart weakened like so many of the displaced by the constant stress during wartime. For she'd grown up in Germany, escaping just in time through France to the Channel Islands only to be trapped there forced into hiding during the German occupation. Surely if he were going to die of loneliness, he'd have passed away ten years earlier, shortly after she did.

"He wants to see you," my sisters had told me repeatedly in the three months preceding his death, but I'd put him and them off for so many years, that I'd say, "Sure thing, this Sunday," automatically and then forget about it when Sunday came.

"Never mind, he just wants to tell you his war stories." My sister Ruby clearly had given up on me when she said this, but for once, my ears perked up. I'd always enjoyed my father's war stories, tales of derring do he'd been telling me since I was five. He'd stopped though when I was in my teens. All right, he'd stopped when I stopped listening, when I wanted to do my own thing, with my friends, not his.

But now he lay in bed, fingers all knotted up with arthritis, as he dictated. "I want you to write down the story of my war, maybe publish it, you think." He looked hopeful. "A tribute to your mother."

I doubted the accuracy of this last, for I knew that for all the devotion he'd shown her, he'd a never-ending stream of other women he'd shown devotion to, at least on a temporary basis.

"So you'll write it down," he repeated eagerly, when he saw the thoughtful look on my face.

"Better than that," I replied from my seat by his hospital bed and whipped out my brand new Dell with its brushed aluminum case that I occasionally polish unnecessarily with my sleeve, 520K RAM, and a 40 MB hard disk. 'Course my ancient Quay 100, 64K RAM, no hard disk, just a 5 1/4" floppy, would have done every bit as well for word processing, but it wouldn't have been as portable or as shiny.

And this is how this book came to be.

1

Book I. The Pilot

Chapter 1. My War

Now, I'm going to tell you about my war, my tiny part of World War II, right from the beginning. Sure, there is a much greater war to write about, with a far broader scope: World War II was fought on every continent but Antarctica. But I wasn't in the desert with Rommel and Montgomery, or on the Russian front when a million Russians died along with several hundred thousand Germans. And I wasn't in the Pacific fighting a constant rear guard action as the Brits fled Singapore, then Burma. Few Canadians were. My war was confined to England, France, Switzerland, and a tiny bit of Spanish airspace over the Pyrenees, and, oh yes, the airfields out at Châteauguay, Quebec and Camp Borden, Ontario where I did my basic. I'll tell you about them, too. And, I'll tell you about the Channel Islands where I met your mother. Claimed by France, these islands were claimed by England also, and, for a few brief unpleasant years, by Germany as well. I lived there twice: once, when I begat you while in a state of near amnesia, and once when I was in charge of the whole shebang.

Chapter 2. A Secular Jew in a Hostile Land

As a Jew growing up in Montreal, my principal memory is of how eager everyone was to remind me that I was a Jew. My uncles, my aunts, and, later, when we'd moved to a more accommodating neighborhood, my playmates. After my parents signed me up at the YM/YWHA (Young Man and Young Women's Hebrew Association), my father so I could learn to box, my mother so I could learn to dance, all my friends were Jewish. Soon, like them, I was an ardent Zionist.

But unlike many of them, I really wasn't much of a Jew, I mean from the religious point of view. My parents, like many of their generation, were secular Jews. That is, they were cultured—dabbled in the arts (abstract paintings on our walls), music (a piano in the living room, which my mother, who'd played for the silent movies, would play for us), literature (good books for them, and for me too, *Tom Sawyer* and *The Prince and the Pauper*), possessed a belief in the future of humanity (while keeping a wary eye on mankind's current behavior), and sprinkled their conversation with a few, a very few, Yiddish expressions.

Like all Jews, they had a near universal anti-Semitism to contend with. What they didn't have was religion.

I wasn't sent to Heder to learn Hebrew until I was 12 (and then only for a brief period as I prepared for my bar mitzvah), nor was I forced to listen to daily passages from the Torah. I had uncles who prayed three times a day, skullcaps on their heads, Tallits over their shoulders, Tefillins on their foreheads and wound round one arm, but my father and my mother, no.

At that time, Montreal had three school systems. These were religious rather than secular as in the States. Catholic schools for the French Canadians where instruction was in French, Catholic schools for the Irish (and a few other English-speaking nationalities), and Protestant schools for the English.

I went to the latter. We didn't have religious classes per se as the Catholic schools did, it was more a matter of atmosphere. I remember walking one morning into my first grade classroom, eager to learn—most first graders are—and being told in a chorus by my fellow students that I couldn't stay, I must go home. "It's a Jewish holiday," they cried. I shook my head, puzzled, what holiday was that? Why had I not been told about it? My classmates led me to the official school calendar, where one might see that two and sometimes three days in a row were marked with the letters j.h. In the current week, only one day, the present one was marked. "It's a Jewish holiday today, see."

I returned home, to my mother's surprise, and informed her that it was a Jewish holiday. "What holiday is it, mom?" She shook her head; she had no idea. "Something to do with the harvest, or maybe the planting, or maybe it has something to do with Torah."

Don't get me wrong; we did observe two of the major religious holidays, sort of— Yom Kippur and Passover—just none of the minor ones. On Yom Kippur both my parents would fast, and, when I was a small child, I would fast too, though it might be only till lunchtime. During Passover, I would play the part of the youngest and only child and be allowed to ask the four questions.

Just as the Jews were a minority within the Protestants, so the Protestants were a minority within the larger Catholic population of Montreal. The exception were certain "cities within the city," largely Protestant communities, where Jews were unwelcome,

Hampstead for one, Mount Royal, and Westmont. (The latter, distinctly upper-class, had just been penetrated by the Bronfman family, bootleggers in the 1920's, who owned Seagram.)

I don't recall being harassed by my classmates because of my religion, nor did I sense any hostility emanating from their parents when I went to play at my classmates' homes. But I knew anti-Semitism was present if only through remarks made by my mother and father.

My contacts with Catholics were oblique. They ran a store, or lived on my street, or, when I was older, they gave me a lift when I was hitchhiking.

Some Catholics were wary, looking for horns. Many a Catholic priest, particularly in rural Quebec, would devote a Sunday sermon to the iniquities of the Jews. Christ killers? It was the Romans for Christ's sake; have those priests no scholarship?

Of course, a Jesuit-educated Catholic would not have made this mistake, but they, too, thought there was something special about the Jew and would always be examining you for signs. Of what I was never sure, and only if they knew you were Jewish.

In my entire life, only one man ever identified me as a Jew and he was newly arrived from Xingjian, the Western-most province of China. He didn't look Chinese, more like a Turk, and explained that this was because he was descended from the raiders of Genghis Kahn as all the Turkamen peoples were. Having told me this, he announced without hesitation, "And you are a Russian Jew."

But as I say, he was the only one to identify me so, apart from my relatives who, of course, knew what I was.

My father had already Anglicized our name twice from its Hebrew origins to Friedgut and then to Freygood, which could have been anything. Norwegian perhaps, wasn't Frey one of their Gods?

I had brown eyes, long eyelashes (when young), and straight dark brown hair. I could have been Irish, or German, or (and this only if you were from Azerbaijan or Xingjian province) a Jew.

When it became evident to one and all that Canada would enter the War as a British ally, the latent French-Canadian anti-Semitism once again emerged.

The reasoning in this instance was rather tortuous. The French-Canadian's ties to Europe were with France. They still felt a strong hostility toward the English, though they'd been living side-by-side with English-speaking Canadians for 400 years. They wanted no part of an alliance with Britain and its Queen. So what if Germany persecuted Jews, the Jews were terrible people (present company excepted). As early as 1939, the government of Quebec informed the Canadian Prime Minister, McKenzie King, that they would resist any draft. And when, very late in the War, the draft was finally instituted, the Mayor of Montreal went to jail for his protests.

But long before this happened, back when war was still just a possibility, I'd already joined the air corps, eager to crush Hitler and, not incidentally, to learn to fly.

4

Chapter 3. Basic Training

In 1937, I was 17, four years older than the Royal Canadian Air Force. I was eager to join the latter, not because I was particularly interested in the military—there was no history of the military in my family, although the uniform was somewhat of an attraction—what would girls think of it?—but because I wanted to fly.

I'd dreamed of flying for years, beginning with those dreams that signal the onset of puberty. In my case, those dreams had become daytime fantasies, and scale models of airplanes, and all the books on flight I could lay my hands on. I could probably have named every major pilot of World War I on the German or British side.

I might well have signed up the instant my final exams were completed had not cooler heads prevailed. "Enlisted is not for you, you want to be an officer." , "A Jewish boy can be a doctor, a lawyer, or a shipping clerk; you wanna be a shipper?" advice that I ignored, and "A pilot has to be an officer," which caught my attention, instantly, though it proved not to be completely true.

"Two years of college, then you can join. That's what it takes." And two years of college was all it did take to be an officer in those days, so off I went to McGill, to take the courses all freshmen had to take, along with as much math and science as I could fit in my schedule.

Now, I'm sure what my uncles had in mind was that with two years of college, I'd want four, then I'd want to study medicine, and by that time I'd have forgotten all about my silly desire to join the military. But by 1939, Hitler had made his intentions clear, to all but Neville Chamberlain, and my uncles were as firm as I in their desire to see me serve my country as they had been that I become a doctor. "Peter will show that Hitler bastard."

With two years of college under my belt, I was having second thoughts—my uncles were right in thinking that the relative independence of a college education would have an appeal for me—but I knew I was a Jew whatever an orthodox rabbi might think of a boy who had barely made it through his bar mitzvah and was seldom to be seen in the synagogue. In fact, once I'd given the matter serious thought, I'd as much desire to shoot down that Hitler bastard as the most patriotic of my uncles.

The Air Force was glad to have me, though it turned out it was for all the wrong reasons. I didn't find this out though until after six weeks of useless drills, and sleeping in a barracks, and wearing ill-fitting uniforms.

Basic training in the Air Force is not much different from basic training in the Army. You even get to carry a pack, though there's not much you can put in it. Your head is shaved, you go to bed when told, you get up when told. You march endlessly. You are inspected. Bloody boring. When do we get to see an airplane?

Basic training was divided into four phases. First was introduction to the service. We filled out numerous forms, uniforms were issued, we received innumerable inoculations, were taught who and when to salute, (rule of thumb: If it moves, salute it; if it is still, white-wash it), and we began our physical training. Plus intensive instruction on how to wear, spit and polish uniform and boots, close order drill (marching at 140 paces per minute), more physical training, introduction to firearms and rank structure, more drill (marching at 160 paces per minute), more physical training.

Phase Two consisted of a classroom introduction to military law, organization and history of the service, military writing, and map reading, plus more drill, firearms, more physical training, and aptitude tests. In the latter, I learned I had the aptitude, if not the willingness, to be a navigator. But more about this later.

As the weeks progressed, we took turns leading the marching drills and calling out the fitness exercises. That is to say, we were given leadership training. Whoopee.

We didn't go up in a plane, but we got to pack and unpack our parachutes. At last, a useful skill. And we practiced jumping off walls into sand, absorbing the shock with our knees.

Phase Three included radio use, aircraft recognition, more physical training (the tired serviceman is the reliable serviceman), parade drill (if it has gray hair, it's at least a squadron leader), and the theory of flight.

An unheralded part of our course required a kid who as an only child had always had his own room to adapt to sharing close quarters with a dozen other smelly males. (We weren't that smelly; a guy who didn't shower often enough got hosed down. A man who snored would be placed under his bunk; a man who wet his bed—it happened—would be ignored.)

My bunk mates consisted of a couple of fellows I'd seen if not known at McGill plus Norman Feldman who because of his name had sat next to me in my college classes and sat next to me in classes now, three Quebecois from the l'Université de Montréal, (thoroughly pissed off once they discovered all our classes were to be in English), a chap from Hull on the western edge of Quebec province, one from The University of Fredericton, one from Dalhousie, and one whose family lived in Montreal but had done his four years of college—yes, a college graduate—at Queens in Ontario. We bunked together, ate together, had classes together, by far too much togetherness. Like being in college (though the classes were more like high school) only you didn't get to go home at the end of the day.

A Phase Four existed too, a flight school located in Camp Borden Ontario, but only if one passed through the previous phases successfully.

All proceeded according to some intricate schedule. We weren't privy to the schedule, of course; this wasn't McGill where you knew that on Monday, Wednesday and Friday from 9:00 to 10:00 am you'd be in English Lit. One did what one was told. One anticipated that someday one would have subordinates who would do what one told them.

As always with the armed services, I did not get to be what I wanted to be. What I wanted to be was be a pilot. What they wanted me to be was a navigator.

Sit in a darkened compartment looking at instruments, playing with a slide rule, when I could be piloting the plane, one with the universe?

"We're desperate for you, people with a solid math background. What good's a bombing mission if we can't reach the target?"

They were impressed it seems by my math courses, math and physics, both. If I'd known in advance that they would be, I'd have studied English Literature. "You want to be a pilot? You'll do what you're bloody well told. Besides, you wear glasses."

"I don't really need them." To prove my point, I immediately removed my glasses and tucked them away in a shirt pocket.

"Thankfully, as a navigator, you're free to use them, bent over your charts and what not."

"I really thought . . . "

"Impressive your math skills. Ideal navigator."

And that as they say was that, at least for the duration of my basic training, much of which was done in the confines of an oversized windowless shell of a plane that never actually got off the ground.

"Navigators really don't need 20–20 vision or windows, you see," a senior instructor reminded me.

My uncles had taught me one thing, (though, because they'd never been in the military, I wonder how they'd learned it): "Never talk back. Do what you're told. Keep your buttons polished." Ok, three things. Still, occasionally in the presence of a superior, I would allow myself a frown as if perplexed. This was one such occasion. "O.K. Freygood, what is it?"

"Will we ever have to help fighter pilots out with their navigation, make our way up and down rivers, chart our course without a map?"

Most training officers might have said, "not your concern," (and most of mine did). But I did have one who was willing to discuss things, (though not the one who'd declared me a navigator). He explained that virtually all fighters were still single-person affairs much as they'd been during the first war. The occasional two-man fighter had been produced in the 1930's; even three-man fighters existed if only in the planning stages. In the latter, a second pilot would occupy the cockpit and man the guns, while the navigator crouched in the back in a kind of half seat. "I'll take you up in one, if you like."

I liked, particularly as I got to sit in the aircraft where the copilot would sit normally, a position from which I watched and tried to memorize every single move the trainer made.

"Where are we now?" he asked, as we were about to turn back. I hadn't a clue for, instead of glorifying in the aerial view that I'd dreamt about for so long, my eyes had virtually never left the controls, except when we were smooth sailing above the clouds with no landmarks in view.

Had I wasted my opportunity? As things turned out three months later, not at all.

No one had mentioned glasses when I enlisted. They were all too happy to have this college boy on board. (The math-physics, I'll bet.) I'd be an officer-cadet with a special insignia on my uniform. Nobody told me that that insignia would mark me to officer and other ranks alike as a wet-behind-the-ears ignoramus.

I suppose my first clue that all was not according to plan came during a week devoted to survival skills. Prior to a late evening hike, part of leadership training, I was handed the maps. Why me? Why couldn't I be leader or equally hapless follower? The navigator, as things turned out, was the one to be blamed, even if I'd told them that it was best to go round rather than up the hill. "Take too long," had said the idiot who was our leader, and we proceeded to get lost immediately.

Not that we were expected to pass all these survival exercises. In some instances we were expected to fail. One particularly twisted instructor—he spent only a brief time with us, thankfully—thought that the best way to teach us we needed to check and double-check our instruments before takeoff was to deliberately give us faulty equipment.

One evening we were sent out on a survival exercise where, unbeknownst to us, our compass has been tampered with. As there was a full moon, we never actually looked at the compass. The instructor was enraged by our failure to do so. Fortunately for him, not us, the skies were overcast two nights later and he again directed the drill sergeant to foul up our compass. Alas, one former member of Baden Powell's Boy Scouts was part of our group, and on noting where the moss grew, he was able to persuade me and several others that our compass was kaput. Not all of us, alas, for when we did show up at the finish minus several of our members, this quick-thinking instructor failed us for "our failure to work together as a team."

Not at all incidentally, the ability to read a map and navigate through the woods at night without benefit of a torch (flashlight) or compass is one every pilot needs to possess. That exercise and the ones in the week following were to save my life many times in all that was to follow. Still the Air Force should have told me earlier in the game, you're not going to be a pilot, boy, you're not going to be a pilot.

As the course progressed, I had the impression that our schedule was undergoing constant revision and that the changes were as much a mystery to our instructors, the noncoms who ran the drills and the officers who provided the classroom instruction, as to us.

I was right, of course. The Canadian Air Force was converting, albeit slowly, from a peacetime footing to wartime readiness.

An unexpected and, for some, unwelcome part of our training was engine maintenance.

A fellow trainee asked, rather recklessly, I thought, as the instructor was the same dreadful Flying Sergeant who daily made our lives miserable on the drill field, "Why do we have to learn this stuff? It's a job for the enlisted."

Our instructor could have told him, "None of your concern," or "Shut your hole," but instead he provided us with an answer that was to motivate me through the balance of our training. "It's not the grounds crew that'll be going up in that plane with the defective engine, it's you."

I needed the motivation. Some of the others, who had taken shop in high school or spent the hours after school in fixing up their own or their father's cars, simply breezed through the course. I, on the other hand, would take the entire engine apart without thought for its reassembly, and would then be faced with an enormous jigsaw. The fact that Feldman who worked at an adjoining bench had done precisely the same thing was cold comfort.

It seems an engine ought to be disassembled a section at a time, then reassembled before proceeding to the next section. Or, if you do have to disassemble several sections before getting at the one you want, then each section ought be laid out separately. Obvious to some, a hard-won lesson for me. And still I would put the engine back together only to find a part or parts left over.

Our instructor would walk by my bench and either rip a tool from my hand and say, "No you bloody idiot, use a ratchet," or worse, simply shake his head and continue walking.

My task was not helped by the manner in which the British (and all our engines were British made) then assembled their engines with seemingly a different size screw or bolt for every component. None of the standardization you'll find today.

Why would not that last bolt go in? Because, "Freygood, you bloody idjit, you've put the wrong bolt in somewhere else. Always sticking it in the wrong hole, you are." At which everyone would laugh, even those who would at the very next moment fall victim to our instructor's bile.

Which brings me to Sunday, bloody Sunday.

The first six weeks of basic training over, and the world still at peace, we airman had the day off and were headed for the City except for a few fuck-ups and a few total fools like me.

"Off to see the nurses?" Eric asked me, for the nurses or, more accurately, the nursing students were our chief source of feminine company back then, our uniforms and theirs contributing greatly to a mutual appeal. I wished Eric hadn't asked, for though I turned him down, whenever something went wrong that Sunday, and things went wrong almost continuously, I would think of the nurses and what I could be doing with my day off.

What I did do after everyone else had headed straight from morning parade to the front gate was to go to the mechanics training hut. My plan was a simple one: I would spend the day taking apart and putting together my engine. An exam, the decisive exam was scheduled for the next day. "Smitty's a right bastard," more than one noncom had been happy to tell us, not that we weren't well aware of Smitty's character. "Plenty of surprises," was the cryptic comment made by the head cook when he heard of our coming test.

Smitty himself had made clear at every opportunity that you passed his exam or you headed for the gate. I would have had plenty of time for student nurses then, though no uniform to impress them with.

So I set to work. I'd never be top boy in that class, but they weren't going to fail me out.

The first problem was the door to the hut. It was firmly locked; apparently, they didn't want anyone walking away with what had to be World War I vintage engines, although perhaps it was the tools they were more concerned with. Any road, the last bus to the City was long gone.

I walked around the building. The left side had two windows high up on the wall; neither was capable of being opened, unless I wanted to break the glass. Oh, I wanted to, but it would only have guaranteed a dishonorable discharge.

The back wall, further back than I remembered the back wall to be, had a door but no windows. I assumed this door too was locked, rattled the handle anyway and almost walked away. Almost. But then I noticed that this door opened out, not in. Instead of pushing, I pulled as I turned the handle and the door swung open.

I had stepped inside some kind of office storeroom. A coat rack held a couple of jackets, instructor size, along with a flying cap. A half empty bottle of beer sat on the desktop. What I wanted, though the beer and some crackers I found in a lower drawer would later come in handy, was the door to the instruction lab proper. Would that one be locked?

It wasn't. Relieved, I made my way through the darkened shop, turned on the light over my bench and set to work. I took my engine apart once, a section at a time, then put it back together. I did this again and again. Thoughts of the student nurses occasionally interrupted my work, and I only stopped thinking about them when the fantasy was getting out of or rather into hand.

I did ten pushups, voluntarily, just to get some fresh air into my lungs. Then I set to work again. After several hours of this, I was hungry and thought of the mess hall. They would be serving some kind of meal there if only bread and lunchmeat for a make-your-own sandwich. But the lunch hall meant other people, noncoms including my instructor who might just ask, "What the hell I was doing there on a day off?" (a bit more colorfully perhaps). And there was always the possibility that while I was out someone would lock the rear door to the shop.

I ate crackers, drank stale beer, and took my engine apart as well as another more advanced engine that two of the whiz kids had been permitted to work on. This last, I only had to take apart twice to get right.

At 1700 hours I headed for the chow line. The noncoms were there and I did get kidded. "Struck out in town did you, Freygood." I didn't care; I was ready for the test.

Or so I thought.

We had a morning run the next day to keep us alert, thirty minutes of drill, breakfast for which I had a not-unexpectedly-hearty appetite and then we were off to the engine lab.

The engines that sat at each station looked nothing like those we'd worked on before. Well, O.K., I could see they had pistons, and a carburetor, and a drive shaft that might lead to a prop, but it was as night to day with the engines we'd been working on.

"How. . .?" some fearless recruit asked. "Use the manual." was the instructor's instant reply. I stared at the engine and stared at the manual while all around me, my fellow recruits were setting to work. Well, some of them were; some were still bitching about how unfair it all was.

I continued staring, manual in hand, running my fingers over the engine, trying to get some feel for its disassembly when I saw the problem, the real problem, "Smitty's a tricky bastard," Cook had told us. The manual I held was for a different engine than the one before me.

At the adjoining bench, Feldman too was staring into space. I picked up my manual and walked over to join him. "Totally unfair," he said. I ignored him and looked at his engine. Ah, hah! Surreptitiously, I reached over and interchanged my manual with the one he'd been given. Alas, not surreptitiously enough. Feldman grabbed at his (really my) manual. A wrench fell to the floor and the instructor was instantly at our side. "Just interchanging manuals," I said as quietly as I could, "Feldman's idea."

(Where had I learned to talk like this?)

"Smart Jew bastard, aren't you Feldman. Maybe, you won't flunk out after all."

Feldman looked puzzled, but kept his mouth shut. And, no, we recruits didn't all leap over and complain about the racist epithet. That's the way things were in those days. Even my buddy Eric had referred to Feldman, not to his face, but in my presence, as that Jew bastard. Feldman with his Jew name and Jew-like hooked nose had been the butt of more than one instructors' ill temper. Which would you rather be, the butt of someone's humor, or the one who stood there quietly, anonymously knowing that but for an accident of genes and your father's good fortune in Anglicizing his name, that you too would be the object of ridicule.

That morning, Feldman simply stared at him.

I tuned them both out, and started over, the correct manual in hand. In no time I'd figured out what I was going to do and how I was going to do it, one section at a time. According to the laboratory clock, I even beat out a couple of the whiz kids who never did realize that their manuals didn't match their engines.

Chapter 4. Learning to Fly I

Unlike the camp where I'd done my basic training, where student nurses and the flesh pots of Montreal were only 45 minutes away, the Service Flying Training School in Camp Borden, Ontario was situated out in the middle of nowhere. I suppose this was so we might fly out over Georgian Bay or the endless forest during training thus minimizing potential damage to civilians. Trainees came to Camp Borden from all over Canada, from Vancouver, the Prairie Provinces, and the Maritimes; the largest contingent coming from Ontario itself. So half a dozen of us Québécois, officer-cadet insignia newly sewn on our blue uniforms, mine by a favorite aunt, headed out by train from Montreal, first to Toronto, and then to Barrie, Ontario.

War hadn't begun yet, so as far as the other passengers on the train were concerned we were just another group of noisy teenagers, annoying ones at that. To them, our rapid patter, loud voices, and hitting on every woman in sight were unwanted annoyances.

"You gotta try," a buddy said, after being shot down once again, this time by an older woman who had only glared at him frostily in reply.

Yes, we were horny all right, and filled with pent up energy. "No more drills, no more stupid marching," Feldman said. But I took a wait-and-see attitude toward the future. So far, the Air Force had provided endless examples of sheer stupidity. And indeed drilling and marching is exactly what we did on arrival, just to see if we'd forgotten how in the week intervening.

But when Feldman was on the verge of saying, "I quit, I go home, Hitler will just have to wait for me," our flying instruction began.

In ground-based trainers, of course, the shells of bombers with mock controls. But if the pilot trainees felt something was missing, how much worse was it for us designated navigators. We did navigation exercises in the classroom, then we did the same thing bent over a navigator table in the plane, while mock engines made noise, and instructors yelled at us.

Two weeks of this and I was ready to go bonkers. Or would have been if I'd not made a habit of coming in during our few off hours—no time away from the camp as yet—and sitting in the pilot's seat.

Everything was new to me; I marveled at each gauge, trying to remember what I'd over heard while working on my own assignments. It took awhile, but eventually I knew those controls as well as the pilots-in-training. Knew them, but could only dream about using them in flight some day.

The citizens of nearby Angus, not yet overrun with airmen as they would be in a very few months, organized a dance for us. No alcohol—Ontario was far more conservative than Quebec, but plenty of girls, supplied by the local Church groups.

Theresa became my girl, not because I chose her—she was short, I liked them tall; wide, I liked them slim; noisy, I liked them quiet; big breasted (I wasn't sure I liked this either at first as big breasts weren't my idea of class) and, not least, a face you couldn't really brag about with a thin darkish line above her lip of what might well turn into a mustache when she was older. Oh, and she was Catholic, not Jewish. I'm not sure there were any Jewish girls in Angus. Anyway, it was unlikely I would ever want to bring her home to my mother.

No, she chose me. She served me punch, saw that I got cookies and cake, and then abandoned her punch bowl to escort me around the community building, not that there was much to see. She made sure that I got to dance, with her. And on our second trip of exploration of the center, she made sure my hands went on those breasts, above the bra, before she gave me her phone number and had me promise to call.

I'd spent weeks with Winnie, my student nurse, trying to get my hands on her breasts, much smaller versions of those Theresa had on offer. Even when I did make contact, my hands had been beaten away. Who cared if Theresa were Catholic? I was a secular Jew.

Don't get me wrong; plenty of other girls were at that dance. I just never got the chance to meet them. And in my bunk that evening, Theresa was all I thought about.

Theresa was my girl and if I'd wanted it any different, I doubt if much could have been done about it. Everyone in Angus knew that Theresa and I were together; she made sure of it.

Theresa and her family and I went on a lot of outings together, even if it was only to drive into Barrie on Lake Simcoe to eat at the train station or to go bowling. Her family made me a part of them. They made me feel as if I'd never left home.

I loved their house, a separate two-story structure with a lawn in front and a garden behind—my parents' home was a duplex, one of a long line of them. A fresh coat of paint would have been welcome on Theresa's house, but it had a screened-in front porch where Theresa's father might sit in the evenings while he smoked his pipe, or where Theresa and I might share a quiet moment on a swing while her younger brother and sister played on the steps.

Theresa and her mother often dressed alike, in long, woolen shirts of yellow and black plaid. The styles in those days featured shoulder pads, shoulder pleats, and pleat yoke backs, with large patch pockets on the front just at the waist. Acceptable on her mother perhaps, but I thought the style did nothing for Theresa's figure. I tried to point out another style once on a trip into Barrie, a long sleeve jacket open at the throat, but it was no sale. Too citified, I guess.

It wasn't total togetherness. Always her family gave us time on each outing to be alone together. Then my hands would be placed on her breasts, sometimes outside, sometimes inside her bra.

One day, we were sitting side by side on her bed—I don't know where the rest of her family had gone, when she unsnapped her bra, pulled up her blouse, and brought my head down to her breast. You'd think I'd never been weaned. We did that breast feeding ritual night after night from then on, sometimes in her father's car, sometimes in her bedroom or that of a friend's, once on a picnic in a grove out of sight and earshot of the others.

She could feel my erection against her while I sucked. I had a constant erection in those days and she would usually arrange things so that I could rub against her thigh. Once her hand came down and began to rub me. The result was a spot on my pants that I was afraid her family would notice for sure. But practical Theresa simply got a towel from the linen closet, pulled my pants down around my thighs and dried the mess while my penis hung there limp and useless.

Five days a week we were in training, and seven evenings a week, except when I had guard duty, I was with Theresa. Our class was going up in the air now. Sometimes in a bomber with a crew of five, usually with an instructor serving as copilot. Sometimes in a twin-engine reconnaissance plane, with me crouched in the dome behind the pilot and copilot.

I can still remember the first flight I made. Dressed in overalls, helmet and goggles, I sat crouched over as we bumped across the grass. When the aircraft stopped bumping, I knew we'd left the ground behind. Forty minutes of ecstasy until we touched down.

12

But bigger thrills were yet to come. We were scheduled to go up one morning and the trainee who was to be the pilot was out with the flu. "Can I sit in the copilot's seat?"

"I don't see why not."

Every chance I got after that—and these were few and far between aside from a week in which virtually every one, myself included, came down with the flu, I would sit up in the copilot's seat, my eyes firmly on the control and gauges, indifferent to the skies I'd dreamed of flying among for so long.

Once I got to go up alone with the instructor in the de Havilland Tiger Moth that the pilots used for most of their training flights. A biplane, powered by the 130-horse power D.H. Gipsy Major engine, its maximum speed with two on board was barely 107 miles per hour. But, back in the copilot's seat, I had my own controls, could let my hands move along with his hands.

The instructor took us off the ground, but once in the air I was told that I could operate the controls. "Really?" "Really."

I did so, thrilled at the prospect.

"Now cut the engine." A breathless pause in which I simply stared straight ahead not quite believing what I'd heard. "Cut the engine." he demanded, irritated.

I did what I was told, cut the engine and waited for us to fall from the sky. We didn't though, but simply glided along until, unable to stand the suspense any longer, I restarted the engine in midair.

"We won't fall when you cut the engine," the instructor persisted, but I no longer needed to be told.

Meanwhile, Theresa had also taken the controls in hand. We would lie on her bed, she would take me to her breast and while I sucked away heartily her hand would reach down, pull me free of my pants (to avoid further incident), and the stroking would begin.

I was addicted to the stroking. If I had merely tolerated Theresa to begin with, a stopgap till I met someone else, I now began to take her seriously. Her family encouraged the prospect. "If you finished your college education, and became an engineer, you could come back here and work half a dozen places." (They meant in Barrie, less than half an hour distant, though as Barrie held less than 9,000 people, I doubted it would offer many opportunities.)

And every night after work, I would suck and play with Theresa's breasts and she would stroke away. Of course, her parents only saw us kissing, I think.

Our class completed the program. A few had dropped out, Eric among them, but not many. We learned to pack our parachutes all over again and completed one jump with fair success. One fellow broke his leg, but did not drop out of the program. He would be back six weeks later to start all over again.

It remained only to complete a solo flight (that is, one without the instructor) back to Montreal and the Châteauguay airfield. I told Theresa this; her entire family gathered in the living room to hear. "And after you graduate?" her mother asked.

"I'm not sure. If there's war (and by now, anyone who listened to the radio was sure there would be one) I'll be sent overseas."

Theresa's mother and sisters gasped, a foretaste of my own mother's reactions. "A man's got to do what a man's got to do," I heard Theresa's father say as Theresa led me back to her bedroom.

"Sit on the bed,' Theresa instructed as I started to lie back on her pillows. "No stand up first. Now sit," she finished, having pulled both my shorts and my trousers down around my ankles. My penis popped straight out and bopped her in the forehead before she had me positioned the way she wanted. She brought my hands down to grasp her beautiful breasts, and then, taking a deep audible breath, her mouth engulfed my penis.

I'd never experienced anything like that before. I'm not even sure that I have since, even with Rebecca. The first time. It was incredible. The warmth of her mouth, her huge jutting nipples. "I love you Theresa," I said as I came and I heard her choking, swallowing, absorbing all I had to offer.

"Now you're part of me," she said. I could see traces of my sperm on her lips and wiped away a spot on her cheek. "Come back to me when your war is over."

Chapter 5. The Trip to Trois-Rivieres

There was no time for us to marry. A good thing? A bad thing? I've never looked back. But I would have married Theresa then, even in the absence of my parents, and worried about the consequences later.

Fortunately or unfortunately, a navigator's job is full time on the ground before a flight; we had no time for extended farewells of any kind and that included marriage. I had to look at weather maps, what there was of them, talk about cloud cover, and decide whether we would travel over the lake (Lake Ontario) or the land. Nominally, an instructor would be close at hand ready to bail me out if I made a serious mistake, but he merely sat around gabbing with the other instructors while I made my plots. I was on my own.

In the morning, I went over the maps with my pilot before we stepped out on the tarmac. Our plane was the twin-engine Blenheim Mk 1F. I thought it was the most beautiful aircraft I'd ever seen, though it was obvious from the varied weathering of the different panels that this model had been cannibalized over its long history from three or four others. Our pilot and co-pilot spent as long as I lost in admiration before they climbed into the cockpit. About 40 feet from head to tail, the Blenheim's wings stretched almost 60 feet across. Its blunt nose was almost in a line with its propellers powered by two 840-horse power Mercury 8s. I'd once disassembled a Mercury 6s.2. These 8s were supposed to be a step up.

"It's a bear," the trainer had said, meaning that the Blenheim would be awkward to maneuver. But I didn't think so. He said it was slow; I guess it was compared with a fighter, but I thought that 250 miles per hour was fast.

We got up to 15,000 feet in the first quarter of an hour, then cruised through the sky at 220 mph. "No rush," said the pilot, an unpleasant brute from the Maritimes who shared none of my nervousness.

The copilot was from the Maritimes, too, somewhere in New Brunswick. We were to fly to Montreal drop our bombs—"I plan to devastate Westmont," said Feldman who was our bombardier—and then proceed to the Chateauguay airfield.

The pilot and copilot were casual, much too casual about our flight. I suspected excessive celebration the night before. Our tail gunner was also pilot-trained but he'd clearly spent the evening with the other two, though being a French-Canadian, he might have gone off on some rampage of his own. Our class in flight school, built as it was from several separate training classes across the Dominion, never really acquired the unity we'd had in basic training. Only Feldman and I of our crew of five appeared concerned that our future would depend on this exercise.

The pilots demonstrated their indifference early on by not taking the path I'd plotted but headed due south, so they could look at Toronto from the air. I'd chosen the course, not at all arbitrarily but because there had been rumors that morning as well as the night before that thunderstorms might pose a problem along a slowly moving warm front from the States south of Lake Ontario.

This indifference led to the first of our many arguments, which, naturally, they, with their hands on the controls, won and I and Feldman hapless in the bomber's midsection lost. In fact, back in my windowless cubbyhole, I only learned about the deviation from our course when I overheard them chatting in the cockpit about the Prudential House and Maple Leaf Gardens passing below. The latter building, at least, should have been invisible from the lake.

"Hey Feldman, you yid, here's something else for you to drop your bombs on." They meant the Gardens. We were all fans of the Canadiens.

The tail gun opened up then, blanks I hoped, to be followed by the chatter of guns from the cockpit.

The thunderstorms did not materialize, so we were hardly in any danger. Still, the pilot did what he could to keep Feldman and I off balance. "Oops," he said a few moments after we'd crossed into Quebec, "looks like we just lost one of our engines." I didn't tell him I knew we could lose both and still keep flying. Feldman said, "We're going down?" phrasing this half as a question, half as a statement. Either way, he was starting to panic. I told him not to sweat it. And sure enough, the dipstick in the pilot's seat had the second engine on again by the time we were down to 10,000 feet.

Our trip probably would have been successful, had we not been instructed as we approached the Island of Montreal to bypass the Chateauguay airfield and head for Trois-Rivieres instead.

Was something wrong? Or was this just a part of our test? an unexpected and unwanted part.

"Hey, why aren't we flying over the city?" This from Feldman.

"Why should we?"

"So I can bomb Westmont."

"Maybe I don't want you to bomb Westmont. Maybe I really like the people there, specially 'cause they hate Jews too."

The anti-Semitic garbage mouth in the pilot's seat was someone who was supposed to help us stop Hitler? But by this time we were well past Montreal and heading up the river. At least I hoped we were headed up the river. A navigator has to rely on what the pilots tell him.

I whispered to Feldman, "Where are we?"

"Over a river."

"Let me know if the river gets wider."

"Its wider, practically a lake. Its the St. Lawrence all right."

"What's all this whispering back there, girls." But the garbage mouths had no more time to chat with us as they began to receive instructions, in French, from the Trois-Rivieres control tower. Fortunately, the co-pilot, who was from New Brunswick spoke the language.

On the flight back to Montreal—yes, the diversion was all part of our test—the tail gunner took the copilot's place as the copilot shifted left into the pilot's seat, and the pilot, our sole English-only speaker, considerably chastened, for now no one was on his side, went back to the tail.

Alas, the changeover did not yield an immediate improvement in our teamwork. I was given next to no time to plot a new course—"You think the Jerries will wait for you, Freygood?"—and after we'd taken on aviation gasoline, we were back up in the air.

The copilot and tail gunner chattered away in the cockpit as if they hadn't seen each other in weeks, ignoring me, who was still finishing up my calculations. With my attention on the plot, and the pilots on each other, it was Feldman who first said, "I think we're following the wrong river."

I pushed forward from my cubbyhole, leaped might be a better description, and leaned into the cockpit. A forest stretched ahead of us, and a portion of the plane's shadow could be glimpsed on the treetops ahead.

"Guys, have you looked at the compass, lately?"

"Shit," from the copilot; "Merde," from the French-Canadian tail gunner sitting in the copilot's seat. The first was from New Brunswick, while the second came from Hull on the other side of the Province, but this was no excuse. For almost half an hour, we'd headed north along the Shawinigan, rather than southwest along the St. Lawrence.

At least, I had their attention.

I went back to my cubbyhole and hollered out compass headings, from time to time asking for landmarks in return. We talked back and forth, pilots to navigator, the way an experienced crew should. As for our worthy former pilot, Mr. Garbage-Mouth himself, he slept back in the tail, never knowing how close we came to flunking out.

Oh, we lost points on our test , all right, but we regained them for our recovery. "Team work pays, boys." the lead instructor said.

"Sir." we replied, a single parade-ground shout.

Chapter 6. Graduation

The following week, we graduated, received our pilot-officer insignia, and attended three separate ceremonies. The first one, formal, in the afternoon, featured speeches by various senior officers, none of whom we had seen before, and all but one of whom I was never to see again. The second ceremony, informal, also held at the field, began in the late afternoon almost immediately after we'd been dismissed from the first, and proceeded, for some, far into the night.

Our hosts, the school staff, had provided large quantities of alcohol in varying forms, going well beyond beer, and steaks, as many as you wanted. This ceremony's true highlight though—apart from the steaks, was a roast of the instructors. I'd not been privy to the preparations for this event, but was surprised and delighted by much of it. A parody of one of our truly boring instructors featured a tousled-haired lecturer wearing a woman's wig backwards. He lost his place in his written notes frequently and finally fell asleep at the podium to much applause (the point of this charade being that it was usually this instructor's students who slept).

Four strippers appeared next from the back of the hall, much to everyone's delight; even a minister's son from the Maritimes joined in the applause. I was led to understand that later in the evening they could be had for a price. But by that time I had gone on to my third and final celebration.

One thing these initial ceremonies did not feature was a roast of Feldman. I'd been lying in my bunk, planning to sleep away as much of the morning as I could—how often did one have that opportunity?—when I overheard an unpleasant discussion. A small circle of five or six men had gathered around the adjoining bunk

and were discussing how to get Feldman. Hide his uniforms, burn them, burn holes in them, scoop out manure from one of the latrines and pour it over his head?

As I've mentioned, no one thought of me as a Jew, and apparently, it was Feldman's Jewishness as much as anything else which offended them.

The principal speaker, of course, was garbage mouth from Halifax. I slipped down from my top bunk no longer content or able to remain passive—and perhaps it was about time too, one can't hide who one is forever, and said, "Not a good idea."

"What's it to you, Freygood?"

"He's one of us."

"You some kind of Jew lover?" This from garbage mouth.

"We're fighting Hitler to protect the Jews. Don't they read newspapers in the Maritimes?"

"Exactement. If it were not for the Jews, there would be no war." This from a liberal arts graduate of the l'Universite de Montreal. Murmurs of agreement came from some but not all of the others.

Garbage mouth came off the bunk where he'd been sitting and stood facing me only inches away. "What are you going to do about it?" My eyes were on a level with his chin and I'm sure it was as clear to everyone there as it was to me that one on one I might hurt him but two or three or four on one I was doomed.

But I didn't back down. I raised my right hand high in the air and snapped my fingers. "Crew, to me," I said.

The copilot and tail gunner of our just completed test flight had a big decision to make. Garbage mouth was their buddy, at least he was the copilot's. Then again, I was the guy who'd saved their asses the day before.

It would have been nice if they'd come and stood by me. Because they were grateful or because they just wanted to do the right thing. But what the pair did was to kind of fade away toward the opposite end of the barrack and take the others with them. Garbage mouth was left toe-to-toe with me.

If I'd been the stick-like figure I'd been 90 days earlier, he probably would have beat the crap out of me. But now I had muscles. Lifting and carrying and running and daily exercise had built them.

He walked away and that was the end of it. Feldman never knew.

The family's celebration in my honor was held at the home of my favorite aunt. Note that the main reason she was my favorite back then was not that she did kind deeds such as sewing on my insignia, but that she had the most incredible breasts. Usually these were prominently displayed in a sweater perhaps a size too small. She was prone to hugs that I'd tried to avoid when younger and dreamt about constantly when older. She was all too aware of my interest and once she saw my eyes were on her would be sure to accidentally stretch or yawn, arching her back as she did so, then look up at me , surprised, waiting for my blush.

The evening of the party, she'd abandoned the sweater-girl look and was wearing a long, form-fitting dress that offered barely a glimpse of her creamy mounds. Noting my disappointment, she suggested that she would be willing to change. I couldn't reply; my lips were glued together in embarrassment. I blushed, had an erection, and wanted to die. Of course, this was the very moment my father chose to come by and lead me off to be introduced, erection and all, to his business associates.

My father, not incidentally, had on a formal suit, the kind one would wear to a bar mitzvah, as did all my male relatives.

My erection subsided as I listened to some bad and ill-informed advice from the men—there would be no war, the German army would collapse the minute they ran into opposition; also, I should avoid certain models of aircraft if war did break out. Everyone seemed to know more than I about our nation's armaments and our state of readiness. Finally, I was allowed to slip away. Only to be swept up by my mother and introduced to relatives on her side of the family as well as old family friends, all of whom insisted on kissing or hugging me, or remarking it was a shame I no longer had those beautiful long eyelashes I'd had as a child.

I bumped into my aunt again, who insisted that I dance with her. When I was on the verge of explosion, she passed me off to one of my female cousins, the deeply religious one who I 'm sure was offended by the boner that I pressed against her.

Perhaps not. I was to fight Hitler, after all, would drop bombs deep into Germany, would free my people. A potential hero might be forgiven any and everything, might be permitted liberties.

Even so, cousins were to be avoided as much as sisters, or aunts. Many second cousins were present though ,along with girls who were no blood relation at all, merely friends of relatives. Everyone (save the Bronfman's) had been invited to the celebration and guests were to be found in every room as well as out on the lawn.

The belle of the ball was a girl much like Rebecca, tall, reserved, extremely graceful, with a head of reddish curly hair, like Rebecca's only not quite as red or as long. No one seemed willing to introduce me and, when I pressed the issue, I was told that she was already committed, someone in the Army, and it would be a waste of my time.

I was scanning the crowd searching for other possibilities when I became aware that I was being subjected to an equally intense scrutiny. At first, for the girl watching me was plump and wore a relatively shapeless dress, I thought she was an aunt or someone from a similar age group. "I suppose I should have worn something else." she said, opening the conversation. "But I've gained weight recently."

She was easy to talk to. Not pushy and forward like Theresa, but equally honest and open. I liked that. I wasn't good at girls' games, at the sort of nothing conversation that is supposed to make up courtship.

"This house is so big," she said, "Have you been here before?" I explained that our hosts were my aunt and uncle and that I'd been there many times. I even gave her a brief tour around the house and lawn. I'd planned to show her the lily pond my uncle had started, but it had been turned into one of the first victory gardens. Rationing was ahead; everyone knew it.

I'd also planned to show her the wood-paneled family room in the basement and perhaps play a game of ping-pong, but frantically necking couples already occupied the room.

"You blush easily," she said. "They're just teenagers."

We settled down finally in an upstairs bedroom among a pile of coats tossed on a bed. I thought we might have run out of things to say, but she started talking about what she was studying, as one of the few women students at McGill.

"Are you going to go back to the Uni, afterwards?" she asked, and then "Would you like to kiss me?" She'd loosened her long dark hair, which had been up piled in a chignon and let it fall down across her shoulders.

"I'd like to touch your breasts," I said. And why not be bold, I was going away the next day, flying to England. Nothing ventured, nothing gained.

"That would be complicated. You should see the apparatus I need to hold my breasts up. You'd never figure it out and I'd never be able to get it back together. I can do something else for you, though."

She got up, walked over to the door and made sure it was locked. Then she came back to the bed and knelt on the floor by where I was sitting. She fumbled with my pants buttons for a moment, until I undid them for her. Almost immediately, she took me in her mouth, her long hair spreading out across my lap. I caressed her neck; she tickled my testicles. I tried to pull her up on top of me, but she refused to budge and sucked away until I had no choice but to release myself inside her.

She stayed a moment or so longer than Theresa had and there was no sign of me on her lips and face when she sat down again beside me. "Now, kiss me," she said. "Now," she repeated when I held back and grabbed me around the neck, pulling me over to her. We kissed. I tasted her lipstick, smelled her, tasted me, I suppose. Then she stood up and helped me to my feet.

When we walked out of the bedroom, my aunt was standing there smiling. "Just come to get some coats," she said. "Now, kiss me before you go downstairs."

I kissed her and knew that she knew everything there was to know about me just as she'd always claimed, "from when you were the darlingest baby, newborn in your mother's arms.

Chapter 7. Northolt Field

Transportation to England was provided partly by train (along the St. Lawrence and down to Halifax, after I'd had time to say goodbye to mom, dad, and uncles, along with another frustrating encounter with Winnie, the student nurse), and partly by plane. Multiple landings were required in those days—supersonic Concordes were decades away. From Halifax, we flew to Goose Bay, Labrador, then to Gander, Newfoundland, Rejecovick, Iceland and , finally, to somewhere in England at an unidentified RAF airbase.

My fellow passengers, apart from five other members of my graduating class, included a dozen paratroopers. These last were large tough looking men and were not to be fooled with.

I'd thought being huddled in the narrow space allocated the navigator on a bomber was unpleasant. Well, the plane used for transporting us abroad had been designed for carrying cargo. Forget about windows. Passengers were an afterthought.

Two long benches faced each other across a narrow aisle beneath a ceiling that sloped continually, front to back. Each bench held six to seven men uncomfortably which left four of us to stand or stretch out on the metal floor.

The paratroopers solved the problem by grabbing some of our number who'd had the temerity to sit and pulling them from the bench to the floor. The paras were large and outnumbered us to boot; we let it alone.

Overhearing several of the paras speaking French, I inserted myself into the conversation. Balancing their distaste for airmen against their distrust of the English, the latter won out, and I was soon invited to sit down beside them, albeit at the tail end of the bench, where my head just grazed the ceiling. The balance of my classmates and fellow officers were left to sit on the hard metal floor.

Since our chamber was windowless, we could never be sure exactly when we were going to land and the bumps invariably took the chaps on the floor of the plane by surprise. (My own trick was to bend over as much as I could as soon as I sensed we were going down. Sometimes I did avoid bumping my head—depending on how many times our wheels hit the ground before we were no longer airborne. Third contacts always caught me off guard.)

We'd been told to bring our parachutes on the plane with us, and I'd an instant vision of a final free-falling arrival. My one sad experience with a jump at Camp Borden had been more than enough, but I did as I was told, better one parachute than none. In any event, the parachute was unnecessary—this time.

Our first stop in England was the last for the paratroopers and for two of my classmates including Feldman. It was also the last stop for the pilot and copilot of the plane. Neither they nor the aircraft would be returning to Canada. We were about to go to war.

At first, my fellow officers and I didn't realize we were to be separated from the others; we were too busy digging into the sandwiches and drinks (tea and ginger beer) that had been provided, cream cakes, too. After which those of us who'd been assigned to other bases were packed into a van, somewhat more crowded than the plane, and shuttled from airfield to airfield depositing more of my classmates at each. The last and very late stop at Northolt Field discharged the one and only remaining passenger, me.

I was shown to a Quonset hut by a noncom, pointed at an empty bunk and told to store my duffle and parachute beneath it. "They'll come for you in the morning."

The next morning when reveille sounded, I was on my feet, still half asleep, when I noticed that none of the hut's other occupants had bothered to rise. Readily adaptable—it really was bloody early—I lay down and slept again amid the snores.

The non-com who woke me was not kind. "On your feet young Sir; duty officer wants to see you. They let you sleep in the Colonial forces do they?"

The duty officer, a flight lieutenant by his insignia, though his yellow-grey hair suggested that he no longer flew, also took a dim view of colonials. Much fuss was made about improperly completed and absent paper work, none of which had been generated by me, but for which I was held responsible.

"A navigator? We don't need bloody navigators. This is a fighter squadron. I'll do any navigating that needs be done. We need pilots. Damn fools are always dying. Can you fly a plane?"

"Yes, Sir," I said, always a wise thing to say when talking with a superior, especially one who has just said you can realize a life-long dream. Then again, was it really safe to send me up in a plane as its pilot, safe for the plane, that is?

"It is my duty to introduce you to the others," he added, ending our conversation and cutting off any second thoughts I might have had. I was escorted to yet another Quonset hut, the officer's mess, where again sandwiches—bacon and tomato, tea and ginger beer were to be had.

The expected round of introductions to my fellow pilots followed. (My "fellow pilots," how I relished the phrase.) They were a sea of immediately forgettable names and faces, though a voice or two could be traced to those who talked in their sleep.

Their names and faces are even more forgettable after this long lapse of time, so I hope you will forgive me if I get the names wrong or ascribe to Smith what was done or said by Jones, or ascribe to Jones what was done or said by Smith. Incidentally, a Smith or Smythe, or perhaps both, might have been there that day.

The group that greeted me consisted mainly of pilot officers like myself, but at least two flight officers were present as well as one elderly flight lieutenant, the duty officer who also did the briefing and the debriefing. A hyphenated Throckmorton-Higgenbottom (or thereabouts) looked down his long nose at me, though he too had only the unimpressive insignia of a pilot officer. And there was flight officer Wilson. He would be memorable if for no other reason than his opening remark proved so highly prophetic. "Don't worry about our names, which I see you've already forgotten. Most of us will be dead by the end of three more missions."

I guess they could look down their noses at me. These men had flown in combat while I'd just gone round and round in a trainer. As it turned out, thankfully, I wasn't the only raw recruit, and together we would share the brunt of Wilson's sarcasm.

But hear me (amid the snores of my new bunk mates): My luck had changed for the better. I was to be a pilot.

Chapter 8. Learning to Fly II

Dinner that evening was a formal affair. Apparently, the plates of cucumber sandwiches, and cream cake, and ginger beer that I'd devoured earlier that evening were what the British call High Tea. As it had been the largest meal I'd seen in a very long while, can I be blamed for thinking it was dinner? Besides, I was a bloody colonial.

It appeared early on that I had worn the wrong jacket to table. Bloody colonial again. As it was the only jacket I'd been issued—apparently, in the British service one was expected to buy the formal parts of one's uniform—I was momentarily forgiven in that I was loaned the proper jacket to wear.

We had multiple courses, soup, salad, a first course, and so on along with multiple choices of cutlery laid out by the plates. I had enough culture and aunts who served a fancy enough table on the Sabbath eve, to know that one took the outermost knife or fork and simply worked one's way in. Regardless, innumerable public-school trained eyes followed my hands to see if I would stumble. Score one for the Colonial.

After the meal, came yet another glass of wine. Yes, we had wine courtesy of our commanding officer's cellar. That worthy gentlemen, a tall man with a surprisingly youthful appearance belied only by touches of gray at his temple, a product of the same genes as Throckmorton-Higgins perhaps, but clearly made of sterner stuff, spoke to us, new recruits and experienced airmen alike, of the plans for our squadron:

In a few days, perhaps only two, Air Command was to begin a series of raids into the Ruhr valley "to destroy the Führer's industrial might." A chorus of "hear, hear's" followed and one could see great grins on the faces of those who served us as well as those who were waited on. Our task as a fighter squadron was to accompany the bombers and beat off any German counter attacks. Again the mess was enthusiastic.

"Any chance we can get in some practice?" a lone voice inquired in the temporary silence. The lone voice was mine. The laughter that followed was immediate and widespread. The Colonial had done it again.

"Come, come, Gentleman. I think Freygood, Frygood is it, has a capital idea. Tomorrow morning we shall run through some practice maneuvers. I heard several voices, evident brownnosers, say, "Why not tonight?"

"Not tonight, I'm afraid," the commander's plummy voice continued, "We may have had just a bit too much wine, but tomorrow for sure."

Hard to believe, but in those early days of war, when the air battles were being fought over the relatively distant plains of Holland and Belgium, night raids were unknown and the squadron had yet to venture forth after dark. This was all to change of course, first at Dunkirk and afterward when the Battle of Britain began.

I slept poorly. I was a navigator, not a flier.

I'd flown a plane, but always with someone in the seat behind or beside me, ready to take over should I falter. No, I was a pilot. I would be a pilot.

I ran over the starting sequence in my mind, placed my hands where the instructor had placed his, checked imaginary instruments, pulled out the choke, ignition. Too much. But I was asleep.

The debriefing office talked to us before the flight, sketching on the blackboard where each of us had a place in the formation. I was in the far right tail of a V centered on Wilson. He in turn was on the left and slightly behind a V or vic centered on our commanding officer.

We looked at a map of the area, new recruits leaning forward in their chairs, old hands continuing to puff lazily on their cigarettes. The squadron leader said, "Stay in formation lads," and then we were out the door.

The squadron leader was actually a wing commander, but as things were then, we didn't have either the men or the planes to put together more than a squadron for him to lead. Which explained my own presence in this group, and later on of members of the other Commonwealth nations.

The cockpit of my new fighter (far from new, actually, it had had far more experience than I) was quite different from the planes I'd trained in. As was the plane itself.

Perhaps, I ought to have mentioned to the briefing officer that the only plane I'd ever flown was a twin-engine bomber with its wings midway up the fuselage. All my not-exactly-new single-engine Hawker Hurricane fighter shared with that bomber was a multi-colored body, with some panels clearly far older than others. It was half the size, 32 feet not 60 feet in length, and its 40-foot wings were beneath the fuselage. It would never fly as far on a single tank as the Blenheim bomber, but it could climb 2500 feet a minute, cruise at 300 miles an hour, 325 if one wanted to push it, and rise to 34,000 feet. I wasn't to know then, and no one thought to tell me that the current model Hurricane was just a tad slower than the Messerschmitt Bf-109 with its Daimler-Benz DB601Aa engine that I'd shortly be facing.

"Every engine has common elements, every plane has a need for similar instruments and gauges." came my training officer's voice. It would just be a matter of locating those gauges on the instrument panel, and the controls from the levers before me. Airspeed indicator—check, altimeter, compass, needle and ball indicator. Nonetheless, I stalled the plane on the runway no more than ten yards out, and though my second attempt was more successful, I barely cleared the trees. "Pecker up, Freygood," I heard in my headphones, followed by "Form at 5000" from the Commander.

I was not going to make it. My plane began to buck as its engine backfired repeatedly and almost stalled. What to do? Push in the choke, stupid.

I found my place in the formation, such as it was; apparently, I was not the only inexperienced flier. A chorus of radioed sarcastic remarks followed to be squelched by the Commander. Slowly, I became part of a team, turning first on command, and then automatically with the lead plane in my formation.

Nearly an hour passed before I felt sufficiently in control to forget about the immediate present and start worrying about the future. How the hell was I going to land?

"Follow me in chaps."

"Slowly." Wilson's voice admonished.

We lost altitude slowly, or tried to. One poor chap, failing to heed Wilson's admonishment, let his plane fall a dive and barely straightened out before he touched ground. No it wasn't me. I wasn't very good, but I wasn't the worst flier there.

My landing was not precisely one to be proud of and I expected a tongue-lashing. But it was a former Public School boy who earned the burnt of the debriefing officer's invective. Stalling his engine well above the ground, he smashed his undercarriage on the final descent, thus putting his plane out of action for a week.

Still, I hadn't landed yet myself, though I was now down to 1000 or maybe it was 500 feet. Where was the bloody field? Turn the plane; I followed a spiral down, my head out the cockpit. I was bound to see the field sooner or later, wasn't I; after all I'd been following Wilson in. Then all at once, the field and the runway were dead ahead of me, not more than ten feet below. Had I misread the altimeter?

I eased back on the throttle, pulled up on the nose, panicked as the engine cut out momentarily, and then I was on the ground going much too fast.

I overshot my ground crew by 50 yards or so, but I did land safely, and, thankfully, the 50 yards were there. Ours was a training field, designed to shelter the inexperienced. I circled back toward the hangar imagining all eyes were on me. They weren't of course. Too many others had missed the field entirely, and were making second passes. The fellow who'd smashed his undercarriage had to be towed out of the way. So much for the previous evening's faked enthusiasm.

Wilson, already dismounted and on the ground, looked completely unruffled. He came up to my cockpit just as I killed the engine. "First flight?" he said.

I did not, despite certain signals of urgency from my bowels, proceed directly back to my hut along with the other officers. Instead, I followed my plane into the hangar.

"Where you going?" came a surly voice, and a short bull-headed gentleman in mechanic's garb stood in my path.

"I'm looking for my ground crew."

"What you want them for?"

"I want to thank them." The man halted dead in his tracks. "Blimy," he said. I continued to follow my plane.

A short man with a moon-like face and red strands of hair across an almost bald pate came around back from where he'd left my plane and intercepted me. "No officers here."

"I'm looking for my ground crew."

"What you want them for?"

It all sounded familiar. A taller man wearing coveralls came around from the other side of the plane. "I'm Birny. This is Stubbs. We take care of this plane."

"Thank you so much. It's in tip-top shape. You fellows did a great job." And I meant every word of it. That Sunday cooped up in the training hut, assembling and disassembling an engine had taught me infinite respect for the men on the ground.

"Blimy."

As my father had explained to me so many times, the trick to success in business lies in getting men to work extra hard for you without actually having to pay them more money. So it is in war, also.

A figure of authority strode toward us. He had sufficient braid on his sleeves to indicate a Chief Technician's rank. "Hear, hear; if you've got something to complain about it, you come see me."

I continued, as I'm sure my father would have advised. "I'm so glad you do have time to talk with me, Chief Technician. Would it be possible to have these two men work on my plane regularly? Their schedules permitting, of course."

By this time an entire hangar full of non-coms and other ranks were gathered round to listen to us. For all I knew, they'd been summoned from other hangars.

"You want these men to work on your plane?" The Chief Technician did not want to surrender his authority.

"They do a bang up job. I'd be butter on the tarmac, but for them."

"Where are you from?" The tension was gone from the Chief's voice, but I could see he still wanted to show his men that he was in charge.

"Canada. Pilot-Officer Freygood, Royal Canadian Air Force."

"Explains the uniform."

"Explains the ruddy accent," came a voice from behind me.

"Don't see why not," said a thoroughly placated Chief Technician continuing our conversation, "Birny? Stubbs. O.K. with you?"

Heads nodded all around. "We were going to install a new carburetor. Pep up the plane a bit." Birny said. "Would you like to see it before we put it in?"

Very much so." I'd not forgotten what our drill instructor had said. "They don't go up in the plane, you do."

Chapter 9. First Kill

At dinner that night, a less formal one though wine was served, Wilson was in top form. He began with the seemingly complimentary, "Canada's breadth, from sea to shining sea, coupled with its small population means that its pilots can travel for hours without bumping into one another. Unless, of course, they're in the air."

To which, having learned early on in basic training not to be clever, I made no reply.

The task of our fighter squadron was to escort British bombers as they attacked industrial installations in the Ruhr. When the German fighters came to intercept them, the dogfights would begin. It was very World War I. We'd been given a weird admixture of planes, some fresh off the production lines, and some that ought to have been mothballed and were until we were given them.

These last were slow, unhandy to maneuver, and stalled readily. Their function one soon realized was to act as decoys luring the Heinkels and Messerschmitts away from our more effective fighters.

One of Wilson's more wicked remarks, directed at a new recruit who was wailing at the sight of the aircraft he'd been assigned, "Not to worry. If you survive, you'll be given one of the better planes."

The catch, of course, was that when you lost a pilot, you most often lost a plane in the process, though not always visa versa.

The exceptions to the rule were, first of all, a pilot who "failed to make effective use of his aircraft," who might be grounded forthwith, a decision that could be made by the Commander in consult with the debriefing officer when a pilot had been seen hanging back, failing to engage the enemy.

Few disgraced themselves in this fashion, but there were more such than are generally reported. Throckmorton-Higgins came close, but a thorough bawling out by the Base Commander, the Adjutant, and everyone else senior in rank, along with a totally silent mess, seemed to reach his backbone, and his first kill was recorded on his very next mission.

The second exception was the arrival of a brand new aircraft, at which point everyone might move up a notch. New recruits, who appeared on a fairly regular basis, would be handed the scraps.

The downside of this method was that one had to get used to a brand new aircraft just when one had mastered the intricacies of the first. Thus, occasionally, one might leap up the ranks three or four levels to a faster, more powerful craft as I later did, simply because someone senior had refused to switch.

We'd flown five or six missions as escorts, the first time finding only empty skies, but we were guaranteed to be fired on thereafter. I was sent out again as one of a group of five or vic on the squadron leader's left. "Just don't get in our way was the only instruction," I received and this was from Wilson. Oh, and the squadron leader told us to maintain radio silence.

Think of migrating geese forming three V's, the center V in front of the other two. I was in the inner part of the outer V, a comforting place to be, providing I did as Wilson said and stayed out of other peoples' way.

It was the squadron leader's order that we maintain this formation at all times. I noticed that Wilson interpreted this command rather loosely, but I'd no choice but to follow him, the apex of my V, which often seemed to lead directly into danger. "Better to attack them, than to have them attack you."

On our initial missions, the German fighters ignored us. Appearing seemingly out of nowhere high in the sky, they would attack our bombers.

We would follow shortly thereafter, raking them with our guns—if we got close enough. Wilson soon had several verified kills, as did one or two other members of my V. I got nothing, though I survived in an honorable fashion, while two others, Throckmorton-Higgins among them, got a terrible bawling out for hanging back.

On the mission of which I'm writing, the Germans came directly at us. If I'd been alone, I'd surely have perished, but I stayed in line with the squadron, or with Wilson, rather, and when he turned, I turned. When he headed directly nose to nose at an oncoming Messerschmitt I did the same. Well, almost. I dipped when he rose, heard bullets all around me, and when I headed up again, a Messerschmitt was directly above me. I fired, then shot upward through the space the Messerschmitt had been a moment before. I followed this with a twisting turning barrel roll in a far from approved fashion—a tongue lashing from the squadron leader could be anticipated—when I found myself alone in the sky.

Everyone else appeared to have gone down several hundred feet as the Messerschmitts, discouraged by the reception we'd given them, had headed down toward their prime targets the bombers.

In the brief skirmish, they lost three fighters (one at my hand, I learned later), we only one. We got one more of theirs on the descent and, again, one of ours was lost, after which our bombers, freed of their loads, were able to scamper out of the way.

Briefing officer, please note: Freygood, one verified kill.

We were halfway back to Northolt from this mission, somewhere over Eastern Francewhen I noticed that my gas gauge read below one-quarter.

"Squadron Leader," I said into the radio, repeating these words quietly when there was no answer.

"Maintain radio silence as requested," came the curt reply. "This is a command channel."

"I'm running out of fuel, that is petrol, Sir."

After a longish pause, the curt voice of the squadron leader asked why the hell I hadn't checked the fuel level before our departure.

"Jerry nipped his gas line," piped an anonymous voice which I'm sure was Wilson's. Nipped the gas line. I knew I'd been shot at. We were always shot at, every mission. Sometimes they hit us; more times we hit them. This was the first time I'd been hit.

"How much fuel?"

"Bit over an eighth of a tank."

"You'll have to land then. France. Find a clear field if you can; find an airstrip with luck.

"You speak Frog don't you Freygood."

"Yes Sir."

"Good luck then." The commander's tone was kindly, the sort of tone you'd use with an old friend who was slipping away after a long illness.

"Keep your pecker up," came from half a dozen almost familiar voices. And then I was on my own. They went on their way out across the water toward England and I went on a diagonal across Pas de Calais.

Lucky for me the war hadn't yet reached France. Lucky for me that I spoke Frog, French that is. But I didn't feel lucky.

Once I was back over land, the atmosphere was crystal clear and I could see vast distances over what were mostly farms, not the long strips I was used to in Quebec, but a smaller patchwork quilt, with a church spire and the adjoining town putting in an appearance every ten miles or so. "L'Avion Force Aérienne Canadienne requesting permission to land," I asked in somewhat fractured French when I felt I might be within radio distance of an airfield.

"La What?

"He wants permission to land," I heard the speaker say to someone at his end, apparently having forgotten to take his finger off the transmit button.

The air went silent and then a new voice, very plummy, very upper class British came on the line. He spoke slowly as if convinced the entire world spoke English if only one spoke slowly enough. "Who did you say you were?"

I gave him my name and rank.

"The Royal Canadian Air Force?" The voice, the same that had spoken a moment before, was near incredulous. "Where are you exactly?"

"Fifteen thousand feet, over Pas de Calais."

"Can you come down to ten thousand?"

"If I do, I won't be able to go up again. And I'll need the height if I have to glide at the end."

"Come down to ten thousand feet. That is an order." No mistaking this tone; I was talking to a British officer, not a French.

"We have you now. Do you see two bridges close together?"

"Dead ahead. Sir." I added to be safe.

The rest of the conversation was not all that unfamiliar; I was given a series of directions, and at the very end, with the field in view, a landing speed. I missed the field the first time round, but made a decent if not impressive landing on the second.

A reception committee was there to greet me, though not a French one as I'd first anticipated. "Welcome to the 17th Squadron," said the plummy voice, and once again there was a round of introductions.

Chapter 10. Digression

Before telling you more about my war, let me digress briefly to tell you the distinction between *my* war and *the* war. Briefly, it's the distinction between tactics and strategy. How we grouped the planes in our squadron, that's tactics. Whether we bombed the Ruhr and destroyed the Nazis industrial base (marginally successful), or Berlin and its civilian population to destroy morale (again, only marginally successful as the Nazis shot any of their people who wanted to quit), that's strategy.

Strategy also included logistics. Ideally, we would always have as many pilots as planes or planes as pilots (there was a temporary shortage of the former while I need wait on my gas line to be repaired). At the beginning of the war, when planes were in really short supply, the decision had to be made whether to hold back some planes to use to train pilots, or put those same planes up in the air for combat where they were needed desperately.

What really decided the war in the Allies' favor (though it was not to be determined until several years after the part I've been telling you about) was the same factor that had forced me to land in France rather than England: The Nazis ran out of fuel.

That's the reason why they found themselves in Russia, creating a second front, and destroying themselves in the process as they strived to capture Baku and the Caucasian oil fields.

But that's another part of the war altogether, one you'll have to look up in someone else's book.

Chapter 11. To France

Gaps and discrepancies in these reminiscences are inevitable. For example, what happened to Feldman? Why did I get sent to Northolt where they needed a pilot rather than somewhere else where they needed a navigator? Why did my entire squadron get transferred from Northolt, England to Arras in France so that I became the first rather than the last to arrive at our new base?

How should I know? And, to the point, why would anyone think that I would know? I was a member of the Armed Services. I went where I was sent and followed instructions. I'm sure the people who sent me did the best they could, but communication was not instantaneous, except perhaps in the field, and then only among units of the same squadron.

Did you think we had email? Or that I could go down to the post and ring up good old Feldman, if, that is, I'd the slightest notion where they'd sent him.

I did receive mail, once. A letter from my mother and one from Ruth, the girl who'd given me the big send off my last night in Montreal. The letter from Ruth just shows that what is typical of war also is typical of real life. I'd spent a year courting a student nurse and received only blue balls for my efforts. I met a girl at a party, received an enthusiastic welcome, and only learned her name after she sent me a follow-up letter.

Anyway, after several days lapse, Wilson, Throckmorton-Higgins, Wing Commander Phelps, the gang, my gang, appeared. No one seemed surprised to discover I was already at the new base. At least no one acted surprised, that was the way of the British.

We resumed our previous efforts, sending planes out in support of our bombers, engaging the enemy, coming back alive. I did not distinguish myself except in one respect.

Our commanding officer spoke French but few of the other officers did. I was one of the few exceptions. Of course, after hearing a few words from me in my Province of Quebec accent, most L'Arme de L'Air (French Air Force) officers with whom we had contact would switch to English. They just wanted us to make an effort.

My chief value came in liaison with the French officials in the nearby village of Roclincourt. They did not speak English. They did not like the English. They did like to have us spend our money in their town. They did not like us to linger there, get drunk, or try to pick up their women. In short, our every communication with them was doomed to failure.

(One could drive to Arras, but it was a long drive. They did not speak English in Arras either, nor care to.)

The local farmers complained that we flew too low, that we scared the cows and diminished milk production. Should they not be compensated? ("No." was the only comment from our commanding officer, along with, "Rubbish," a comment I did not care to relay. As he was unfailingly polite on a face-to-face basis with the local officials, it was always left to me to deliver the bad news.)

They also complained that our flights were the cause both of too little and too much rain. Somehow, we had created air currents that had displaced a cloud that should have poured its rain upon one field to a field two hundred meters to the left that had no need of it.

Meanwhile, boys would be boys and girls would be girls. Later, there would be cries of rape, never substantiated, but how else explain unwanted pregnancies. The language barrier also meant much misreading of signals. We were faulted both for unwanted advances and for a failure to advance. Hawkins and Smith-Smythe discovered they were both in love with the same girl. The briefing officer, yes the same one we'd had back in Northolt, tried to explain that love simply wasn't on in wartime, but they'd have none of it.

Meanwhile, and I hope you have not come to the opposite conclusion, the daily flights over Belgium and the Ruhr continued. Occasionally, I would be privy to a discussion among the senior officers over optimal routings and, cleverly, I held my tongue. I was a pilot now and not a navigator and I wanted nothing to change that.

One afternoon I came back from another fruitless discussion with the local officials and discovered the majority of the pilots gathered in a loose circle about the commanding officer. As it was it explained to me in a quick-catch up briefing, Throckmorton-Higgins and at least one of the other pilot officers had failed to distinguish themselves on a recent encounter with the enemy. In RAF speak, this was as close as a senior officer would come to calling someone a coward.

In Throckmorton-Higgins's case, this was far from the first time. As always, he had delayed his attack till the worst of the fighting was over , while the other officer had failed to cover his flight leader's tail. Moreover, Throckmorton-Higgins had had the temerity to suggest on his return that he might be assigned to one of the commissary runs to England.

I should explain that our commanding officer was rather well to do (had a private living as the British would say) and we dined rather well for Air Force officers, chiefly at his expense. I would be sent to town to purchase cheeses and other local produce, while someone else might fly to Northolt, which was located near the commanding officer's estates, to pick up wine from his cellar along with the roast beef of old England, desirable supplements to Air Force rations.

You got the commissary run if you distinguished yourself in battle, or were way ahead in kills, or were just plumb wore out. What could Throckmorton-Higgins have been thinking? Our commanding officer was not one for a public reaming. Throckmorton-Higgins was the exception, and Prentice-Jones, the other slacker that day, unluckily got a public chastisement as well.

No use turning to one's brother officers for sympathy, none was to be had. Throckmorton-Higgins tried to be friendly with me—a first for him, but I would have none of it. And both officers' ground crews were shunned by their comrades, purely by association.

The next day we were medal bound had anyone actually been handing out medals, counter-attacking a somewhat superior force that was a mixture of Messerschmitts and the more maneuverable Heinkel 112's. Wilson got two kills; Prentice Jones got one, and was promptly rehabilitated in the opinion of the mess. Even I got a pat on the back, not for a kill—I'd missed again, not yet having mastered the necessary coordination between one's plane and one's armament, but I had driven off a Messerschmitt who'd been on Smythe-Smith's tail.

Chapter 12. A Night on the Town

As a result of a series of successful missions, or perhaps we were just held up by a lack of aviation fuel, which had to be extracted painfully from the less-than-cooperative French, we pilots were given the evening off beginning in the late afternoon and told we need not return till morning.

Somehow, perhaps because no one else would have us, I ended up in a party of three—Wilson, myself, and a kid who had just joined us. I'll call him the Kid, simply because he was to be shot down and burned alive the next day, and as Wilson said, there was no point really in learning his name.

Roclincourt as a liberty destination wasn't going to cut it. I knew both of the raunchy hangouts in the immediate neighborhood of the village, knew just how raunchy they were. And I hesitated to move upscale, for fear I might be caught trying to pork one of the local official's daughters. Fortunately, I was able to persuade the other two to drive with me all the way to Arras. They didn't care; they just wanted off the base.

We parked the truck somewhere in a maze of back streets and alleyways; yes, we did find it again, after a bit of a search in the late night hours. Wilson suggested we first visit a series of taverns, something we could have done with the other men back in Roclincourt. The Kid said he didn't drink. Wilson asked why, and the Kid, he was a kid, said he wasn't old enough. "This is France and your mother isn't around." The kid said he didn't want to get drunk.

I was no help, for when Wilson asked for my opinion, I said I'd rather meet some girls. "And risk the clap?" Respectable girls, I said.

At this point, the Kid did prove useful, for he pointed back in the direction we'd come—we'd been walking more or less aimlessly through poorly lit streets lined by shuttered shops, and said he thought there'd been some kind of dance back there.

Indeed, a dance was in progress in a hall adjoining the local hospital, a hall that proved to be filled with young nurses. We had some difficulty getting in at first with much discussion among the adult chaperons. Wilson kept pointing to our uniforms and doing his best to force his way in. I observed, in French, that as we were here to die for France, we should be welcomed.

We could come in, it was agreed, but a fee must be paid as required of all guests. British pound notes were produced along with a Canadian dollar on my part. The female guardian at the door looked at both and shook her head. The male guardian, her superior I gathered, whispered in her ear, and waved us in.

The girls inside were indeed respectable, some whose sheer ugliness accounted for it, but, thankfully, there were others who were downright sexy. The first girl I danced with was quite shy, almost withdrawn, the sort I'm normally attracted to. Alas, as she began to feel more confident, she began to giggle.

But there were many other girls there just like her—"the odds are in our favor tonight"—all slim, small busted, extremely feminine.

The one who chose me was buxom and extremely forward. "You English," she said in a charming accent and a low contralto voice. "Quebecois," I replied, and for a while we switched back and forth between languages.

She was a student nurse, much like the student nurses I'd been dating back in Montreal, though less restrained as she soon demonstrated. Her large moon-shaped face had a shockingly large amount of blond hair piled up around it, and she had full, very red lips. But it was the glimpse of skin between her ample breasts that I kept looking at, whenever, that is, she gave me the opportunity. She pressed close when we danced and it was not quite clear who was leading whom.

At that point my eyes were still roving over the crowd, seeing if I might better my hand with a new partner. But my new friend was not to be content with a single dance. "Stay with me," she said, and tucked herself closer into my arms.

Inevitably, her breasts would brush against me each time she turned. When my hand accidentally grazed one—it was quite substantial—she exclaimed, "Mon Dieu, you fliers are fast."

My reply, "That depends on the model of plane we're flying," appeared quite logical at the time, until I realized what she was really getting at. The next moment or, at least, a short time later, we were in an narrow alley, pressed against the wall, having sex upright, a manner new to me, as, come to think of it, was intercourse itself. The process was quite enjoyable, better than anything I'd had back in Canada (and lasting longer). I hoped my companions were having an equally good time.

We made our way slowly back to the dance hall, me, happily confused, still trying to tuck in various portions of my uniform, she looking like the cat that had swallowed the proverbial canary, which indeed she had. At the same time, she appeared as fresh and virginal as when she'd first put on her blouse that night. As I went to open the door, ever the gentleman, we encountered Wilson and the Kid being ejected, and not too gracefully.

"I was misunderstood," Wilson said, "Language barrier." Sign language, perhaps. I gathered from the comments of the French authorities that the young lady in question had been forced to slap away Wilson's roving hands. Alas, I too was barred from the hall, my uniform my ticket to rejection. Tant pis.[1] I got one last look and a wink from my friend— what was her name? what was her phone number?—and then I was back on the street with my comrades.

"You damn blagard," the Kid said to Wilson, "Tonight would have been the night. François was more than willing." (Did people really say blagard in those days? Well, the Kid did.) I gathered that the Kid's apprehensions concerning strong drink did not extend to women.

"How'd you make out?" Wilson asked me. I said nothing, though the answer was written on my face, apparently, for I was soon being pounded on the back to a chorus of "you lucky so and so." The two must have spread the word when we returned to base, for the next day I also received pats on the back from the members of my crew. Even our debriefing officer treated me with a new respect.

---

[1] The meaning of this French expression is somewhere between "too bad" and "tough shit" depending on the context.

Chapter 13. Training Flight

I would like to tell you more about Wilson. Not just because, as another of the very few heroic survivors of my war, he crops up again and again in these memoirs. But because throughout my first year as a pilot, he served as both my mentor and my role model.

Wilson had an elongated oval for a face, which made him look forever sad, a look exacerbated by his persistent refusal to laugh at the laugh-invoking, his own special brand of humor being a cross between deadpan comedy and vicious sarcasm.

He didn't have many friends; check that, he didn't have any friends and he didn't seem to care.

Not a particularly tall man, he seemed taller than he actually was. He had a certain presence. He could sit quietly in a chair smoking throughout a discussion, yet somehow you knew he was there.

He might have been educated at Eton or Harrow like many of the other British officers or he may have been educated at one of the more obscure public schools. School was not something he talked about or felt he needed to.

Perhaps he'd gone to school with the Prince of Wales, or perhaps he was the Prince of Wales; he just radiated that feeling.

I suspect it was his this attitude along with his undeniable flying ability that had won him his rapid promotion to Flying Officer. (And by the same token would see him end the war a grade or two below where he ought to have been.)

When I say he served as my model, I don't mean that I imitated him slavishly, as I had, say, that émigré math professor Lambek during my freshmen year, matching Lambek's haircut down to the part on the left side, copying his gestures. (Cutting my hair to match Wilson's would have been counterproductive. Already only a few sandy hairs remained strewn across his near bald pate, whereas I had that thick head of dark brown hair that I possessed till very recently.)

Nor did I go about deliberately alienating every one I met. No, it was in the air that I did my best to imitate him. He was a pilot extraordinaire and already had more kills than anyone in our unit, save for the briefing officer who'd been a World War I ace.

I'd talked to my ground crew and learned that Wilson generally used less fuel than anyone else unless he'd been in an extended dogfight. In other words, he knew how to get the most from his plane with the least expenditure of energy.

I wanted him to teach me, and treasured my position behind him in the flight as it allowed me to mimic his movements, turning when he turned, launching into the air only a few second after he did, at precisely the same speed.

But I'd learned all I could learn from a distance. I wanted lessons from the master, himself.

Wilson must have thought more of our night out together than I did for he took me aside not very long afterward and suggested, not too kindly and in a manner far from pleasant, that perhaps my flying could be improved.

He asked if I would like to follow him into the sky for lessons. (No more than Brer Rabbit would wish to be thrown into the briar patch.) The idea was that I was to trail his plane, the mother duck, like an eager duckling, banking my plane when he banked his, feathering my engine when he feathered his.

I allowed as I would be pleased to do so and told him I wanted to learn as much as I could. He scowled as if he expected no better.

Birney and Stubbs having both gone into town, he watched while I checked and rechecked my plane, his own check long since completed, but said nothing. He spoke to me only once before we took off after first pointing at his radio repeatedly till I finally got the message. "Leave your radio on; keep your mouth shut."

We took off at a normal speed and settled into a slow steady tapered climb into the sky with none of the sudden maneuvers I expected. At about 10,000 feet, we leveled off, began a series of spirals down to 5,000 feet, and then went back up. Again, nothing I wouldn't have done in pilot training had I actually had pilot training.

An isolated altocumulus cloud hung at about 12,000 feet and we went up through it at an angle leveling off just above it at perhaps 15,000 feet.

"Cut your engine."

If he thought he would scare me by that action, he was wrong. I had done this one exercise in training though with a trained instructor beside me.

"Bank right." I couldn't see naught all, of course, not inside the cloud into which I'd quickly descended, and was tempted to do a steep bank. Without an engine?

"Descend to 13,000."

Where was he? Where was I? I was already at 13,000 feet and felt I'd no choice but to start my engine.

"Good."

Where was he? How the hell had he known what I'd done?

The answer was that he was right behind me as could be seen as we passed briefly beneath the bottom of the cloud.

A moment later, he was ahead of me. He dove, I followed, and the next moment we were doing a loop the loop, the top of the loop passing in and out of that same cloud. Then, we were in and out and all over in the trickiest possible game of follow the leader. We did loops, slow rolls, "flick" rolls, not so much follow the leader as lose the follower.

Whenever I lost sight of him, which was not often, but more often than it ought to have been, I'd find him on my tail, my radio announcing, "Bang bang, you are now dead."

Then we would level out for a bit, something that would be unlikely to occur in an actual dogfight, and I'd find that my hands had been clutching the controls, my fingers dead white. When this happened, I'd shut my eyes or at least blink them a few times to clear them for I'd become disoriented in the cloud and by the many abrupt movements. Finally, I realized that I was making more of this exercise than I needed to. I wasn't engaged in a life or death struggle, merely a game of follow the leader.

The ability to remain calm helped. He didn't lose me after this—not as often, anyway, and so we headed for the ground, but not back to the airfield, not right away. Instead, we skimmed the tree tops and the cows—yes, there was hell to pay later and the commanding officer reamed me out side by side with Wilson and, later, in my own private reaming.

We were sailing close to the surface of the stream that ran next to the base, when we came to the first of the bridges.

I've already noted that Wilson was the best flier in our squadron. He was also far and away everyone's superior at flying close to the ground, a skill that had already won the disapproval of the local farmers and a bawling out from our commanding officer.

He had the not-entirely-necessary ability of being able to guide his plane with pinpoint accuracy through tight and narrow spaces. He was fond of telling the entire mess, sometimes while we were on quite another topic, how he'd flown beneath this bridge or that, though he preferred to hear second-hand descriptions of his efforts.

His piece de resistance was a set of two bridges placed close together that did not do much more than ford a stream near the airfield. A sensible flier that knew his limitations would approach the bridges, perhaps even venture close to the first of them, but quickly lift off again. Others would scoff, say it couldn't be done, then watch in horror as Wilson did it. The less sensible, and there had been only one of these men so far, would dally on the way back to the field, head for the bridges, pass successfully beneath the first, then clip their wing on the second, dying rather horribly in the subsequent crash when their plane caught fire.

I heard what our commanding office had to say to Wilson about this last or rather had his words repeated to me several times by those who had overheard the interchange or had had it repeated to them. "I don't mind losing X, he was a damn poor pilot anyway, but I do mind losing his plane."

Wilson's punishment—after all he hadn't actually forced X to do it, merely taunted him unmercifully for days, was to carry the briefing officer's clipboard for almost a week watching while other less-skilled pilots headed for the skies.

So there I was, the distance of my landing wheels above the surface of the stream, following close after Wilson. We went under the first of the bridges without my really thinking about what we were doing. Then we were heading toward the second and there was all sorts of time for the thoughts to rush in. 'This bridge isn't as wide as the first.' 'There can't possibly be enough room.' 'I should be higher, lower.' 'shift left.' 'shift right.' But I never once thought about escaping up and into the clouds, but let my plane follow Wilson's under the second bridge exactly between the struts where he had placed me. Then, after a final salute to a farmer's cows, we flew back to the base.

Chapter 14. Dogfight High in the Sky

The next morning when the squadron set out, I was able to join in with renewed confidence, my hands light on the controls, caressing, not choking them.

Our squadron cut a single unswerving image in the sky, as pretty as a flock of geese, leaving the minimum of ripples behind, using the minimum of fuel. We cruised along in this fashion, totally unmolested for what seemed an unreasonable length of time. Finally, our squadron leader, acting solely on instinct, an instinct I trusted completely, announced plus five, and we rose another 5000 feet in the air, fairly close, if I recalled correctly to the Hurricane's rated ceiling.

The Heinkel that appeared without warning at twelve o'clock had to rise to meet us. I greeted him with gunfire and, as usual, missed. Unusually, he failed to shy away, but quickly reappeared on my tail.

I launched a quick loop the loop to avoid him and found myself confronting a Messerschmitt on the way down. I fired and missed but the trailing Heinkel caught him in a burst of gunfire. No kill to be added to my tally, but definitely an assist.

Another loop the loop failed to shake my pursuer, so I rose in a steep sloping bank; he fired, missed, and again I tried a loop the loop. I was definitely at or beyond my rated ceiling now, but as my statistics prof at McGill would have said, an average like the rated ceiling is just that, an average not an absolute. The Heinkel had at least another 2000 feet to go he before he needed to level out—if you believed the specs and I guess his pilot did. Nonetheless, I heard his engine cough as it missed briefly, and I immediately launched into a wider, longer loop, which this time ended with me behind him.

I fired. He dove, whether because I'd hit him or because he just wanted to get away, I couldn't tell. I followed him down looking for any sign that I'd scored a hit, smoke, fire, anything.

We dove through a group of German fighters chasing ours and I fired again hitting at least one of them, I think. The Heinkel continued downward but I maintained my distance. He wasn't going to get away and he didn't, leveling out finally. I must have hit something the first time and now I fired again.

The sky around us was full of falling aircraft, two Messerschmitts and a Hurricane that looked a lot like the one Prentice-Jones flew.

All of a sudden I found myself surrounded by unfamiliar aircraft, not that the swastikas on the wings weren't familiar enough. Junkers, I guessed, but only because they were bombers, large, slow moving bombers.

I fired and fired again until I was out of ammunition. The result wasn't all that good a feeling; I now had absolutely no defense on the long way home.

I checked my gas gauge. The level was about normal for me prior to the return flight to the base, a little under half a tank, but then, normally, I didn't engage in all this frenetic activity. I turned northwest by west and headed toward home, inching toward a higher, less-fuel-consuming altitude along a relatively gentle slope. With luck, I'd rejoin my squadron and fly home in company. My luck held and I landed with the group.

For once, the debriefing was exciting. I had something to contribute other than verifying others' claims. We began with the Messerschmitts. I said I'd got one and maybe a second. Wilson said I'd gotten three, which seemed unlikely but the briefing officer wrote down three.

"Who got the three Junkers?" Nobody answered; I guess they were wondering what

Junkers were or, at the very least, how we'd happened to come across them. I raised my hand. "Freygood, three Junkers."

"And what about my Heinkel?" I asked, when it looked like the meeting was over.

"I've no record of a Heinkel." Was the debriefing officer's reply.

"I can give you its number." My voice was that of a little leaguer robbed of a hit by the official scorer.

"Please do so." The debriefing officer's voice dripped icicles.

Almost three years passed before I got credit for that Heinkel. We had to reclaim that portion of Belgium first.

Chapter 15. Promotion

Promotion in rank came easily in those days. All you had to do was survive. And as a group, we weren't very good at that. Some of us, as Wilson was wont to remark, were simply poor fliers with too little training and too little natural ability. But the real reason was there were simply too many of them, too few of us, and, at least at the beginning of the war, Jerry's planes could fly higher and faster than ours.

I'd been lucky, that was all there was to it, really. Or, maybe, God was on our side.

The day I got my Flying Officer's insignia was the day the Wing Commander called me in to bawl me out.

"You're supposed to stay in formation," he snapped.

"Sir, I was mirroring Wilson."

"Wilson!" Wing Commander looked over at his adjutant. It was clear they'd discussed this topic more than once. "Forget Wilson, I want you to stay in formation."

"Sir."

He looked over at the adjutant a second time. Was there to be more than a mere reprimand? "Tom Churchill's dead," he said, "Died in the same bloody dogfight, where you took out the three Junker's and a Messerschmitt."

"It was three Messerschmitts," said the adjutant, who was also the debriefing officer.

It was also the same bloody dogfight in which I'd broken formation to follow Wilson, but I said nothing.

"Not confirmed," snapped the Wing Commander. "You." He looked at me again, so I guess "you" meant me. "You're now a Flying Officer. Did you know that?"

"No, Sir."

"Well you are. Got a letter here about it somewhere. Even if you weren't, but it's better that you are. I want you on the other wing, away from Wilson."

Now, I was in trouble. Wilson was my mentor and good luck charm rolled into one. "You'll be in charge, the other four will group around you. Throckmorton-Higgins and. . . who are the others?" This last was directed at the adjutant. "Dead for the most part, I'm afraid. Hawkins is left, and I'll see Freygood gets a few of the new chaps."

"Don't mind working with a new chap do you, Freygood?"

What was he talking about? I was a new chap.

"Anyhow, you stay in formation; they stay in formation."

"Yes, Sir."

"Dismissed."

"Hold a moment," said the adjutant to me. A series of whispers were exchanged between the two senior officers. "Quite right," Wing Commander said and fumbled in a desk drawer. He drew out a set of Flying Officer's sleeve and shoulder insignia and handed them to me. "Get these sewn on as quickly as possible." After which he and the adjutant got into an intense discussion and it was several moments before I realized that I'd been sent away.

But where and how was I to get the Flying Officer's insignia sewn on? No favorite aunt lived nearby to help me here, not even a student nurse. Well, I did know one student nurse, if not her name or where she lived.

"Wilson," I said that evening, "We're going to town." I'd have preferred to ask the Kid, the Kid would have jumped at the opportunity to visit his François, but the Kid, of course, was long gone. There'd be a new kid tomorrow, reporting to me, God help him.

Wilson was not keen, though the possibility of my failing to find the girl did intrigue him. "You don't know her name, her phone number, or where she lives?"

"I know where she works."

Wilson commandeered an old truck and off we went, picking up a variety of other ranks that wanted a lift on the way out of the base. We dropped most of them in town, though one stayed with us all the way to Arras.

"Do you remember where the dance was?" I asked Wilson who only looked back at me with an "I told you so" grin.

"Stop the car." He stopped; I hailed the first passer-by and asked the way to the Hospital.

"The Hospital," he repeated. "You are English, yes." I explained, again in French, that I was Canadian and the way to the Hospital was desired. He looked at me skeptically, but eventually, after much unnecessary chitchat, pointed the way.

We were walking up the hospital steps when I saw a young lady who looked vaguely familiar. Apparently, she remembered us, too, as the moment she saw Wilson she began to shy away. Just what had he done at that dance?

I interposed myself between the two of them and began with my, "Excusez moi." "You are Marie's friend," she said and her scowl turned to one of welcome. "She misses you."

"I miss her."

"You have indeed. She has just gone home. But I will take you there," she added when she saw the look of desolation on my face.

If Wilson thought this was about to turn into a double date, he was soon disabused. Tonette, Marie's friend, made sure to keep me interposed between her and Wilson as we walked along, thus forcing Wilson off the sidewalk and into the street for most of the way.

"I leave you here," Tonette said as we reached Marie's narrow doorway and scurried off even as Wilson was opening his mouth to call out to her in an English she would not understand.

Marie's mother came first to the door. She resembled a Marie who had allowed herself to grow much plumper, her face that of a Marie with jowls and an extra chin or two. But she was as pleasant as Marie and eager to invite us into her home, which I took as a good sign.

"Marie," was hollered up a long stairway. We waited at the bottom while a Marie wearing only a slip appeared briefly at the top then disappeared. A satisfactory amount of time later, she appeared wearing a green sweater with a deep V-neck and a white skirt, both perhaps one size too small.

"She is something, uh," said the mother, and I could tell that plans were already being made. I had my own plans (besides the insignia I'd brought with me, of course) and they involved standing up in back alleys or, better still, lying down in the back of the truck.

"What is happening?" A swarthy man in a short-sleeved undershirt appeared in an inner doorway carrying a newspaper just as Marie was kissing me full on the lips. "Who is this man?"

Some hurried explanations followed that, it seems, were not entirely adequate in his opinion. The man walked up to me. "You are English," he said, "The English and the Jews are the cause of all our problems."

"I'm a Canadian," seemed an inadequate response, and I wondered if I could just leave the insignia and go, perhaps to pick the sewn-on product from Marie later at her work place.

But I'd not reckoned with Mrs. LeBlanc, nor, apparently, had her husband. A flurry of rapid French ensued, followed by a retreat of man and paper to the living room for a further discussion, though the raised voices of Marie's mother and father hardly made their subsequent conversation more private.

Finally, he reemerged, this time without the paper and wearing a work shirt. "I am going to the tavern," he announced. "You will be gone when I return."

The door slammed and Marie was in my arms again.

I was barely conscious that Mrs. Leblanc had led Wilson away to the back of the house. "Perhaps, we could go somewhere," I suggested when Marie and I came up for air. Believe me I was stiff and hard against her, and the kissing and occasional feel of her breasts while wonderful, was not all I wanted.

"It is not necessary," she said and led me up the stairs.

"But your mother."

"She approves."

She approved of Wilson also for when we came downstairs some hours later so that Marie might get her sewing kit, neither Mrs. LeBlanc nor Wilson were to be seen, though a great deal was to be heard.

To give Marie credit, she blushed. Wilson reappeared just as the last of my new Flying Officer's insignia was sewn in place, he looking like the proverbial cat that had swallowed the canary , and Mrs. LeBlanc all smiles.

"Alas," she said, "There is not time for me to give you a real meal." But then she proceeded to set the kitchen table with beef that had been cooked in wine along with carrots, onions and potatoes, a small salad, and a wonderful apple tart to give us strength for the return journey.

Thus fortified, we kissed our respective partners farewell, and set out for the street near the hospital where we'd parked our truck. Neither of us had the energy nor the desire to talk. I was a Flying Officer!

Chapter 16. The Fog

Today, we live in an era when we can predict the next tsunami within hours, (providing one lives in the right country) and, unless we're George Bush or his head of disaster preparation, establish just when and where a hurricane will hit the mainland by watching the Weather Channel. But once there was a time when we couldn't tell what the weather would be that same afternoon, much less the next day, or the next week.

Before the war, we simply didn't have enough weather stations. And we were just beginning to understand that to predict the weather on the ground, you needed to know what was going on 1000 feet, 10,000 feet and 30,000 feet up in the air.

World War II forced us to develop the necessary skills for weather prediction, to establish more weather stations, and to take radio balloon soundings the way a riverboat pilot might cast a weighted line to see how the currents were flowing at various depths.

The war forced us to develop many new skills, not only weather prediction, but cryptography, computers, snorkels, sonar, and on and on. No, I'm not saying this is an argument for war. It's just that during wartime, politicians who normally would rather let the country fall apart around them than stand accused of spending, must invest or die.

The weather that morning as viewed from our observatory, the officer's hut, was fog, a dense thick fog. My question for the briefing officer was how far this fog extended and how long we could it expect it to last. Yes, I was eager to go up in the air again, I was eager to add to my kills.

He said he didn't know how far out or how far up the fog extended. He thought it might burn off in a couple of hours.

I said it was safe to take off then, as the fog would burn off well before we needed to return.

The Wing Commander said he wasn't sure this was within policy. The burnouts and suck ups among us nodded their heads.

I said I'd volunteer to find how high and how far the fog extended. "Maybe Jerry is already out there."

"But our bombers are not." the Wing Commander said decisively.

"If you followed a specific compass course which I would draw up for you, . . ." the briefing officer thought aloud.

"You could swoop out of the clouds and strafe that Jerry airfield near. . . where all our troubles have come from lately." This from Wilson.

"If they have fog, that is." The Commander again.

"Cloud cover in that region is expected."

And the two senior officers got into a discussion of weather forecasts that they may well have continued in heaven even to this day.

"Could we give it a try, Sir?" This from Hawkins, who needed a kill or two to impress his French girlfriend.

The raiding party I took with me included five in all. Wilson, Smith, Hawkins, and, of course, Smythe-Smith who was not be outdone by Hawkins.

I'd rather hoped Wilson would lead, but he immediately developed a false modesty and insisted I lead the formation.

Of course, the fog extended only a few hundred feet in the air, but then came a low-lying layer of clouds. With the clouds screening the fog from the sun, it might not burn off before we returned to base, at which time we would be hard pressed to figure out where to land and how. Maybe this raid hadn't been such a good idea after all.

(If you're wondering why we just didn't make use of radar, get a grip; while ground-based radar existed all over England, though not yet linked completely, and airborne radar was available in prototype, it just wasn't in our hands, yet.)

On the plus side, the cloud layer extended well into Belgium and perhaps over the Netherlands as well. Perhaps, we would surprise the Germans.

The long uneventful flight across Eastern France gave me time to think about just what we were going to do when we got near the German airfield. We wouldn't be able to see it from our present altitude. And though I was confident that we were on a course and speed that would bring us near the airport by a specific time, I wasn't sure how we could translate 'near' into 'there'.

I saw the solution in my mind first, then sought to translate it into the minimum number of words. It was never a good idea to break radio silence.

Ten minutes out from where our target might or might not be, I brought us down to 10,000 feet and then just above the cloud layer at 6,000. "Wilson, Hawkins, down on go. Report miles, direction."

Out of the silence, I heard, "eins, zwei, drei, vier, fünf," to be followed shortly by "nörd, ost, Süd, Westen." Scared the shit out of me till I recognized the voice of Smythe-Smith delivering this morning's German lesson.

"eins, zwei, drei, vier, fünf." I strained to remember. Brilliant idea. By speaking in German, we were less likely to reveal our presence.

"Go." Wilson and Hawkins streaked off at a steep downward angle. A long frustrating pause. What if there were fog below?

" fünf. Süd." came from the radio. Translated, the German base was five miles away somewhat to the south of where we were headed. Correcting for Wilson's and Hawkins' increase in speed on the dive, and the distance we had traveled before their report reached us, and the time it took me to make the calculation, "Go," I said, and Smith and our German instructor Smythe-Smith headed through the cloud cover toward the ground.

Then it was my turn. Ten seconds later, I discovered there was no fog below to provide cover. Descending the last 500 feet totally exposed to the guns of the field, I banked and began shooting, first at the control tower and then at a line of planes. I sensed rather than heard shouting and then heard the rapid firing of my comrades' guns mere seconds behind me. Banking, I saw towers of smoke and flame arising all around the depot as fuel stores ignited. No time for a second pass, alas. Men were pouring out of the barracks, guns in hand, though Wilson and Jones were firing down on them sending them scurrying back. I wish we'd had bombs with us, we could have taken out the hangars, too.

I headed back up into the clouds. The others followed shortly thereafter. No damage to us and anywhere from eight to ten of their planes destroyed along with some if not all of the equipment the control tower had held.

Far off to the East, where other German airfields were located, black dots appeared in the sky. These may have been German aircraft now on the alert to defend their own airfields, or German aircraft dispatched to chase after us, or simply black dots. My focus was on what lay ahead of us on our home field. Fog or no fog?

The way back appeared to take a lot longer than the flight in. No plans could be made ahead of time; we would only know what to do once we'd arrived.

When we were in radio range of Arras, I said in English, "Arras field, fog?"

"Fog still, rangers," came the cheery reply. I had an eighth of a tank of gas left. "Got gas, chaps?" I radioed to my flight. "Some.," "Enough to land." came the responses.

How much could we rely on our altimeters? Not a great deal. Even a five-foot miscalculation could mean the difference between a bumpy landing and a lethal crash. The total insanity of what I'd talked the other four men into doing hit me.

"Lights on." I heard from below. "We'll have a light on top of every building and lights along the main runway."

'Candles in the rain;' wasn't that the title of a recent song? The lights along the runway seemed no brighter than candles. Still, I coasted easily between the lines of lights, wishing only that they'd though to mark the end of the runway as well.

Smythe-Smith followed close on my tail. I heard his engine die and took this as a sign to cut my own, traveling only a short distance into the underbrush at the edge of the field before I came to a stop.

"Spot on, Sir," hollered Birney as he came running out of the fog. "Formidable," said the first of the two Frenchmen who worked for Birney as mechanics. But my ear remained tuned to the sound of engines as one by one all five of us landed safely.

We received modest congratulations from the other pilots, in the form of smiles and slaps on the back, for the British are not much given to celebration, and looked forward to lying about for an hour or so while the news of our success leaked around the base. But a busy serviceman is a happy serviceman. Those fliers who'd stayed home had already endured a series of bad training films, including one warning of diseases one might contract with improperly cleansed French girls.

We joined them, once our planes were secured, for a morale building speech by our commanding officer—why we are here, followed by one on navigating under hazardous conditions by the debriefing officer who, it soon appeared, had stumbled across the appropriate pamphlet while we were en route to the target.

Dinner—quite a good one including several bottles of a very good wine that the Wing Commander said he had been saving for just such a special occasion—was followed by the usual bull session. We covered the day's events, but briefly as most had already heard them and it was considered bad form to brag about one's current exploits. After which we went into a game of "do you remember when" whose sole objective was to leave everyone newer to the service than the teller with the feeling that nothing they had done or would ever do could possibly top events of the lost and legendary past. Thus, of course, the appellation "bull" session.

After which we got into our usual useless discussion as to why Air Command did what they did, particularly concerning the timing of the raids. One group held that the raids should be limited to the late afternoon, when we would be coming out of the sun invisible to the defending planes. A second, slightly smaller group said that the time of day was a matter of indifference—surprise was the most important element. And a third group, who appeared to have confused west with east, opted for an early morning run. What difference? Air Command would do what they would do, ignorant of and indifferent to our desires.

Once each of us had drunk his limit and felt braced for sleep, we went to bed. What a dumb idea our flight through the fog had been; how wonderful the way things had turned out.

Chapter 17. The Village

My trips into the village of Roclincourt, that at one time had provided me with a sense of self-worth, now seemed an intrusion on time better spent in the air. What a collection of yentas (gossips) the townsfolk were. Not enough that we British airmen should be the focus of their quarrels, we must now become privy to them.

The local priest, I was told, had an eye for women, yes, even now in his late sixties. Hawkins and Smith-Smythe's common girl friend was also the focus of much vicious conjecture. Perhaps, she was just such a slut as was described to me in detail. More likely, Hawkins and Smith-Smythe, being particularly handsome specimens, were desired elsewhere (as lovers by the other girls, as husbands by their mothers). Or could it be, for it was here the males of the village had taken their stand, simply because Hawkins and Smith-Smythe weren't French.

Economic factors might be involved. Had I bought cheese from Cedan? Did I not know his cows had the fever, his storage sheds leaked rain in winter and were filled with flies in summer? The lives of Canadian fliers should not be risked on such foul stuff.

Politics were as important to the French as their pocketbooks and their women and were allowed to ride roughshod over common sense. Just as the Israelis were later to stand accused, it took only three Frenchmen to form a new party. Every traditional brand of French politics was represented in this tiny village, socialist, communist, monarchist, Catholic-conservative, along with some truly undesirable new ones that were prepared to welcome the Nazis with open arms.

From being reserved and standoffish, the villagers had become entirely too friendly. Not merely the girls (of all ages, for the lack of teeth, or the presence of wrinkles and excess chins appeared no barrier to flirtation) but those like the Delebaire brothers who thought I would like to join them in a daily chorus of the communist Internationale.

The war was on all their minds, too, how could it not be, with the possible exception of current members of the French L'Armee de Aire and their L'Armee de Terre who, it appeared, would be content to posture and collect their pensions till the end of time.

I was sharing a morning snack with the town baker—I had supplied some of the cheese I'd just purchased, he the bread and coffee, for the French still had coffee to drink at that point in the war—when the wife and daughter of the would-be-Gauleiter of La Ville de Roclincourt appeared in the doorway. The 17-year old naturally blond and buxom daughter had early on expressed a preference for me. Perhaps, the homemade, form-fitting and rather short dress she wore that morning had me as its target. What was there about a city-raised Jew that could be so attractive to this almost-woman who'd clearly been bred to work, pitchfork in hand, alongside the men in the fields while discarding babies between her ample thighs? I didn't want to know.

Her mother, it seemed, would not be opposed to the idea of uniting two cultures, but had to tiptoe around the topic due to the rather anti-British, anti-Semitic, anti-everyone views of her husband. Like many Frenchman of his time, his anti-Semitism translated, despite the long-standing French distrust of anything German, into identification with the Nazis. I suppose, too, in his case, he imagined himself in the tight Nazi uniform, distended belly somehow melted away, barking orders to a group of devoted subordinates.

Father and daughter did not get along at all well and any appearance of the family in public was sure to be marked by an extended screaming match among them. The screams from the daughter were off-putting for a second reason, the possibility they might be directed at me some day stiffening my resolve to avoid what was, after all, not an entirely unattractive female. (Arras was just too far away for the daily encounters my body craved. Men at arms, like their civilian counterparts, are not hungry for combat in the mornings but for coffee, a croissant, and a woman.)

The girl stood next to me, tongue-tied, while her mother talked to the baker, with the occasional, "Good morning, how are you, how is your distinguished commanding officer?" addressed to me. The baker was a socialist, though , as he'd confided, with some monarchist leanings as this would restore order to the country whose governments came and went far too often for his comfort. The arrival at the bakery in search of his daily baguette of Pierre Delebaire, who along with his equally rapidly communist brother ran the only garage in town, completed the triangle of views. Gabrielle, the daughter, had to quickly decide whether the handsome Canadian flier or the handsome communist mechanic would be the better choice for producing babies.

She was spared the choice, for at that moment her father appeared in the doorway. What was keeping his wife? Why did she prattle on so? He glared at me, he glared at Pierre, a long time enemy. He would have frowned at the baker had he dared.

Mother, loaves in hand, and daughter pushed passed us to the door hoping to shut off this tirade, the daughter giving me a light shove with her hips to indicate she cared. Pierre began to sing the Internationale and the would-be-Gauleiter was immediately on the boil. There would be changes, he announced. Order would be restored. (Here the baker nodded his head in agreement.) The British would be sent packing, and the French and Germans, natural allies, would live together in harmony.

The mayor of the village, owner of the more agreeable of the local taverns patronized by the airmen, came on the porch then, attracted by the sound, and expressed his great and continuing admiration for the British, though there was still the question of compensation for the now dry cows. The would-be-Gauleiter began to scream at him, too; wife and daughter began to scream at the would-be-Gauleiter and I longed to be back in the air, where at the very worst one could be killed.

Chapter 18. Dunkirk

If one's ambition like mine were to kill Nazis, kill Germans, and, ultimately, to kill Hitler, or, as the Public School boys believed, that now Britain had entered the War, Hitler would soon back down, then the Spring of 1940 brought nothing but disappointment.

In May 1940, Germany invaded Holland, Belgium and Luxembourg as well as attacking French positions in Western France. The Luftwaffe flew more than 1,000 bombing sorties in support of the offensives. Our fighters and those of the French won victories in the air, 85 of them, but the French still couldn't decide whether they were in or out and the bombers of the Armee de l'Air were not committed to action.

The repeated successful missions had won me a measure of respect, even from Wilson, but this may only have been because he now so many new targets, that is, junior officers on which he could vent his sarcasm.

A transport had ferried a group of our still living pilots back to England, and when they returned it was individually each one behind the controls of a spanking new Hurricane.

They were accompanied by a new flight of pilots, mostly colonials like myself. Not all were fully trained as one Australian proved on landing. Fortunately, we were able to repair his aircraft.

The new additions included an American for the first time. America, itself, still hesitating to enter a foreign war. The Yank was named Levinson; like me, he was not there to prove himself in combat, but to kill as many Nazis as he possibly could. A fellow Canadian (also named Levinson), a Rhodesian, and an Australian would make up my flight.

The Rhodesian had a long, rambling, but intensely interesting story to tell. His elementary flying training had been out in the African bush where the roads were just rolled dirt. The airfield was grass, no runways, so most take-offs were into the wind. The aircraft used for training were Tiger Moths—World War I vintage biplanes. To start them, the propeller had to be rotated by hand, usually by a ground mechanic. When the engine was primed, the pilot would call "Contact" and the mechanic would swing the propeller to start the engine. The Rhodesian's first lesson was in how to move the airplane on the ground. One had to apply just enough power—not too much—to be able to use the rudder pedals to steer, as it was necessary to constantly zigzag the airplane to see where one was going.

As in my own training, they'd practiced stalls. The Rhodesian was able to do a rather spectacular turn, called a stall turn, followed by a spin originating from the stall. Their failure rate, not incidentally, was higher than ours, four out of ten trainees falling by the wayside.

He got a bit cocky early on in his training, and, once, stalled the engine while hanging upside down, something I'd yet to try. (And never did). On another occasion, while up alone on a fairly hazy day, he lost sight of the airport. (I'd done that often enough, myself.) Not to worry; he found a railway single track and followed it. When he saw a farmhouse with a good open field close by, he decided to land. Remembering the drill, he made an initial low pass over the field along with a wind check. No problem. The subsequent approach and landing went smooth as silk. He thought he'd gotten away with it, when he heard a sickening crunch. An instant later, the airplane slewed around and tipped forward onto the propeller, which immediately shattered.

Stopping the engine, and stepping out of the plane, he discovered the problem. Not one he was likely to run into in France, or England for that matter. He'd struck a termite hill, only a small one, but tough enough to smash the wheel. An African appeared and fetched the farmer, who in turn called the airfield for assistance. Somehow, the people at the airport thought he'd come down by or rather on the railway, so they alerted Rhodesian Railways, who in turn stopped the trains till they could find out more.

The result was he had to wait five or six hours for a lift back to the base. He was given food, but the wait was tedious. A car showed up, eventually, driven by the Duty Officer, and it was pitch black by the time they returned to the airfield. He received a negative assessment from the flight school following this incident, but in my book, he was a fine pilot, one who clearly learned from his mistakes.

Meanwhile, Throckmorton-Higgins had decided that I was his good luck charm. He came sucking up to me that evening after mess, and declared that though he may not have given his all before, he was a changed man. "I'm now willing to die," he said.

"But are you willing to kill?" I looked him directly in the eye and he looked away. But he must have talked to one of the higher ups, because the next day when my flight went up for our evening constitutional, he was there in place of the Rhodesian. Pity.

I learned several things about my group from that maiden flight. Levinson the Canadian could fly—he'd already seen combat with the 17th squadron. Levinson the American could not. But he did respond to simple commands. The Australian, who'd been a crop duster until he enlisted, could fly rings around us all. He was incredibly reckless, though; Wilson would have loved him; I marked him down for an early grave.

The mechanics kept the radio going all day in the hangars, two radios actually, as the base had hired some locals to work alongside our men, and they spoke only French. What was creepy, as I who spoke both languages soon noticed, were the discrepancies between the two sets of news broadcasts. British radio didn't report all the disasters, but their reports were tempered. From listening to French radio, you'd hardly think there was a war. The French continued to say reassuringly that the Maginot line was impregnable and it was merely a question of holding fast in Belgium (or, at least, in Walloon, or French Belgium).

We had shortwave in the officer's mess, and the German government broadcasts presented yet a third view. Even correcting for the many obvious lies generated by Goebbels and his crew, clearly things would get much worse before they got better.

The next day we learned that Chamberlain had resigned as Prime Minister—Yay! and Winston Churchill had replaced him as head of a coalition government. Most of the mess seemed to think Winston would make a great leader. Not surprising, these Public School types all stuck together.

I was planning more training flights for my group, tightness in formation was essential, but it was not to be. Immediately after breakfast the following morning, we learned from the base commander that the British army was to be evacuated in its entirety from the Continent.

German radio hadn't lied after all. The French had done themselves in. Their vaunted Maginot line had fallen in hours, not months, and the Germans were everywhere including Calais and Boulogne on the coast of northern France. Dunkirk remained the only port available for the evacuation of our troops. We were to provide two of the 16 fighter squadrons assigned to the protection of the port.

"You'll be in the air pretty much all of the time." the briefing officer told us. "Squadron A under the command of Flight Lieutenant Greer will fly out immediately after this briefing. Squadron B will fly out on their return."

49

I was in Squadron A and had already visualized the layout of my flight: The two Levinson's would be immediately behind me—I'd have at least one competent flier to watch my tail, Throckmorton-Higgins would fly on the inside rear, the Aussie on the outside.

We looked at maps. The Southwest portion of the German line was to be our squadron's ultimate responsibility. We were to fly due south of Arras on this first day in support of a British counter attack.

Our flight went out as one, over-confident, zealous, with nothing to change our attitude during the first 40 minutes. Fighting could be seen to the north, but where was the promised counter-attack at Arras?

"Reconnaissance aircraft at 10 o'clock," reported Wilson from his lead position on the left flank. "You have five," came the laconic reply from the Flight Lieutenant, which meant that Wilson's group could go after it but couldn't spend more than five minutes in the endeavor.

Five minutes did not prove adequate. I learned later that one of the two fighters Wilson had sent after the aircraft experienced engine trouble and had been forced to return to base. The other had continued the pursuit, but after several minutes in which he'd barely gained on the fleeing reconnaissance plane had returned to the squadron.

"Reconnaissance plane at 2 o'clock," Levinson the Canadian reported on our own group's channel, "permission to engage."

I passed on the request for permission to the Flight Lieutenant. "We'll go as a group," I radioed when permission was granted. A minute later when the reconnaissance plane was in our sights, a flight of Messerschmitts appeared on our left from out of the clouds and we as quickly switched targets. I dispatched the Aussie to finish off the reconnaissance aircraft and focused on the Messerschmitts. They came down, we went up, faster than they expected, I think. Shots were exchanged. Two Messerschmitts went down, my kill and I think one of the Levinson's. I noticed the Aussie had returned and then only a single Messerschmitt was left hanging there. "Mine," Levinson the Canadian hollered as it disintegrated.

We picked off another reconnaissance plane on the way in, or rather, the Flight Lieutenant did, but saw no more German fighters before we had to return, passing the second squadron on our way in.

One by one we reported to the debriefing officer, then ate lunch (or else the other way round). The good times were over, no waiting about for things to settle down. Wilson was interrupted during the meal to do his debriefing, returning to cold fish and chips. "Tea's still hot," he said.

Birny chased me out of the hangar. "I've got 'elpers," he said, pointing to two Frenchmen. "You're to sleep. You'll be going up again today."

That's what the briefing officer had told me. I went to my bunk as ordered but got out a paperback. Who could sleep in the middle of the day?

The briefing officer was in our hut in what seemed only a few minutes later. "Go to sleep." he commanded.

I closed my eyes as ordered and went over the morning's flight in my mind, thought about Marie—did I want to marry her?—and then I was asleep as ordered.

We indeed did go up again that same day, sans the Canadian Levinson, who we'd left somewhere over Arras on our first flight, two kills to his credit, and short two pilots from Wilson's flight whose engines were still on the bench waiting reassembly.

Priorities had changed in the hangars, and whatever could be back in the air in the allotted time was taken care of first. Birny assured me that he'd gone over my plane personally. "But some of these new fellows . . ." He shook his head ruefully, his voice trailing off. The two French mechanics stood at attention, hands in a salute as my plane rolled down the runway.

We passed the Wing Commander's squadron on the way out. They, at least, were at full strength.

Two more reconnaissance planes appeared on our outbound flight and when we chased them swarms of Messerschmitts appeared to chase us. The Messerschmitts were a mixture of models and we were no match for the 109E2s; the longer range of their 20mm cannon were sure to hit us before we could hit them. The Aussie refused to accept this, as did a man from the second squadron who was to die a day later from his injuries.

If you would ever doubt the courage of an Australian, don't. Our man was in his final dive, spinning madly on one remaining wing and yet he managed to record a kill no more than 1000 feet above the ground.

Still, a single day in the air and I'd lost forty percent of my flight, our squadron, only slightly less.

Meanwhile some 300,000 men were being evacuated across the channel at Dunkirk leaving behind them as we could see from the air most of their equipment. We only hoped our troops had sabotaged the gearboxes on their trucks and put sugar in the gas tanks before they left.

But I'm getting ahead of myself. By evening, the British counter attack at Arras had begun and the Germans were doing everything they could to stop it. Two air battles were going on simultaneously all along a lengthy front, one at high altitudes fighter against fighter and one at low when the German planes went down to strafe our troops and we went down after them.

Not all our planes were lost to enemy fire. Our Flight Lieutenant had waited till the last possible moment to turn the squadron back and some of the lads, low on fuel, were forced to walk home. Thankfully, most turned up in the next day or so.

Chapter 19. The Wedding

The next two days were a great deal easier on us, not for a good reason, but a bad one. The counter attack south of Arras had failed and our troops had pulled back. For whatever reason, the Germans held off from pursuit for our base would have been overrun had they done so. The rumor after the war was that they'd held back because Hitler's astrologer had warned him to wait a day or so until the stars were favorable. The other rumor, which I made up myself, was that Hitler's astrologer was a British agent. The result, whatever the explanation, was a relatively quiet series of days, although we still went up twice each day with twice the potential to kill and be killed.

A week earlier, our commander had found a solution to the ongoing conflict between Hawkins and Smith-Smythe over Nanette, the local girl they were both crazy about. The better man would marry the girl. Hawkins won the toss and the bans were posted in the village to much amusement there.

As I might have told the two Flight Officers, had common sense not dictated I keep my mouth shut, it was not just that both had slept with Nanette, but other men had as well. If Hawkins wanted to marry a slut instead of a virgin, that was his problem. Besides, he'd been saying over and over how much he loved her.

And don't get me wrong, Nanette was beautiful, certainly far more attractive and presentable than the common whore one of the enlisted men had decided he was in love with. Nanette taught school when not at work in the bar and for all I know would have made a good wife and mother.

The commander arranged a shift in our squadron schedule, so that Derek [Hawkins] and Nanette might marry that afternoon. I contemplated marrying Marie that afternoon as well—a double wedding—but it would have been too complicated to arrange. Besides, I had my own doubts about Marie's virginity.

The Hawkins-Lafarge wedding wasn't quite as ornate as the one depicted in the film, *The Sound of Music*, held as it was in a mess tent rather than a cathedral. Moreover, the ceremony was performed by a parish priest in faded patched vestments with the aid of a single altar boy rather than an ornately-clad bishop with a choir of assistants, but it had in common with the movie wedding the combination of religious and military ceremony.

An escort of pilot officers in formal uniform (mine borrowed as usual) met the bride at the mess hall door and trailed bride and bridesmaids up the aisle to the makeshift altar. The tavern keeper took the place of the bride's father, a prisoner of war of the Germans.

We were at that point in the service where the groom is supposed to say, "I do," when the alarm went off. At least I thought we were at that point. This was the first wedding I'd ever attended in person rather than on film, though later I was to have plenty of experience with weddings, including four of my own, well, three plus a wedding rehearsal. The service, in Latin was, Greek to me. In fact, I don't suppose anyone there really understood Latin apart from the priest and a few of the Public School boys who'd had to decline irregular Latin verbs while they were in high school (the fifth form, I believe the Brits call it).

The alert rang out a second time, a loud clanging alarm that sounded throughout the station. My first thought was that the briefing officer was responsible, a prank, sort of like a Prairie Chivaree. My next was that Smythe-Smith was behind the joke, a last final jab at the groom. But no, Smythe-Smith, the groom's best man, was standing next to him, waiting with the ring.

I thought all this, but at the same time I was running toward the door, my training dominating any second thoughts about schoolboy pranks. When I did reach the field, the briefing officer was already there, megaphone in hand, waving his arm and shouting, "take off in your plane, take off now."

My fighter was still parked outside the hangar where I'd left it earlier for inspection. I'd barely reached it, when Birney and Stubbs practically tossed me into the cockpit. At the same time, I could hear the loud drone of engines, not Rolls Royce engines, but Jumos; a near dozen German bombers were close at hand. Bombs began to drop at the far end of the field behind me and I heard the sound of machine guns firing.

Forget the checklist; as soon as my engine turned over I was accelerating toward the end of the runway, hoping I had sufficient clearance. Again came the shots, much closer now, practically in my ear. I banked on takeoff into a more favorable wind, looked behind me and saw planes on fire, some exploding just as their pilots climbed into them.

Heading upward on as steep an angle as I dared while staying clear of the field, I heard more explosions below. Bombs had been dropped on the mess hall, and on the runway itself. A boom, a flare of harsh yellow light, and a steep column of black smoke announced the Jerries had hit our fuel dump.

But where were they? And how many of us were left? I intended to kill as many of them as I possibly could, on my own if necessary, but I was not to be a hero. Two minutes free of the field my gas gauge indicated I had only half a tank left. Well and good, there hadn't been time for a refueling, then. But the needle continued to drop; I'd been hit, after all. I continued to climb in pursuit of the bombers, but the gauge read only 1/4 full by the time the bombers had turned and were headed back to . . . to where? Germany? Belgium? Or just a few miles to the southeast in France? The war had reached out to us now; we were in as much danger on the ground as in the air.

Still, three of our fighters were nosing in and out among their bombers and two Junkers fell from the sky. As for me, I'd no choice but to return to the field, hoping for a usable stretch of runway, riding on fumes.

The mess hall had been destroyed, collapsing in the middle after its supports gave way. People were still emerging from the wreckage, some injured, others half dead and having to be assisted.

The priest had been spared, though he was bleeding profusely from a head wound. The bride's father was dead; the bride was dead. Smith-Smythe was dead having been killed as he was getting into his plane. Hawkins had been freed from the wreckage of the mess hall but was doubled over in grief, his wife and his best friend dead in the space of ten minutes.

My flight which now included the Rhodesian gathered round me as one by one they returned to the field. All had survived along with their planes or so I thought at the time. Levinson the Yank, the raw beginner, the ultimate survivor, later was found dead, stuffed in a bomb crater, useless.

Throckmorton-Higgins was the last to arrive, beaming all over, as if totally unaware of all that had happened. "I got one," he announced full of pride.

"The blagard finally got it together," Wilson said in memory of the Kid.

But by that time I was standing in the middle of the wreckage of the mess hall, helping the briefing officer to identify bodies. Several of the wedding guests, four or five members of the ground crew who'd been invited to look on, and our beloved commanding officer were among the corpses.

Throckmorton-Higgins stopped smiling when he saw the latter's body; other men cried. I just stood there, stunned, suddenly realizing with absolute certitude who had betrayed us, how the Germans had known to stage an attack on the very afternoon we'd be least alert. I vowed to take care of that one man in the morning and I did. But first, I needed to get back to separating the living from the dead, organizing work parties to clear away the debris, inspecting the damage to the hangars—minimal; how had the Germans missed?—helping our briefing officer to verify his counts.

I wasn't alone, of course. Everyone who could walk was lifting lumber, shifting corpses for later burial, checking out planes, and moving those that could be repaired back toward the hangars.

Derek Hawkins tried to help, but got in the way. Who could blame him for his grief? Wilson had the bright idea of sharing a glass of scotch with him in memory of his beloved Nanette. The Rhodesian, a Brit from Wilson's flight, and I then shared glasses with Derek in turn. When he passed out, we put him to bed.

The briefing officer, our acting base commander, face set in tight angry lines, had no choice but to head off for never-ending radio conversations with Group Command, and Flight Lieutenant and Acting Squadron Leader Greer took over the clipboard. By evening, we had the final count: Fourteen operable planes and four possibles including mine. Six pilot officers and two flying officers dead. Our Base commander. Ten enlisted men. The Chief Mechanic had been killed standing out on the tarmac shaking his fist at the Germans. Birney had been appointed to take his place and would as soon as he got out of the medic's hut. Some kind of operation was necessary and would be performed that evening.

Pity, for the next morning, when I woke deliberately an hour before dawn, I could have used him at my side.

We ate together that evening, officers and men alike, food intended for the wedding, plus vin ordinaire in small quantities. A man who reached for a second glass would be restrained; we still had work to do.

I went to bed late, though earlier than some, and woke early, stole a truck (the one that still worked and was not lying sideways on the dirt like some dead animal) and drove to the home of Jean and Pierre Delebaire. They were flaming Bolshies, but come to think of it, so was my mother.

They did not like being woken that early, but their experience in the Party had taught them to obey orders. They showed no surprise when I asked them to supply me with a pistol and to bring pistols for themselves.

We drove to the opposite end of the village, perhaps a half-mile out into the country, and parked behind the house of the would-be Gauleiter of Arras. The damn fool had even left up the radio aerial which could be seen in the glow of dawn clamped to his smoking chimney.

The dogs set to barking. We didn't wait for the house's occupants to come down to greet us in response, but kicked in the door. Monsieur was first down the stairs, wearing a nightshirt, followed by Madame in nightdress and robe. and shortly afterward by Mademoiselle. "What is the meaning of this?" Monsieur began. I showed him my pistol, "Take us to the radio."

"But you are mistaken." he protested.

"It's in the attic," Mademoiselle told us. Her father started toward her then and there as if to strangle her and I shot him in the thigh. I wasn't aiming for the thigh.

"Take him upstairs to get the radio," I told the Delebaire brothers. "Then bring it down."

I waved Madame to a seat at the table. "You have coffee perhaps?" Mademoiselle volunteered to make some and I let her pass behind me, but not too closely.

The Delebaire brothers reappeared. Both had their hands full of radio, their guns put away, but the would-be Gauleiter who staggered down the steps ahead of them already had lost a good deal of blood and did not look as if he would have put up too much of a fight.

"Put your new transmitter in the truck and then come back," I told the brothers. As soon as they were out the door, I shot Monsieur. I'd intended a gut shot, which would have meant a slow painful death, but got him in the heart instead. I'd never be a marksman.

Madame remained calm. Amazing fortitude, the French. "You may kill me too, Monsieur Canadien, but please spare my daughter."

"I intend to do just that." The brothers returned and after we all sat and had a quiet cup of coffee, always the best way to start the morning, I had them escort Mademoiselle to the truck. They were happy to oblige. They were good boys and I did not think Mademoiselle would come to any harm; perhaps a marriage might even result.

Moreover, their newly acquired German-made radio transmitter would prove of much value to the about-to-form French resistance.

I removed the remaining bullets from the pistol, wiped it clean of prints with a dishtowel, and tossed it to Madame. "You will tell the police you shot your husband, a philanderer. Otherwise, I cannot guarantee your daughter's safety." Had I read too many detective stories, listened to too many radio mysteries? Would she keep silent other than as instructed? In any event, a day later, I would not be around to find out.

Chapter 20. Flight over Dunkirk

The bombings during Derek Hawkins' wedding had taught us that neither skill nor luck would save us, that we were as vulnerable on the ground as in the air.

On a personal note, Stubbs was dead. Birny walked around with a patch over one eye, the result of a flying glass fragment, but the doctors had told him he might soon remove the patch. No one said anything when I set to work beside him and even those officers who normally would have scorned to work with their hands found that clearing away fallen lumber and the fetching and carrying of tools did fall within their job descriptions.

We spent the morning, relieved for the moment from active duty, in sweeping up the debris, and in seeing what if anything could be salvaged from the mess.

I worked alongside Birney, determined I could at least salvage my own plane, but it was not to be. At noon, we received the orders to fly one last mission from Arras and then to return together to Northolt, back in England, for our new assignment.

There were many tears and much hugging on the part of the Frenchmen we would leave behind. I'd already said my goodbyes in the village earlier that day and did not intend to return there a second time. Marie would just have to wait.

We'd enough men, planes, and petrol remaining to put together a single squadron with the Flight Lieutenant in charge. He was a good man, reliable, and I'm sure if he'd lived through the next week, he'd have been promoted to Squadron Leader, or even jumped a grade to Wing Commander.

I now had the Rhodesian out on the right where the Aussie had been. Levinson the American's place had been taken by a Frenchman, highly qualified, though I'd doubts about the Bloch MB 152 he brought with him. He said he'd pieced it together from two half-completed prototypes. The last member of my flight was Doyle, a newbie straight from Eton. Well, he'd been new a week earlier when he'd joined the Wing Commander's squadron, but now he was a seasoned veteran, one wise enough not to show it.

The morning had gone well for Group Command as a whole. The debarking from Dunkirk had continued and every passing hour saw the departure of another four or five thousand men. Every hour also saw the slow advance of German troops as they closed in on the pocket they'd established between Abbeville and Nieuport Either Hitler's astrologer had ended his warnings or Hitler had ended his astrologer. Our job was to keep the Heinkels (the bombers) and the Junkers away. And we did that by being constantly on the attack. In theory, we ought to have held back our forces until there were more of us than there were of them, but as the German circle tightened around us, more and more of their planes could be brought to bear in the increasingly smaller area.

Our group was zipping back and forth supporting one squadron after the other. Everyone recorded a kill that afternoon. The Frenchmen got two before they got him. Throckmorton-Higgins got his before they hit his gas tank and he began a long slow spiraling descent. It looked to me like he might be able to walk home—assuming he landed in French-held territory, but I didn't have time to watch him land.

The Rhodesian, Doyle, and I had company. I went up to avoid the Jerries, which may or may not have been a mistake. It cost fuel, which I really didn't have, but it gave me a longer time in which to glide to safety after a random bullet hit my engine and smashed my coolant system. A mist of glycol spray and smoke from the engine immediately spattered across the canopy.

"We're turning for home," the Flight Lieutenant said.

We were far inland then, and I might have returned to Arras had there still been a base there—Arras itself was now overrun by Germans along with the base and the nearby town of Roclincourt. A return to England across the channel would be next to impossible. Behind me the air was filled with enemy planes.

I headed southwest only to see roads filled with German tanks and streams of refugees. I headed west toward Abbeville, saw a glimpse of the sea, blue and white, as unsettled as the land. Suddenly, as I crossed the boundary between land and ocean, the air was filled with anti-aircraft fire. The Germans had moved their batteries into place at a rapid rate no one could have forecast. I was hit a second time, knocking a gaping hole in my port wing; still my plane continued to fly.

I headed along the coast of France toward Cherbourg. If I could find a landing spot free of Germans—where had they come from? How had they gotten so deeply into France so quickly?—then I would try to bring the plane down in some farmer's field or, at worst, in the water close to the beach.

My compass was useless. Whatever ammunition had hit my tail had remained there, providing the compass with a new north pole. But I did have the coastline to follow. I headed inland, no more than a mile, and cut my engines, or rather heard them die. I was out of fuel again.

Was it better to land on water or on land? Too many rocks, too many trees on the land below me, then I was out over water once more having traversed the Cherbourg peninsula. I spied a fishing boat, changed my glide into a spiral that would bring me down next to it, freed myself from the seat, half-inflated my vest, and hit the waves.

Book II. Mad Harry

Chapter 1. The Fishing Boat—28 May 1940

The concussion I received when I landed in the water had two immediate consequences. First, I was unconscious when Robert Le Tournel hauled me aboard his fishing boat and, later, when he conveyed me the fifteen miles to Guernsey. The life jacket I wore, though only partially inflated, kept me from drowning while he brought his vessel near to where I floated. He inched it closer to me, a few feet at a time, until he was able to perch on the boat's ladder, reach down with one hand and haul my dead weight up and into his boat like an enormous cod.

The second consequence was that when I did regain consciousness a day or so later, and then only for brief periods of lucidity, I neither spoke nor understood English, only French, a condition that was to last for several weeks.

I've no memory whatever of my actions or indeed of anything that transpired during this period, but was gradually able to build up a picture of what did happen to me by a series of interviews after the War with those with whom I'd come in contact.

A native of Guernsey in the Channel Islands, Robert Le Tournel, despite his family name, was English not French, the Channel Islanders being a mixture of both, though in their politics and loyalties they were primarily British. His given name, Robert was pronounced in two equal syllables "Raw-Bert" as the English do rather than with the accent on the final syllable "Rowbarre" as the French affect.

The water in the Channel is incredibly cold, and his first act was to strip off my wet uniform, towel me dry and wrap me in a set of blankets he kept in a storage locker below. He'd brought my wet uniform up on deck to dry when he heard an approaching boat.

His next actions are understandable, given that the radio broadcasts had been filled with the news of the German advance across France. He wrapped a line and an anchor around my clothing and dropped the bundle overboard. The consequence for me was that my identity (and pay book) vanished along with my uniform. If I fell into German hands, I would be treated, sans uniform, as a spy. No Geneva Convention, no Red Cross parcels, just torture and a firing squad.

But the arriving vessel was French not German. In fact, it was the very boat he'd been waiting for. Like many Islanders, Le Tournel did a little smuggling on the side. Parcels were exchanged—no mention was made of me, and back at the Northolt airbase, I was recorded as missing in action, presumed dead.

Le Tournel then went back below, held my feet one by one against his bare chest until they warmed up, rubbed me again with the towel and then, because I wasn't ready to receive the hot tea he'd poured for me, steered for home, his hold only three-quarters filled with the fish he'd hoped to land.

The gulls were disappointed when instead of stopping to clean a portion of his catch after anchoring in the bay beneath his home, Le Tournel tossed me over his shoulder in a fireman's carry and brought me up the slope to his home.

Le Tournel's family were surprised but pleased to see him—he'd come home a day early, and with his wife's aid, he brought me up from his dock to his farm house.

There, a mild fuss was made over me, particularly by his elderly mother who kept insisting that what I needed most was a hot cup of tea. She could not be dissuaded and, in

58

the end, held me propped up in her lap, while she succeeded, a teaspoon at a time in getting the warm liquid inside me.

I slept then, while Le Tournel's family did what farm families do after one member's absence. Get reacquainted briefly and then get on with the chores.

Le Tournel had a son and a daughter. The daughter's new drawing had to be admired, and the son, who was a bit wild, had to be scolded.

The life of an invalid is a relatively pleasant one. The wife Estelle fussed over me— when she could, what with her garden, and the chickens to be fed and their eggs to be gathered, and preparing meals for her family, and getting her children to do what they were supposed to do. The husband's mother fussed over me. And the children? Ah, the children. Little Emily, eight years old, was a delight most of the time, though she could be annoyingly persistent when in need of attention. Robert, Junior, Age 14 (emotional age varying daily between nine and eighteen), was a holy terror. It was he who first named me 'hairy,' later changed to Harry in Cockney fashion, when I'd stumbled in on the family the second morning completely nude. Le Tournel's mother said, "Nothing I haven't seen before," and Le Tournel, "Jesus Christ." His wife had rushed to get me a shirt of her husband's and a worn-at-the-knee but otherwise presentable pair of pants (saved initially for Robert, Jr to grow into from a time when Robert, Sr had been somewhat slimmer), Emily had giggled, and Robert, Jr had branded me 'hairy' on seeing that, like all members of my family, I'd not a single hair on my chest, whereas he already had the beginnings of a fine pelt.

He called me 'hairy' thereafter every time he brought by some of the teen-aged rapscallions he hung out with, making me a regular part of their afternoon tour.

Just as well I couldn't understand English, as he and his friends no doubt said a great many other uncomplimentary things about me once they understood that I could not understand and would be unlikely to retaliate or tell their mothers.

In fact, it was Robert Jr. whose latest mean prank would send me up and on my way. But I'm getting ahead of my story.

The reader may wonder why Le Tournel had not rushed to bring me to the attention of the authorities, but let me lie about his house eating the family's hard-won food and occupying Robert Jr.'s bed—this theft of Robert Jr.'s bed along with some articles of clothing he felt were intended for him may explain some of his later antagonism toward me. The Le Tournel's were nowhere near rich despite long hours of hard work , except in love and family and the quiet beauty of the Isle of Guernsey. But Le Tournel had no car, only a bicycle (and his boat, of course), and town was a long way off. Moreover, the never-ending farm work left him little room for side excursions. Besides, the wife's brother was expected at the end of the week. The trip to the authorities could be and was put off till then.

It was the brother-in-law incidentally who regularly carried the parcels obtained from the French to the fisherman on the other side of the island who would pass it on to the English smuggling team in return for a parcel from them. This strange custom of passing parcels back and forth between France and England by way of the Islanders had gone on for centuries, ever since the days when the two nations had begun to impose burdensome custom duties on the produce of the other.

The brother-in-law arrived on schedule, and Mr. and Mrs. Le Tournel both went into town with him, Mr. Le Tournel to call on the army post there, army and air force being all the same to him, and Mrs. Le Tournel to do some shopping, exchanging garden produce for the items her family needed.

What they discovered in town, where everyone had a different somewhat distorted story to tell, changed everything. Simply put, the British army was packing up and going back to England, later to be dispatched to the desert to fight against Rommel. The Islanders were advised by the British government to think seriously of "going back to England" themselves. An odd choice of phrase as most of the Islanders had lived on Guernsey for many generations. They had their own government, independent of England, their own language—Norman French, and certainly their own way of doing things.

Regardless, all over the island, entire families spent the next few days trying to decide should they go, should they stay, should they send the children away to England for safety. The British army departed, leaving nothing in the way of weapons behind. During the next two days the Island Government issued several communiqués: England would not forget them; England would return. It might be a matter of a few weeks, a few months, a few years. Perhaps, if a family had small children, they should consider going to England after all, or, if they must stay, then send the children off to England where they could be safe.

The Island already had a small contingent of mostly well-to-do Mosleyites (British fascists) in residence that felt that only good would come of the abandonment. Churchill was mad and things would only improve under German leadership. A few German agents in place, who'd been sent in under cover during the mid 1930's, contributed their views to the discussion.

Not surprisingly, with so much to discuss, and the phone constantly ringing, that is, when the party line was not tied up, it took some time for the Le Tournels to notice that I was gone. And then the best they could do was to emulate the wife, shake their heads, say, "I hope he'll be all right," and get on with the packing.

I was gone because a party of 13-and 14-year olds finding me asleep on my bed—fully clothed thankfully, I had lain down exhausted as I still needed to rest several times a day— had thought it would be great fun to light a firecracker beneath my cot.

They'd already been kind enough to introduce me to the stinking iris and the slimy toad, but this latest prank was far more unsettling. I heard the bang, interpreted it as the sound of bombs dropping and ran from the barrack, no, the home, scattering the adolescents before me—they now as frightened as I. I had to get to my . . . to my what? Bewildered, I just kept running, running through the fields, plunging through the hedge rows, coming to rest finally on a haystack perhaps two or three miles from where I'd started out.

When I woke, I didn't even think to find my way back, my mind assuming that the Le Tournel's home must have been destroyed in the explosion. Instead, I began to walk with no particular destination in mind, not 120 paces per minute, much less 160, but a low measured pacing that ate up the miles toward some unknown destination.

That night, I slept in a field. The night after, in a barn.

The smell of breakfast drew me to an adjacent farmhouse. "It's Mad Harry, " said the young man of the house, one of Robert Jr.'s band of young criminals, when he opened the door. "Invite him in," came a woman's voice, "Let him share our last breakfast."

I was not a prepossessing sight. I hadn't shaved in a week and was developing a beard. Though my hair, cut short military style to begin with, might now be mistaken for a bad civilian haircut. The woman might have regretted her hasty decision once I was inside the house and fully visible, but feed me she did, while her husband scurried in and out of their home packing the car.

"We've decided to leave the island, see that young Michael is safe in school," she explained.

"No use talking to 'Arry. He don't understand English or nothing," that worthy young gentlemen piped up and received a good cuff on the ear from his dad for his rudeness.

"He speaks French," Michael's father explained. "Perhaps, he ought to stay with the Guilberts. I wonder if he was in their army."

"A deserter," young Michael said and again received a bang on the ear.

After a discussion with his wife as to whether the Guilberts would or would not be staying, the man gave me directions to the Guilberts' farm using a mixture of hand gestures and the few French words he knew.

He also gave me a bicycle, which would prove invaluable then and later. "You may have to walk it some. Guess I'll retrieve it from you when we get back."

"We won't get back if we don't go," said his wife who had finished cleaning up the dishes by then. I stood outside leaning on my new bicycle while they made their preparations, and waved goodbye when they took off down the road in their overloaded automobile.

From what I learned later, it was chaos in the St Peter Port harbor that day and the next two or three days after that. Not all who wanted to go to England got to go. And though an evacuation vessel was promised for later that day, the one that showed up finally was reserved for children.

Families were separated never to be reunited. And some who had planned on leaving, changed their minds and came on back again. Neither the family who had offered me hospitality that morning, nor the Guilberts, who had indeed decided to go to England, was among them.

I was tired by the time I got to the Guilberts' home, for I'd had to walk as often as I pedaled across the back fields in the direction the man had pointed. I was tired, though I'd already rested several times, and hungry.

The house, a graying concrete block similar to the Le Tournel's, had boards nailed across its doors and windows. But I thought, 'what the hell,' after circling it once and made my way in with a minimum of effort.

Inspecting the cupboards, as well as a vacant chicken coop and an empty barn where cows had once rested between milkings, I realized that I wouldn't eat well, but I would eat, at least until the canned goods ran out. The electricity was still on, but I imagined it would go off as soon as the power company got round to it. The well would have to be pumped by hand then, but I'd have water to drink, whether the electricity failed or not.

I was neither the first nor the last person on the Island to break into one of the newly vacated houses that day and throughout the next week. The following morning when I heard a truck pull into the driveway, I walked round the house to meet what might well be the Guilberts returning. With luck, I could provide an explanation before they leaped to fatal conclusions. But on seeing me, the driver of the truck as quickly pulled around in a half circle and drove off again. One set of looters stymied.

The balance of the day, I spent either in uninterrupted sleep—what paradise to be free of the Le Tournel children and their friends, or in exploring my environment. (Those children incidentally were already on their way to England.) Some chickens had made their way back to the hen house from which they'd lately been freed and I had an omelet for lunch. But by the next day, the urge to keep walking was on me again.

Whoever I'd been in my previous existence, it was not someone who'd enjoyed remaining quietly in one spot enjoying nature's beauty.

Meanwhile, at the harbor, chaos continued to reign. Just as some folks were about to pay great sums to fishermen to ferry them to England, yet another vessel appeared, chartered by the British authorities to carry landward any remaining Gurnseyites who wanted to leave.

This particular boat, of course, came along well after the ship that had been designated to carry children only. So that a family who already had bade a tearful farewell to their offspring need now decide, and quickly too, whether to follow after them or go back to their shops and farms. Moreover, the new ship had been designed to carry cargo not passengers, and those who elected to leave with it found themselves crammed into holds that normally held coal or tomatoes. The struggles of those who did reach England and then sought to regain their children would fill another book.

The Guernsey government continued to hold indecisive meeting after indecisive meeting while waiting for more information from England that never quite arrived in the form desired. Go. Stay. The opinions one received from someone in the know varied from hour to hour.

But none of this was known to me, along with much else besides, on the morning I finally decided to leave the Guilbert home . Walking up the gentle slope behind their house and barn, I caught a glimpse of the sea and what, far off in the distance, might well be a harbor and a town. I'll go there, I thought, taking no account of the distance involved.

Chapter 2. Mad Harry

By the time I drifted into St. Peter Port, my bicycle in the back of a truck driven by someone who spoke Guernsey French, as different from my Canadian patois as my own speech from that of a Parisian, things had fairly well calmed down.

My appearance hadn't improved. M. Guilbert had not left a razor behind and I really hadn't thought about how much I might need one. I'd had a bath, several, beneath the Guilbert's outdoor pump. Nonetheless, people avoided me in the street, sniffing audibly when I passed near them.

The streets of the town were little more than alleyways for the most part including the narrow pedestrian way that paralleled the harbor. Several dozen fishing boats lay at anchor there or were pulled against the quays. Two long breakwaters marked the harbor's boundaries and kept the ocean's strength at bay. A castle, straight out of some Elizabethan romance, stood on guard near the far end of one of the breakwaters.

Notices were pasted at intervals along the walls of the alleyways, with the words 'Don't be Yellow' printed in black on a yellow background, though with the part of my mind that understood English still closed off, they were meaningless to me.

I did not go far into the town itself, for the narrow east-west streets that led from the harbor climbed a steep hillside, interrupted only occasionally by flights of steps. Instead, I remained near the water, a street or two above the harbor, itself.

I was hungry. I'd brought some food with me, but had eaten it along the way. A woman, seeing the look I gave the shopping basket she was carrying, handed me a tomato. I also received a half loaf of bread and a bit of stale cheese from a clerk who saw me staring through the window of her shop.

Gradually, I worked my way out of town, directed by a friendly Bobby wearing helmet and all, strap tucked beneath his chin. I suppose he was moving me along, actually, but he went about doing it in so very affable a manner that I was not offended.

The road that led up and out from town, winding as it did across the hillside, represented a steep climb, and I stopped many times to rest and look back upon the town or the water, whichever was then in view. I stopped, finally, well after dark, and again slept out of doors, perched on a hillside overlooking the sea.

The chill wind from the Channel roamed everywhere, the sound of its passing added to the noise of the waves lapping at the rocks below, but I'd brought a bedroll with me from the Guilberts and, wrapped within it, I soon fell asleep.

That morning, very early, I slipped down to the water's edge, walked out over the stones and plunged in. Bloody cold and, as I shortly discovered, bloody deep.

How deep, I wondered. I took a couple of deep breaths and plunged straight downward. Almost twenty seconds went by and I popped back up to the surface still without touching bottom. I selected a large rock from the surface and repeated the process, this time going down far enough that I felt a pressure on my ears. Dawn glinted on the downward sloping bottom. Deep. They could have brought a submarine into shore here.

I got out of the water, rubbed myself down with a towel I'd acquired from a clothesline along the way and, after dressing, climbed back up the hillside to where I'd stashed my bedroll. Soon I fell asleep a second time.

When I woke again, it was well toward noon. Maids and waiters bustled about on the shore below. A long deep green lawn lined the shore to my left and led along a gentle slope toward a mansion above. On this side of the narrow bay—perhaps, fjord might be a better description given its depth, sat three mansions in a row. Hardly row houses; each two-or three-story structure was surrounded by its own extensive grounds.

Immediately beneath me on the lawn, servants in white jackets were setting up tables along with a green canopy to protect those who might so desire from the sun. Maids in uniform followed along afterward fetching plates from the mansion's kitchen. When all was in place, a large punch bowl at the head of one table, and plates of food everywhere, the guests began to arrive, all elegantly dressed.

A trio of Jackdaws had thought to steal from the plates and it was the noise of their being driven off that had awoken me.

I was not alone. Near me on the hillside sat a young woman, the most beautiful girl I'd ever seen. In her early twenties, she reminded me in a way of the girl I'd seen at my graduation party, the one that was already committed to someone else so that I shouldn't waste my time. This woman, who was later to become my wife, also had golden-red hair, though hers was much longer. Tied neatly behind her head, it fell in waves, naturally curly, almost to her waist. She smiled at me, but did not speak, her attention riveted as mine had been but a moment before on the scene below us.

The smell of the sea, seaweed and salt water, was omnipresent. Now, added to it, was the smell of food. Perhaps sandwiches, and cream cakes, and tea as well, would be found on those linen-draped tables, though it was roast pork whose smell lured me downward in the end. Food takes precedence over sex when one is hungry and without exchanging words with the girl I began to make my way down the hillside toward the garden party, her eyes following me as I descended.

Perhaps I was not dressed appropriately for the occasion. After all, the other guests were in formal afternoon wear. My beard and haircut ran together, which may explain why I never got closer than twenty or twenty-five yards from the tables before I was stopped.

"It's 'Mad 'arry,'" said one of the guests with a great toothy grin. "Probably hungry," said another, a tousled blond-haired man with an infectious smile, "Shall we feed him?"

"I hardly think so," said a third, very tall, dark-haired man, who was probably the host. He gestured to one of the waiters. "Remove him."

The latter, along with a second waiter whom he summoned to help, came over and took me by the arms. My attention continued to be fixed on the plates of food and the women in their long dresses and scornful looks and I hardly noticed that I was being dragged away.

When we reached the edge of the lawn and were momentarily out of sight of the guests, they threw me down on the lawn and one aimed a kick at me. They spoke together then, laughing in a language I did not recognize. I did sort of recognize it though; it wasn't this incomprehensible English that everyone on the Island seemed to speak, but it was a language I'd heard before, on the radio. A second kick was aimed at me, but I was alert now, rolled away, and then quickly ran off, the men's laughter ringing in my ears.

I made my way painfully up the hill—I guess that last kick hadn't missed after all, and tried to crawl back into my bedroll wanting to forget the entire incident.

"Vous avez faim? (You are hungry)," the girl said in French in an accent I could comprehend.

"Yes, I am," I replied truthfully.

"You can walk? You are all right?"

I nodded.

"Come with me then." She remained in a crouched position as she moved away, her body hugging the ground until we were out of sight of the garden party below. When she stood up, I saw that she was tall for a girl, perhaps only two or three inches shorter than I.

Her walk, one of elegance and grace, revealed a woman, but one who felt no need to flaunt it.

"You don't need to walk behind me," she said after a few moments. "You're not a dog."

I caught up to her, my cheeks flaming red, though my blush must have been well concealed by beard and sunburn. Admittedly, I had been looking at her hips and rear as she walked.

Apparently, she wasn't aware of this latter or at least she wasn't going to mention it. "They are Nazis," she said as I came alongside her, "Concerned only with themselves. I think, too, they are spies."

I nodded, though I wasn't sure I knew what Nazis were. I'd heard the name though. And spies, I knew, were bad.

"The three families that own those big houses, they're all new to the island. Very British, all Mosleyites, perhaps, but more likely they are Germans pretending to be something else."

Her smile was bitter but very warm when she shined it on me. Her teeth were not quite white and one was chipped. Her face had known care and premature responsibility, suffering, fear, and sorrow. A mole, a beauty mark really, dotted her right cheek. All making her, perhaps, even more beautiful.

"Submarines," I said, the thought having just popped into my mind. "Deep water."

"Perhaps, you are right," she replied after a moment and looked at me thoughtfully. Perhaps, I was not quite the helpless idiot I'd appeared to be at first, though I gather that my doglike smile of admiration persisted, suggesting that her first impression of me might have been correct, after all.

Her home was over a shop in town, a jewelry store, which we passed through quickly on the way upstairs. She sat me down at a small table and soon appeared with bread and cheese and several fresh tomatoes. Tea was brewed, though I'm afraid I embarrassed myself by gobbling down one of the tomatoes and a hunk of bread before it could be served.

She brought out a knife then, and cut the bread for me, putting bread, cheese, and tomato before me on a plate before serving the tea.

"It's good to watch you eat," she remarked after watching me put away food for several minutes. I'd tried to eat slowly, demonstrating that I did have manners, but was so very hungry that I may not have been successful in the attempt. "Somehow, I lost my appetite along the way." she continued.

I burped, thanked her profusely, and then, feeling I needed to go to the toilet, made my way down the stairs and out the door to search for a secluded spot in which to attain relief.

Once so relieved, I thought of returning to the shop and the apartment above, but instead, giving no further thought to the woman who had fed me, I made my way down to the harbor. There, I spent most of the remaining afternoon and evening gazing out across the water at the boats and their reflections, and listening to the sound of the waves lapping at the old granite landing steps till I fell asleep.

When I see a homeless man today, I often stop and wonder whether he too has lost his memory, deliberately or through some accident. I'll have one of my children give him a dollar or, better, go into a shop and buy the man something to eat.

65

Chapter 3. Passover

The first stirrings in the harbor woke me well before dawn as the fishermen (those who had not fled to England) left in their boats in search of the morning's catch. The putt-putt of their motors, and the smell of their exhaust slowly faded away along with the ripples from their passing. I remained unmoving on the shore.

By the time the fishermen returned, several families had already come down to the port with their suitcases. But they were destined to disappointment. No further ships were dispatched from England till the end of the war, five years later. Some bought from the fishermen, then made their way home. Some just stood around with blank faces. Only the gulls and the fishermen went about their normal day.

The Bobby whose job it was to move me along, though lately he'd been too busy discouraging looters to bother with the likes of me, gave me a wave. Wanting to avoid trouble for both him and me, I took my bedroll and made my way back in the direction of the Le Tournel's.

Near the airfield, I came across a rather peculiar ceremony though perhaps I may have misinterpreted it. A group of town dignitaries were standing at the start of a long grass runway and appeared to be listening to a tall blond man, the same man who had wanted to feed me at the garden party the day before. A pert brownish-blond secretary stood next to him, clipboard and pen in hand, taking notes as he spoke.

She wore a demure pink print dress of cotton broadcloth that had puffy sleeves with gathered trim and a bit of ribbon at the center of its low-cut bodice. I imagined that all the men might be staring at her, too, but their attention was focused instead on the man who was speaking and on the field around them.

"Airplanes," I said in French moving toward them, "you've got to rip up this field." Where had this idea come from? "You don't want the Germans to land."

They all looked at me blankly, except for the blond man who said, "Harry?" by way of greeting and the blond girl who seemed to understand what I was saying.

"What the hell is he saying?" asked a florid faced man whom I'd also seen at the garden party. He had a bushy Guardsman mustache and a military bearing, so I suppose that at one time, perhaps in the previous war, he'd been an officer in the military.

"Something about aeroplanes," the girl in the pink dress said, her name was Angelique Martel I found out later when I slept with her. Her pug-nosed face was bright, alert, the eyes wide apart. "He's speaking French. Shall I talk to him and find out what he wants?"

The men's comments varied from "Yes, find out what he's on about," to "Just send him away, this meeting's gone on long enough." This last from the military man.

The blond man, who appeared to be some kind of facilitator, if not actually in charge, waved his hands helplessly but indicated that perhaps the girl ought go and talk with me. I found out later that he had been the Island's Attorney General and since the evacuation of the Island along with its chief ministers was now the acting chief of Guernsey's Governing Council who formed the balance of the group around him.

I tried to explain to her that this was an airfield (how did I know?) and that it must be destroyed, else the Germans might land here should they choose to invade.

Angelique translated what I'd said to the men. The blond man nodded thoughtfully, although, "He's mad, quite mad," one of the other men said. There were general murmurs of agreement to this last; certainly, I looked the part of a mad man. But then the man with the military bearing nodded in my direction and said something along the lines of "This ...

person may be correct. Our Island is the oldest and closest representative of the British Empire. Herr Hitler cannot but help recognize the inestimable propaganda value of its occupation."

The man who spoke next, a tall lean man with wavy blond hair, had also been at the Garden party, a next-door neighbor of its host, if two men both owning very large estates can be thought of as next-door neighbors. "But Sir Abraham, by the same token, England will do everything in their power to maintain possession."

"Hear, hear."

"Tell, Harry," the blond man said to the girl summing up the consensus, "that we appreciate his comments, but we need to keep the field open in case the Royal Air Force plan a return."

The spirit of compromise embodied in his words was utter foolishness given the exigencies of wartime, but how could he have known. The group of men drifted away back toward the town, and only the girl, after checking with her superior, was left to talk with me.

"Are you hungry?" she asked. Women did seem to see Mad Harry as an object worth feeding. I allowed as how I was, my last meal being the previous day at the beautiful girl's.

"You need to go to my mother's shop. They'll feed you. Talk to my sister if you can. Tell her Angelique sent you."

She gave me directions and then skipped on her way after the departing men. I followed slowly afterwards.

My inquiries at the shop were not particularly successful. While it appeared initially that the woman behind the counter might give me some produce that was on the verge of being thrown away, she was stopped in the act by an older but still very attractive version of Angelique, Angelique's mother I presumed, that appeared in the middle of this putative transaction. Not only did the latter toss the still edible produce in the rubbish bin, but she wasted no time in ordering me from her shop, then following me to the door to see that her order was complied with.

"You are very attractive," I said as I backed away from her, but she turned on her heel and went back into her store without making a reply.

The balance of my day was spent in further wandering, and gradually the town's shops and alleyways grew familiar to me. I waved at the policeman when I saw him again as well as at other persons whom I remembered having seen before but I kept on walking. I was all the way out of town along the uphill road I'd taken the previous day when it occurred to me that I knew a place where I might be fed.

By then, it was evening. Most of the shops had closed, and the streets of St. Peter Port were deserted. No compassionate shopper was likely to offer me a tomato from her basket, now. I tried the door of the jewelry store, which at first glance appeared closed, also. But a slight pressure on the handle allowed me to slip inside.

The shop itself was deserted; the sign on the door read 'closed, ferme', but evidently the proprietress had failed to close the door securely. I made my way slowly and quietly up the steep flight of stairs as I had the day before and found Rebecca sitting alone in her kitchen surrounded by all the trappings of a Seder.

For those unfamiliar with the Jewish ritual let me explain that the Seder is the Passover evening meal, the one depicted in the paintings of Jesus' last supper.

The table held a stick of celery, a small bowl of water, salt water presumably, a larger bowl of water in which to wash her hands, a tiny plate containing horse radish, a larger plate on which sat a lamb bone, a tray of water crackers (as close, I guess, as one could come on the island to the necessary matzos), and, finally, two glasses of wine, one in front of her, and one across the table to await the coming of the prophet Elijah.

"What makes this night different from all other nights?" I began, interrupting her reverie.

She looked up at me and smiled, breathtakingly beautiful. "On all other nights we eat leavened and unleavened bread," she continued in Hebrew "but on this night we eat only unleavened bread?

"That on all other nights we eat all kinds of greens, but on this night we eat only bitter herbs?"

Then I, who was once and still the youngest and only son, replied, drawing from memory, "Matzoh reminds us that when the Jews left the slavery of Egypt they had no time to bake their bread.

"Maror reminds us of the bitter and cruel way the Pharaoh treated the Jewish people when they were slaves in Egypt."

"Why do we dip our foods twice tonight?" she asked, then answered, "We dip bitter herbs into Charoset to remind us how hard the Jewish slaves worked in Egypt.

"We dip parsley into salt water. The parsley reminds us that spring is here and new life will grow. The salt water reminds us of the tears of the Jewish slaves."

Her voice broke midway through the last sentence and she began to cry. I put my arms around her and tried to comfort her. She did not pull away, but rose out of the chair, her hands on my shoulders, and clung to me, her breasts against my chest.

She took me to her room, then, leading me by the hand and slowly undressed while I sat on the bed. I have never seen a more beautiful woman, then or since.

I undressed too and lay down beside her. It was she who guided me inside her. I kissed her tears; I kissed her lips. Later, I kissed her breasts and her thighs. After we'd made love, her thighs were spotted with blood.

"Perhaps it is crazy to celebrate Passover in June," she said as we lay side by side afterward, "but somehow the ceremony brings me peace." She told me how she'd been smuggled out of Germany two years before, had crossed thorough Luxembourg, Belgium, France. Had paid a fisherman to transport her to the Channel Islands where her uncle lived, only to find him gone, one of the lucky passengers who'd caught the last boat to England.

"I found his notes, though. He could see what was coming. He knew about the spies we looked down on yesterday. Do you know there is a radio transmitter in the attic?"

We fell asleep then, side-by-side in her narrow bed, to wake in the middle of the night, and make love once more, a continuing voyage of discovery.

The next morning, Mad Harry set out before breakfast and walked down toward the harbor carrying money he'd been given to buy fish from that day's catch. Mad Harry never returned.

68

Chapter 4. The Bombing

On the 28th of June, 1940, many of the Guernsey farmers, the ones that had remained behind after the mass exodus two weeks earlier, were driving lorries filled with tomatoes down to the harbor to be shipped to England, hopefully to yield a handsome profit there. Three German bombers swept in, bombed the line of carts and killed 29 Guernseyites, farmers and townsmen.

Some say today the Germans made a mistake, misinterpreted the line of carts as preparations for a resistance, others that the Germans just wanted to ensure that when they did invade a mere two days later all resistance would be broken.

Either way the falling bombs served to trigger the resurgence of my memories and when Angelique came running down to the harbor a few moments later to see if she could help with the wounded, it was Flying Officer Freygood who replied to her.

"I'm sorry," she said as she passed by. "About my mother, I mean. If you come by later, I'll see you get fed."

"Thanks awfully," I said, though I'd no idea at all what she was talking about. She was an attractive girl though, close to one's physical ideal, brownish-blond hair, small but evident breasts, a very pretty face. Feminine.

"You speak English," she said.

"Always have."

"But aren't . . .? What's your name?"

"Peter. Flying Officer Peter Freygood. Shouldn't we go down and help?"

She took my hand unselfconsciously and we walked together down to the harbor, she gripping my hand tighter and tighter as the sheer numbers of dead and dying, and the smell of those incinerated became more evident.

A tall blond man with a horse-like lined face was hard at work, lifting aside cases of tomatoes, and directing the work of others. He reminded me of the ill-fated over-bred Throckmorton-Higgins. "Tell Harry, we can use his help," he said to Angelique.

"He speaks English, and his real name is . . ." she began when I stopped her. I'd suddenly realized I was not wearing my uniform, that I could be shot as a spy. I remembered now crash landing in the water, but nothing else. "Don't tell him," I said in French, and then in English to the blond man, "I help."

I helped for the balance of the morning. Partially incinerated corpses had to be dragged from the wreckage and set aside for later burial. Others lay half in their trucks and half on the ground, blood and intestines mixed with the juice of the tomatoes. But there were bodies that could be mended if given a good stiff drink before pulling a dislocated shoulder back into place. And there were bodies, barely alive and bleeding copiously, that died even as we were pulling them free.

Mid-afternoon came before the work was complete. Angelique reappeared bearing sandwiches, her mother by her side. I was no longer conscious of the smell around me, though I could see she held her nose. "This is Peter," she said to her mother, "He's going to have supper with us."

"He is?"

"Yes, he is."

Strangely, the daughter was allowed to win this contest of wills, though she was admonished to clean me up first.

The work at the harbor done, sandwiches eaten and coffee drunk, we headed up the hill to her home, which was set both above and behind the grocery.

She led me upstairs and fetched me a razor, a straight edge. "Would you like to clean up? " she asked. "It's my dad's. He's in the service." I looked at the razor with suspicion. I was definitely a Gillette man, used to a far safer cutting tool. My hand shaking slightly, I picked up the instrument I'd been given, prepared to go to work, whatever the consequences.

"Let me," she said.

Have you ever been shaved by a woman? Nothing is more intimate. Filling a basin with hot water from the stove below, she produced shaving brush and soap and proceeded to lather me up. Then it was to work with the razor, which appeared to yield almost a pound and a half of hair before she was through.

"We'll have to give you a haircut next." She rubbed her hand against my cheek. "Smooth," she said.

I rubbed my cheek against hers. "Smooth," I repeated. Then I kissed her.

She appeared taken aback, so I kissed her again.

"No," she said, "Stop. What are you doing?"

But I couldn't stop; I pulled her along the hallway, found a vacant bedroom and pulled her inside. There, I clawed at her clothes, ripped her blouse, pulled her down next to me on the bed and began to rain kisses on her face and hair. She did her best to fight me off, but unsuccessfully. Something is to be said for the training the Royal Canadian Air Force provides in hand-to-hand combat.

Strangely, she did not scream, perhaps unwilling to alarm her family in the rooms below, perhaps because she was attracted to me. Or perhaps, like me, having viewed death so close at hand, she was eager for life. I grew angry, more impassioned still. We rolled on the floor.

"Stop," she said and lay passive, "If that's what you want, that's what you will have. But can we go to bed like normal people."

I stood and pulled her straight up in front of me. "Take off your clothes," I ordered.

She stripped, slowly, almost teasingly and was soon wearing only a slip. Such clear pink skin had never seen the sun. Translucent blue veins could be seen just below the surface. Her long nipples jutted straight out from small round breasts.

Now, she led me toward the bed. I still had on all my clothes, though somehow the top button of my trousers had come unbuttoned and my willy was showing through. "I'll undress you," she said. Sitting on the bed where I'd been moments before, she loosened my trousers. I reached down to free them from my legs, but she pushed my hands aside. Unbuttoning my shirt, she pulled it over my head along with the undershirt beneath, "Hairy," she said, and giggled.

She kissed my chest and my breasts, stuck her tongue into my navel and then kissed the hairs that protruded from my underpants. She yanked the latter down along with the pants themselves until they sat around my ankles. "Very beautiful," she said. "I always wished I had a brother so I could look at one whenever I liked."

I felt very naked and very childlike, the very opposite of the beast I'd been a moment before. I also noticed suddenly that the room had two beds. A sister?

Now comes something I am very embarrassed about. I began to cry. Maybe the events of that morning, the bombing in the harbor, the bombing back at Arras field, the dying and the dead had all caught up with me. I clung to her the way a small child would cling to its mother. We lay side-by-side and I made absolutely no attempt to penetrate her. All the passion and the rage that had been present only a moment before had fled. She held me against her breast, put her nipple in my mouth and we were one.

70

This idyll didn't last of course. The stirring began again in my loins and a moment later I penetrated her, a long lasting penetration that ended with her giving a little scream of joy and clinging to me unwilling to let me out again. When I did slide out at last, blood was on her thighs and on the sheets as it had been the day before. My second virgin in only twenty-four hours. But Flying Officer Peter Freygood remembered only the one.

Chapter 5. Awakening

The lack of a uniform began to haunt my days. Where on earth had it got to? In uniform, at worst, I would become a POW when the Germans landed, entitled to receive letters and packages via the Red Cross from my mother, Ruthie, and perhaps Angelique, now that we were lovers. Without, I was merely a spy, entitled to be shot. Very well, I would be a spy.

"Can you get me some maps of the Island? Topographic ones," I asked Angelique.

"I'll ask Andrew."

I assumed she meant the tall blond man who was her boss, the deputy bailiff. "Don't. He'll want to hold meetings and round table discussions, build a consensus, and then decide that the possibility of future repercussions means they should do nothing at all."

She laughed; apparently my single meeting with Andrew had indeed taught me all there was to know about him.

"And I'll need a radio."

"I think I know where one is."

"Who knows about me?" I asked at supper that evening, "I mean that I can speak English, that I'm not mad." Both Angelique's mother and her sister Madeline, the latter far different from Angelique in appearance, buxom rather than slim, dark rather than fair, had given us strange looks when we appeared at table. I wondered if Madeline, the sister, who looked if she couldn't be much more than 15 or 16, had tried the door to the bedroom while the two of us were otherwise engaged.

"Just my mother and sister. I haven't been out of the house."

"No, you haven't," said her mother, and Madeline giggled.

"Do you really think the Germans will come?" her mother asked me. Before I could answer, she continued, "The Council raised our taxes, a special supplement to aid England's defense, and now this!"

"Yes. I think. . .' I paused, then changed my mind about what I was going to say, "The Germans will be here soon. It would be best if I could walk about, disguised as Mad Harry, the poor crazy fool that no one thinks twice about."

"You'll have to let your hair grow," said the mother, "And grow that dreadful beard back."

"But mother," Angelique interjected, "I was going to have Rebecca cut his hair. He'll look so much better."

"If he's going to be crazy, he'll have to look crazy. In fact, it would be best for him to sleep outside tonight." Despite this last exercise in subtlety, one could tell there were limits to her mother's patience.

"But, mother," said this spoiled petulant lover of mine. Having tasted ecstasy once, she clearly wanted to dine on it again.

"Outside." And so Mad Harry went back to sleeping rough—this time in the shelter of a haystack. Though I did drop back for supper at Angelique's home the next day, ostensibly to pick up the maps, and while mother and sister went to visit a neighbor, Angelique and I played doctor in her bed.

The map she'd provided was not entirely up to date. I made a tracing of it, then set out, bedroll behind my bicycle, to spend the night well out of town. After making my way several miles up and down hills, I came across a second natural harbor, long and narrow and apparently in private hands.

In the morning, I discovered by repeating the process I described in my adventures as Mad Harry that what the channel lacked in width, it made up in depth. (Though as far as I was concerned then, this was the very first time I'd seen the deep channel.) From my resting place on the hillside, one could tell how deep the fjord was by color alone, the steep slope down to the water's edge lined with palm trees continuing on, once past a layer of fallen rock, to a depth of 30 or 40 feet only a few yards from land, a natural landing place for submarines. It offset Guernsey's other coast where at low tide acres of mudflats extended the island's boundaries into the sea.

That next day confirmed every Islander's worst suspicions. A Luftwaffe officer landed in a reconnaissance aircraft for a tête-à-tête with the local officials.

The only bright note was that he had to make a quick getaway when three Bristol Blenheims took on his air cover. The downside was twofold. Two of the Blenheims were shot down and the very fact these antique trainers were used at all meant that England was desperately short of planes.

I made a second tracing of the map that evening, leaving the first behind at Angelique's house as a master copy. The airstrip I'd urged the destruction of was already blocked off and in enemy hands. A company of German soldiers had been brought over from France in the belly of modified Junkers and landed there as I (or, rather, as Mad Harry,) had predicted.

I'd no choice then but to return to Angelique's house. Her mother did not appear glad to see me. Perhaps she was more worried about a possible pregnancy than Angelique appeared to be; perhaps she was worried about the Germans.

"I need to get access to that radio we spoke about."

Curfew had not yet been decreed by the invaders, though it would be imposed the very next day, followed by the need for travel passes, and restriction of all boats (fishing or otherwise) to the immediate neighborhood of the Island. Indeed, to all intents, the Channel Islands were now totally cut off from one another, and each would follow a quite different path through history as the war progressed.

To get to the radio, Angelique and I simply walked through town till we came, yes, to the shop where Rebecca lived.

Our appearance in her doorway must have been incredibly traumatic for her. Not only because I, who'd taken her virginity, though freely-offered, did not appear to recognize her, but because Rebecca and Angelique were already the best of friends and had been so for some time. For Angelique, Rebecca was almost a second sister, closer to her than even Madeleine, while Angelique was virtually Rebecca's only friend on the Island. Worse still, if worse were possible, Rebecca's best and only friend appeared to think Rebecca's home ideal for assignations with this same man, Rebecca's first and only lover.

Angelique was wearing another pink print dress, newly pressed as if had just come from a box, looking every bit as enchanting as when we'd first met. Rebecca wore the same faded blue dress she'd worn when we first met, one that was clearly home made and had been patched in places. They stood side by side, dressed as I've described, yet one could only marvel at how beautiful Angelique's friend was, and secretly wish I'd met her before I met Angelique.

Angelique was eager to go to bed, too eager, perhaps—Rebecca's presence unsettled me for reasons I could not understand. (In hindsight, the reasons are obvious, the result of memories creeping outward from a buried section of my consciousness.) But the radio was at the top of my priorities and I was forced to put Angelique off, at least for the moment.

Rebecca led the two of us upstairs and into her bedroom. Opening the closet, she pulled down a set of steps hidden in its ceiling that led to an attic above. We climbed them to find a windowless attic, though fresh air drifted in at irregular intervals through screened-off orifices. The attic's low sloping ceilings forced one to walk in a crouched-over position. And to use the transmitter, one had to sit on pillows arranged on the unfinished floor, rather than in a chair.

The transmitter setup was fairly easy to understand, its weakness being that it was much too bulky to be concealed readily should the Germans choose to search the home above the shop. The transmitter's aerial began at floor level, then emerged, cleverly disguised, alongside a plumbing vent through the roof.

I turned it on—it appeared to have been preset to a specific frequency. It took some time to warm up, but even then I heard only the crackle and hum of white noise. Perhaps messages could only be transmitted and received at a specific time.

A search of the attic revealed no mention of either times or frequencies, but Rebecca said she might know of a place where her uncle had hidden the specifications along with a codebook.

While Rebecca went to look for her uncle's notes—they were down in the repair shop so they might easily be confused by an enemy with a record of customer's purchases, I brought Angelique to a particularly noisy finish on Rebecca's bed. At the time, I felt only pride in this accomplishment, today, only embarrassment that I would force Rebecca to listen to such a thing.

On her return, she looked at me long and intently, searching for, I imagine, some sign of recognition. Angelique only made things worse by remarking, "He looks really tired, doesn't he? I really tired him out." Angelique, of course, looked fresher than ever, Rebecca only depressed.

Her uncle's notes were in Yiddish, Hebrew, German, and English. Thankfully, Rebecca knew all four plus French, Swiss German, and some Italian, the product of her education as well as her travels.

My education, particularly my training in math also came in handy, for the transmission time and frequency were related to the month and the day of the week. As it turned out, I finished the calculation with only seconds to spare. We heard a voice tell us, in German, that the clock was not open. We replied, also in German, that 29 Lilies had been sold and 2 Junipers acquired. The voice thanked us, and said it would like to know if the Junipers sprouted branches.

"What does that mean?" Angelique asked. But I was not yet sure I knew the answer.

Chapter 6. Departure

The Junkers continued to bring over men the next day, while a French merchant ship, impressed into service by the Germans, brought anti-aircraft guns and ground vehicles as well as their crews. Along with it came the S.S. Holland, which served then and subsequently to convey German troops back and forth among Guernsey, Jersey, and the other Channel Islands.

A day later, a curfew was imposed and passes were required to travel anywhere on the island, anywhere by road that is. Oh, and all clocks were ordered set ahead one hour (to conform to German time)—an order particularly vexing to Angelique who was charged with moving the hands ahead on each of the many indoor clocks within the government building. It took awhile for all the churches on the Island to comply and, if one were devout, one could never be sure on hearing the bells summoning parishioners to mass whether one ought come running or wait the hour out.

I adapted my spying methods to the new regulations, traveling by foot, mainly at night, and by the backfields, avoiding roads. The great thing about being Mad Harry was that I could wander about late at night or early in the morning without interference, and sleep during the day if I liked, behind a hedgerow or in an abandoned building.

To be sure the townspeople became used to Mad Harry's presence, I deliberately left my hair uncombed. And if straw had not worked its way in among the strands during the night, then I had made sure to sprinkle some on my scalp before setting out. "Arry," they'd shout when they'd see me walking by. I'd call out some gibberish in return or merely wave my arm. "Arry" was their good luck charm against the gradually dawning horror.

I did encounter Germans from time to time or, rather, they ran across me. On two occasions, I appeared to be fishing off the rocks, though, in reality, I was spying out potential landing sites at a distance from the existing harbor.

On the first occasion, I'd been yanked to my feet and was about to be marched away, when a tug on my fishing line attracted my captors' attention. The friendlier of the two soldiers who'd apprehended me reeled in the fish and then proceeded to persuade his companion to release me.

I suppose he was just a farm boy who remembered the good times fishing with his companions back in Bavaria or wherever he hailed from. We parted with an exchange of friendly gestures for they had only a few words of English and I was still feigning not to understand.

My next contact again was with two soldiers, but this time, they only hailed me as they passed by on the road, "Ça va 'Arry." The soldiers, too, now knew who Mad Harry was, a mentally bewildered, bewhiskered man living rough off the countryside.

Of course, the Germans were not the only ones to accept my existence. Wherever I roamed, whether along the coast or into the farm-spotted interior the Islanders would greet me. It might be a farmer's wife who would holler "Viens ici, 'Arry," (Harry, come here) and provide me with bread and cheese and perhaps a tomato or a peach, or someone fishing from the shore, eager to show off his catch, would offer to share with me.

No one was really hungry yet this early in the occupation; the food they provided me with was not being stolen from the mouths of their family. Then, too, as the islanders grew increasingly restive under the restrictions imposed by the German occupying forces, Mad Harry in his madness, in his forgetful simplicity, came to symbolize that most precious of all possessions, freedom. To touch me was to share however briefly in the life on

Guernsey as it was before the Germans came.

So I could roam more or less freely and stay well fed as long as I avoided St. Peter Port proper, and the airport, and one or two spots on the Island where the German troops had their encampments. One day, I might cross the island, east to west, pass by a twelfth century church, an 18th century mansion, a half dozen farms, till I looked down on the tide flats to the west. On the next, I would venture south to the grounds of the Sausmarez manor and the gates of the St. Martin's churchyard where a Stone Age menhir, ancient ancestor of the present Episcopalian cemetery had survived 10,000 years. But of greater interest to me were the places I could not go, to the south for example, all along the coast road from St. Peter Port to Fermain Bay. The Germans had placed their headquarters there, making use of Fort George which had held the British garrison's own headquarters before they fled the month before. For me, it was a structure to be properly labeled and placed on my map along with the troop dispositions.

The real trick, of course, was getting in and out of St. Peter Port and into the jewelry store without detection to make my radio broadcasts. If this proved impossible, I would just have to spend another night sleeping outdoors on a hillside or in a farmer's barn, or another day hiding in the attic waiting for nightfall when I could leave while customers, the majority of them German soldiers, came and went in the shop below.

Occasionally, if Angelique's and my lovemaking had gone on too long, we would sleep three on a bed, as Angelique would be unable to go home.

We ate well courtesy of Angelique's mother even though the Islanders began to suffer various food shortages. The Germans kept changing the rules and no one could be sure from day to day what was and what wasn't permitted. Angelique's mother—Marcie was her given name and I shall try to remember to call her that—had made a deal with the German equivalent of a Quartermaster and goods continued to flow into her shop. Throughout the occupation, Marcie's shop would make a steady profit and the Quartermaster a much larger one.

I woke one morning in bed, not yet having gone up to the attic, to the sound of crying. I rushed downstairs and, after checking first to see if the shop were empty, found Angelique with her arms around a wailing Rebecca.

The explanation testified to the increasing Nazification of the Island. The shop had maintained the name of Rebecca's uncle, Jacob's Fine Jewelry. But Jacob was a Jewish name and "Jeuden Verboten." So read the white painted letters that now besmirched the shop window.

In a way this was a good thing. The shop had experienced a marked increase in sales as a result of extensive purchases by the German soldiers, all of which had been paid for in the near-useless Reichskredit currency which I'd heard described by gentle Rebecca as "useful only for wiping one's ass." Call these sales "respectable looting." But it was the disease and not the symptom that had frightened Rebecca.

As she'd not yet been recognized as Jewish, indeed, Angelique had never thought of the possibility—I guess it takes a Jew to recognize a Jew (or maybe a descendent of Genghis Khan from Sinjian Province), the solution, I thought, was simple: Change the name of the shop. Simple, yes, but for Rebecca abandoning the name meant giving up yet another link with her past.

The next morning I looked out the bedroom window, peeking beneath the curtain, to see a tall blond German airman helping Angelique to install a new sign, one presumably with an Aryan name.

Again that evening, Rebecca was in tears. I put my arms around her and we lay down in bed together. When she fell asleep, I fell asleep also.

Ten o'clock rang on the nearby church steeple, and still Angelique had not returned. Perhaps her mother had put her to work and she'd failed to leave their shop before curfew. I was preparing to go to my attic bed, when Rebecca's hand reached out and touched my thigh. It didn't take much to give me a woody in those days. I leaned over and took Rebecca's nipple in my mouth. She gasped. I probed between her legs and found her dripping wet. In no time at all, I was on top of her, her naked breasts against my chest, my lips on her lips, deep inside. I knew her. Knew every inch of her. Her thighs began to move uncontrollably and any control I had vanished at almost the same time. If she hadn't been pregnant before, she surely would be now.

(This was it, you see, the secret of my first child's birth, for on either our first or second bout of love making, Rebecca became pregnant and would bear a child in the midst of the German occupation.)

Dare we ask why one woman, whom I'd sex with exactly twice, got pregnant, and the other with whom I'd sex on every possible occasion, albeit with scattered attempts at contraception, not. Because this is the way things turned out.

When morning came, Rebecca and I looked at each other both with guilty expressions on our faces. She felt guilty because Angelique was her best friend, I because I knew how much Rebecca had already suffered and worried what effect my inevitable departure might have on her. Did I worry about the possibility of children? No I did not.

On my peregrinations around the Island, I thought once that I saw a man in civilian clothes taking photographs of military installations. Taking photographs when Germans soldiers were likely to march round the corner at any time was incredibly dangerous. Dangerous enough that I doubted I'd seen what I'd seen. Any pictures I took were with my mind, to be transcribed that night or as soon as possible to the master tracing.

But when I mentioned the possibility of his existence to Angelique, she said, oh yes, that was Bert, Andrew's first born, he was hoping to get the pictures to England somehow.

Good luck. What would happen to him if they caught him in the act, or with the unprocessed film upon him? And if Angelique knew of him, might not Bert's presence be known to everyone on the Island, Nazi sympathizers included?

My master map was gaining more and more detail. An evening came when it was sufficiently complete that I sent out a message asking to be taken off the island. No one replied on the designated channel. Was I to wait forever until the spymasters in England contacted me?

The following evening, I again sent out a message at the prescribed time. And again, there was no reply on the designated channel. But on a different channel I found while twiddling the knob, a message could be heard: "Submarine available." How was I to know this message was aimed at the mysterious 'Bert.'

"Next Sunday." I requested.

"Confirmed," was followed by a set of coded coordinates. I flipped rapidly through the codebook and consulted the map. A half-mile out in the ocean? How the hell was I supposed to get there? I responded with a new set of coordinates, those of the potential submarine anchorage I'd discovered. The answering reply was not in the uncle's code books, but I'm sure would translate as," you're out of your bloody mind."

I repeated the coordinates of the deep-water channel and waited. But there was no reply.

The following evening, the time of the submarine's arrival was repeated by my unknown communicants along with the coordinates they'd transmitted originally. I countered with their time and my coordinates. They sent a new set of coordinates: Those of the St Peter Port harbor. They couldn't possibly be serious. Perhaps they just wanted to be sure we were working from the same map. I duplicated the harbor coordinates and sent them back. The coordinates of Vale Castle, a near ruin several miles to the north and west of St. Peter Port that dated to the 14th Century, were sent next. I duplicated these also. Then I retransmitted the agreed on date and time, along with the coordinates of the landing place I'd chosen.

"Confirmed."

Four days left to evade capture. Four days left to complete my map and get the equipment I would need. I'd need some way to wrap the maps and keep them dry and I'd need some way to wrap me and keep me warm while in the water.

When I went to Angelique's house again, her mother was not happy to see me. "What if somebody sees you come here? You'll be arrested." which could be more accurately expressed as, "if somebody sees you come here, I'll get in trouble."

Not that Angelique's mother, Marcie, wasn't helpful. When both Angelique and her sister blanked on how to keep the maps and me dry, it was Marcie who thought of an oilskin wrap for the map and some kind of diving suit for me.

But where would we find them? Again, Angelique's mother had the answer. There was, or rather there had been before he left for the mainland, a diver in St. Peter Port who made his living scraping barnacles off the hulls of fishing boats and the yachts of the idle rich.

Angelique and her sister Madeline were dispatched to the harbor that evening to get me a diving suit, an oilskin pouch or two, and a heavy pipe wrench from the diver's abandoned shop. More about that wrench later. What I didn't learn till the following day was that Angelique decided to take that oh, so helpful German aviator along with her.

"To slip past the guards and break into the shop?"

"No, to lift me over the sill, and afterwards to carry home all the stuff you've sent me for."

"But he's a German soldier."

"He only does what he does because they tell him to. They'd kill him if he didn't. And he's not a soldier; he's an airman."

"He's a German airman; he drops bombs on innocent civilians."

"And you shoot them."

While Angelique broke into the diver's shop with the aid of her German helper, her sister's job was to distract the guards. The guards, three of them, weren't there to watch the shop of course, indeed the diver's possessions were left alone for almost a year, before the Germans thought to break in and inventory the shop's contents along with those of every other abandoned structure. No, the guards' job was to patrol the harbor and prevent sabotage.

At first, I found the notion of Angelique's sister playing the part of a femme fatale to be ludicrous. To me, she seemed hardly more than a child. A view formed in part by the way the other members of her family treated her.

I've written that Angelique resembled her mother, and that she and her sister were physical opposites. Well, it was the same way with the two sisters' personalities. While both Angelique and her mom were petite bourgeois constantly on the lookout for number one, (sparing only members of their immediate family from their avarice), Madeleine took more after her absent father, all lovable innocence, a rescuer of sick birds and abandoned cats (not that her mother would have permitted any of the latter near their house or store).

But in discounting Madeline's femininity, I'd forgotten one thing: The German sentries, all three low-ranking privates, were also still in their teens. In no time, they gathered around her competing for her attention, leaving Angelique and her new consort (was she already preparing for my departure?) to complete the job of breaking and entering. "And he carried everything back to the house for me. The wrench and dive suit were heavy, too."

The sequel to all this was ironic. Madeline's consorting with the German soldiers did not go unnoticed by a sharp-eyed passer-by, albeit one who was out to do his own late-night looting. While Angelique and her mother might well have been so accused, Angelique with her pilot, Marcie with her German quartermaster, it was Madeleine who was to be branded with an entirely unwarranted reputation as a "jerrybag."

Saturday night, I put the final touches on my map, wrapped it and a copy of the Deutsche Inselzeitung, the island's military newspaper in the oilskins, and said goodbye to Angelique's family. Her mother hugged me. "You are a very handsome, very brave man," she said. "Thank you for saying I look attractive. Do not think badly of my future actions." I understood almost nothing then of what she was trying to tell me, though I thanked her for the compliment.

Sunday, having had sex for the last time with Angelique—let the German aviator think on that, I gave Rebecca a hug, and made my way out the back of her jewelry store with my newly-reinforced bedroll. The pipe wrench and wet suit added a large amount of weight and I was panting by the time I reached the first hilltop, close to exhaustion by the time I reached my destination above the submarine landing.

At 19:40 precisely, (that's 7:40 civilian time), I made my way down the hillside to the rocks below. At the foot of the hill, I removed my clothes—let them be found, proof that Mad Harry had finally surrendered to despair, and began to piece on the wet suit. I soon discovered the latter was both shorter and wider than I was. The extra width was convenient for it offered room for the oil-skinned wrapped map and newspaper as well as the wrench that I would need to weigh me down should I want to swim despite all the trapped air. The suit's inadequate length meant that a rip immediately developed along one shoulder leaving a large patch of skin exposed; oh well, at least I wouldn't die of hypothermia—I hoped.

Shit. Someone in the nearby mansion had let loose their dogs. Probably it was those dammed German thugs turned waiters who were responsible. I could hear the hounds racing toward me, and shoeless, smashing my toes at every step, I ran out across the rocks toward the Bay. The dogs had a rough time of it, too, their claws screeching across the stones as they pounded on toward me.

I reached the water well ahead of the dogs, but those Alstatians must have had spaniel blood in them, because they came splashing after me. Shit, shit, shit.

I was perhaps thirty yards from shore when I first heard the submarine's engines. The sound grew louder still when I put my head under the water. The dogs weren't too keen on the sound either, because they stopped several feet from me and reversed direction, or maybe someone had called to them from the house.

I became conscious of something dark beneath me, and dove down, hand outstretched. The hand soon made contact with the length of cable that connected the series of stanchions that ran along the outer edge of the submarine's deck. I grabbed hold of the cable and found myself being dragged along back toward the waiting dogs.

Shit. Somehow, I extracted the wrench from my wetsuit, letting in a flood of icy cold water in the process, and bending down, I began to pound on the deck.

Chapter 7. The Submarine

Fortunately, the onset of my banging coincided with the submarine's reversing its engines. When the engine had come to a full stop and the sub also, a single bang came from below. I answered with a single bang back. Two bangs from them were followed by two bangs from me.

The engine started up again and we began to move out toward sea, staying, I was pleased to note, just below the surface. Good, I didn't fancy a long swim. Still, as we grew nearer the opening of the bay to the ocean, the waves grew larger, and my head began to dip below the surface with fair regularity. I wished the sub would slow down; it became harder and harder to catch a breath between one wave and the next.

Finally, just beyond the mouth of the bay, in the ocean proper, the sub broke the surface. A hatch opened on the deck and a voice called out to me, "On the double."

I slip-slided over to the hatch, where I was dragged inside by a pair of strong arms and handed down the ladder. The hatch was closed, fastened securely, and down the submarine went again, or so I imagined.

"And who might you be?," "And where did he get that ruddy uniform?" voices called.

"Commanding Officer, please." I knew how to behave in civilized society even if these squids didn't.

A burly chief, the same man who had brought me aboard, escorted me five yards to where his commander stood. "Army lout," the chief said. "Air Force," I corrected, "Flying-Officer Freygood, Royal Canadian Air Force."

"You don't look much like a Canadian," the commanding officer, a Commander, judging by his insignia, said. "Or like the commando we were supposed to fetch back with us. And where's your uniform?"

"You didn't come for me?" I asked, plaintively.

"We did not." he turned to his crew. " Up periscope. Ensign, see if you can spot a light on the shore. Engines, reverse. We're going back in. Your uniform, where is it?"

His last remark, I slowly realized, was directed at me. I explained that my uniform had disappeared following the crash and mentioned my bout with amnesia. "I have my dog tags though. Afraid my pay book is with my uniform. Pity, I could use a few dollars if we're going ashore. By the way, I do need to get to England. I have a map the Wing Commander will want to see."

"Oh, will he? Let's see this map of yours. I'm not at all sure we'll be taking you anywhere."

"Searchlight on the shore, Sir, scanning this way." piped the ensign, "Is this what we're looking for?"

"Dive!" hollered the commander in a voice that made me jump and sent the appropriate members of his crew scurrying to oblige.

"Reverse engines. Full ahead. We're going home. Same course."

"We may not have been seen, Sir," said the hapless ensign.

"And we might well have been. I can't take the chance. Our friend the commando will just have to wait for another day."

He turned to me. "Now, one more time, who are you, what are you doing on my boat, where did you get that ridiculous outfit?"

I more or less went over my previous responses, finishing by peeling my wet suit down to my waist—the heat within the sub was stifling, the stench unbelievable—and extracting the oil-skinned wrapped map I'd secreted there.

"And how do we know this map is not a gift from the Germans designed to lead us astray?"

"That's for the Wing Commander to decide."

"You mean the Admiral."

"This map is Air Force property."

"This sub is Admiralty property," said the burly Chief who'd first handed me down, "Perhaps, you'd care to walk, no, fly home, Sir."

"That's enough Holmes," said the Commander, though you could see he was amused. He rolled my map up then, the fruit of eight days labor and the constant risk of death by firing squad, and placed it in a tube.

I reached for it. "Uh, uh," he tut-tutted, snatching it away, "Like the Chief says, if you're unhappy, feel free to fly away anytime." Whereupon, he and his crew of thieving pirates proceeded to ignore me completely, at least until we were approaching land. Oh, sandwiches were produced at one point; I got a half, purely as an afterthought from an already well-stuffed seaman.

As for Second Lieutenant Hubert Nicoll, the native of Guernsey, whom I'd seen wandering about taking photos, would he have made it aboard the sub if it had gone to the original landing site? The point was moot; a week later, he made the rendezvous and was brought back to England, only to discover, as I did, shortly, that no one really wanted the information.

At a point when the combination of diesel fumes and stale body-scented air made me wish I'd attempted to swim to the mainland, the Commander's voice sounded again in my ear. "Shore tells me Flying Officer Freygood is missing in action somewhere over Western France. What have you to say about that?"

"Like I said. . ."

"As you said," he corrected my grammar, "You Canadians speak a strange brand of English."

"As I said. . ."

"No matter," he interrupted, "We'll be going ashore together shortly. Now if you don't mind, get the hell out of my way while I prepare for the landing."

I got the hell out of the way, and a short time later, we were walking together along the quay, the Commander holding the tube containing the map, the burly Chief holding me by the collar.

I had to get that map to the Air Marshals, had to.

Two Pilot Officers, tourists one gathered, were leaning against a railing looking out to sea. The harbor was impressive, had been for some 500 years. It was even more impressive at that moment with dozens of small vessels—trawlers and mine sweepers, and large—submarines, destroyers and cruisers, lying at anchor and a single large battleship that was already heading down the channel. I waited until we were a mere ten feet away from the two airmen and hollered, "Help me, help, I'm being kidnapped by the Navy. Flying Officer Freygood."

They looked up, unsure exactly what was happening. The commander sealed his fate when he said to them, "This is Navy business, nothing you have to worry about."

"I'm not so sure about that," said the larger of the two Pilot Officers. Not one to wait about for orders, the Chief released my collar, stepped forward, and shoved the man full in the chest. A bad mistake. Releasing my collar, I mean. Meanwhile, the Pilot Officer had charged the Chief in turn and blows were exchanged. I grabbed the tube with the map out of the Commander's hand and ran for a bank of taxis a good hundred yards away, as the

Commander and the second Pilot Officer came together.

The Commander must have been a rugby player in his youth, for he brought me to the ground half way down the quay with a flying tackle. I'd never played rugby, but I knew enough about the game to quickly pass the ball on. I heaved the tube at the second Pilot Officer and hollered, "Get this to Air Command, quickly."

He took off at the run, and the Commander, pinned by me, was unable to follow.

The Chief appeared then towing a much-battered Pilot Officer behind him. We were frog-marched to the Shore Patrol office and turned over to them for safekeeping and further harassment while the Commander went off to report to his superiors. The Chef stayed behind an additional moment to sneer at us and then followed his master.

The Shore Patrol placed us in a deserted room, which by the smell of it served primarily as a drunk tank, and told us to shut our holes and wait.

The Pilot Officer introduced himself, "LaGrandeur," he said.

"Freygood. Vous étés un Québécois?"

"Mais oui. Vous aussi?"

We continued to chatter away in French, much to the chagrin of the Shore Patrol. They couldn't do much with us, of course. We weren't exactly under their jurisdiction. "But disturbing the peace, fighting, those are civilian crimes." The police were called. And in a short time, a Detective Inspector appeared, which I thought was pretty grand for petty criminals like us.

"Aren't you going to handcuff them?" the SP's asked as the Inspector, an older man with a sad and slightly bemused expression, started to lead us away.

"Are they particularly violent?"

"You should have seen what they done to our men," one of the SP's began before his partner shushed him. The Navy did not want to come across as particularly delicate creatures.

The SP's contented themselves by coming out to watch us being escorted down the quay to the Inspector's car, an impressive black Ascot. A good-looking WAC sat behind the wheel and their attention quickly shifted to her, our attention as well, as the Inspector helped us into the rear of his automobile.

"Where would you boys like to be dropped?" he asked as we drove away.

"Aren't you going to arrest us?"

"I'm not sure my son, Flying Officer Moyle would approve. Incidentally, Flying Officer Frygood is it?"

"Freygood, Sir."

"I'm a civilian, Sir isn't necessary. By the by, do you have a more traditional uniform?"

"I'm afraid I don't have any clothes with me at all."

"He had to parachute over France," LaGrandeur chipped in.

"In the water, actually."

The WAC whispered to the Inspector. "Hadn't you ought to feed them, before we let them go?"

"I really would like to get some dry clothes first."

"Quite understandable," the Inspector conceded and gave a short series of instructions to his driver.

While we drove to our destination, the Pilot Officer and I focused on the cropped back of the red-haired WAC's trim haircut. The Inspector, silent for the most part, occasionally looked back at us and grinned.

"There goes my day in London," LaGrandeur groaned as we pulled up before Air

Command headquarters. But the Inspector had it all sorted out. First, they dropped me in front of the headquarters where it was to take me pretty near forever to wangle some dry clothes; next, the Inspector had the good-looking WAC (who was actually a member of the Home Guard) take him back to his office, after which she was assigned to drive Pilot Officer LaGrandeur wherever he wanted to go that day.

Chapter 8. Northolt Again

I'd not expected much in the way of a greeting once I did reach the Northolt airbase, as the British are not much in the way of demonstrations. What I did not expect was to see so few familiar faces there to greet me.

Mind you, it took more than a day and half for me to get to Northolt. Was I me, Air Command needed to know?

"Dog tags?" I offered.

"Maybe you stole them off his corpse."

"Fingerprints?"

"And send over a bloody convoy to Canada to fetch them? I think not."

Eventually, Northolt was telephoned. They found someone, my old friend the briefing officer, who could describe me and then came the trick question. "He wants to know what planes you shot down."

"Tell him a Heinkel, a bloody Heinkel." Since the Heinkel was not yet in my records, nor would be ever if the briefing officer had his way, I was quickly identified.

Of course, there were other stages that had to be got through. But at that point, I was at least permitted to change out of the prison coveralls I'd been given in exchange for the wet suit and into an officer's uniform, without insignia, of course.

A voice asked in French if the uniform was a good fit, comfortable, and I replied, in French, that it was. Second test passed.

My map had already been passed on by the young Pilot Officer and the next day, two men came to chat with me about it, one in uniform, one in civilian clothes. They asked me a great many questions and had me walk them through the map as well as through my days on the Isle of Guernsey confirming much it seemed that they already knew.

"Will you be landing there soon?" I asked, "The Islanders are hoping you will come to their rescue, all but the Nazi spies and the Mosleyites of course."

The two men said they did not know about that, it was not their job, but later that day, that night rather, two other men came to chat, both civilians. They wanted to know about the Nazi spies and, as important, how I knew they were Nazis.

"An agent of yours was in place, a Jacob Goldstein [Rebecca's uncle]; he identified them." They wrote this down too, but again neither man told me whether this was a good thing or a bad.

The Inspector telephoned during the day, bless him, but I only heard about the call several hours afterward, and, no, I was not released into his company, nor did I get to dine, then, at his club. I did get fed though, which was more than the Royal Navy had done for me, barring the half-sandwich previously mentioned.

I was not a prisoner, not officially, though a couple of provost's men were to accompany me from London to Northolt. They stayed close by my side until the debriefing officer, looking up during a break from his morning duties, said "Ah, Freygood, slept in again, did you?" after which they quietly disappeared.

The debriefing officer continued speaking. "Do not tell me all about it; there simply isn't time. We may even have to have you go up later today, if only to act as a decoy while getting in some flying time.

"Every day we need to put men in the air," he said, "Every night. Go get lunch."

Men were scattered about the large mess hall eating in groups of at most two or three with none of the camaraderie I remembered. It was as if they'd all just arrived from somewhere else, like freshmen at a college. I saw no one I knew well, and only one or two I thought I recognized from the airfield at Arras. One man looked up as if he recognized me also—what was his name, Tyne something or something Tyne, or was Tyne the name of a river I'd seen on a map? But instead of coming over t o greet me, he signaled with a hand wave that he'd best stay for the moment with someone whose identity he was surer of. The longer the war continued, the more men would only feel comfortable in proximity to those they knew.

A Flight Lieutenant came up and wanted to know where my insignia was, then interrupted me half way through my explanation. "You'll need to see the debriefing officer."

An enlisted man came by a short time later, bearing a flying officer's insignia. He wandered about the mess for a few moments, mainly to give himself a break between errands, I suspect, as I was pretty sure he'd spotted me the instant he entered the hall. Before he could hand them to me, I asked, "And how the hell am I supposed to sew these on?"

"May I have your jacket, Sir?" I handed the latter over to him and shortly before supper, my new jacket, insignia now in place, was returned to me.

This time as I entered the mess hall, I recognized three, no four familiar faces, though I couldn't have assigned a name to any of them. They looked back at me and in a couple of cases I could see that they, too, were searching their memories.

Wilson, a much older-looking and, if possible, somewhat balder Wilson, looked up from his food, saw me, said, "I see you've yet to purchase a dress uniform." He got up then and left the room. I'd swear there'd been a tear in his eye, but he left the hall so quickly, there was no way to tell.

Of course, one could tell. I was glad he'd missed me, even more so that he'd shown it. I'd always wanted to be more like Wilson, well, like Wilson appeared to be. Now I realized that the real Wilson was more like me, that he had feelings, that he cared, that he suffered as I did when all around him men died. He was simply more adept at concealing how he felt. We should all strive to be more like the dour-faced Wilson, to remain unaffected by the horrors of war, though we will all fail to varying degrees.

At the meal's conclusion, the Flight Lieutenant who'd cautioned me earlier reappeared to tell me, "You're in my squadron. You'll find your plane on runway three parked in line with but behind mine." He turned to go, then turned back. "You've flown Hurricanes before?"

This last was a question. "Yes, Sir."

"You'll be on the far left wing. Mainly to act as a decoy and get some flight time in. I'll have someone watch you. You know acting Flight Lieutenant Wilson?"

"Yes, Sir. Can I check out my plane, now?"

"If there's time."

But I didn't have time; the alert sounded and we ran out on the field. Damn, I needed to piss.

Wilson went running by. "Follow me."

"What's the flight plan?" I hollered after him.

"Don't need one. They Jerries are coming to us. Follow me, stay out of the way, and keep your radio on."

Where had I heard all this before?

Much later, it was explained to me that our radar stations now were networked; the network informed Air Command when and sometimes where the Germans were on their way. The Germans would usually fly in on a course parallel to the English mainland to keep us guessing then abruptly turn and head for their real targets. Air Command informed Group—ours was the No 11 Group out of Uxbridge, Group informed Sector and, as in the present instance, the number 1 squadron, that's us, was sent on its way. (55+ squadrons in all, with between one to six of our planes, though not quite so many of our pilots, shot down each day.)

Directly ahead of our squadron on an inbound course was a force of twenty-four German-built Dorniers, slightly faster than their Junkers, but virtually standing still compared with our Hurricanes, thus, just begging to be shot from the sky. That is, they would be shot down as soon as we got rid of the forty much faster Messerschmitts that were accompanying them.

Squadron 74's Spitfires showed up to help us and a Dornier and a Messerschmitt fell to earth. Then the anti-aircraft batteries opened up from below, more bad news for the Germans, but not exactly good news for us either, there being no way for the batteries then to distinguish friend from foe. The Flight Lieutenant and the rest of his squadron, Wilson and our vic excepted, went in ten abreast toward the Dorniers as if neither Messerschmitt nor anti-aircraft batteries existed. The rest of us were held back to cover their tails.

After both the Spitfires and our squadron had made second passes at the Dorniers, the final score was RAF, 20 German planes down (one to Wilson's credit), and for the Luftwaffe, one RAF pilot-officer killed, four of our planes permanently out of commission.

Chapter 9. On With The War

Wilson and I finally had a chance to catch up on past events as we were waiting together the next day outside the debriefing officers' hut. We were there together at the same time, I suppose, because the debriefing officer would be asking Wilson whether he felt I was altogether ready for duty.

I could imagine Wilson's answer, "Well, he didn't fly into anyone, but he's not that much use yet either." And, roughly, that was what he did say once he was ushered into the inner sanctum. I knew Wilson would want someone reliable out on his wing; he was serving as Acting Flight Lieutenant with a permanent appointment soon to follow.

The briefing officer approached what he was about to say to me obliquely, an approach far scarier than his usual direct manner. Perhaps, the bombing at Arras had changed him, too.

"Your countrymen have come over now in great numbers, much appreciated; in consequence, they have formed a number of squadrons of their own, RCAF and all that. Perhaps you would like to join them?"

"No, Sir."

He smiled briefly, a thing rarely seen, and went on to his next, quite unexpected question. "Wilson. What do you think of him as a leader?"

"He's a crackerjack pilot."

"We all know that; it's his leadership I'm asking about."

"I'd follow him anywhere."

The debriefing officer wrote something on a piece of paper and went on to his next question, again skirting around what he wanted to know instead of coming at it directly. "We've got in a new type of plane, well not that new actually, but new to us. They did well during the evacuation, Defiants, do you know about them?"

I shook my head.

"They're two-seaters. Pilot in front, gunner in back with four 0.303-inch (7.7-mm) Browning guns mounted in a mobile turret. Bloody dangerous."

I did not know then, but would know soon, that their chief danger was to those who rode in them.

"I'd be the pilot, not the gunner." I wanted that desire on record immediately.

"If you like. We're putting together a very small squadron of them, a half-squadron, really, they're a bit slow; we'll send them out with a flight of Hurricanes for cover, and put you all down among the bombers. You do well down among the Junkers as I recall."

Again, a smile! "We'll be letting the Spitfires handle the dogfights from now on."

Spitfires, Defiants, I didn't know much about either one.

"Flight Lieutenant Billingsly will lead the squadron. You know him?"

"We just met, actually."

"You'll need a gunner; have to be one of the new fellows, I'm afraid, and they're very new. Sure you don't want to be the gunner?" I knew this was a joke, as he made no attempt at a smile.

"Send the next fellow in, will you." and the interview was over.

Wilson was waiting for me outside the hut.

"Wanted to know whether you'd make a good leader." I told him.

"Wants to make sure that my rank as Acting Flight Lieutenant stays just acting."

"Maybe. What's a Defiant? What's a Spitfire for that matter?"

And that was when he told me about the days after I'd gone down in the Channel:

The squadron had made it back to England safely enough and established themselves again at Northolt, absent a few like Thockmorton-Higgins and myself who'd already been shot down before the Channel crossing. After a brief hiatus, the Germans who were now in total control of Northern France had begun their attacks across the Channel on England itself. The squadron soon discovered they would have to contend not only with the Germans but with three additional enemies: The first was the weather, the second, the other British services, the last, their own planes.

In early June, mists had blanketed the English channel. The good news was that this had held off Luftwaffe attacks for several days during the evacuation from Dunkirk during which our troops had crossed back across the Channel unmolested. The bad news was that British pilots returning to base had to remain circling in the air for hours searching for a place to land. Squadron 72 returning to Manston airbase nearly hit the cliffs. They'd gone on to other airfields, found them closed also, and then had to settle to the ground as best they could, one Spitfire hard by a farm tractor, three others crashing after repeated passes at the Manston airstrip.

Though the RAF lost a total of ninety-eight planes during the nine days the evacuation required, the British soldier, who seldom caught a glimpse of our high-flying aircraft, felt he'd been abandoned. He often took it upon himself to fire at our planes, purely out of spite. The Royal Navy, traditionally hostile to the other services, also made it a practice to shoot at anything they saw flying by.

But the biggest problem lay in not recognizing friend from foe in the air, so that Spitfires fired on Hurricanes. It all got sorted out later, but that didn't help any of the pilots who'd been downed in the initial skirmishes.

Hurricane squadrons along with the Defiants now were assigned to attack the German bombers. The fighter-to-fighter dogfights our squadron had engaged in out of Arras were over mostly, unless the Messerschmitts and Heinkels came down to greet us, which they often did, Wilson assured me. "That's where the Defiants come in. They clear the skies. Bit sluggish though, so you may just find yourself alone and vulnerable. If you're lucky, maybe they'll just send you up at night."

Years later, my wife and I were to live out in the country when our children were in their pre-teens. We'd enough acreage then to have dogs, gardens, a small orchard, and a section of woods. We had two dogs, a serious, remarkably intelligent German Shepherd, and a brainless but speedy Irish Terrier. The pair used to hunt squirrels together. The Terrier would run round and round after the squirrel, panting, and the Shepherd would wait, paw raised in the air, until the exhausted squirrel was fool enough to run under it. I gathered this was how Wilson's squadron of Hurricanes (the Terriers) and mine of Defiants (the Shepherds) would work together.

Two of the RCAF squadrons I'd scorned to join flew the Spitfires that had taken over the task of engaging the German fighters in the dogfights. The Spitfires were more than a match for the Messerschmitts (much less the Heinkels). They could do 346 miles per hour at 15,000 feet and get up there in less than seven minutes. They were true state of the aeronautical art with two-position variable pitch propellers and elliptical wings, and could do a tighter turn than anything else in the air. And they were "bloody beautiful" as every pilot who ever laid eyes on one was wont to say.

The Spitfire did have one flaw, Wilson was kind enough to point out. If a roll were attempted at high speeds, the aerodynamic forces upon the plane's ailerons would often twist the entire wingtip in the direction opposite of the aileron deflection. In plain English, the bloody plane would end up by rolling in the opposite direction from the one the pilot intended.

But this was not something I would have to worry about. For I'd be moving sluggishly along in my Defiant waiting for the German planes to come to me.

Chapter 10. Flying Officer Moyle

The briefing officer had just finished dispatching the two squadrons of Hurricanes the next morning when he closed his notebook. Two hands shot up but were ignored for the moment in the mad exodus from the briefing room. Ignoring me still, he indicated that the other man might speak, a lanky sandy-haired Flying Officer, whom the Yanks might have called 'string bean' or 'slim,' though he was not all that tall.

"Sir, what about the Defiants?"

"Nothing on till this evening."

Sounds of relief came from the remaining junior officers, who were immediately shushed by both the sandy-haired lad and I, seemingly the only adults among the Defiant's crews.

I shot my arm up in the air again, and again was ignored. I could pilot a Hurricane; why couldn't I go up in one now, then go up in the slugs later.

"Sir," the sandy-haired officer continued. "We need practice. Couldn't we at least take a practice run after the other flights have left?"

Groans from the juniors, including one who'd almost made it through the door and was due for a reprimand. I thought the sandy-haired officer's proposal a smashing good idea. I'd been too long on the ground. Besides, he had a Kirk Douglas dimple in his chin, if not Kirk Douglas's build, and an air that inspired confidence.

His smile revealed a gap in the teeth along his upper left quadrant. I though it might have been the result of a collision with a downed plane's instrument panel, but he explained much later that it was the result of a mishandled cricket ball early in his teens.

"We have limited fuel," said the briefing officer, "Every flight must count." And that was that.

"Moyle," said the sandy-haired lad and extended his hand.

"Freygood," I replied and took it.

"Mad Harry; heard about you from my Dad."

"Saved me from the Shore Patrol; I'll be forever grateful. Hope to take him up on his dinner invitation, some day. Food here's not what it was in France."

Moyle looked at me with new respect. I was one of the squadron's old boys then. "What are we going to do about these?" he waved his hand despairingly at the junior officers, many of whom were still there, uncertain whether they could go without our permission.

"Kids." All right, I was still only twenty then, but these newly-minted pilot officers, ninety-day wonders who'd yet to see a single day in action, all seemed like kids to me.

Moyle and I looked at one other. When not frowning at unwarranted behavior, he had an infectious grin . That Kirk Douglas dimple helped. He turned to the others in the room. "Follow me chaps."

More grumbling and moans of complaint immediately arose and we pointed to our Flying Officers' insignia. RHIP. Then we led them outside and to the airfield.

The Paul Boulton Defiant Mk I was a beautiful machine, a true flying battleship, with that impressive turret right behind the pilot's seat. Still, it became apparent after an hour in which we'd started the engines (though we'd not left the ground) so that the gunners had a chance to crank away at their hydraulically-powered turrets, that absent several hours or weeks working together as a team, pilot and gunner were going to have difficulty in coordinating their activities.

Moyle signaled for a halt and, after dismounting, walked over to where I stood on the ground. "Perhaps we ought call on the briefing officer."

I did not need to be told what he intended us to talk to the debriefing officer about. Our crews, still without flying experience, would not do. "Talking has never worked with him before," I counseled. But we crossed the tarmac anyway after dismissing the others and headed for the debriefing officers' hut.

"Very well," said the debriefing officer after hearing us out on the need for further training. I'd a suspicion he may already have heard a good deal about the Boulton Paul Defiant from other sources. "But you'll both be going up in Hurricanes with the others this evening."

Oh throw me in the briar patch, do.

Chapter 11. Dinner at the Moyle's

The following morning—our squadrons having failed to encounter the enemy the previous evening, we were permitted to spend some time in the air with our Defiants.

I might add that our failure to encounter the enemy was not unprecedented. The Germans were very good at concealing their flights' intentions until the last possible moment. In this instant, squadrons from two different RAF regional groups including our own had been put on the alert, and the Luftwaffe had surprised us by launching their attacks upon our radar installations instead. Damage had been done, but the word was that by midday, all but two of the radar units would be back on line.

As for the Defiants, the results of our morning exercise were not impressive, but at least my gunner and I parted on speaking terms. If that evening, the enemy did not come upon us too quickly or in too large numbers, we might at least survive, and might, just possibly, be credited with a kill.

But this was not to be, at least not that evening. We confided to our debriefing officer that our little flight of Defiants if not truly ready for battle were at least as ready as they would be in the time allotted, and received two pieces of good news in return. Sector had decided the squadron could stand down for the evening. And, "You've had a phone call, Freygood, from an Inspector Moyle of the London police, your colleague's father, I believe."

Moyle and I went to the pay phone together, Moyle handing me the necessary coinage as it was requested. Could I come for dinner? Tonight would be fine. "Could I bring a friend?" I asked, not that I could have said anything else with the younger Moyle standing there beside me grinning. "I believe you may know him."

Would that we could have left immediately, but we did not, the interval permitting a Pilot Officer from our tiny squadron to seek me out for counseling. Why he sought me out, I'm not quite sure; perhaps, he was impressed by my Flying Officer's insignia, which once upon a time had seemed so important to me. Later, I was to become a magnet for Pilot Officers, fresh-faced innocents barely out of training. I know that none of the other ranks saw fit to call upon my expertise; I'm sure they realized my intrinsic worthlessness; if they had a problem, it would be a Flying Sergeant for them or, if a signature were required, to take compassionate leave for example, then a Squadron Leader.

The Pilot Officer wanted to know if I'd ever been afraid of dying. This was a first for me, not that it was the last time I'd be asked this question. Dying simply wasn't something one discussed. Anyway, I'm sure he did not want an opinion from me so much as an opportunity to vent his own feelings. I might have listened, first sharing with him all the many things I was afraid of, like fucking up in front of the other men, stalling on take off, or damaging my landing gear on the return to the field. But I merely said, "No," which pretty much ended the conversation.

The Moyle's lived in a section of London I'd not known existed. The self-contained neighborhood might as well have been in some small isolated country town albeit it was only a short walk from a Tube station. Here the neighborhood green grocer, there the neighborhood pub, with next to it an Italian restaurant with checkered tablecloths, and around the corner, one after the other, a series of narrow two-story houses.

We turned out to be four for dinner. The unexpected but undoubtedly welcome fourth was Dorothy, the Inspector's driver. Out of the shapeless Home Guard uniform and into a cream-colored linen suit, she was truly gorgeous. In a nice way, I mean. You could imagine her serving tea to her father, the vicar, along with his guests at the parsonage. Her father was a small-scale C of E minister, by the by. She and her dad could both well serve as representatives of the British lower middle class, not really enjoying any of the British Empire's privileges, but loyal to it still to the death. They say that when Beaverbrook announced the creation of a Home Guard, they had almost a million sign ups for it within the week.

I wondered naturally if she and the Inspector had anything going on between them. They did spend a lot of time together. I would have liked to spend a lot of time together with Dorothy myself but, face it, I owed the Inspector a great deal.

"This home cooked meal is not really what I had in mind for you," the Inspector said at that moment, "but as my son chose to come along with you," he gestured toward the company gathered round the table and did not finish his sentence. "You must come and have lunch with me at my club, someday."

"You have a club?" Dorothy said to him and we all turned toward her, silent till now, amazed that she spoke in an incredibly feminine voice that had nothing of the Home Guard in it. "You've never dined at the club."

"I don't really," the Inspector began, "Not often. But I thought Flying Officer Freygood might . . ."

"Oh, Dad, Freygood is perfectly happy eating here with us." the junior Moyle put in.

"I am, more than happy, overwhelmed and truly grateful."

"Let's see if you are all still happy once we've eaten," Dorothy said, ending a display of genuine feeling among us that might well have gone on indefinitely. The Inspector was outrageously happy to see his son, and by extension me. And I was outrageously happy to be in the bosom of a family once more. If Dorothy should be drawn my way, it would only be lagniappe.

And the meal was delicious. The roast beef of Olde England, potatoes and Yorkshire pudding both cooked in the roast's juices, and, an investigation having taken the senior Moyle and his driver out into the country, carrots and parsnips. Carrots and parsnips and other root vegetables were what we spent the winter living on in Quebec. I loved them.

And a salad, of course. "I mixed the salad," Dorothy said. The salad outdid any the French had had on offer and we all ate tons of it. It was clear we all loved Dorothy and I wondered again if the Inspector's love was purely avuncular.

I intended to ask the junior Moyle that very thing once the meal was over, but while we were waiting outside his father's house, ready to walk Dorothy home as arranged, he turned to me and said, "Isn't she a wonderful girl." I realized at that instant that he'd known her for a month and a half longer than I and that this month and a half had been more than enough for him to fall deeply in love.

12. The Defiant

No complete history of the Defiant aircraft has ever been written, nor will one ever be. Few who flew it in combat were alive at the end of the war, and none are alive now. I was not really one of them, more about this later.

The Boulton Paul Defiant was one of those bright ideas conceived in a one-man brainstorming session. Or, worse, by one air marshal chatting with a group of his brown-nosing subordinates. No, I've too much respect for my commanding officers to think that. More likely it was some Beaverbrook or Bevin wanna-a-be from industry who conceived the design ignoring his engineers' warnings. Intended to be the battleship among fighters, it had neither the armament nor the armor necessary. It carried only four .303 guns compared with the eight aboard the Hurricane and the Spitfire, or the seven 7.9 mm guns of the Heinkel 111 bomber. Intended to relieve the pilot of the burden to fire his guns while trying to outflank the enemy, instead it forced the pilot to think about what effect his maneuvers might have upon the gunner sitting behind him in the rear cockpit. By the same token, the gunner was obliged to keep his gun turret in constant motion to compensate for his pilot's actions.

During the evacuation from Dunkirk, Air Command had finally accepted that the unwieldy, slow-moving Defiant was useless in daytime engagements. A somewhat twisted mode of reasoning was used to establish their continued use at night. But as the Defiants lacked their own AI radar, this meant that pilot and gunner must constantly strain through the darkness to see what was going on around them. Would the Defiant be abandoned then? No, they would be renamed as "cat's eye" night fighters as if calling a goat a "horse" would make it easier to ride.

The Defiants, everyone admitted, had at least one good feature. It took so bloody long to get them up to altitude that they would still be below the desired level by the time the German bombers passed above them. The result was that the bomber now presented a large target against the sky and was far easier for the turret gunner to hit.

This was all according to plan, it was announced. The Defiant had been designed to fire upward, indeed, it had no forward-firing armament. A perfect arrangement as long as the bombers, and the bombers alone, sailed on above us. But let a German fighter descend from above and fire at the Defiant from just below its tail, and it would be goodbye yellow brick road.

We were spared this discovery on our tiny squadron of Defiants' first night in the air. Trailing well behind the squadron of Hurricanes, we'd barely reached the site of the action, when the German bombers, forced to turn back by the fury of the British counterattack, headed for home. Score two for our Hurricanes, none for us.

The following day, we reluctantly said farewell to our slugs in the sky. They were sent to a base further South where they might be Johnny on the spot during the German's next appearance. Moyle's gunner took his place in the pilot's chair; a newly arrived Polish pilot took mine.

We were more fortunate than they. Five Defiants went up the next night from their new location and only two returned. The Pole, thankfully, was the pilot of one of them. He'd come too long a way merely to die his first time out.

As already noted, flying a Defiant in combat required a huge amount of coordination between pilot and gunner, coordination that the new set of fliers lacked, and that Moyle and I, having had only a few training flights in the beasts, probably lacked, also.

The remaining Defiants weren't mothballed, incidentally, but were combined with the surviving Defiants from another squadron, fitted with the new Airborne Interception radar (a true "cat's eye") and repainted black so they could see without being seen.

"Bad news, chaps," the debriefing officer said to Moyle and I the next day. He meant, I think, that we would never get to fly a Defiant in combat now, rather than the loss of the men who had so recently flown in them. "But I do think I might have something on the field that would interest you."

This something proved to be the Hurricane II. Physically indistinguishable from the Hurricane I, the debriefing officer invited us to step forward and inspect the engine, a supercharged 1390 horse power Merlin XX, a big step up from the 1030 horse power Merlin II that had served the earlier model.

The differences in performance may seem tiny on paper, a ten mile per hour greater top speed, a half minute less to get up to altitude, a 2000 foot higher ceiling, but it's the differences in performance between you and the enemy, not the actual values that count in the air. Imagine sitting in a parked bumper car at the fun zone, while a second bumper car doing a mere ten miles per hour zooms down upon your flank. Equip those bumper cars with guns at the front end of the car only, and it's easy to see why Moyle and I had big smiles on our faces when we got our new assignment.

"You'll be going up this evening," the debriefing officer added. "Get some rest."

I didn't, of course, at least not immediately. I had to see Birney, yes, Chief Mechanic Birney, no longer merely acting—he was at Northolt too, and brag on the new plane. Birney knew all about it, had checked out the incoming engines personally and was as proud of the new superchargers they were equipped with as if he'd invented them himself.

Of course, my own presence in the hangar meant that I had to be introduced all round, and be bragged on with tales of impossible feats including a dozen downed German aircraft that I'm sure were not to my credit.

Chapter 13. Mad Harry Returns

The word filtered down one morning that a high muck-a-muck from The Royal Canadian Air Force (un grande légume as the French would say) had appeared on the base. Probably didn't take more than five minutes after he'd passed through the gate before the grapevine brought the news to me.

I'd been told early on my return to duty in England that I might join one of the all-Canadian squadrons and, remarkably, I'd said no, that I felt at home where I was. Was this man here then to make a personal appeal?

Not till sometime after lunch did Wing Commander (later Group Leader) Douglas Gordon Raffey of the RCAF just happen to drop by. As suspected, it wasn't an accident; I'd been his intended target from the beginning.

He had deep-set penetrating eyes that summed me up in an instant and, I hoped, did not find me wanting. Like me, he'd been raised in Quebec but had lived in England since 1934.

"They were quite impressed with that map of yours down at RAF Air Command. You took a lot of risks to put it together."

I gave him an 'aw shucks' smile but remained rigidly at attention. "The Royal Navy wasn't that much of an obstacle."

He chuckled and stroked his well-proportioned moustache. "I heard a bit about that, third hand, of course. Perhaps, you'll tell me the whole story later. Look, could we sit down somewhere, have a chat?"

My bed didn't seem such a good idea, the mess hall a long way away. Besides, what good could come of a chat with a senior officer?

"Sit." We sat side by side on my bed. "The thing of it is there are no plans to follow up on your map yet. The boys at the top don't think we can afford to commit the troops or the planes to an immediate counter attack on the Islands and we'd lose far too many men in the process. Also, it's Winnie's thinking, and I certainly agree with him, that the more men the Jerries put over there on Guernsey, the fewer they'll have available for use in the desert or on the continent."

He must have noticed my crestfallen expression, for he added, "It's not as if you have family or friends on the Island."

None except two wonderful young women, four if you count Angelique's mother and sister. Bastards, I thought, thinking of the Air Lords safe in their cubbyholes. Why don't you help them?

"The weak part of the plan, I think," the Wing Commander continued," is how to keep the Germans on the Islands. Perhaps, we could convince them that we will be counter attacking at some point. Would you have any suggestions?"

A senior officer asking me for suggestions? It hardly seemed real.

"We could drop leaflets, keep their spirits up." I improvised. And I could fly back to Guernsey with the leaflets, see how things were going if only from 5000 feet up in the air.

"Hmm. We wouldn't want the Islanders to get too excited, launch a resistance. That would only lead to unnecessary killings. No one wants that."

"The message could be in code, not an obvious one. Just a message in plain English that could be interpreted several ways, directed as much at the Germans as the Islanders. Keep the Germans off balance, while letting the Islanders know they're not forgotten."

I was raving now, making it all up as I went along, but Wing Commander Raffey was listening.

"The leaflet would contain a story, about a porcupine, no a hedgehog, that's what the British call them, surrounded by wolves.

"And the porcupine—it will be a porcupine, this is a Canadian plan," said the Commander, getting into it, "will wrap itself tightly in a ball, quills outwards until the wolves get tired and all go away." We finished the story together.

"And we'll sign it, 'Mad Harry.'" I added.

"'Mad Harry,' I'm not sure I understand that."

I told him everything then that had happened to me on Guernsey. Crashing in the water off the coast of France, the presumed rescue (or had I swam ashore?), my amnesia, my wandering about the island in a daze and living rough. And then, when I'd regained my memory, how I'd continued to live rough so the Germans would pay no attention to me while I worked on the map of their installations.

"You see, Sir, the German Command on the Island will want to know who Mad Harry is. Some of their own people, if not some of the Quislings will rush to tell them. This alone will persuade them that something is up, that an attack might come at any moment.

"A little tramp, symbol of the passive resistance, how appropriate," said the Commander who was clearly a Chaplin fan. "I'll see what can be done. Do you want to fly the mission? Probably get fired on."

I smirked. We always got fired on; it went with the job. He stood up. I stood up. We shook hands; then he was gone.

It took a week before I heard from him again. I was still alive when the message arrived; Wilson was still alive; Moyle was still alive, though he'd flown back twice in a crippled plane. The mission to Guernsey was on.

I drafted the pamphlet, and took it by the briefing officer for approval before sending it off to the printers. He added a pen and ink drawing of a porcupine in its corner. "Mad Harry, himself," he said with one of the very few grins I'd ever seen cross his face.

The job seemed to take bloody forever at the printers, but soon, the pamphlets, a Blenheim trainer, and I were ready to go. A fresh-face youngster named Beckham sat at my side in the copilot's seat with the pamphlets in his lap. Wilson and Moyle were to fly cover in their Hurricanes.

I stayed low over the water the entire distance engulfed in a dense mist with Wilson and Moyle way above me over a thick layer of altostratus clouds. My plan, which I stuck to, was to come in from the north-west bypassing the principal German gun emplacements, cross the island dropping the occasional pamphlet, then come down the coast over the airfield and the port raining pamphlets over friend and foe alike. I'd turn back inland then and if still alive treat the southern part of Guernsey to a visit from Mad Harry.

The trip went surprisingly well, the Germans reacting unexpectedly slowly with only occasional rifle fire from an over-eager German soldier (and one irate farmer who thought I was the Germans out to stampede his cows) presenting any real danger.

This route made my return trip to England longer than necessary, and might well have been fatal, but I soon had mist again to cover me. Several German planes did take off in pursuit, but they were called back even before Wilson and Moyle had a chance to engage.

The real mystery was what the effect on the Guernseyites had been. We didn't really know until after the war, but we did have one clue, a message that evening on the regular channel at the regular time: "I love you, Harry."

The rest is history. The German authorities on the island did indeed puzzle their way through the pamphlet, convince themselves there was a conspiracy in progress, and call for

97

reinforcements that Hitler was only too happy to provide. The Mosleyites on the Island had convinced him that as long as he held the Islands, he held the hearts of the English people. Not.

A week or so later, several air raids were carried out by the RAF against the Guernsey aerodrome to keep up the pretense that the English might be landing in force. One German soldier and five Islanders were killed. Further efforts were abandoned.

But I'd been right about the airstrip, as had Sir Abraham or whatever his name was. Once the airstrip had been expanded using Islanders desperate for any job that paid a wage, it eventually housed the equivalent of almost four German squadrons, two of fighters, the same two that daily escorted the bombers on their runs over England, that daily tried to kill me before I killed them or the bombers they escorted.

Chapter 14. Night on the Town

From time to time after that, at least during the early days of the Battle of Britain, we might be permitted a day or two in London, no more than one or two of us at a time. The duty officer would look us up and down, decide that today's lucky winners were bloody close to useless and off to town they'd go, frequently to do no more than sleep, but sometimes if one had a girl friend or family simply to spend a relatively quiet day with them.

I was fortunate in that the senior Moyle had more or less adopted me, perhaps because in my presence father and son seemed to relate more easily. Flight Officer Moyle also seemed glad of my company. After all, we'd fought together and each of us had now saved the other's life or thought the other one had, at least once and perhaps several times more than that.

The senior Moyle could be counted on to prepare a bang-up meal—he was an excellent cook, albeit in the rather restrained British tradition, and, on occasion, he might take us out to a restaurant. I'd even dined once at his club, not one the average person would have heard of, as it catered mainly to senior police officers including those who might have served in one of her majesty's police forces abroad.

The quality of our own mess had declined radically since we could no longer count on our commander to supplement RAF rations from his own stores. The new head of our squadron was as reliable a pilot and a leader as the old; he just didn't have the former commander's palate. The result was that I was always grateful for the senior Moyle's invitations, and the junior Moyle and I would usually take off for his home together.

Dorothy, the senior Moyle's driver was a frequent fourth at these occasions, and we were all glad of her company. She had wit as well as looks, was a bright and sparkling conversationalist, and had a certain freshness about her that made one feel content and at home. (A mystery to me was how with the black particles of soot that always seemed to hang in the London air, her face could always seem so well scrubbed.)

If she did not so obviously favor Flying Officer Moyle's company, I would have made a play for her myself. He, needless to say, was hopelessly in love with her.

Which was why I grew increasingly irritated that when the meal was over and he would leave to see her home or, having dined alone with his father and I, he would set out for her house, somehow, I would always be dragged along.

Remember Winifred, the student nurse? She, too, had been a lovely, spirit–warming girl, though not quite so attractive as Dorothy. She, too, had left her escort sated with kisses but otherwise unsatisfied. It had been bad enough parting from Winnie of an evening, my body stiff, my balls compacted, but now I had to stand by, often no more than a few feet away, while Dorothy, that delightful, warm, this-is-the-one-to-bring-home-to-your-mother girl, drove my squadron mate crazy.

Kisses would be exchanged, hands would be brushed aside gently, and when we arrived back at her door—she lived, she claimed, with a never-seen maiden aunt, he and I would be sent off with a handshake. Well, I would receive the handshake; he might receive a final peck on the cheek.

In our first visits, a girl might be brought along for me, a Mildred, or a Maude, or a Susan. None was prepossessing in appearance, and the broad-shouldered dresses they wore were not that much different from their Home Guard uniforms (or the uniforms American girls attending Catholic high schools were forced to wear in the 1950's and

60's). But they were girls. Alas, neither Mildred, Maude, nor Susan appeared to see anything in me that rated a handshake much less a peck on the cheek.

We were walking away from the aunt's house one such evening, when I thought to ask, "what happened to your mom?" I was thinking Moyle's mother must have taught him great patience to allow him to put up with so limited a display of affection.

"Leukemia, the white cells crowd out the red ones." he said, then added in an unexpected and somewhat unwelcome display of emotion, "She died when I was twelve. But first, she was sick all the time, and I could hardly stand it. You know how mean and self-centered twelve-year olds can be. I must have made her life miserable."

Understand, Moyle and I were not close buddies. We were more like two-half brothers, the product of two different mothers, that had only just met. I'd never suspected his heart held a pent-up sadness. What could I say; what could one say?

I walked a few steps ahead, not wanting to meet his eye in case tears were in it, and called back over my shoulder, "I bet she loved it when you walked into her sick room after school. Probably, the happiest part of her day."

"She used to run her hands through my hair, say I was her loving boy."

Understand, this man had gone into battle almost daily for more than six weeks in a row, watching as other men, men he'd had breakfast with that morning, dinner the night before, died all around him.

For a moment, I thought he might be going to cry. Crying in my presence would not be a good thing, much worse than being allowed to kiss your girl only when your best friend stands near by.

I continued to stay a few steps ahead of him, silent, walking along solely to release the tension, for perhaps half an hour, when I couldn't help notice that the neighborhood had changed and not for the better.

"Looks like the sort of area where toffs like us might get mugged." I said.

"Rather."

"The uniforms might scare them off."

"Oh, they wouldn't steal our uniforms," Moyle answered, a statement I did not find particularly reassuring.

I turned at a right angle then—we had come uncomfortably close to the docks, so that if the muggers did not get us, perhaps the Royal Navy might, and marched us up a narrow alley-like street away from the water.

We were passing by a tavern, when its door opened suddenly and a dwarf stepped into our path. Moyle looked at the dwarf, and the dwarf looked at Moyle. My gaze went from one to the other and finally I looked only at Moyle eager to discern what the dwarf found so fascinating.

No one had said anything, which I found nerve racking, so finally I broke the silence. 'You're bloody tall, you know," I said to Moyle, though he was at best only an inch or two taller than I. "Must create problems for you, I mean, banging your head on door frames all the time, unless you remember to bend over as you enter."

"Bugger you," said the dwarf and stalked off. Moyle laughed. The black fit that had possessed him was over.

The next block held a strip joint (a private club, they called it over there), two of them in fact, side by side. Strip joints really weren't our cup of tea, but what the hell. The barker, excuse me, the doorman held the door open a crack and we could hear loud music along with a glimpse of flashing lights. "Private Club, Gentlemen. Two pounds membership fee, but then you can come and go as often as you like."

We were in the process of negotiating a lower membership fee for men in uniform when the air raid siren sounded drowning out the music from the club.

"Bloody hell," said Moyle, "we need to get back to the base."

"Bloody hell," I contradicted, "we need to get down into a shelter."

"Where's the shelter, Scroggins?" This from Moyle to the doorman.

"I could let you in for perhaps a pound," the latter replied, "say, rather, a pound and a shilling."

Moyle repeated his question, his hands around the doorman's throat. "Where ... is ... the ... shelter." Moyle was on the thin side, not particularly muscular, but I didn't give much for the doorman's chances.

A man in the uniform of the Home Guard passed by then carrying a darkened torch (flashlight, that is; hard to remember sometimes when I tell this story that I'm a Canadian). "Why aren't you down in the shelter? And you, shut that bloody door and keep it shut till the raid is over."

We merely had to say, "Where?" for the Home Guardsman to lead us off in the direction of the Tube where we'd spend the night.

"Stupid place for you young officers to be." The man said.

"Girls not clean, then," I ventured, still in a chuckling mood.

"Too near the docks. That's where the Jerries are aiming night after night."

"Have to get through us first," Moyle said.

"Can't do much to stop them when you're on the ground, can you , Sir." which ended the conversation.

"We needed the break," I said to Moyle, once we were inside. I didn't want him feeling guilty.

"Dorothy," he said and stood up as if to go outside again.

"She'll be O.K.," I said and yanked him down. She was. We were, too. Forty people were killed in that raid elsewhere in London and fifteen houses were destroyed along with two government buildings.

Chapter 15. Mr. Jacoby

Mad Harry's flight over Guernsey had an unexpected result, a visit to the air base by a Mr. Jacoby. They didn't let him on the base of course, but he left an address and a telephone number behind. I telephoned, then called on him the next time I was in London.

Dressed conservatively in a well-worn black suit that now hung loosely about his frail figure, he invited me inside his home and immediately offered me a cup of tea. 'We will have something to eat later," he said, "Not much but something."

What Mr. Jacobson, who now called himself an Anglicized Mr. Jacoby, had to show me was a Red Cross postcard sent from Guernsey by his niece Rebecca. She said that she was well, that she was getting plenty to eat despite the ongoing conflict and hoped that he was, too. Her friend Angelique had fallen in love with a Canadian aviator named Freygood and wondered if there was any way Mr. Jacoby could let her know what had befallen him.

Of Mad Harry's flyover and the German-imposed restrictions on the Islanders, there was no mention whatever.

"Undoubtedly, she knew such comments would be censored. Now, tell me, who are you and how did you happen to become acquainted with my niece?" Of how he had happened to track me down to Northolt in turn, no mention was made, then or later.

I explained how I had come to be on Guernsey and meet his niece, violating in the process a number of injunctions the men who'd interviewed me so many weeks before had placed upon me. "She was greatly disturbed to have just missed you."

A shadow crossed his face. Years before, a young, not-very-long married Herschel Jacobson had watched as his young bride succumbed to consumption, what we today would call tuberculosis. They'd left Germany together to spend some time in the Swiss mountains at a sanitarium hoping she would recover. When she did not, he'd moved on first to Austria, and then to France, leaving behind a mother, a father, and a younger sister, Rebecca's mother.

"We weren't that close a family. My fault really. My parents had not approved of my wife. They took greater care with my younger sister and saw that she married a fine young man of a fine Jewish family. I really didn't know that I had a niece until years later in the mid 1930's when my parents finally realized that the madness in Germany would not end, that safety lay only in flight.

"Not for them, of course, they were too old, too set in their ways, but for my younger sister, her husband, and their child. Could I help?

"Of course, I could help. I could send money, I could provide a place for them all to stay temporarily. But I could not help with the other things they needed, exit visas, passports. My brother-in-law lost his post at the University, then he was arrested. The very last letter from them asked if I could find a place for Rebecca.

"If I'd only known that she'd escaped, that she was on her slow painful way, a country at a time to Guernsey. But I'd no warning of her impending arrival and almost the instant the Germans crossed into France I knew it was time for me to leave the Island. I've heard about all the confusion in the weeks following, and I gather this was the best thing I could have done.

"The key to the shop was left with Stewart Martel's wife Marcie. Do you know her?"

I said that I did, omitting the details of just how well I knew her daughter or his niece. I explained though that Rebecca had obtained the key and that the Martels were her good friends. "I used your radio, Sir, to communicate the news of the German's arrival on

Guernsey to the British, and later to arrange for my own departure."

I told him then about the map and the submarine, and about my recent over-flight of Guernsey distributing pamphlets to Germans and Islanders alike.

He laughed at that. The British authorities had checked with him to verify my comments about the Nazi spies but had not given him my name. As was characteristic of the spy trade, everything was compartmentalized, nothing divulged except on a need-to-know basis.

"Does it bother you," he asked, "the thought of dying?"

"I'm here to kill Germans," I said.

"It's not good to think about killing. But, I suppose, it is better than to think about dying. Perhaps, I should have stayed on the island, though I'm sure that by now I would be in one of their camps. Here, with nothing to do, I can only think about dying, can only worry if my house will collapse in the next air raid."

"You could join the Home Guard, keep busy," I suggested.

"That is the joke, my young friend. I am a German national, a refugee to be sure, but, because of my nationality, barred from anything in the way of service. I even have neighbors that look at me askance. Some because I am German and talk with a funny accent, some because I am Jewish and they blame the Jews for their troubles."

"Do they blame Churchill, too?"

"People like that blame everybody. Mark my words, when this war is over—yes, I believe we will win, Churchill himself will go down to defeat, blamed as the Germans blamed Otto Braun, and the Russians blamed Kolchak for the exigencies of war and the sins of earlier administrations."

I saw then that he was old and tired. If I helped him the very next moment to get up and serve the promised supper, it was only to be sure he would not forget to eat, himself. I ate sparingly, though he pressed food on me, explaining to him—not quite a lie, that one could not eat too much before going on a mission, for I suspected that he could ill afford food for guests.

I left only after first extracting a promise that I might take him to lunch in return one day.

"If you live," he said.

"I will live and I am going to marry your niece."

Which, of course, is exactly what I did, but there were years to live though before my declared ambition could be realized.

Chapter 16. Battle of Britain

The Battle of Britain went on and on, or so it seemed to me. The Germans staged air raids daily striking at sometimes half a dozen different targets. Our squadron could count on being in the air at least once a day and sometimes twice. I recorded kills; Moyle recorded kills; Wilson recorded kills.

The task had grown more complicated. We now had barrage balloons to be avoided, along with tethered mines that had been ballooned aloft. The Germans were supposed to be held back by the wall these formed and often were. But a barrage balloon couldn't judge whether you were Axis or Ally.

More anti-aircraft batteries were in place than ever before. They shot down German bombers. They shot down Moyle. He brought himself and his plane down safely, a large hole in one wing, but he was not at all happy about it. As Wilson had remarked weeks before, we now had multiple enemies to contend with.

Still, our squadron was rather fortunate, for when our pilots crash-landed either they died instantly or , like Moyle, they walked away intact regardless of the damage to their planes. Other pilots in other squadrons had been burned from head to toe when their gas tanks caught on fire, or were hit by shrapnel, or had their spines crushed on impact with the ground and would spend the rest of their lives confined to a hospital bed.

I wished only for something to break the monotony, a night spent with Dorothy perhaps, or with Marie or Theresa or Ruth, with Angelique or Rebecca, or even with the Mildred, Maude, or Susan who hadn't cared for me all that much. I longed for change, for the D-Day when we'd be punishing the Germans, instead of barely holding our own in defense of England and Democracy. On the plus side, I enjoyed flying, the thrill of the take off, of looking out across either wing and seeing my comrades flying beside me.

According to the debriefing officer, we were shooting down more planes than they were at something like a 2.2 or 2.3 to 1 ratio, 2.2 planes of theirs for every one of ours. But if you listened to German shortwave, and Mr. Jacoby could and did and passed on the bad news to me, the Germans felt confident of the inroads they were making and an all out invasion of Britain had been scheduled, first for Mid-September and then, put off for some reason, for the following month.

America was still not there to help us, the poisonous Joseph Kennedy, Irish-American ambassador to the British Court, would just as soon have seen the Nazis land at Windsor Castle. But we did have Americans to help us just the same. Remember how during the Viet Nam war, Americans would flee to Canada to avoid the draft, well, in 1940 they were crossing over to Canada in droves to swear an oath to the British crown and enlist.

Of course, we also had Australians, South Africans, New Zealanders, and Rhodesians; some Commonwealth countries like Canada and Australia fielded entire squadrons. Let Germany invade another country and immediately we'd have some of that country's pilots—Poles, Belgians, Czechs, Frenchmen, Romanians. What ought to have pissed Kennedy off, hopefully, were the ten Irishman that joined us.

The names of the aces of all nationalities were familiar to us—Peter Townsand, a Brit, Jimmy Davis, a Yank, Josef Frantoisek, a Czech, twenty-eight planes to his credit before he died in October 1940.

I didn't come across too many Jews in the service, though perhaps they, even as I, had slipped by unnoticed. Those I did meet were all enlisted men, having joined up when I did or soon after war broke out. They'd been excluded from the ranks of officers for the same reasons they'd been excluded from the exclusive gentleman's clubs, the Public Schools and colleges from which British officers were selected. The few Jews who did serve as officers were almost all from the Commonwealth countries where breeding and family connections were less of a factor in selection.

I did encounter one chap in our squadron, a Throckmorton-Higgins in fact, though not our Throckmorton-Higgins, but a younger sibling, who insisted on parroting a remark made originally by Roald Dahl, the author of *Willy Wonka and The Chocolate Factory*, not once but several times. "Never seen a Jew in the front line."

The boy had the same supercilious look his older brother had when we first met and I hated him instantly. Perhaps, I said, aping Wilson at his best, this was because he (and perhaps Dahl) had never been in the front line.

"Love the Jews, do you?"

"Which part of Germany did you say you were from?"

A regular music hall routine we were.

We could have continued this dialog in its present vein for some time, but I elected instead to say, "Your brother was in my squadron at Arras."

"My brother. You served under him did you."

"Actually," said Wilson who'd been listening to this exchange with the concentration music-hall audiences reserve for only the headline acts, "your brother served under Flying Officer Freygood, and this was only after your brother had gone down on his knees to be allowed the privilege."

"My brother died a hero."

"Yes, he died that way." from which statement I learned that Throckmorton-Higgins had not landed safely in French-held territory that last day out of Arras after all.

But the Battle for Britain continued. Day after day for four months, the Luftwaffe focused their attention on the British Isles. Some grew more depressed as the battle continued—Moyle Jr. and Mr. Jacoby for example. Some did not. When we first learned of the ratio of downed Luftwaffe to British fighters in a morale-building speech, some had cheered, the glass was half full. Some, like Flying Officer Moyle, thought only of their now dead companions; for them the glass was half empty.

Some were too busy to be depressed; they kept on keeping on, doing the job they'd spent their lives training for; our debriefing officer and the senior Moyle were good examples. I merely longed for change, a single day without having to take my Hurricane up and fly straight into an oncoming attack. Let me return to Guernsey and play the spy. Let me fly a one-man mission to Berlin and bomb Hitler's headquarters.

Chapter 17. New Friend Down

We had three debriefing officers now, including two long-retired men, World War I veterans, newly recalled to active service. Too much was happening for a lone officer to handle. But it was my long-time nemesis and guide who spoke to me after that morning's run, "Flying Officer Moyle failed to return to the barracks last night."

"No harm done, as long as he went up this morning."

"He did not."

Bugger. We'd had our hands full that morning, too, as we'd had our hands full the day before, and the day before that. Some days, Moyle and I had time only to have a cup of tea while our planes were being refueled and then it was back in the air again.

The Germans kept sending in their bombers, further and further up the Thames each time, and we kept shooting them down.

"Maybe he got tired of walking home," I joked. Moyle had been shot down two days earlier on our inbound flight by one of our own anti-aircraft guns, an increasingly dangerous hazard. He hadn't walked home all the way, of course, but had been picked up early on by an observer, then received three quick lifts in succession. Most of his walking had been done on the way in from the gate.

"This is not a joking matter."

"Sir. Permission to take a day's leave." This request wasn't as outrageous as it sounds; Moyle and I normally went on leave together.

"One day. You'll be back no later than noon tomorrow. After that, this becomes an official matter. You're both good men and have shown inspired leadership for the new recruits."

Which, translated, meant I'd exactly 24 hours to find Moyle and bring him in or he'd find himself in jail or before a firing squad for desertion. Both the debriefing officer and I much preferred that he keep going up in the air if only because Jerry would want the exact opposite.

The idea of sending me out to find Moyle was ludicrous. Never mind that he might or might not want to be found. I was a foreigner, not a native, and the maelstrom that was wartime London lacked street signs or other identifiers that might aid the enemy or me. But Moyle's father was a police inspector and so the Central police station was my very first stop. (My second, actually, as I got off the wrong exit from the Tube to begin with.)

"Ah, you're here to have that lunch we talked about. Unfortunately, Dorothy and I are on our way out. I have to be elsewhere for a bit. Perhaps, we might meet for a late diner."

"I've come about your son."

Dorothy's hand went to her heart. "He's not . . . " the senior Moyle began. As always, his voice remained calm and controlled.

"No, but it's worse. He . . ." I stopped and indicated Dorothy's presence with a nod of my head.

"She might as well know, too, bound to pry it out of me sooner or later." They exchanged glances like a long-married couple, no, like a daughter with a beloved father-in-law.

"He failed to report for duty. Twenty-four hours and it will all become official."

The smile became a grimace as the Inspector's lower lip shot upward. "I've no choice, but to go now," he said at last. "Can't take you along. But here's my house key. Think you can find my place, wait there for my return?"

My face must have revealed my confusion—I'd been to the Moyle's several times, of course, but always in Moyle Jr.'s company. Dorothy immediately set to work to write down a series of directions. "You won't get lost," she said, "No you won't. Just take it one step at a time."

I took it one step at a time, found the neighborhood restaurant the two of us had dined at one evening, found the tavern we'd gone into several times for a drink, Dorothy, Moyle Jr, and I, and only then did I find Moyle's home.

No lights and the black out curtains were still drawn. The senior Moyle must have had expectations that morning of a very long day along with the possibility that he would not be back until well after dark.

I didn't bother to turn on the lights, and banged into a low table with my shin while looking for a place to lie down. Perhaps, I ought to have gone off on my own, but I knew no one in London but the Moyles, and would be sure to get lost should I venture outside. Instead, I stretched out on the sofa to wait for the Inspector and immediately went to sleep.

The light from a desk lamp woke me. Inspector Moyle had turned it on before he realized I was there. He'd come in alone; Dorothy was not with him.

"Had a good nap then?"

"Don't often have the opportunity."

"Saw you boys in action once. I had a case out in the country. Streaks of fire in the sky. Saw a plane you'd fired on hit the ground, then burst into flame. We tried to save the pilot."

Enough bullshit. "When did you last see your son?" I asked.

"Thought we'd get around to that. He was here yesterday evening; we had a conversation we'd had several times before, once with you chatting away to Dorothy in the next room.

"He was worn out and he was afraid. You must all be afraid, at one time or another."

"At one time or another." I echoed.

"Told him I understood. Gave him a hug, though I'm usually not very demonstrative. Not very much one can say at a time like that. Can't get inside a man's head, make adjustments he doesn't want to make. Can't get inside your head either. Well, I can to a degree; I'm a policeman after all. I can tell you I truly appreciate what you are doing, but I can't make you go on doing it. That's your decision."

Both of us said nothing for a few moments. "Look, what do you think we should do?" he asked.

I told him that I knew, more or less, the names of all the gentleman's clubs and taverns we'd been to, I'd just no idea how to get to them.

"Or have the membership fees you might need when you get there." He smiled. Smiling was good, I thought.

"Well, let's begin our round of the pubs."

We made the rounds, sometimes by cab, which he was kind enough to pay for, retracing a half-dozen evenings Moyle and I had spent on the town. Occasionally, the Inspector would say, "My son and I once had a drink in there," and we would visit that pub, too.

The air raid sirens went off twice while we were out, but the all clear sounded shortly afterward each time. Thank God for the bad weather, threatening but not quite delivering rain.

We reached the street on which the Moyles lived, again without success along the way, had one last drink at the local pub just as it was in the act of closing, and went into the Inspector's home.

"You'll stay the night of course." I nodded, half asleep already. We could start again in the morning. Perhaps Moyle Jr. had returned on his own to the base.

I had that same thought in mind when I woke to the smell of frying bacon. Absent a shake awake from an enlisted, I'd have slept the day away. "Breakfast," Inspector Moyle said, when he saw I was awake. I'd a mouth full of bacon and eggs that needed to be chewed when I though again of phoning the air base. "Let me do it," he said, "It can take virtually forever to get through sometimes and you might as well go on eating. Whom shall I ask for if I do get through?"

It did take a long time and meanwhile I'd discovered the piece de resistance on my plate. "A tomato, how on Earth!" I exclaimed.

"Not from the Channel Islands, I'm afraid." He remembered my history, "Told you I had a little job to take care of yesterday evening. Hello."

He had got though apparently, but only to the base, for after he'd handed the phone to me, it still took several moments before I had the right debriefing officer on the line. "Could have used you last night," he said in a not particularly friendly tone.

"Is he?"

"He is not. I'll expect you both no later than 1300 hours."

After hanging up—the debriefing officer had already hung up on me, I told the Inspector that we were more or less out of time. "Any chance he's at Dorothy's."

"He wasn't there last night. Anyway, she lives with . . . ."

"But he is there now?"

Again the senior Moyle hesitated, but finally he picked up the phone and dialed. A conversation began that one could only strain to overhear. Even then, I only could make out every third or fourth word.

"And?" I asked when he was through.

"She says he's not there."

"And you believed her."

He would not meet my eye at first, but after a moment he did turn back toward me, "No."

'I should go see him then."

"Shouldn't I go?"

"You've already tried. I can give him the old, 'I was in your shoes too, old boy, but gradually I accepted it ' speech."

"You were never afraid? of dying?" he added after a pause.

"Never. I'm operating on hate, not a sense of duty."

"You're Jewish, aren't you. Saw it in your papers, but never really thought about it. Do all Jews hate Germans?"

"All Jews hate Hitler. Except the dead ones of course."

Flying Officer Moyle was at Dorothy's and there was no maiden aunt. The latter was an abstraction used solely to preserve Dorothy virtue. I gathered this virtue might well have been compromised the previous evening.

"I'm here to bring you back," I said.

"I'm afraid," he confessed and did not look me in the eye.

"Aren't we all? But I'll be far more afraid with you not there to cover my tail."

"I could die; I will die; there are so many dead." Dorothy stood up as if to walk over to console him and I waved her away.

"I won't die before you do. I need you there," I said.

He got up reluctantly—he was a good lad, as his father would have said, kissed Dorothy, a real kiss, not a mere peck on the cheek, put on his uniform—did I mention he'd been sitting at the table dressed only in his skivvies while we chatted, and we went out the door together. I would get him to shave later.

The debriefing officer greeted us coldly—we'd not expected more, and announced that Moyle was late for his new assignment. He had been transferred to the Midlands to serve at a training station. "We need fliers, skilled fliers. You will show them how."

"But Freygood . . ." Moyle began; I suppose he was thinking of what I'd said to him in the kitchen, about covering my tail and all that.

"Will fend for himself," the debriefing officer concluded.

"You don't mind?" Moyle turned to me and I knew that the last thing in the world he wanted me to say was that I did.

But I was not given the opportunity to reply. "Flying Officer Freygood will do as he is ordered. So will you. Dismissed." And that, as they say, was that.

Chapter 18. Postcards from the Channel Isles

I tried to see Mr. Jacobson as often as I could, not only because he was my one remaining contact with those I'd known on Guernsey, but because he reminded me of my own absent family, as if he were a long deceased grandfather who has suddenly reappeared when one is twenty looking exactly as he did when one was five.

He would ring me up whenever he received one or more of the Red Cross postcards the Islanders were occasionally permitted to send. (Not nearly as often as we would have liked to receive them.)

The news always had to be spelled out between the lines. The sender had to avoid the German censors, while the limitation the Germans placed on the number of words required all the messages to be telegraphic in nature.

Two cards had arrived on this occasion, one from Angelique and one from her sister Madeline.

Angelique had written about food. "We are all well. We eat full meals, though we cannot have all the items we would like. Tomatoes and tinned salmon are particularly missed."

"Tomatoes, it makes no sense," I said to Mr. Jacobson. "All they grow there are tomatoes. And as for tinned salmon, the fish fairly leap out of the water into the boat."

"Perhaps, they are not permitted to grow tomatoes. Perhaps, they have been asked to grow something that is more of a staple in the German diet, potatoes for example."

"Potatoes in a greenhouse!"

He shook his head in response. "I only supposed."

"And the tinned salmon?"

"Fish will jump into a boat only if there is a boat to jump in. Perhaps, she is telling us that the Germans have taken away their boats, the better to keep them captive."

Madeleine had written about love or something worse. "Many admirers for all among the soldiers, some too persistent. Strong German leadership fourstalls [misspelled] problems. The French girls provide competition. Rebecca O'Malley, mother very strict. I sing."

"Shall we decode this one," I said.

"Like two Talmudic scholars wrestling with a pilpul? Why not. What do you make of Rebecca O'Malley?"

"That they got Rebecca an Irish passport."

"Very nice, if true. The Irish are neutral; the Germans won't want to offend them."

"The Irish are still pissed off at Cromwell. Tough fighters though, wish they were on our side."

He laughed, which surprised me, not everyone knows the history. But Mr. Jacobson was very widely read and I gathered that he probably knew as much or more history as I and as many languages as Rebecca. Certainly, he knew more than I did. "Gaelic, also," he'd admitted once. "Shall we have a drink?"

"One," I allowed, for by then I knew the little man had a heart condition and, to the extent it was possible in wartime, that he tried to obey the strictures laid down by his doctor. Well, he occasionally tried.

I poured us a brandy each. "The French girls?"

"Whores for the enlisted men. What does 'I sing' mean?"

"That Madeleine's mother has finally permitted her to sing in public, other than in

110

church, I mean. Perhaps, this new occasion is somewhat less respectable."

"To sing for the Germans?"

"Let us hope not. They don't deserve the treat. I've been there when the Martels gathered around the piano and was entranced. Madeleine has a beautiful soprano voice, somewhat on the deep side, and her mother plays. "

"I play a little piano also," he said. I looked around the room, but of course in the tiny apartment he currently occupied there was no room for one. There'd not been a piano in the apartment above his shop in St Peter Port either. He shook his head sadly as we shared this realization. Perhaps the last time he'd played had been on the Martel's keyboard.

"I must go," I said, "But I'll be back."

"God willing."

I only wish he were sitting there still.

Chapter 19. Mission to France

Flying Officer Moyle came back to us in Northolt a month or two later. We'd already flown a mission or three with a few of his gifted trainees; some were still alive when he returned. I suspect he'd had a chance to see Dorothy in the interim as well, because he looked very happy.

I'd my own concerns then, though I'd seen Dorothy once or twice too and got to meet her maiden aunt, a very cute though somewhat plump member of the Home Guard named Doreen. Doreen and I hit it off famously but that's another story.

RCAF Wing Commander Raffey had paid me a return visit bringing me a Flight Lieutenant's insignia and a new assignment. I suspected the two went together.

"They'd like you to go into France, liaison with the resistance. You speak French— you're from Quebec, and you've worked underground before."

I had worked under cover in Guernsey, true. Had I been afraid then? Yes, I had, but not any more than I was now, being shot at twice a day. As for my French, never the best—I'd gotten terrible grades in school, my familiarity with the language was not quite the asset they thought it was.

"Where will I be going?"

"Midi-pyrénées. Gasconne.."

"But that's in Vichy France."

"For the time being. " A truth I was to reflect on much later.

"And they don't speak French there, exactly."

"We Quebecois don't speak French either, not really, not as the French know it. But somehow you got along in Arras; you got along in Guernsey. You are an incredible mimic."

The last was true enough, for I now spoke English as the Brits did though with varying British accents depending on with whom I was speaking. I might even have had a faint German accent while talking with Rebecca.

"You'll get along fine," the Commander said.

"And I'll get there, how?"

"By flying a plane."

"You'll want me to fly reconnaissance over Gasconne?"

"Not right away, but we do want you in place when and if reconnaissance is needed." After which we went into the details of the plan: whom I'd be meeting, how I'd recognize them, how they'd recognize me, how London would send further instructions.

"One direction only, I'm afraid; you won't be able to communicate with us. We'll let you know when there is a change in your assignment."

This assignment, all but the first part of it, was pretty dull. Hide the plane and my uniform after landing, blend into the populace, gather fuel for a return flight (how this was to be done remained unspecified), lend encouragement to the slowly forming French resistance (again the details were omitted), and await new instructions. Which would be received, how?

"You'll know. And don't get caught, you won't be wearing a uniform."

Pity, now that a Flight Lieutenant's insignia would adorn it.

And as for that first part of the assignment, the part I haven't yet told about, it was merely to get to the Midi-pyrénées somehow, via a route to be determined.

Relieved, for the moment, from active duty in the air, I set about determining the optimal route, playing at being a navigator again under the debriefing officer's watchful eye, reviewing my options with Wilson and Moyle whenever they were available.

"Have you considered the Cote d'Azure instead?" Wilson suggested, "It's really lovely this time of year."

A seemingly practicable idea was to fly out over the Atlantic in the direction Mad Harry had taken, only further west. When well out to sea, I would alter course to parallel the French Coast, cutting inward once I was on a line with the town of Auch near where I would be landing.

This had looked like the best route when sketched on a map. Then I learned that German weather-reconnaissance planes flew out over the Atlantic regularly and were very likely to report my passing and/or try to shoot me down. The very first part of the proposed flight would also expose me to incredible danger were I to stumble into a squadron of Germans on their way to attack southwest England.

My final plan or, rather, our final plan, for Wilson and Moyle really did get involved, finally, was to go up with a regular fighter group, stand off from the battle, and when the Jerries turned for home, follow them in, indistinguishable to their land-based radar from their own planes.

This still left me with several hundred miles of high altitude travel over land, but how likely would it be for the Jerries to search the sky for enemies where no enemy was ever likely to be?

It remained only to choose the plane and the time, and to say goodbye to old friends.

The ideal plane would be a Messerschmitt or a Heinkel, one the Jerries would never suspect.

"We can only hope neither Moyle nor I are the ones to shoot you down if that's your choice," said Wilson.

"No," said Wing Commander Raffey when told this idea.

I knew the Hurricane. Perhaps, it would be best if I flew one of them, the older model Mk.I I'd flown in France, though. No use giving the Jerries one of our better planes should I be caught.

The solution provided by the Wing Commander, or those he worked for, was the Moraine-Saulnier 410 produced by the French and considerably modified before it got to me. Among other changes its engine had been replaced with the more powerful Hispano-Suisa 12Z. A working prototype of the latter engine had been loaned to the Brits before the war broke out and never returned. I guess you could say I'd be returning it to French soil.

Thus modified, the MS 410 could fly faster than the Hurricane (once it was up above 5,000 feet, that is) and if it didn't have the Hurricane's armament, well I hadn't been sent over France to fight. Supplied with ample gasoline, it could readily fly the entire distance to Auch without refueling. The best news was that the Germans were making use of them, though not in Western Europe, and I might well pass inspection from below.

"Again, what's to keep our boys from shooting you down?"

To forestall the early termination of my flight, Wilson and Moyle were assigned to fly alongside me on the day of my departure. They were to drive off all planes, friend or foe, that approached nearby, at least till I was well out over the channel in the wake of the retreating Germans. After that, I'd be entirely on my own.

On my test flights—for I had to get familiar with the Moraine-Saulnier's controls and handling, our ground observers along with British civilians were constantly radioing (and phoning) in reports on my progress through the surrounding skies. One could only hope the French populace was less observant or less organized.

There remained to choose a time for my departure, not an easy decision to make, as it would depend on when and where the Germans chose to make their attacks.

I'd want a late evening or nighttime departure, and the ideal weather conditions would include a cloud layer somewhere between 10,000 and 15,000 feet with clear skies above and below. These conditions had great appeal for the attacking Jerries also, so they weren't that restrictive.

The problem was that while such conditions were common over England and Northern France, we'd no idea how far the cloud layer would extend into the sunny south. Tant pis.

The other bit of bad news came when I telephoned Mr. Jacobson to say goodbye. He told me he would be going away too, that the British had decided to intern all foreign nationals. "Absolutely crazy, bloody ridiculous, one could not imagine a more determined opponent of Hitler," I said to Inspector Moyle when at last I got through to him. He said he'd see what he could do, in a voice that, to me, did not sound at all reassuring.

The evening for my departure came, finally. The weather reports looked ideal. An already weary debriefing officer had been checking and rechecking the Wing's flight plans along with mine when section headquarters sent the signal to scramble. German bombers were headed our way.

Wilson, Moyle, and I gave the rest of the squadron a five-minute head start—best to stay away from the forth-coming battle, then followed shortly thereafter. I climbed slowly, an irritable Wilson far in advance of me, but by 15,000 feet we were able to fly in formation at a speed more to Wilson's liking. Two Hurricanes from another squadron arrived immediately, in pursuit of me apparently, and were driven off by Moyle.

By then, we'd reached the limits of the dogfight off Dover and Wight, most of which was taking place below the cloud layer, invisible to us. We could only cut our speed, monitor the radio, circle and hope the fight below was going the Allies' way. Finally, we received the signal that the Germans had been driven off.

Spitfires and Messerschmitts appeared out of the cloud layer ahead of us, all headed back to Calais, the Spitfires in pursuit. Below, our Hurricanes continued to harass the German bombers, though now that the latter had dropped their loads they were far more maneuverable and dangerous. Still, on balance, it was another unsuccessful day for the Luftwaffe.

The Messerschmitts dropped below the clouds on their descent into France, and the Spitfires turned back toward England. They headed toward us, then veered away. Wilson and Moyle followed shortly afterward. "Keep your pecker up." And I was alone over Northern France.

No antiaircraft fire, no pursuing planes. Good. I estimated 45 minutes till I need begin my descent and then? what? I now was passing over Normandy, if my compass did not lie. Did I see an aircraft far to the West? I could hear the beating of my heart, an impossibility, for it would have had to be drowned out by the engine. Calm down, Flight Lieutenant Freygood. Remain calm as long as the sky remains free of tracer bullets.

When I flew over Poitou-Charentes, the sun had already crossed the Atlantic and reached Quebec. My parents would be waking. An hour later when I landed in the Midi, it would be Theresa's turn to rise in Northern Ontario. The radio was filled with chatter over Aquitaine. Nothing about a Moraine-Saulnier MS 410 passing overhead.

The cloud layer below gradually dissipated in the night air, and I glimpsed the peaks of the Pyrénées. The time to descend had arrived.

I was headed to the town of Pavie to the south of Auch when I realized the flaw in the plan. How was I to tell where Pavie was or distinguish it from Beaulieu or Auch or a thousand other towns in Gascony, not that the towns themselves could readily be discerned in the dark? At 5,000 feet, I had part of my answer. Pavie, they'd said, lay astraddle the division between two valleys. I spoke, "Lenin" into the mouthpiece at the prescribed frequency when I saw the gap ahead of me and a few moments later saw a flare break out no brighter than a match head perhaps five miles to the southeast.

I dropped down to 1500 feet as I traversed the miles and again spoke, "Lenin" into the mouthpiece. Again came the flare, more like a distant campfire. Surely they could hear my engine now flying above them, but following the drill, I said, "Trotsky," into the mouthpiece, a strange choice given the enmity between the late War hero murdered in Mexico and the current Soviet government.

From 700 feet, I floated a further 200 feet down and then to the left to follow a line of suddenly lit flares below. I landed safely, and, abruptly, all the flares but one were extinguished. "Piss on it," I heard someone call out in tainted French, the Gascon accent I imagined. Then I was standing on the ground to much applause. Hands clasped mine, men shouted victory, while the man in charge tried to obtain order. Soon the men—seven of them in all, I discovered counting quickly, at least six too many who knew of my landing—and I had wheeled my plane between a line of trees, and together covered it with branches. We dispersed immediately to two cars, one a tiny Citroën, one a farm truck.

"Let him sit in front," came the order, a flask was pressed into my hand, good brandy. "The best," the same voice said, and I was off to new adventures.

Book III.   The Alps and the Pyrenees

Chapter 1. The Kiln December 1940-February 1941

My host during my first few months in the Midi was Paul-Henri Leduc the Trotskyite leader of the small group of men that had helped me to land and hide my plane. A short man with broad powerful shoulders, a broad forehead and a jutting brow, he appeared to be formed from a mixture of all the races in the area, Basque, Gascon and Gallic.

Paul-Henri lived on a farm and expected me to help with the running of it. I had no problem with this at first, even if I seemingly was to be delegated the most menial of chores. I need earn my keep after all. I 'd been supplied by the Wing Commander with French francs in limited quantities, but had been advised these might be required to bribe my way out of certain situations rather than be used to cover day-to-day expenses.

I began to build muscles in new and unexpected places lifting sacks of grain and tossing pitchforks of hay to the animals. I learned new aspects of animal husbandry. One can chase a chicken or a duck, but never ever chase a goose, that's a job for a dog, a clever, nimble dog.

My assistant in these tasks was Paul-Henri's daughter, an attractive girl of 16 named, or nicknamed, Bébé. Or, more accurately, I served as her assistant since she had long since learned how to do what needed to be done around the farm with the minimum of wasted effort.

While she soon left me to do the heavy chores alone, she persisted with the milking, laughing at my own initial efforts. "Apparently, you do not know how to stroke these properly," though what she indicated with a gesture was her own ample breasts set on a block-like torso strongly reminiscent of her father's but with the afore-mentioned feminine additions.

However much I enjoyed Bébé's company, particularly after she introduced me in the hayloft to the game of doctor, I soon saw that the real weakness of my role as farm laborer was that it kept me isolated unable to perform my task of consolidating the resistance.

Paul-Henri recognized and accepted this complaint. I think, too, he felt somewhat guilty for the tasks he'd been forced to assign me, many of them make work, for he had Bébé to help him on the farm, and a sister named François to help him in the house.

Fortunately, he was also the owner of small kiln used for producing charcoal that he then sold throughout the neighborhood. In addition to gathering the wood, and keeping the kiln fed, it would be my job to make deliveries, thus giving me a plausible excuse for traveling about the neighborhood.

"But I think you will first need to correct your accent." This is how I came to meet Madame Simone Printemps.

Simone taught at the école secondaire in Auch; Pavie was too small to have such an advanced educational institution. She had studied in Paris, it was said; (I was later unable to verify this claim). I would surely enjoy her company for it was obvious I was an educated man.

Simone spoke some English and knew the French grammar well. "I am embarrassed," Paul-Henri, said to me one day, "that my speech is too much of the farm, too little of the town." This from a person who genuinely believed in the equality of all men, save perhaps for women and Moors.

Was there not a risk, I asked him, that Simone might be too well educated, that she would instantly recognize that my accent had only been honed in Northern France and was from some other country entirely, Canada, for example? Moreover, I was not sure that a cultured French accent would be entirely suited to my new role, working as I would need to among all classes of people. In any event, the lessons did get me off the farm and into town. And Simone Printemps proved to be an excellent teacher. I never felt confused or helpless in her presence, but always that I was learning, learning to talk like a true Gascon.

I had some trouble explaining the latter to her at first, that though I wanted to correct my grammar, I did not want to sound like some educated toff from the North. Indeed the more slang I could learn along with the local dialect, the better for me it would be. She agreed after some argument to provide the accent, but not the vocabulary. "You may pick that up from your farmers," she declared with a sniff.

On the down side, while Madame Printemps' hips were broad and suggested great comfort for the weary traveler, she was flat as a board above, and had just the suggestion of a small mustache. (Perhaps, Paul-Henri felt these small defects would make little difference to me. More Simone would mean less risk of pregnancy for Bébé, and Bébé, as we both knew, was as man crazy as they come at that age. Our game of doctor being but one example. Of course, Bébé, too, had her drawbacks, not the least of which was that she was barrel-chested and broad-shouldered like her father.)

My days now were filled with activity. In the morning, I would tend the kiln. In the afternoon, I would accompany Paul-Henri on his deliveries with the admonishment to keep as quiet as possible till my accent was improved, and in the late afternoon or early evening hours I would be dropped off in Auch to study with Madame Simone.

Feeding me supper was part of Simone's duties. Thankfully, the British had supplied me with the necessary currency to reimburse her. She was not a rich woman. In fact, no one in the Midi, at least outside of Toulouse, could be described as rich. After supper, Paul-Henri would appear at her door to pick me up and he and I would go to the meetings of his resistance group.

I should have been warned about those meetings, if not by British Intelligence, then by my own experiences in Rochincourt. Foolishly, I assumed that a group of ardent communists, albeit of the Trotskyite rather than the Stalinist variety, might exhibit some cohesion. Nothing could be further from the truth. Indeed, neither a majority of votes much less a consensus could ever be obtained on any issue. Nor were there ever a mere two sides to any question, but always three, four, or seven (as the men who had assisted me to land were the entire cadre).

One thing only did they have in common. Always after the meeting, or occasionally during a break, one or more men would come up to me, assure me of their loyalty to a cause (a cause that was never quite specified but one assumed included freeing France from the invaders and then installing a government based on syndic-anarchist principles), and then tell me that I must avoid becoming involved with or adopting the principles of any of the others.

Only two of the men seemed at all interested in developing a consensus. One, Paul-Henri assured me, was a plant from the local Soviet-dominated Communist party. They tolerated this man only to prevent the party from sending another man whose sympathies might not be so easily recognized. The other was a Spaniard who'd fought on the losing Republican side in the Spanish Civil War. He'd learned his lesson early in the infighting that occurred there and I hoped he'd pass the lesson on to the others in our group: We hang together or we hang separately.

Much later, I was to discover that he was one of the few lucky ones to remain free after escaping over the Pyrenees from Spain into France. The French authorities had tossed almost all the escapees into prison and the Vichy government had no intention of releasing them soon.

As the days went by, I continued to develop my body as well as my mind. The cutting and carrying of wood added muscle, particularly around the neck and shoulders, bringing me close to the frame that I carry today (or that I carried till recently). The demands of my appetite picked up as well. Fortunately, François the Aunt was a gifted cook and the food, straight from farm to plate, was plentiful. Commonplace treats included delicious pieces of duck and a whole range of pâtés. Paul-Henri would occasionally lend a hand to produce certain local specialties—he had his own variation on the cassoulet, and various neighbor ladies (particularly those left adrift when their husbands had gone to fight with the free French or been taken prisoner by the Nazis) would bring a dish.

"I made too much," one would say, "I am not used to Pierre's absence," and she would smile warmly at me. Immediately following such a woman's departure, Bébé or François would fill me in on various scandalous details in the woman's past in the hope that any attraction I might feel for her in return would die stillborn.

I continued under Madame Printemp's guidance to improve my French. At the meetings of our resistance group, the men now remarked on it. As a result, I was less hesitant in making suggestions. Of course, all my contributions like those of anyone else at those meetings were followed by a "yes, but," and the 50 reasons why my suggestions would be impossible to carry through.

As time passed, the bowls of soup Simone provided me with each evening were gradually replaced by stews, then supplemented with salad and dessert, and 'souper ' gradually became 'dîner.' Madame Simone's black dresses, "I fear now my spouse will never return," yielded to lightweight frocks, and flesh could be seen above the stockings and deeper and deeper in the line below her throat.

An evening came when Paul-Henri was unable to return for me—a crisis on the farm. I lay down on the couch, Madame Simone shortly lay down beside me, and I soon discovered the great comfort one might find between those sturdy thighs, the security provided by those ample hips.

The next day, I suggested to Paul-Henri that perhaps I ought spend the night again with Madame Simone. He did not object. It had become clear to him that were I to remain a guest on his farm, Bébé, too, would soon lay down beside me. (Indeed, she already had, but this was knowledge was not be shared with her father.)

Auch was to Paive as Arras to Rochincourt or Montréal to Chauteguay. The river Gers ran next to it, not just a tiny steam that ended in a duck pond. Paive held a small church. A cathedral towered over Auch.

Halfway up the cathedral's steps stood the sculpted figure of a man. He wore elegant calf-length boots, a full-length cloak around his shoulders, and a broad belt buckled diagonally across his chest. A sword hung from the belt, the man's left hand caressing its handle. D'Artagnan. I was vain then, indeed I'm vain now save when I look in a mirror, and it was easy to imagine myself standing midway up the stairs, Wilson and Moyle by my side, the Three Musketeers. But Wilson and Moyle were not here, nor did I have a briefing officer or squadron leader to advise me. Whatever I would have to face, I would face alone.

The shift in quarters to Auch provided me, Musketeer and man, with the opportunity to meet with two new groups of partisans. One group, Gaullists all, waited only for the General's orders. The other, Soviet dominated and Soviet financed, were ardent communists. I was not surprised to find that each group despised the other and had no use for the Trotskyites of Pavie either. This discovery was not altogether encouraging. Where was the opposition to the right-wing policies of the Vichy government to come from? Free

France did not exist and would not in the absence of unity.

The two groups appeared to accept my cover story that I was a downed French pilot—though not one from the immediate neighborhood. Their guesses varied from a birthplace in far off Normandy to nearby Bordeaux, a partial credit to Simone's teaching. Both groups promised to supply all they could of aviation grade gasoline and the communists actually followed through.

Does it seem unreasonable with my work going so well that I would spend a bit more time with Madame Simone than necessary, and do so solely to experience the physical pleasure, or that I would again take up duties on Paul-Henri's farm, tending to Bébé at the same time I tended to his kiln? In Paive, the sounds of 7mm guns firing, bombs dropping, fuel dumps exploding were far, far away.

Simone and I were in bed one night engaging in the pillow talk that is often as emotionally satisfying, though not as physically so, as sex itself. She was talking about her education at the Lycée, which she had been forced to cut short due to the fear of war. Her husband, if she'd actually been married, had left her then to go with the French Army to fight in Belgium.

I told her that I, too, had been forced to cut short my education, dropping out of the University after only two years to train as a pilot.

She asked which University I had gone to. I said the Sorbonne in Paris as this was the story Paul-Henri and I had agreed to.

Her brow furrowed in puzzlement. "But are you not a Canadian, a pilot for the British?"

"Who told you that!" I demanded, though the answer was obvious. Paul-Henri had told her. If he had told Simone, who else had he told, breaking his solemn pledge? And what of the men in the group? Who else had they told? Who else had Simone told? How long would it be before the news of my identity leaked to the Vichy authorities and then to the Germans?

Chapter 2. The False Escape

I had to get away; start over in a new hiding place.

One cannot tell just one person a secret, as I cautioned Paul-Henri the very next day. With the word of my existence widespread, it was only a matter of time till I was detected and dragged away, by the Germans, by their helpmates the Alliance Français, by the Vichy government or, when and if it suited their purposes, betrayed by the Soviet-backed communists.

No, I must assume that I was already known to these organizations—had Paul-Henri not said that the communists had planned a spy in our midst. Already, some person or persons might only be waiting for a convenient time for my arrest, perhaps until my detention would be of some bargaining value with the German invaders.

I had to make plans. While my arms around Simone's shoulders that night as we lay together, unable to sleep, the plans poured into my brain. Too many of them; which to choose? All suffered from the same inevitable flaw, someone local would know something, would betray me accidentally or under the threat of torture.

And there was the problem of my aircraft, the MS 410. I might retreat to some other distant hiding place, but the plane would have to stay hidden in the wood near Pavie until it was called for.

In the morning, the solution came to me: I would follow through on all the plans. I began with Simone, explaining the need for me to go another hiding place. She protested. Were we not together, now? She would protect me.

Of course, but would it not be better if we were to separate briefly? Perhaps she had a friend or relative who lived at some distance from Paive, one she would have a plausible excuse for visiting at regular intervals.

An old school chum, perhaps; where had she gone to school?

"Bordeaux."

But Bordeaux was in occupied France! This would not prove to be a problem, I was assured. She had already been to Bordeaux many times since the invasion. Life with the Germans was not that bad and few were in the city. (A lie as it turned out.) The city mainly ran itself just as it had before the occupation. (Another lie. Bordeaux outdid even the Vichy government in its anti-Jewish policies.) And she had a friend whose large apartment could accommodate us. One who could be trusted to the death. This woman also had a boyfriend while her husband was in jail; she would welcome Simone's company (while not, one assumed, coveting Simone's own man). We would spend weekends together amid the vines; dine fashionably during the week. (How true that each of us has his or her own unique perspective on life.)

Then arrangements must be made, I said. How soon could these be completed? And without alerting the occupation authorities. "They don't bother to read our correspondence," Simone answered, though this assertion too was surely built more on hope than on fact.

"How often can you come and visit me?" I then asked, for the success of my master plan required that Simone be convinced of my sincerity.

"Often," she assured me, "Yvonne is my oldest and dearest friend."

Next, I called on Paul-Henri, returning to his home for the day and night. I began by asking him how many he had informed of my presence, though I already knew the answer.

"Just the men who greeted you on landing," he assured me.

"Including the Stalinist, the spy."

"Well yes."

"Who you will kill."

He blanched at this, then agreed it would be done. I could tell he had in mind some far distant future in which this act would be performed and not, as my plans required, the very next day.

"And did you tell Simone I was English?"

He confessed he had done this. "And anyone else?" Bit by bit the list of those he'd informed grew. Customers for his wood, a neighbor down the road, always some dear person who could be trusted.

"As to the election . . . ." I concluded. The Trotskyites chose and rechose their leader regularly, not quite in the form of an election with a sealed ballot box, but more an endless discussion. Paul-Henri was leader mostly because no successor could be agreed on. "I shall not be voting for you."

"But why?" His cry was one of desperation.

"Because you are unfit, unworthy, a violator of trusts. I cannot support you. Indeed, you ought to consider resigning from the party."

"No!" He was a broken man. He needed to be offered hope. The Wizard had given Dorothy hope: "But bring me the broomstick of the Wicked Witch of the West." Might I not do the same?

I explained carefully that he would tell the group that night that he would be going away for a few days. He was to leave for Montauban the next morning to search for a place for me to stay, though this latter purpose would not be shared with the others.

'You will return secretly the day after your departure and kill the Communist. Then, you will go away again."

He appeared unable or unwilling to understand the intricacies of the plan, not even the part I was willing to share with him, and so I had to go over it with him a second and a third time. I knew why he was reluctant. For all his talk of revolution and Trotsky at the head of the Red armies, as well as the gun he would occasionally wave (unloaded) during a frenzied discussion, he could not kill. Few men can; they say for all the rifles fired in wartime, only one in ten is aimed accurately at its target.

We agreed finally on this: He would speak at the meeting and then depart as scheduled. He would come back two days later and try not to be seen doing so. Yes, I knew it was inevitable that in such a small community he would be seen and recognized. The important thing was that he be officially absent when the deed was done so that he would not be arrested. While his culpability would be widely accepted, particularly given the known enmity between him and the man in question, the authorities would lack sufficient evidence to arrest him.

"But who will . . . ?" he began.

"You do not have a need to know. But I will need you to give me a gun." A nod is as good as a wink to a blind horse; he retrieved his pistol from its hiding place and lovingly unwrapped it, practically having to have it pried from his hand. Bullets were a problem, too, it seemed, but these were ultimately located in their long neglected location. The pistol was well oiled, though, equally clearly, it had never been used except to fire at rabbits and wine bottles set atop fence posts.

The balance of the plan, his plan, that is—one should not forget that my own plan was one of many different plans, only one of which would actually be fulfilled—simply called for him to go back to Montauban for the balance of the week as discussed previously and find me a hiding place.

"And the airplane?"

"The plane is to remain hidden and never, ever talked about. Jamais!" One could only hope he would honor this latter command.

The third plan pivoted around Bébé and was discussed with her as soon as her father had announced to the family that he would be going away for a week. "We can make love in his bed," she said, for till then we had been forced to make use of straw in the barn and more often the hard ground behind the kiln. "Why not yours?" I responded for I doubted the integrity of his sheets. Paul-Henri was not one for the excess use of soap and water. "Too small."

We talked then of my need for a new hiding place. "You are going away?" she practically wept in response. Could this self-centered creature actually miss me and not merely the sex?

"You told me of a cousin you spent some time with when you were younger, shortly after your mother went away. She lives in Saint Gaudens."

"Begoña, of course."

"Could we stay with her?" I emphasized the "we."

"You mean permanently. Leave my father?"

"Man and wife." She would have celebrated our forthcoming wedding then and there but, of course, her father was still in the house. As things were, he was not gone five minutes and we were in her bed. It was too small as she'd said, but we improvised. Our activities continued throughout the day as we explored various bedroom possibilities, indoors and out, and then I sprung on her the other aspects of the plan.

Of course, we were not alone in Paul-Henri's home. I've already mentioned the third member of the household, his sister, Tante François, a sharp-faced blond woman, with an amply breasted but otherwise spare body that she normally kept hidden away in shapeless clothing. Her husband had left her early on, first to join the French army and then De Gaulle's, after which, unable to run the farm on her own, she'd come to live with her brother in Pavie. He needed a woman in the kitchen as well as someone who might be able to manage his increasingly-out-of-control Bébé.

François and I had had a discreet accommodation for some time. Mainly kisses, though I had come between her thighs once.

I explained to Bébé that without her Aunt's cooperation, our whole liaison would be impossible. Already we had signs that her aunt did not approve of what we were doing. Only one way existed by which that cooperation might be enlisted and I begged Bébés indulgence on that score. Bébé assured me she was not jealous, that all that was important to her was that I not forget my own marital duties.

This situation might seem idyllic for a young man in his early twenties, Bébé in the morning, Tante François in the afternoon, and Simone in the evening, though the latter would be sent off the very next morning to Bordeaux to confirm that I had a place to stay. But I also had a man to kill that night.

This last had not been difficult to arrange. The men in our group were always trying to arrange private meetings with me. Bumping, not at all accidentally, into the Communist spy the previous evening, I'd suggested that as Paul-Henri would be going out of town, the next night would be ideal for our long-put-off private discussion.

The next evening, from four o'clock on, the air was filled with electricity. One could smell though not see the far off thunder storms, the product of a day of intense heat. The Communist and I met at the landing site, for I'd explained that I needed his help hiding the plane. The lightning was closer now, one could see the flashes and hear the thunder though as yet we had no sign of rain. He watched while I removed one or two critical parts from the engine, and then as I dug a hole in which to bury them. "I cannot trust Paul-Henri to leave the aircraft alone. He is not reliable."

A moment later, I raised the shovel on high and brought it down on the man 's head. My aim with guns had always been bad and I might well have winged rather than killed him had I actually made use of Paul-Henri's pistol. The rain began to fall in earnest then packing the earth atop the grave I buried the spy in.

The next morning it was necessary to further enlist Bébés aid. "You mentioned to me once, a traveling salesman, very handsome."

"He is not as handsome as you," Bébé rushed to assure me.

"We will need him to drive us to your cousin's. You mentioned that he will be coming by here this Wednesday."

"But heading in the wrong direction."

"He will return again on . . . ?"

"Friday."

"Then here is what you must do." and I explained to her the plan, that is, her part of the plan.

Accordingly, she waited by the road and flagged the man down on his way to Tabor the next day. As expected, he was thrilled to learn they would be going together that Friday to spend a night in Toulouse while her father was absent. In fact, he arranged to be back our way on Friday morning rather than evening which, I suspect, meant that he would fail to call on a client or two that trip.

He was not pleased to learn after she'd climbed aboard his company-owned Peugeot that Friday that she needed to stop on the other side of town. Even less so when he discovered that the person they were stopping for was me. 'But you must understand, it is so if my father finds out, he will think I have left with Pierre."

"And I need a lift."

He was positively enraged when she got out of the car a moment later. "We must not be seen leaving together. But I will be at the hotel no later than five. Please have the room ready."

"Was this story really true?" he asked me suspiciously after we'd gone a few miles in his car, "had she and I not . . ?"

"She is a child," I protested, "And I have a real woman waiting for me in Foix."

"Foix! I thought you were going to Toulouse."

"She thinks so. Her father, too, the old skinflint. He may not like all I have brought away with me. He works me hard. He pays me little; it is only fair." And, so help me, I winked.

With such an admission, he shared his own little secret. He was married, but he said, he "enjoyed the companies of little and not so little girls like Bébé," everywhere he traveled.

He really was a nice man and went out of his way to drop me on the road to Foix before going on his way into Toulouse. "There will be time," he said, and licked his lips.

Whereupon, I immediately doubled back on the road to Paive.

123

Chapter 3. The True Escape

Bordeaux with Simone? Montauban with Paul-Henri? Saint Gaudens with Bébé? Toulouse? Where was I really going? Why had I laid so many false trails? The answer to this last question is obvious. (Of course, the existence of these additional escape routes did create the possibility of further hiding holes should such become necessary.) But for the moment, I was going back to Paive and Bébé's Tante François. After that time would tell.

I have described the aunt, François as full-breasted. This was not strictly true. She was more an example of what the French call 'la faux maigre,' the false hunger. Not an ounce of spare flesh anywhere except in the oh-so feminine breasts and thighs. The overall effect was breathtaking. If François had sharp fox-like features, a nose a bit too long, hazel eyes a tad too close together, one does not always need to look at the face.

Besides, she was a gifted partner in bed; by comparison, Bébé, while enthusiastic (sometimes exhaustingly so) lacked experience. François prepared meals fit for a three-star restaurant, her omelets alone worth a special trip into the country, and when truffles were in season, her cooking was to die for!! How is it she never gained weight herself? It had taken almost no time after my arrival in Paive to convince myself that if I wanted a woman who would always hold me first in her heart, this was the one.

I looked forward to spending the next few months with her. Not once did I anticipate that it would not be for just a few months, but for more than a year.

The next few days spent on Paul-Henri's farm in Paive together with François, were truly idyllic. With Bébé and her father both away, she and I had no need to rush our love making.

As instructed, Paul-Henri had sent word via a friendly truck driver on his third day in Montauban so we knew he would not be home soon. The police would also learn of this when they made inquiries sometime in the future.

Bébé had long since set out for and reached her cousin's home in Saint Gaudens. Though I'd not be surprised if she'd stopped off in Toulouse for a bit of fun along the way with the intention of fobbing me off later with some cock and bull story. (I had met the bull and was aware of her interest in all cocks.) François and I assumed that after Bébé had waited an additional day or two for my appearance at her cousins, she would then be too frightened at the possibility of what her father might do to think of returning home for some time.

As for Paul-Henri, he would not know what to think, would suspect the communists, and they, in turn, would suspect him. In fact, they had already called once at the farm, but to look for me, not him. I'd not thought the man I'd killed would have had time to pass on the news of his meeting with me, but perhaps I was wrong.

At any rate, life would go on, and the plane and the aviation fuel hidden near it would soon be forgotten. Who would imagine that Air Command would forget me for so long a period also?

Our plan was to go from Paul-Henri's farm to that of François' some three to five days away by foot in the direction of the Aude River and to remain there together until I might be called away. I had not and did not intend to lie to her about my military duties; she had already seen too much of the war.

We packed for the trip, taking as little as we possibly could. This was not an easy task. Slickers were required for it was sure to rain in the late afternoon. We would need blankets for the nights though it might get insufferably hot during the day.

Had we been able to remain at one altitude the trip might have been easier also. But we would need to go up and down, in and out of the foothills of the Pyrénées as we headed for Quillan near where her farm was located.

We would bathe in streams having no need to hide from each other. We would eat bread and cheese and apples, all of which we brought with us.

"You will need to take the gun," she said, when I thought we were through packing. "Some items may have disappeared from the farm in my absence and it may take a tough man with a gun to retrieve them."

Given the short time it had taken the French army to collapse in the face of the advancing Germans and the fact that most of the men in the area of her farm had neither volunteered for the army nor joined de Gaulle to fight for a Free France, I anticipated that a tough man with a gun could probably accomplish that very thing. Indeed, I was only obliged to shoot two men to do so and that it took two was on account of my bad aim. But I am getting ahead of my story.

Last, came a truly pleasant surprise: we would not have to walk, at least most of the way. "We shall take the horse," she said referring to a dappled gray that did double duty on Paul-Henri's farm behind a plow and, from time to time, in hauling the small cart used for carrying charcoal or some other light load.

I protested at this, for while I might rob Paul-Henri of his cook and his child, I could not see stealing his livelihood. "The horse is mine," she said. "He has a tractor in the barn and you've seen his Citroën. He is just too cheap to buy the gas."

I could only hope this did not mean he would dip into my own supply of gasoline. If he did, he would only burn up his engines with the high-performance aviation fuel, while I would be robbed of a vital commodity. In fact, before we departed, I left him a note. "My gracious host, M. Paul-Henri. I am sorry we must part, but it is only temporary. Please continue to collect as much aviation fuel as possible. I will return when it is time. Should a message come for me, you will know where to deliver it." This last was a lie but would provide him with some comfort in that he'd feel he could reach me if need be. Hopefully, also, he now would be too intimidated to make the attempt.

We set off in mid-afternoon, hoping that while some might see us leave, they would assume that we had returned after dark when they were at supper or putting their animals away. Indeed, we only came to the attention of a few dogs. Or so we hoped.

We continued to travel long after dark until we had reached the boundaries of the area in which I, at least, felt at home, traveling eastward and occasionally to the south as we went. We stopped around midnight, ate our bread and cheese, took water from a stream, made love in a seated position, an interesting innovation which she instigated to save her clothes, lay down on top of the blankets and went to sleep.

A few hours later, I woke and rearranged the blankets so that one lay on top of us. To the North and West, the sky was brilliant with stars; to the South, the night sky lay hidden behind the Pyrénées.

The next day I chose to walk, not for the horse's sake, for she appeared content with her double load, but because my bottom was ill-prepared for such a lengthy trip on horseback. By the afternoon François had joined me on the ground. I am sure my Simone would have lasted longer, having more padding. Thereafter, we walked beside the horse for the most part, though it continued to carry our belongings.

We were able to avoid towns that day, though not avoid being seen by men and women working in the fields. These may have wondered at our passage, but none left their work to inquire.

The next day, we boldly went through a town, Saint-Lys I believe, and then at nightfall Muret where we saw and were seen by a single old man sitting outside a dilapidated building who waved as we passed.

We could have headed farther south and avoided seeing anyone, but to do so would ultimately mean rising to higher elevations. In the end, we had no choice but to turn south; we went first to Pamiers—another two days of walking—then due east to Mirepoix staying well to the north of the mountains.

North of Pamiers, near LaVernet, we had our first real scare when we saw two army vehicles—trucks, coming one after the other down the road.

"They are going to the camp," François said.

Pressed for an explanation, she said this was the camp where they had interned the Spanish soldiers. "But why?" "They do not want trouble with the Spanish. "

The men interned here then were the losers in the Spanish civil war. Given the sympathies of the local people, many of Catalan origin, I was amazed they'd not yet been broken free.

That war had ended years before. Then how explain the new arrivals that we saw from our hilltop being unloaded from boxcars on the tracks below? François had no explanation.

Once we had moved on to the west and south of Mirepoix, the people were a bit too friendly, asking too many questions. For these questioners, we had one simple answer: François had left her husband; she was now with me. More we could not, did not wish to say.

The road to Chalabre went up and down between narrow passes; we could almost reach out and touch the hills to the South. If a car passed—they seldom did, we would be behind our horse, staring at the fields.

Then to Camp Ferrier. We had no choice now but to climb, not so far, a couple of hundred meters at a time on average. We deliberately went north to avoid one steep rise. Surprisingly, she knew a family here. They asked no questions, but invited us to stay for dinner. Meat, what a welcome change, though the meat was goat, something I'd never eaten before but would soon get used to eating on a regular basis.

The amazing thing about all this, considering the trips by car, train, and plane I've taken since with my family, was that never once did François and I argue, never did either of us complain. If we smelled bad and we often did, then we smelled bad together. If we had to hold back our hunger, then we did so as one. And if one or the other was too exhausted to make love, that was all right, too. Well, I was the more impatient of the two of us, but often I'd no more than inserted myself inside her, when I, too, fell asleep. We would still be a single body, though not quite so connected, when I woke hours later under the stars.

On day seven of our journey, the road wound back and forth, north to south, staying at approximately the same level as the hills around us grew steeper and steeper. A stream ran beside the road determining the path the latter had taken over the years.

Then, at last, we were in the valley of the Aube River. We headed north once more, our back to the Pyrénées and gradually the land opened before us, field after field until we came to François's farm.

For seven days, we had walked till we were exhausted, eating bread, cheese, and sometimes an apple, having sex, and sleeping. Our brains were given little to feed on. One could watch the scenery, but it changed so slowly that after an hour or so, one simply tuned it out. The first hour after waking was exciting, of course, as the combination of shadow and a fresh mind recorded detail overlooked the day before. But from then on, the body simply trudged along holding the horse's reins, while the mind wondered why one was there, on Earth, I mean, what was the purpose? After Hitler was dead, what we were to do with ourselves? What was I to do?

Chapter 4. The Farm

On arriving at the farm, finally, we were sufficiently tired and hungry to content ourselves with unlocking the front door and doing the minimum required before going to bed.

François proved to have the front door key hung about her neck where it had remained, she said, save for when she bathed, since she'd left the house she'd shared with her late husband almost a year and a half before.

We stripped the coverlet from the bed, and replaced it with fresh sheets and a down comforter extracted from a sweet-smelling cedar chest. We stripped off our own clothes next, and took turns standing under the pump in the yard while the other worked away on the pump handle. Bloody cold. We made love then, it would have been impossible not to, and went to sleep immediately, though we'd promised ourselves that we'd finish off the last of the bread and cheese we'd brought with us first.

Not till the next morning did we discover that everything else that might be taken from the farm had been. The tool shed was almost empty; it held only a broken rake and a broken shovel both of which she said had been intact before she left. Surprisingly, chickens nested in the coop still—their eggs provided the basis of our breakfast, and a small bag of feed lay nearby. The main feed supply, a huge bin, had been emptied.

The source of many of these disappearances, the neighbor who'd offered to watch over the property in return for permission to farm the acreage adjoining his own, appeared at this point, indignant over the disappearance of what he termed his eggs.

François proceeded to offer him a list of the many items that had disappeared from barn and tool shed. The man stammered, said that he had only taken them to his home for safekeeping, and that they would be returned the next day.

The next day, the neighbor did not appear, and François suggested that it was now time for the tough guy with a gun act. I observed that with so many items that needed to be returned this effort might be premature; we would need both a truck and even a helper; ought we not wait for the man to honor his commitment?

The neighbor to the left of her farm was her brother in law, one with who she'd never been exactly on speaking terms. (This explained why the neighbor on the right had been given the task of overseeing her farm.) The brother-in-law had plowed and harvested the acreage adjoining to his own farm during her absence though and was grateful enough to loan us both his truck and his son. The latter, I notice, went flaming red when hugged by Tante François. He would need to be watched.

The trustee of our tool shed was not pleased to see us. He babbled how things had cost more than he expected. Perhaps, he should be allowed to keep certain items in payment thereof. I took out the gun and shot him in the thigh. As with the Gautlier of Roclincourt, this was not where I had aimed. People came running from the house when they heard the shot, and later even François took me to task. "Could you not have first tried to negotiate?"

"L'Armée de l'Air did not teach us how to negotiate. They taught us how to kill."

Not one to panic, I directed our young helper to start loading such items as his aunt might choose to point out and succeeded in ignoring the shouting until this task was completed.

I've already mentioned that I was forced to shoot two men, the consequence of my having such terrible aim. The next day the neighbor showed up with his younger brother, a sturdily built, vigorous lad who undoubtedly wrestled bulls in his spare time. I shot him in the balls. It was the resulting protests of his wife who proceeded to complain long and loudly throughout the village that I believe were responsible for the gradual return of so many items to François, some of which had yet to be missed. These last often arrived mysteriously during the night to be left at the top of the drive. Even François's sister-in-law appeared one day with some china which she said she had been standing guard over—"to prevent their theft"—until François returned.

The presence of my gun and my willingness to use it also proved of value in negotiations with the local merchants for we would need their assistance in acquiring the seed we needed for the next harvest. We had animals to purchase also, though François' cow and a pair of pigs were retrieved from the neighbors' farms.

I liked the taste of goat and thought a pair of them would prove useful in putting down the grasses that had been allowed to rise all about the house and drive. We acquired three, a buck and two does, in the hope, realized the next spring, of both milk and young goat meat.

Barley and hemp were both winter crops and as we simply took over acreage already planted by our two neighbors, we were able to feed our animals from our own stocks by spring.

Tante François took over the garden as she had in Paive and we soon had fresh vegetables, though I didn't quite care for all she raised, cabbage not being one of my favorites.

The land itself yielded bountiful harvests of asparagus, apricots and cherries in the spring, figs and olives the following fall, and delicious wild mushrooms of various kinds throughout the year. Under François' tutelage, I learned to make cabécous of Rocamadour from goats' milk. And these in turn would be eaten along with mashed potatoes, garlic, and fresh cream.

Quillan was, if anything, more isolated than Paive. Was a war still in progress? Or had there been one? Men like François' husband had left for the army and not returned. But was this because of the war or simply because they chose to stay away? Much excitement might be found elsewhere in the world. Here the teller might wink but then reassure me that he, personally, much preferred the simple country life. After which he would stroll away down the main street toward one of the two petanquier courts.

Meanwhile, of course, I waited, waited for the message from my superiors that would indicate I should finally complete my mission. One might argue that my moving away from Paive would prevent this, but as François was in communication with her brother (careful not to mention my presence at her side), and he was in communication with her (and he could not keep a secret) we had no reason to believe that a message had arrived.

I have already discoursed several times on the size of François's breasts, a natural enough obsession in the adult male. But after we had lived together on the farm for two or three months, it became evident to me that François's breasts were larger, and that her face, once drawn and sallow, had filled out and was now fully fleshed. A new color suffused her cheeks and altogether she looked totally radiant.

No more than a few years later, I would have had no trouble in recognizing these changes for what they portended, but I was very young then. A month later, the breasts still larger, and the belly, too, no explanation was required.

"I want to get married," she said.

Now François had once talked me into going to Church with her, a late-morning mass on a Sunday, so that we would not be rushed in bed. "But I'm not a Catholic," I'd cried, "I won't know what do, when to rise, when to sit down."

"You rise when I do, you sit down when I do."

"But won't I have to go to confession?"

"Only if you wish to receive communion. And I have no intention of going to communion while I am making the beast of two backs with you outside of marriage   .

"Confession is for those who feel the need for absolution. Do you feel such a need? Do you have something you feel you must have absolution for?"

Whereupon, as she had been talking to me raised on her knees and elbows over the bed, she gradually lowered herself down, fitted me within her and made me come again for the second time that morning.

"You know I'm not a Catholic." I said when she first brought up the subject of marriage. "Were we to marry, would I have to take instruction? Promise to raise my children as Catholics? Would your Church be willing to marry you and me at all?"

"Do not fret. Of course, the Church will not marry us; divorce is not permitted."

"But I'm not divorced and I thought your husband was . . ."

"I don't know if my husband is or is not dead; that is the problem." (A not uncommon problem in France and many occupied countries at that time. In Britain and in Germany no woman whose man was in service could be completely sure, nor would be sure till the war was over when or whether her man would or would not come home.)

"But what I want from you is a declaration, some sort of ceremony."

"Then you shall have it."

Since that time, I've learned that the simple ceremony we performed out on the lawn in the presence of her brother-in-law and his family would, at least among the Quakers, or the Religious Society of Friends as they are more accurately known, have qualified as a marriage. At least, it would, if François were ever to succeed in establishing the death of her former husband.

We both repeated, "In the presence of God and these our witnesses, I take thee [insert Peter 's or François's name here] to be my [husband or wife, respectively] and promise to do the things that a [wife or husband] would be expected to do."

The ceremony was moving enough that her sister-in-law cried. Her nephew may have also. (Like me, I'm sure he had a thing for his very attractive aunt.)

130

Chapter 5. The Christening

The next real mention of religion in our new family came shortly after the birth of our child. "We must arrange for a Christening," François said.

I wondered how easy this would be for a couple that had attended Church exactly once since living together in the village. But apparently it would be only a matter of talking with the priest, making the appropriate arrangements, a small contribution to the church, and so forth.

Still, my previous visit to the church in Quillon had left me wary, not because of the hostility, but because, to the contrary, the villagers had been all too warm and friendly.

To avoid the problem that had arisen in Paive (or may have arisen, for I'd left well before trouble could materialize) I'd tried to keep my distance from the villagers. This was in keeping with the tough guy, "le mec" version of myself that I was projecting. But, alas, this was all the more reason why my friendship was desired.

Would I join them on the green that afternoon following the service to play football? (A discussion followed concerning which team I ought join.) But football (more correctly, soccer) was alien to me. Only put a hockey stick in my hands and I'd demonstrate the prowess I'd exhibited as early as the sixth grade (well, I wasn't all that good). But of course, this knowledge of hockey and the corresponding lack thereof of soccer were not to be shared with these others. I'd responded then by pointing to François and shrugging helplessly, but one could not repeat this gesture often and still be thought a man.

Visiting the church meant we must pass though town, meant I must shake a dozen or more hands, and accept congratulations—a step up from the ribald humor that had accompanied previous visits to buy supplies when François was ballooned outward.

Fortunately, François was at my side; together we pushed onward in the direction of the church, capturing congratulations and cries of enthusiasm from the women as we progressed, dispensing invitations to the yet-to-be-set date for the Christening.

Once in the church, I was hard pressed not to gawk at the side table set with candles, at an old woman no taller than a child in the act of lighting one, at portraits in wood hidden in darkened alcoves, and, at the same time, to feign interest in a discussion of the details of a Christening that held little or no interest for me.

This was the baptismal font; an altar boy assisting the priest would stand there, various godfather's, the brother-in-law and his son, would gather here, my bride (well she was not actually my bride, call her the mother of the child), would wear thus and so. Soon, I'd tuned it all out and was gawking after all.

Then, abruptly, the meeting between Priest and mother was over. I had a dozen or more questions to ask about what I'd seen, but as none concerned the Christening, I decided to hold the questions till later.

The priest, Father Ignatius, took my hand and shook it vigorously. He was pleased I had come, perhaps I would come again. And, by the way, did I play chess?

Glad to be on a less sensitive topic than my close-to-nonexistent church attendance, I replied in all honesty that while I did know how to play the game, and was familiar with several opening lines, I was afraid I lacked the necessary patience to succeed.

"I'm surprised," he said, "my friend Commander Raffy said you were an excellent player."

Had I heard him say what I thought I'd heard? His friend Raffy! I looked around me quickly; François had gone on ahead; the old women whom I'd seen earlier lighting a candle had disappeared. "Have you a message for me?" I asked.

"Not at present. But were we to meet regularly to play chess, it would not be difficult to pass one on."

Recall, I had only set foot in a Catholic Church twice before, once in Quillion the previous year and once back in Montreal, when a group of us seventh-graders had walked what then seemed miles to the Shrine of Saint Andre where cripples were said to throw aside their crutches never to need them again. (Indeed, the crutches could be seen lying against the wall outside the door of the shrine.)

Now began a series of almost weekly visits to the rectory. Such a tough guy playing chess, what would the locals would think—perhaps he'd learned it in prison, questions were not to be asked. Father Ignatius looked pretty much the tough guy himself. Prematurely bald—he was only in his mid-thirties, with sharp chiseled features, tall and imposing, only the priest's collar modulated his gangster-like appearance. Our two altar boys scampered at his slightest command and some older ladies in the parish crossed themselves whenever he came near.

I brought a cabécou of Rocamadour or a tapenade François had made to the priest each time I came as a gift. By such gifts Father Ignatius lived. A Jesuit, and an exception to the poorly educated clergy who normally staffed small parish churches such as ours, Father Ignatius had not been far short of a degree in math and physics himself before at last heeding the call of God. Thus, we discussed a number of contemporary topics, radar, and the possibility of splitting the atom to obtain energy.

"Do you think it might be used as a weapon in the present war?"

Neither of us wanted to pursue this line of questioning.

I expected him to know more about these subjects than I, which he did, but was surprised to discover that my teachers had taught me some things of which he was unaware. Unlike today, when the Internet connects us all, the scientists on his side of the Atlantic were not familiar with all that was going on in America and vice versa.

The priest became my link with the outside world. He read newspapers, one of the few in the village to do so—newspapers are not a normal part of a farmer's regimen, though the ones he received were usually a week or two behind.

And he had a radio, two of them. We could listen to the farm broadcasts, all the farmers did so; we could listen and comment on the various promulgations of the Vichy government, and, at night, we could listen to the BBC.

In occupied France as in the Channel Islands, one could be arrested for listening to such broadcasts or even for possessing a shortwave radio. But here in Quillon, the priest and I were the only ones who bothered to listen.

Yes, the Christening was held as scheduled. I would have at least one child who would be spared a life in Purgatory (though I hear the latter has now been abolished by the Catholic Church). And she would have godfathers to watch out for her interests should I be called away.

I continued to visit the priest. The good news was that Britain was no longer alone, both the United States and Russia were now in the war. Unfortunately, much bad news was mixed with the good. The Germans had launched massive air raids against purely civilian targets in England. Rommel had launched a counter-offensive in North Africa. The Hurricanes and Spitfires that had won the Battle of Britain must now flee from the far superior Focke Wulf FW-190.

The news that would affect me the most according to Father Ignatius was that Germany had asked the Vichy government to provide it with laborers. Though the Vichy government under Laval had not leaped to oblige, it had agreed in principle to do so.

132

"Sooner or later, they will come here to look for men. Laval and Pétain are so eager to be cozy with the Germans. The people hereabouts will say, why should they take my son or my husband, what about that man of François?"

"I've been living here for more than a year."

"You could live here for five as I have or for twenty-five and you would still be a stranger. Hopefully, the ones who sent you will realize the risk, also."

I discussed the possibility with François. I could hide when they came for me if I had enough warning, but sooner or later I would be found. I could use my pistol but that action would cost not only my life in the end but also that of my family. What could I do?

Air Command solved the problem for me with a call to active service in late May 1942. I was to proceed to Lyons and establish contact there with a Pierre Laval (no relation, despite the name, to the second-in-command of the Vichy government). Laval would arrange for my transport to Switzerland where I would receive further instructions at the Canadian embassy from a Miss Giselle Murray.

"Anything else?" I asked the priest. What of the hidden airplane?

Nothing. Father Ignatius had passed on the entire message.

"You decoded it?" This had not been necessary; the message was in French, well, Catalan. Like the bible itself, it had gone through many translations.

"Then the Germans may know the entire contents, may know about Pierre Laval."

"I would assume so."

Chapter 6. Crossing Vichy France, June, 1942

Barley is a demanding crop. If the rains come at just the right time, one can harvest two crops each year. But the rains need come at just the right time and you have to know your birds.

During the growing season, one needs birds, insect-eating birds to drive off and consume the grasshoppers faster than the latter can eat your crop. But as the grains come to maturity one needs to drive off the birds, not the insect-eating birds, but the grain-eating birds that are as hungry for the harvest as you.

To tell the good birds from the bad takes experience. I had the experience, and a crop only a few weeks from harvest that May, a child I doted on, and another one on the way, when my orders came.

I was to proceed to Lyon and from there to Switzerland, where I would obtain further instructions from the Canadian embassy.

In many ways, Francois was braver than I. The morning of my departure, she packed me a lunch—she would not say what was in it—"you will have several surprises, my husband, pleasant ones," and sat nursing our child while she watched me eat the big Canadian-style breakfast she'd prepared. I wanted not to eat, though as always the food she'd cooked was delicious, but to take her back to bed and stay forever holding her and the child.

Arrangements had been made for me to go to Carcassone with a local farmer seeking markets for his cabbages. Once in Carcassone I would look about for a ride north.

What I could not know, what I could have had no hope of knowing, and would not have become aware of had I not set out on my journey, was how little the attitudes of the people I'd been living among for the past year bore to those in the balance of Vichy as well as in the occupied provinces.

I refer here not to the Germans, nor the German collaborators, but to the vast mass of the French people, Anglophobic and anti-Semitic. Had I landed anywhere else in France (or at least to the North or West of where I did), I would have been exposed and killed within months, if not weeks or days.

In Carcassone, dozens of pairs of eyes questioned my existence. Who is this young man? Why is he not a prisoner with the balance of our armies? Where is he from? Is he French? Would he not make a good substitute for one of our men who has been committed to work in Germany? And the real question: What profit for me in this young man's existence?

Fortunately, for a limited period of time at least, while the market was in progress, I could wander about Carcassone, the walled city, a simple farm boy taking in the sights. I walked along both the outer and inner ramparts, testimony to a city that had faced more than one siege, albeit sans airplanes raining destruction from above. The skies were clear now. I wondered, for I loved to fly, if we might start over after the war, with gliders, say, that would be too light to carry armament.

Inevitably, the walk led to yet another Catholic Church. The Basaltique St.-Nazaire, still a tourist destination today, is formed of bits and pieces dating back anywhere from the 11th to the 16th Century.

What ended my sightseeing tour was not my fear of detection, but the realization that the farmer I'd caught a lift with would soon be on his way back to Quillon, cabbages sold, and I had better be on my way as well.

Ideally, I would have liked to wait till I was assured of a single long ride. Preferably all the way to Lyons, if not, then all the way to Valence, or Nîmes.

To be avoided as drivers were men with strong political opinions, whether they favored the Vichy government or opposed it, men who would be curious to learn their rider's views. It was safest to shake one's head and say, "They are all from the same basket," and continue to sell one's cabbages.

But a choice had to be made and quickly; my ride was leaving for Quillon and without him, a trip to the local police station was guaranteed and a trip from there to Alsace to work in the coal mines.

It may seem strange that the one thing I did not fear was exposure as an English pilot. For a man in his twenties, it was as dangerous at that period merely to be French.

As for my being labeled a Jew, my Carte d'Identité read Catholic, and nothing in my clothes or hair belied this. A true Jew would have let his beard grow, would have kept his scalp covered in the presence of the Lord. But I have already discussed my lack of consideration in these matters.

The farmer I'd caught a lift with would, I hoped, turn over the money earned from our share of the cabbages to François. He would not be surprised that I had chosen to ride on farther. This is what many men did in that era, the young ones, they left their wives and went off to seek their fortune in the world.

Besides, who in Quillon did not know that I was not a farmer's son, but one who had learned the trade only to pursue a relationship with François and hide from the Boche.

I needed a lift to Lyon, I told the men and women behind their stalls. They looked at me strangely. Why did I need to go such a distance? I knew a girl in Lyon; I wanted to see her and bring her back with me to my farm. I had to go to Lyon now or wait till after the harvest.

Surely, it was foolish to go all the way to Lyon for a woman. Plenty of single women, and some single enough, hereabouts. Besides, one had a sister, a niece, an aunt who would welcome the company of a strong man like myself. A girl from Lyon would be of no use on the farm.

The ride I obtained finally was with a long-distance trucker who lived in Valence. He had a full rich black beard, a great roaring laugh, and appeared to be well known to the others in the market. He walked with a slight limp favoring his left leg, which explained why he had not been sent off to the mines.

Not once did we discuss politics on the ride, though we talked of virtually everything else as my driver had unlimited opinions on women, food, bad roads, and compulsory miseducation.

The first clue I had to his feelings was when we stopped in Nîmes, where my driver said he had a female friend with whom he must spend the night. He advised me that I would probably be safe there providing I stayed well clear of la Légion des voluntaires français contre le bolchevisme, a fascist group.

I could sleep in the truck or, (this final thought accompanied by a wink) it was possible I might find a young woman in search of masculine companionship myself. "So many men are away."

In retrospect, a man with an eye to the future would have gone with the latter suggestion. But encountering no desirable females on the walk I took toward dusk through the surrounding neighborhood, I slept in the truck.

A much-refreshed driver appeared the next morning, whistling, to offer me cheese and bread with which to start the day. I procured bowls of café au lait from a nearby cafe for the two of us and we set out for Valence. No roadblocks, no problems, the war seemed to be a long way away.

In Valence, our final destination together, the driver revealed his true sympathies. He was part of a Trotskyite cell that a German named Victor had established. Their organization's task was to identify German soldiers as well as Frenchmen who might be willing to oppose Hitler.

I was not ready to match confession to confession but asked if I might stay with him on my return from Lyon. Perhaps, a branch of his organization existed in Lyon with whom I might stay also, providing, that is, that I did not receive quite as warm a welcome from my girl in Lyon as I anticipated.

He looked at me strangely. I don't think he'd ever bought into my story about a girl in Lyon. "You must understand," he said, "our organization is cloisonnement (compartmentalized). I know no one in Lyon, but if you wait, I'll see what I can do."

The wait was at the man's home where I was given the luxury of a mattress and a meal. The latter was the occasion for a lengthy discussion between man and wife. Food it seems was difficult to come by and the expense of running a household great. I had some gold coins in a money belt but did not wish to reveal their existence unless absolutely necessary.

Fortunately, the husband won the argument having just been paid by the people for whom he drove. We ate well that evening—sausages, and the next morning as we left the house—he'd offered to drop me on the road outside the city—I surprised them both with a gift of a 5,000 franc gold piece. "For the gasoline, for the bed, for the meals, and for the company of a beautiful woman." I felt the inclusion of the last with his wife standing at his shoulder would make it difficult for him to refuse.

I should add that he had already given me a name and a telephone contact in Lyon. "Mrs. A."

"As in the alphabet?"

"Exactly. But be warned, she or they may not be as trusting as I. They may or they may not help. But I think you are a good person." And he gave me a hug before he set me down on the road to flag my next lift.

Chapter 7. Vichy Lyon, June 1942

My first ride that morning was a worrier, and that was the least of his problems. He was tall and thin and had an equally thin moustache, of which, considering the few long hairs it consisted of, he was inordinately proud. He worried about the risk he subjected himself to in picking up hitchhikers—so many robberies and beatings had occurred on this very stretch of highway. Of course, I looked a decent sort. He worried that a decent sort like myself might attract the wrong sort of driver and that I might be robbed and beaten. Of course, I was safe with him.

"Where was I going?" I was going to Lyon to see my girl. "I liked the ladies?" Very much. "Just the ladies?" Alas, they were my sole weakness. He dropped me off shortly afterward remembering an appointment, but as I stood by the side of the road waiting to flag down my next ride, I noticed his car, an ancient deux chevaux of a Citroen, heading in the opposite direction.

Well, at least he hadn't been the police, brimming over with questions I couldn't have given a proper answer to. No was my next ride, a long distance truck driver, heading with a load of raspberries for the market in Lyon. He was also a long distance talker, his principal topics being women and politics. A girl in Lyon? He too had a girl in Lyon. Fabulous, they were all fabulous girls in Lyon. He had a woman, a fabulous woman in virtually every city whether he drove there to pick up goods or to deliver them. As for politics, he believed in no one. The politicians had been an evil bunch before the war, and those of Vichy were no better. Pétain a has-been, Laval an opportunist. Any modern historian would agree with his views.

He dropped me in a Market Square near the center of Lyon and I could tell he regretted not being able to take me farther if only to have the opportunity to tell me more of his likes and dislikes.

Mrs. A. answered the phone on the first ring, told me to remain where I was, not to talk to anyone, and if by chance she could not come immediately—she would do her best—then to stroll about the market place, perhaps buying one or two items to avoid suspicion.

I had a sack in my hands containing one or two tired looking potatoes, and a paper tray of raspberries courtesy of my last driver when Mrs. A. arrived. She reminded me in some respects of Simone, if only because she had the same tightly curled coal-dark hair, though without Simone's gray touches. Mrs. A had narrow hips, a modest bust, and undeniable presence. She wore the clothes, grey skirt, white blouse, and stern look of a schoolmistress. A stain on her blouse revealed that she had a young child, one who was still breast-feeding.

Mrs. A's smile would have lit up a hall, much less the narrow stall we sat in with our coffees before us, and now that smile and all her attention were focused on me.

"What do you want from us exactly? A room? weapons?"

"I need you to point out a man, Pierre Laval."

"Because?"

"I wish to observe him."

"Nothing else, no further demands. You are sure you do not wish a place to stay?"

"I thought I would stay in a hotel."

"This would not be advisable. Too much attention is paid to even the casual visitor to Lyon. Your Carte d'Identité—I assume it is forged, would soon be under intense scrutiny by the police."

"Then what do you advise?" I was weary of this game of cat and mice.

"I advise nothing."

"Perhaps an empty building, belonging to the recently deported, from which I might observe M. Laval."

"That might be arranged. But there are many Pierre Lavals to be found in a city as large as Lyon. Could you be more precise?"

I could be if I had known anything besides the name. "I believe he is in the same business that you are."

Her expression was that of one who has bit into a pickle expecting a crisp white cucumber. "I don't think so. But now I know who you mean."

"He is supposed to live near . . ." and I gave her the address I'd been given.

"He has moved," came the immediate response, "Into the home of, what does one term it, the recently deported.

"We will meet again tonight, a different bar. I will have a place for you to stay by then and someone who can point Laval out to you. Such was your desire?"

I nodded.

"Ben. Thank you for the drink. We meet tonight."

But at 7:00 the appointed meeting time, Mrs. A. did not appear. I nursed a Campari for a while till a squat man wearing a black leather jacket joined me. Was he from Mrs. A?

"May I join you?" he asked. The bar was crowded, but not that crowded, still I indicated that he might sit down.

He ordered, briefly consulted a newspaper and then looked up at me. "You are new to Lyon?"

"New, old." I shrugged.

He pressed on. Apparently he desired more than a newspaper for company. I hoped he did not desire me. "I like this city very much. To me it has the excitement of Paris but not the crowds." I allowed this was so though I hadn't the slightest idea whether he was correct in this or full of shit.

Our non-conversation might have gone on for some time had not a pert young thing with short-cropped hair approached our table and begun to chastise me. 'You were not where you were supposed to be," she proclaimed in a voice loud enough for everyone in the bar to hear.

"But, but, I thought we were supposed to meet here," I stammered. This being 100% correct, I thought it might have the ring of truth.

"We were supposed to meet outside the theater." She stamped her well-shaped foot.

I stood up. "I should pay. Where is the waiter?"

"Never mind," said the man in the leather jacket. "I'll take care of it." It was clear that he wished me to introduce him to the young lady. This would have been difficult, as I did not know her name. She solved the problem by tucking my arm under hers, turning me about, and striding off so that I had no choice but to follow.

We headed immediately toward the cinema a mere half block away. "What were you doing with that informer?" she demanded.

"Was that Pierre Laval?"

"Of course not. About Pierre we have only suspicions. About that man, we know for a fact that he reports daily to the police."

"He was overly friendly." I conceded, "I thought perhaps he was after my body."

She laughed. "Never mind, buy the tickets."

We walked into the theater and took a pair of vacant seats close to the middle so that the seats all about us were already occupied. "In case that man gets curious and plans to follow," she explained. "Now watch the picture. I have wanted to see this one for some time."

We had, it appeared, come in before the start of the main feature. The news was first.

Marshall Pétain came on the screen. Silence prevailed for a moment, until someone broke wind and a great wave of laughter accompanied by fart-like noises swept through the theater.

The girl squeezed my arm; I took this as a good sign.

Leaving the theater, we walked down the street arm in arm as before, but now she was pressed closer against me, her hip brushing against mine with every step. I was on fire, but we had more walking to do. We came to her door finally and she handed me the key. "Pierre lives across the street," she said once we were inside. 'You may sleep here," she opened the door to a room facing the street. All the furniture had the equivalent of paint covers thrown over them.

"And you?" I asked.

"You may stay as long as you like." She turned then and left the room. I watched, listened rather as she headed down the hallway toward the rear of the home. A door opened, then closed and I realized I was alone in the house.

I woke shortly after dawn and discovered that bread, jam, and coffee mixed with chicory, Napoleon coffee as it was known, had been provided. Once I 'd eaten, I'd nothing to do but watch the house across the street through the curtains, unless I wished to make a piece-by-piece inspection of the covered furniture.

M. Laval slept till noon. A swarthy, dark-skinned man with eyebrows thick as caterpillars, he descended his front stairs sleepy-eyed about twelve-thirty and disappeared up the street. After a short interval, he reappeared bearing a baguette, a newspaper, and a lit cigarette. I supposed the balance of the fresh pack was in his pocket.

A short time later, a car pulled up before his house. An ornate desk was brought forth from the rear seat and with great difficulty a man and his wife carried it up the stairs to his front door. They left bearing nothing tangible that I could see.

This ceremony or its equivalent was repeated two more times that afternoon. It was clear to me that at least one of the couples, perhaps two were Jews. The third set of arrivals, a father and a son, both wore skullcaps.

Around five, a truck pulled up before the building. Two men wearing workers caps raced up and down the stairs carrying Pierre's newly-acquired furniture to their truck on each downward trip.

A fat man in ill-fitting but expensive clothes, the worker's boss I assumed—he'd been the last to emerge from the truck and had yet to touch a piece of furniture, stood at the top of the stairs and chatted with Pierre. When the workmen were through loading, he pulled out a billfold and handed Pierre what I assumed were several thousand francs.

A meal would have been nice about then, special delivery by the cute girl with short hair, but none materialized. I dashed out of the house via the back door, acquired cheese, some pastries, and a bottle of milk in the nearby stores and resumed my watch. I needed to know more about this man I was about to trust with my life.

At nine p.m., Pierre emerged and walked to a nearby bus stop. I followed. After an interval, he checked his watch and continued walking. We did not walk far but soon came to the entrance to a train station where some eight or nine people, among them two small children, waited for Pierre. Documents and tickets were produced; everyone smiled; the men shook hands with Pierre and he walked them to their train.

I was left with two choices, follow Pierre for the balance of his evening or stay with these people to find out what became of them. Pierre solved the problem for me when he reversed course on the way back from the train and stepped into the tunnel between the tracks. His new vantage point allowed him to keep an eye on the train bearing his grateful clients and me to keep an eye on him.

A group of policemen came down the corridor from the entrance to the station. The one in charge, an officer judging by his bearing and the deference the other men showed him, stopped and spoke with Pierre. Again, money and documents were exchanged. Pierre got the money; the policeman got the documents.

The police continued on toward the train, which had appeared on the verge of departing, at least, until the police reached it. Words were exchanged between the boss cop and the conductor; a cry went up, the engine ceased emitting steam and the policemen boarded the train. Not long afterwards, they returned with the three families Pierre had sold them firmly in tow.

I turned to see if Pierre appreciated this set of events, but he was no longer lurking in the tunnel.

Walking back in the direction of Pierre's house and my own quarters, I was not surprised to see him hard at work in a corner bar, a drink in his hand and a young lady on the stool next to him. I was about to step inside when the young lady must have said no, for he stood up, smacked her in the face, and walked back out to the street.

I followed at a somewhat faster pace—clearly he was heading homeward, until matching my steps to his, I pulled up beside him.

"Suppose you had to leave Lyon suddenly," I asked. "Where would you go?"

"Such a thing could be arranged for a price," he began, but I cut him short.

"Not me. You. The details of your transactions with the police have been provided to the Resistance. Now, one last time, where will you go?"

"Who are you?"

"Your traveling companion."

"It will take time to arrange."

"You have no time."

"Merde. I have no money with me."

"Give me the key to your house."

"Are you crazy?"

"And tell me where the money is. Trust me." I led him to the rear door of the house I'd stayed in the night before and indicated his home directly across the street.

"Merde," he said again, but he gave me his house key and some directions to what, I suspect, was only one of his hiding places.

Crossing the street, I retrieved some 5,000 francs and a pistol I found hidden beneath a floorboard nearby, returning shortly thereafter to our common astonishment. He was still there and I had returned as promised.

I handed him the money. He looked even more surprised, his eyebrows raised in astonishment like some cartoon character.

'I know where we must go," he said.

"Genève," I replied.

"But that is not my choice!"

"I paid you 5,000 francs. Surely I get to choose."

"But it was my money."

"Your money, my money, we are together."

And indeed we were. To my surprise, we did not return to the train station we'd both visited earlier that evening but took a slow-moving trolley to the suburbs, first.

140

"Reste (be calm)," he said, putting a hand on my arm when it appeared I might either bolt or do him harm. "They watch always at the center."

I realized then that I was in the hands of an expert and British Intelligence had done well to steer me into his hands. Not that my own contribution, a direct threat to both his livelihood and his life, hadn't played an essential role in his cooperation.

The Rhône-Alpes were prominent enough that I knew we were headed in the right direction. First, by train that we boarded at Meyzieu, a relatively minor suburban station, and then via a car that he had parked in someone's garage in a small town northeast of Ambérieu-en-bugey. The car, an old one, made it up some surprisingly steep grades. But at Ballegarde-sur-valsérine, we left the main highway, "It is heavily patrolled," and began our walk through the foothills.

The nighttime air was fragrant with the scent of pine, of berries, of crushed fruit.

Betrayal, I knew, was inevitable. I did not know when he had contacted the German authorities, but I was sure that he had. I only hoped they did not have dogs.

They had dogs. Fortunately, I'd already been walking for some time in Laval's shoes having left his corpse buried beneath the leaves a mile or so back. Abandoning the path and heading up a steep hillside a further quarter mile, I shinnied up a tree from which, after a moment, I bounced his shoes back down the slope into the ravine. A Tarzan-like maneuver was required to reach the next tree, but I did so, remaining there when dogs and men arrived and they pressed on with their search. They would tire eventually. I slept, hoping the soldiers would be gone by morning. They were.

Chapter 8. How Had It All Begun?

How had it all begun? The ease with which I would take another man's life? After the Arras bombing, when in my certitude of whom the betrayer had been, I'd shot and killed the would-be Gautlier of Rochincourt?

Or now that a second person, a despicable person to be sure, one not worthy of the honorific "man," lay dead by my hand behind me in an Alpine forest.

Or, had it begun when I'd engaged in dog fights in the skies over Belgium with no more thought to the planes I was shooting down than years later I gave to joining my grandchildren in a game of Space Invaders at the arcade.

Mind, I had not shot down those planes because they were shooting at me, but because I wanted to impress my messmates, as later my grandchildren, with my score.

Angelique had said to me that her new boyfriend merely dropped bombs on unseen people, while I killed.

François had said that I did not know how to negotiate, to shoot a man in the thigh or balls was far easier for me.

Hadn't my life was a killer begun when I agreed to go to war, when I set out with determination to kill Hitler?

During the Vietnam War, my son, seeking to avoid the draft, attended a non-violence seminar run by the Quakers. They discussed the possibility of employing the nuclear option. I forget which side my son advocated. But midway through the discussion, the Quaker facilitator spoke. "Does it matter whether you go to war with a stick in your hand or an atomic weapon? Once you elect violence, all methods are the same."

Chapter 9. Girl from the Embassy—July 1942

When I'd thought of Switzerland, when young, when I'd thought about it at all, it was of a land of Swiss cheese and cuckoo clocks, and tall snow-covered mountains. What I saw instead were vineyards, gentle flowered-covered slopes, and, far off, a lake of light blue. An invitation to rest and relax.

Perhaps, I shouldn't have gone to sleep once I finally crossed the border, but I'd been on the move (or up in a tree) for close to 24 hours.. The problem was that when I finally strolled into Geneva proper, the Gendarmerie stopped me immediately. The Geneva police, that is, the ones who investigate traffic accidents, not border violations.

They asked me a number of questions, but regardless of their official role, the question they kept returning to continually, was, "Where is your passport?"

"In Giselle's apartment. My girl, Mme. Giselle Murray."

Her name and role at the embassy were familiar to them apparently, for the one in charge said immediately, "That explains your strange accent. You are Canadian, also."

I acknowledged that I was, and forbore from mentioning that the strangeness of my accent might be due to the overlay of my native Quebec with the Gascon, the Languedoc, the Normandy, and a day or so of Lyon.

"Well, we shall take you there to verify your story of a morning stroll," they said and ushered me into their vehicle. I thought this mighty thoughtful of them for I was rather tired of walking.

What I had to do was avoid gawking about me like a tourist, though little could be seen that was novel save when we crossed one of the many bridges. I must have been successful in the deception, for they asked me no further questions before we arrived at her apartment building, one of many on the Rue Schaub.

The girl who answered the door had near perfect features, model like, and no, not one of the skinny models they have on the cover of a fashion magazine, but something more of the movie star, and she was blessed as well with sensuous Brigit Bardot lips.

Under the circumstances, accompanied as I was by a police escort, I did the only sensible thing and kissed her. I stepped back afterward—the kiss had gone on longer than I expected, and looking straight into her eyes, my back to the police, said, "These gentlemen need to see my passport."

"Then I shall get it for them," she responded with an impish grin.

"Really, Mme. Murray," said the older of the two policemen. "That will not be necessary. We just wanted to see that he belonged here as he claimed."

"He very much does," she replied, putting her arm around my waist and turning me so that we faced the two officers like some old married couple.

They left, I turned to kiss her again, and a small hand appeared at the level of my chest to hold me back. The honeymoon was over. "You are . . .?" she asked.

"Flight Lieutenant Freygood, RCAF."

"And you've come to my door because?"

"I was instructed while in France to do so."

"You know why the police stopped you?"

"I look like crap?"

She laughed, her open mouth closing to an incredibly beautiful smile. She looked at me; I looked at her. Some spark of romance might just be growing between us but, then, I so desperately wanted to believe that very thing.

"You look like a farmer who has slept in his clothes."

"I am a farmer, at least I was one while on my last assignment, and I have been sleeping in my clothes."

"We will get you new ones. It's a good thing that you are a pilot as we have a budget for their clothing while they are compelled to remain here. Were you a Jew, I could do nothing for you."

"And if I were a Jewish pilot?"

She shook her finger at me in reply. I wanted to take the long slender finger between my teeth and nibble on it. "While I am gone," she said, "You will take a bath and throw away your clothes."

"And you are going?"

Without answering, she took out a tape measure, and proceeded to walk around me, writing down numbers and sniffing audibly as she did so.

She did not leave immediately afterward, realizing at almost the same time I did that I had not eaten in a long while and was ravenously hungry. A cheese omelet with potatoes fried in the same cheese was soon put in front of me. While I ate, she sat down at the table to keep me company. We talked about our common, yet somehow different experiences in Montreal before the war began. I had gone to a Protestant High School located downtown across from the University; she had attended a Catholic girl's school in the same neighborhood. She had taken courses at the Quebec equivalent of a Lycée and then joined our foreign service. I had gone to McGill and then the RCAF.

We discussed streets we'd both walked along many times. She may have gone to a nightclub I'd never visited upstairs from a restaurant she'd never visited several hours after my friends and I had eaten there.

With a final admonishment to wash thoroughly and throw those clothes away, she left. Taking the repeated hints and her more explicit instructions seriously, I shaved as well as showered. When she returned, I was sitting on her couch wearing only a towel. The latter slipped off, alas, while I was helping her with her packages.

We did not go to bed immediately. Some foreplay occurred first, a lot of kissing, and the occasional accidental touch. "Would you like something to eat?" she asked again, which I chose to misinterpret, greatly to her pleasure, and then we were on rather than in her bed.

"I will have to go to Bern to get your passport," she said when we did sit down at the table to eat again later. "This is only a consular office we have here. Our function is to assist any of our pilots or those of the British or other Commonwealth nations who happen to show up in Genève."

I nodded. It might have been me she was talking about had I continued to fly missions over Belgium. Perhaps this meant, as I'd heard but not quite believed, that the Battle of Britain was over and the Allies were now on the attack again.

"While I am gone to Bern, you will have to stay in the apartment. There is just too much risk for you without a passport."

"Couldn't you just telephone Bern?"

"Alas, no. Telephones are too easily tapped and everyone in Switzerland wants to know what everyone else is doing. The nation itself is only officially neutral. No, I must go to Bern or they must come here to transmit information.

"Someone is coming here in three days, actually. Would you mind waiting till then?"

Wait with a beautiful girl whom I will be forced to make love to repeatedly. Oh, throw me in the briar patch, do.

But after a day and a half locked in the apartment together, in which I took many showers and ate many wonderful meals, I decided I needed to go out after all.

"I've heard Genève is the most beautiful city in the world, after Ville de Quebec, that is."

"And Montreal," she said loyally. "Well, all right, we shall go out and walk by the lake but only on one condition, no, two. You will be totally attentive to me at all times and you will hold my hand."

I followed her instructions to the letter; we walked along the river's edge holding hands, first on the left bank so I could look on the buildings of the city, and then along the right so I could look at the French Alps, Mont Blanc foremost amongst them. We kissed, often ; we sat at an outdoor café, drank a glass of Moselle, nibbled at a plate of andouillettes, and lust gradually developed into love.

The next day, though, she was obliged to leave me for a bit. "I have to see to my pilots' needs."

"I'm *your* pilot and what needs are we talking about."

"Razors, shirts, that sort of thing. The authorities have a half dozen British pilots stashed in a hotel in the suburb, interned for the duration. I pick up any letters they wish to mail, though the Swiss deliver their incoming mail if they have any."

"Can I go with you?"

"When you have a passport." But she did make sure to kiss me long and passionately before she left.

An hour and a half later, I was sitting on the couch, fully dressed this time, or at least in shirt, slacks, and a pair of socks, when I heard the key turn in the outside lock. I'd stood up to greet her when I heard a man's voice say from the hallway, "Giselle?"

I'd tossed my pistol in among the trees back near the German-Swiss border, once I was sure, that is, that I would not be running into any more Germans. I looked about me for alternatives. The kitchen, a sure source of weapons, was a fair distance from where I stood, but a fireplace and fire irons stood close at hand. When he came through the doorway, I put the hooked tip of the poker at his throat.

He stained his pants. "That's not necessary. I'm Morris Thompson, Giselle's boss."

"Mme. Murray."

"Mme. Murray. Exactly. Look, you must be Flight Lieutenant Freygood. I have your paperwork right here, see." He held out the envelope he was carrying. I took the envelope, removed the poker from his throat, and walked back into the living room. He followed me shortly thereafter.

"No passport here," I said after I'd leafed through the envelope's contents.

"We'll need a picture for that. Not a problem. It's just that we weren't expecting you, this soon, I mean. If we had, I'd of been here sooner if you know what I . . . "

I waved him down. His babbling was a natural reaction to the death that had stared him in the throat only a few minutes ago.

Morris Thompson was of medium height, an inch or two shorter than I, and overdressed in a tie and vest that seemed hardly appropriate for the season or the setting. He had a head of brown-blond hair with a slight wave to it and, clearly, was very tightly wound. I assumed he'd looked and dressed the same way in high school, a B student rather than an A, and again in college where, a C student at best, he was never to realize his parents' dream of the law.

"Doesn't say what my new assignment is." I said, after sifting through the envelope a second time.

"I think they just pulled you out for a rest, really. You've been working undercover in France for a bit, haven't you."

"Rest for a bit!" Canadian Intelligence had pulled me away from a newly planted crop, a child, and a pregnant wife so that I could rest for a bit! I'd gone 200 miles through Vichy France subject to arrest at any moment, and killed a man so that I could rest for a bit!

"I see you two have met," Giselle said as she stepped into the room. "In case you haven't, Morris, this is Flying Officer Freygood. Peter, this is Morris Thompson, my superior."

"Yes, I was just coming to tell you about the Flight Lieutenant's arrival." To give Morris credit, he did stress my correct rank.

"Well, he's already come on his own." She gave me an impish grin as she spoke the words.

"How are our pilots?" Morris asked, eager to assert his authority as well as to avoid any discussion of his earlier encounter with me.

"We've a bit of a problem," she said and lowering her voice led him away to the other side of the room. He followed and soon they were having a serious discussion just out of earshot. After a moment, I followed also, not quite willing to be neglected or ignored.

"It's a private matter," Morris began.

"Someone shot at a British pilot as he was walking through the woods. Naturally, they're all upset."

"I don't think Flight Lieutenant Freygood needs to know. Besides, are the woods within their allowed area?"

"Yes, he does need to know. The Germans not playing the game. And who cares about the location."

"If you mean the German diplomatic service, *they* are playing the game. But apparently, some members of the local Bund are acting under orders from the SS."

"You never told me that."

"It's not official." Morris used his hands and arms to emphasize this latter assertion.

Remembering the dead man I'd left lying in the forest, and the would-be-Gautlier of Roclincourt, I offered to be of assistance in adjusting the matter.

"How?" This from Morris. Annoyance, frustration, and outright anger were wrapped up in the single word.

"I kill people."

"You do it from an airplane. You fire at people who fire at you."

"Not always." We exchanged glances and I think he realized then that he'd had a perfect right to piss in his pants when we first met.

Chapter 10. Reunion

The three of us ate supper together at a restaurant on the Right Bank that evening; we all had steak with a small green salad; Morris had his well done, the clod. But Morris paid and he acted the perfect gentleman, a benevolent uncle who was glad to finally see his niece in safe hands. A glance at Giselle's face revealed that this was utter bullshit and that Morris was not to be trusted.

After paying the check Morris asked if he ought return to the apartment with us. "I usually just sleep in the spare room." I looked to Giselle for a decision. "Not this time," I said.

We saw that he checked in to the hotel next door to where we had dined, then walked home, giggling like newlyweds, which we were very close to being.

The next morning, I had a picture taken for my passport and we saw Morris off on the train to Berne, thus giving me the opportunity to see more of the city. Giselle would be following the next day bringing the developed photo with her.

I was shown the Palais des Nations where the League had failed to stop a war, and then it was back along the right bank along the aptly-named Quay de Monte Blanc with its view of the mountains. We took a bridge out to the Ile Rousseau to see the statue of the philosopher the city had erected there (72 years after they'd thrown him out of the country). "Surely you are the Noble Savage he wrote of," she said laughing and looking at me, having in mind, I gathered, my costume when I'd arrived at her apartment two days before.

We stopped in the Basilique Notre Dame on the way back, where she genuflected, lit a candle, and proclaimed that while she wasn't sure she believed, one might do worse than try to remain in favor with Le Bon Dieu.

Again that afternoon, she had to see the pilots, bringing them the materials Morris had brought to her, and again I asked if I might come along.

Yes and no. We took a trolley to the general area together, but I was not permitted to visit the hotel where the pilots were staying. "The State police observe all visitors and they are not as trusting as the Genève Gendarmée."

She left me in the tavern around the corner from the hotel, a pleasant enough place. I ordered a spritz and waited for her to escort me home.

Two men sat down at my table uninvited. The State police? No, they carried drinks in their hands. "Mind if we share this table?" Flying Officer Moyle, no, Flight Lieutenant Moyle said with a smile. The dour faced individual who started to sit down next to him was smiling, also. But I was already on my feet embracing Flight Lieutenant Wilson in a bear hug.

"What are you doing here?" I demanded.

"Shh. Don't talk so loudly. The Swiss do not care for demonstrations." Wilson tried to look calm but I saw that he was both pleased and embarrassed.

"So. What are you doing here?" I asked in a voice several decibels lower.

Moyle leaned across the table. Apparently, the pair was dead serious about not wanting to attract attention. "Shot down," he said.

Aside from their starting point—the Northolt airbase, their target—in Normandy, and the fact they were both now interned in Geneva, the stories the two airmen had to tell were quite different.

Shortly after Moyle reached the target area, his Hurricane III, yes, a still newer and faster model I could only envy his piloting, was hit by flak. Despite the hole in his wing, he was able to restore the plane to its position in the formation, but only momentarily. With a "Cheerio, chaps," he flew off toward Switzerland under control, but barely holding altitude.

Two Swiss Air Force ME-109s guided him to an airfield, which he thought a friendly enough gesture on their part. At least, they didn't shoot at him.

Unfortunately, flak damage had made his flaps inoperative and resulted in a high-speed final approach and landing. He overran the runway and only came to a halt in a nearby meadow. The Swiss were not pleased. "I was alive." He smiled; I saw he'd lost a tooth in the landing.

Interned till the end of the war, the accommodations the Swiss had given him at the hotel were spacious enough, no complaints, and the girl from the embassy who brought them civilian clothing was a looker.

"The girl from the embassy is mine."

Moyle did his best to look properly embarrassed. Wilson made no such effort.

Wilson had experienced somewhat more success both in the air and on the ground. He'd managed to record two kills before being shot down that evening. "The Germans have newer fighter models, too, but they're simply not as good as ours." He'd parachuted out of his crippled plan and landed near Lassy where he took refuge with a French farm family.

After a month or two, the Resistance had plucked him and a second pilot from the farm and guided them to the Swiss border. Once across, the pair had been interned at the hotel for a brief period before being classified as escapees. Unlike airmen who were shot down or landed in Switzerland like Moyle, escapees were given full travel privileges. The other pilot had taken off immediately, but by then Wilson had discovered that Moyle was living at the hotel. "I'd of had to learn the other fellow's name if I'd gone off with him. Moyle is hard enough."

"Well, you're lucky you did stay with me."

The door to the bar opened then and a woman walked in. Our three heads turned automatically. The new entrant was not Giselle but a far older woman with dyed platinum blond hair. Wilson seemed pleased to see her and immediately rose to his feet. "Back after a bit." The two left the bar arm-in-arm , both smiling, or on Wilson what passed for a smile.

"Why is Wilson lucky?" I asked, returning to the conversation in progress. "That woman?"

"Well," said Moyle lowering his voice again, this time almost to the point of unintelligibility. "We were walking in the forest the other day, really farther from the hotel than we're supposed to go, but you know Wilson.

"Anyhow we're walking. As usual Wilson is a hundred feet ahead, for him a walk is a walk, never mind if alpine strawberries are to be picked and eaten or an interesting mushroom is to be examined. I look up from one such inspection and see a man in a black shirt standing behind a tree. Darned if he isn't aiming a rifle at Wilson.

"I shout a warning; the man misfires, but then he swiveles around and takes a quick shot at me. I ran, Wilson ran. We're not that far into the forest yet, thankfully, and when we're back on the street the man has disappeared."

"Do you know who he is?" I ask.

"Yes, I know who he is. Wilson's girlfriend identified him. He's some local Nazi."

"And did you kill him?"

Moyle looked at me amazed as if the idea of killing someone struck him as a brand new concept.

"Never mind, we'll do it tomorrow."

Giselle came in the room then and I had eyes only for her. Besides, she didn't need to be introduced to Moyle, she already knew him. And if I'd never tried to birddog Moyle's girl, then he could stay away from mine.

Chapter 11. Spy vs. Spy

Two days later, Giselle had to go to Berne to collect my passport and take care of other embassy business. She telephoned me the day following from the embassy and began to babble about the passport. I heard Morris say, "Not on the telephone." and then heard Giselle counter, "You tell him!" before she returned to me. "I love you darling. I will be home in two more days."

The interval gave me the opportunity to meet with Moyle and Wilson on two occasions. Moyle repeated what he had told me about the man with the rifle and Wilson provided his own version of the story. Their account wasn't unique. Shots had been taken at the other interned airmen, but only if they strayed from the limited space in which they had been confined. These were not warning shots, they were shots intended to kill. If none had been fired in the area immediately surrounding where the airman lived, it was probably because this area was too populated, with too many potential witnesses.

An airman had been killed a month or so earlier, but the embassy (British) and the Geneva Criminal Investigation Bureau remained in denial. They knew who had taken the shots, though, everyone did. He was a member of the local Bund, or rather, its French equivalent. His orders came out of Bern, the adjoining canton.

"We cut off the head, then we kill the hands." I proposed.

"I'm not sure about killing," Moyle said, "perhaps, we ought to vote."

"Then you lose," Wilson responded immediately.

"Regardless of how a vote might go," I informed them, "I'm your senior officer." (By approximately three months, I estimated.)

A genuine grin lit Wilson's face and he gave me a snappy salute, his hand motion upward mirrored shortly afterward by Moyle. After which, we began to make plans.

We needed guns, we needed transportation, and we needed a fake id for Moyle. Absent a passport, he was pretty much confined to the hotel and the surrounding neighborhood. "We don't need to take the train, there are cars," I pointed out.

"Which we don't have."

Both the solution and the problem (a new one) presented themselves the next day when I met Giselle and Morris at the train station. Giselle immediately leaped into my arms and we kissed passionately while her boss stood by looking uncomfortable.

We got into a taxi together with Giselle pressed close at my side, refusing to look at or talk with Morris who sat next to her. Only when we were inside her apartment did she demand, "Tell him."

Instead, he reached into an envelope and handed me a passport. I looked through it, admired my picture briefly and tucked it away in my neck wallet. "You need to look at it." Giselle said.

I took out the passport and leafed through it a second time. "It says you are a Jew," Giselle said.

"I am a Jew, technically."

"Exactly," Morris cut in only to receive a withering look from Giselle.

"You are my Jew and I love you. It is not safe."

"At this time, the Swiss have no official policy." Morris began.

"At this time, at this time! What about next week, or next month? The Swiss are doing everything in their power to placate the Germans. Already, Jewish refugees are being stopped at the border. And soon, all foreign-born Jews will have to register."

She stopped for breath, but only briefly, "Change it to Catholic," she said to Morris. She turned to me, "Do you have any objection to being Catholic?"

"None. In fact, if we were to marry, wouldn't I need to . . ."

But she had already turned back to confront Morris, her hands on her hips. "Change it to Catholic."

"As I told you back in the office, I can't do that. His records show. . ."

"Forget the records, you have the power." her voice broke; she was close to tears.

I made a cutting motion with my hand, then gestured toward Morris. "Perhaps, we might make a trade. I will do something for you, then you will do something for me."

My suggestion received only a sneer in reply but I could see he was listening. "And what would you do for me?"

"Kill the Nazis who are killing your pilots." It was as if Dorothy had suggested to the Wizard that she retrieve the broomstick of the Wicked Witch of the West.

"Here in Geneva?" Ben. Our negotiation had advanced from a potential, "No, out of the question," to a discussion of terms. Little did I realize that his interest lay not in defending our pilots but in pleasing his opposite numbers in the German embassy. Apparently, they were as much dismayed as I by the killings, performed as they were without their authorization.

"No. In Bern, where their headquarters is."

I could see he was impressed by my knowledge of the area. "And you will need?"

"Two passports including my own, and three machine pistols."

"You can't have the passports. I'll get you the weapons—at least, I'll try."

By the next day, still without Morris' aid, Wilson had somehow obtained both a machine pistol and a grenade on his own. We'd sent Moyle off to the Christlicher Friedensdienst to see about passports and transportation as he'd the most honest face. (As the name of this organization suggests, they did wonderful Christian work transporting and hiding refugees, Jewish refugees in particular.) The lady in charge had turned him down flat, but an older man with a scar-pitted face had come up to him as he left the woman's home and offered the services of his automobile—for a price.

We still did not have passports, and indeed Morris would not provide them though he did grudgingly hand over two machine pistols and a rifle.

As Wilson had a pass to travel about Switzerland, he sat in the front seat alongside the owner of the automobile, while Moyle and I either sat or lay down under blankets in the back. Wilson also spoke German, something he was not to reveal to the driver. Away from Moyle's presence, I had explained to Wilson that it might be necessary to kill the man as for every individual and organization anxious to help the refugee, an equal number hoped to profit from his betrayal.

"The kindest always use a knife," Wilson observed and showed me one of the sort thoughtful hunters carry to ease a wounded animal's misery.

Alas, much to Moyle's displeasure, it did become necessary to kill the man during an argument over a change in routing late that afternoon. Wilson, too, was unhappy for he'd hoped to use the car to ride around Genève with his girlfriend had the man's blood not stained the upholstery.

Moyle began to babble. He'd come along mainly to provide moral support; while he would have no objection to killing in defense of Wilson and I, we should probably not count on him for aid in any further killings of civilians. I don't think Wilson or I had expected much more from him. Anyway, we knew we could count on him to cover our backs just as he'd said he would.

Also on the plus side, we could now be sure that the automobile would be waiting for us when we returned from the hunt.

The Nazi leader, a German, lived in a chalet just across the border between Bern and Genève near Chateau-doex. A location chosen, I imagine, so that he could mess up the lives of those living in both cantons without too much extra effort.

Just after we crossed the border, we turned south at the town of Saanen, and soon saw the incredibly tall peaks of the Italian Alps looming ahead. If we'd been traveling singly or in pairs, we'd probably have taken the time to go on and explore those mountains. The copper beech and chestnut trees that lined the streets of Genève had already been replaced by fragrant pine and cedar as well as larch. Years later, had I been traveling that same road with my family, I'd have stopped half a dozen times along the way to look at the scenery, explore a trail, or eat a picnic lunch. The Swiss countryside is incredibly beautiful and we'd been cooped up in a town, a charming town, admittedly, too long, a month for me, and several months for the others.

We had a car; what couldn't we do? But we also were three men from a squadron, used to flying together, ignoring all we saw along the way, focused on a target. So we continued without stopping to our intended destination; the mountains could wait.

The SS chief lived halfway down (rather than halfway up) a hillside near Gifferhorn. A secluded location, the house itself hidden among the trees, chosen, one supposed, like the surrounding area for its distance from prying eyes.

The house, a two-story chalet, the size of any three houses in town, could only be reached on foot or by a single winding road. Still, it was rather poorly situated for defense. The chalet's occupants would be unlikely to spot unwelcome visitors drifting through the trees until they were close upon them.

Late that afternoon, we took up residence under the trees somewhere on the hill above them. We imagined the Nazis would have dogs, but we could not see or hear them, forgetting that as the day grew colder the winds would reverse and bring our scent down the mountain.

As Moyle had volunteered to serve as a decoy, or so we informed him, we sent him down the hillside to a streambed in line with the house, while Wilson crept toward the chalet at an angle so that he might come down on it from above. I held my position for the moment prepared to fire with the hunting rifle at whomever showed themselves.

Two guards emerged first heading in Moyle's direction, the dogs—two Rottweilers, running just ahead of them straining at their leashes.

Our earlier count had revealed eight men in the house including the leader who was our primary target. Figuring that Moyle would handle the two guards or die, I put down the rifle, picked up the machine pistol and headed for the house along a line slightly below the one Wilson had followed.

The dogs were confused; one straining toward Moyle, the other eager to get up the hillside after me.

The guard went for his walkie-talkie then and I shot him. Well, I shot at him, hitting the other guard and one of the dogs as my pistol sprayed ammunition in a seemingly aimless fashion.

Immediately, two other men came running around the edge of the house from approximately the same spot the original two guards had emerged. I shot at them, racing along the shaded ground toward them, wishing at the same time that I still held the rifle.

The guard I'd missed took aim at me, and Moyle, true to his word, shot him. The remaining Rottweiler began to mourn releasing a dreadful howl.

The earth shook then, rocked by an explosion. Wilson had entered the house and tossed his grenade into the living room where the leader and three of his followers were killed instantly.

The explosion caused the guards I'd just shot at to turn toward the house; this time, with their backs presenting a larger target, I hit them.

We heard an automobile start then, but neither Moyle, who had come up to join me, or I chose to follow it. Instead, we circled behind the house where Wilson had entered. He was exiting from the back door at that moment; he saw us, waved, and headed in our direction, seemingly careless of whatever might still be behind him. Moyle and I remained where we were, fully alert, machine pistols braced, eyes fixed on the house, until he'd walked past us heading up again to our car.

One man had escaped in an automobile, with Geneva plates, Wilson said; the others were dead or would die before they could receive treatment.

We headed for home. The mountains and picnicking would have to wait till we had our passports.

Chapter 12. The Passport

Those familiar with the Wizard of Oz will realize that the Wizard didn't exactly live up to his promise when Dorothy returned with the broomstick. I'd rather hoped for better from Morris, but was not surprised when I barged in on him in his Bern office (unexpectedly I might add) to find him trying to welsh out of it.

"It's simply against policy. If you were to convert to Catholicism, but even then, it's your religion at birth that counts, don't you see."

"Only to the Nazis. Change it," I said, "Give me a new passport."

"And if I don't." A sudden smile crossed the son-of-a-bitch's face. Policy be damned; since the beginning he'd been out to get revenge for making him piss in his pants. And as for my sleeping with Giselle, this was something he'd evidently been making attempts at for a year, despite the family he had with him in Berne.

"I'll kill you."

"Ah, yes, a risk I'll run as long as you stay out of custody. A new decree was issued this week. The Swiss are now cooperating with the Nazis in providing them with lists of foreign-born Jews. And then, you didn't exactly check in at the border when you arrived, did you. The new Swiss policy requires the rejection of all refugees who are marked as Jews in their passports. I believe your passport is, is it not?"

"Giselle," I began.

"Oh, you've already fixed that. Nothing to be done about that. Just something else to see you rot in hell for. Do you Jews have hell?"

I stepped into the hallway and summoned a waiting Wilson. "Morris, do you know Flying Officer Wilson? He was kind enough to accompany me on a recent climbing expedition into the nearby Alps. Perhaps, you may have heard about it?"

"If I don't kill you, Flight Lieutenant Wilson will. Now get me that passport."

Morris folded, though not without various attempts at a stalling action: A replacement passport would take time; a new photo would be required; perhaps no blanks were then available. Wilson cleaned his fingernails with the hunting knife I described earlier. He wasn't much of a hunter; he hadn't bothered to wipe off the blood from our earlier expedition or oil the knife before putting it back in its sheath.

I got the passport, after some preliminary discussion about the religion I ought elect. "Wilson, would it bother you if I were a Catholic? Or would you prefer Anglican, which is what we call the C of E in Canada?"

"I am a Catholic."

Which pretty much settled that. One seldom really knows one's fellow man till push comes to shove.

Chapter 13. Zurich to Lyon—December 1942

If one doesn't care for the cold, then winter in Switzerland will not be enjoyable. And winters there do come early and last a long time, though not as early or as long today as in the 1940's because of the global warming.

But I 'd been raised in Montreal as had Giselle. The winters there are cold and long also. When I was three, I'd be dressed in a snowsuit, skis fitted to my feet, and put out in the back yard to spend the morning. My father would have built a ski slope for me, perhaps no more than a few feet high, but seemingly enormous. All morning, I would traverse its contours, up, down, and around.

At lunch, I would be brought into the house, where I'd be warm and snug and find a big bowl of habitant pea soup waiting on the table.

When I grew older, winter meant a trolley ride to the center of the city halfway up the mountain. I would walk up the rest of the way, then ski down, finishing indoors again, though this time to confront a big bowl of hot chocolate.

I was soon to learn that following the German occupation of Lyon in November 1942, it would be cold inside the Frenchman's fuel-starved homes as well as out, and no chocolate was to be had unless one sold one's body or one's soul.

But I was not yet on my way back to Lyon. Six weeks would intervene first. Six weeks in which Giselle and I would take advantage of my new Canadian passport, Swiss entry stamp backdated and in place.

Skis were procured for me, and Giselle and I passed the time on Alpine slopes that were not all that far away from her home in Genève. In fact, the only difference from Montreal was that instead of taking a trolley in the city and halfway up the mountain, we would take one out into the countryside.

Wilson joined us on several occasions. His family had vacationed frequently in the German Alps and he was an excellent skier. Families like Wilson's were the ones Hitler had counted on to bring England in as an almost equal partner of his Aryan supremacy. Not, as the children would say today.

Our idyll together did not last long. Less than six weeks after I had the corrected passport in my hand (and had reported with it to the Geneva police as instructed) a sealed envelope was delivered to the embassy with my name on it.

I was to travel to Lyon and liaison briefly there with the Resistance. They would arrange transport to Yssingeaux, located in the Massif Centrale, the mountainous region of central France, 60 miles southwest of and 2500 feet higher than Lyon, where a plane (!) would be waiting. Use it to fly to Foix. More instructions were provided than these, of course, more names, all in all far more to read through and memorize than the brief message I'd received from the priest in Quillon.

I'd assumed that Wilson and Moyle would buy me one last drink, wish me God speed, and see me on my way. "We're coming along," Wilson said, "We're every bit as bored as you and we want to be part of this War." Moyle's head nodded in agreement. In my heart, I agreed immediately; these were two good pilots and the Allies would be far better off with them serving in the front lines than idling away their lives interned in Switzerland. But what I had no choice but to say, over and over, was, "No, no, no," until the last of my objections were overcome. And who would not want to go off to war with Aramis and Athos by his side.

For the initial lap of our journey, we would need skis for Moyle, and, as it turned out, we would need to teach him to ski.

"You never have?" Wilson could only shake his head in amazement. But the Moyles were from a different social class than the Wilsons, one similar to my own, and could not afford to go abroad to learn to ski.

Thankfully, Moyle was a natural athlete. While he would never be as proficient as Wilson, given six months he would have been a better skier than I. But we did not have six months. At least, I didn't think we had. As usual, my orders merely read go, not how long I might have in the going.

While the instructions I'd received from Air Command were far more detailed than that first cryptic set passed on to me by Father Ignatius, much had been omitted or was of questionable value. I was highly suspicious of the route through the French Alps they'd provided and planned to look into one of my own. A curious omission was how I was to proceed to Lyon after leaving the mountains. Again, I had an idea how this might be accomplished.

In Lyon, now occupied by the Nazis who had done away with the corrupt and inefficient Vichy government and replaced it with an equally corrupt and still more brutal rule of their own, I was to meet again with Mme. A, who would now be my official as well as my unofficial host. (I wondered if I would see the short-haired, good-smelling girl again?)

From Lyon, I or, rather, we, now that Wilson and Moyle were coming with me, would be transported to a location where several planes had been hidden, between four and seven of them. (The note did not specify what we were soon to discover, that these planes were of World War I vintage.) I was to fly one of these planes to Foix in the Midi near where I'd hidden the MS 140 a year before, meet with a new set of resistance workers, and again await orders.

Moyle and Wilson determined to retain their uniforms, albeit covered by the insulating great coats Giselle has procured for them. At worst, if caught wearing their uniforms, they would become POW's. Of course, stripped of their coats, the uniforms would mark them out immediately as member of the enemy.

We had to procure documents for the three of us, though these were relatively easy to obtain, over time, that is, from the very few refugees who'd made it out of occupied France and into Switzerland. Identity cards, work permits, military discharges, and laissez-passers to Lyons were handed to a gentleman of Wilson's friend's acquaintance to be suitably altered. We would need ration cards, too, but these we learned changed color at irregular intervals and would be best obtained in Lyon.

I had been given a very modest amount of gold plus a stack of Reichkredit Reichmarks by Morris, who waved his hands helplessly at the possibility of providing more. Regardless, I had a fair amount of gold left from my previous incursion into France that I saw no reason to tell Morris about. I divided the gold among the three of us—the other two might need it abroad, and kept the majority of the Reichmarks for myself.

Giselle insisted we spend the day before I left together in her apartment. No Wilson, no Moyle, no visitors, just the two of us. Heaven on earth, she fed me my favorite things not excluding herself. One day turned into two. After all, we were not to leave till late afternoon.

The bise was already hard at work when we hit the cross-country trails. All the traffic was inbound to Genève headed toward warmth and hot chocolate. We were guaranteed a hellish near-freezing night as we crossed the border into France, the only good news being a cloud cover that kept the temperatures at or just below freezing and hid the moon.

Moyle and Wilson both had excellent night vision and spotted the Nazi guard post waiting like some witch's hostel near a well-established upward trail.

We easily slipped around the guards—their attention was focused after all on refugees moving from the other direction, and were soon on our way into France not far from where I'd left Pierre Laval's body so many months before.

We soon encountered several corpses half buried in the snow, though none was Pierre. The corpses were those of escapees, shot on their final passage toward the Swiss border, and left unburied as a warning.

Though not a particularly effective one. From a hiding place near the trail, we watched as just such an upward bound group of escapees moved passed us. "Shouldn't we warn them?" Moyle whispered. He meant, I think that we ought tell them about the Germans waiting in concealment further up the trail. I merely shook my head in response. I'd tried several times to explain to him that for a man to be French was no guarantee he was on our side. The leader of this new party of escapees might well be another Pierre Laval hoping to receive so many Reichmarks per corpse when they reached the guard post.

At Ballegarde-sur-valsérine, my intention was to board the train, skis astride our shoulders, but I soon saw the difficulty. I still doubted that anyone would bother to inspect our identity cards; all the attention of the authorities would surely be focused on the outbound trains. But Wilson and Moyle looked far too healthy to pass for French. The German occupation following hard on the heels of the misdeeds of the Pétain administration had left most Frenchmen looking emaciated and malnourished—which they were, apart from the very few excessively wealthy ones who were profiting from the war.

Wilson had an idea and soon disappeared with Moyle trailing at his heels. When he reappeared, an ashen-faced Moyle beside him, both wore the great coats favored by the Gestapo. Our new roles were clear. I was the guide to the slopes, dining well by virtue of my courting favor with the occupiers. They were who they were.

On the train, Wilson and Moyle sat together while I stood in the aisle, having stowed everyone's skis in the overhead bin like the bootlicking lackey I appeared to be. Our coach held mainly German soldiers returning to duty from a brief respite in the French Alps. While the presence among them of a Frenchman (as I appeared to be) might not have been tolerated, one serving as guide and mule for two Gestapo officers was not to be questioned.

I did my best to stay awake, exhausted both by the long hike and the constant tension. My feet were cold, my head on fire, all the heat in the car having gathered near the rooftop. I would fall asleep, jerk upright. If in falling, I fell against the sitting Wilson, he would simply rap me on my thigh with his outstretched arm and go on with his conversation.

As Wilson told me later, he spent much of the trip discussing in German my virtues as a guide. Moyle may have had some knowledge of German, too, but he did not contribute much to their one-sided conversation.

When we exited at suburban La Muletier—we were not fool enough to press our luck all the way into Lyon, I went to shoulder all the skis, a fair load in the days of long heavy wooden slabs and bear-trap bindings. First Wilson and then Moyle yanked them out of my arms, Wilson shouting something in German along the lines of his having no intention of allowing a fool like me to drop his precious skies again.

Chapter 14. Occupied Lyon—January 1943

Once on the street outside the train station, I got on the telephone immediately, dialing the number I'd been given, a different number than the one I'd been given before. A bored male voice responded, "Oui?"

"Madame A, s'il vous plait."

"You are mistaken; perhaps, you've dialed in error."

Shit. No, merde. Switching from one language to another was confusing then and is confusing now. "Ah, what a pity, I was looking so forward to her hot chocolate after a day on the slopes."

A woman's voice came on the line then, but not Mrs. A's, younger, saucier. Did I recognize it?

"You say you have been skiing?"

"To the northeast of Ballegarde-sur-valsérine. With my two friends."

"Two friends would be awkward at the cinema."

I did recognize her voice. Would she remember me? Would she still be as attractive? Nothing I saw around me now was beautiful. The once clean streets of the Lyon suburb were gray with ash mixed with snow and slush, ugly, neglected. Just as remarkable, the streets were almost vacant. I did not like the fact that my two comrades and I stood out on an otherwise empty block.

"Perhaps we can find a place to put them and their costumes," I continued, "so that you and I can again be alone. Is there a matinee, today? Can we meet now at the theater?"

A pause ensued. I knew she was conferring off the line with someone else. "Let us meet first at the bar on the corner for an aperitif. Where are you now? And tell me about your friends."

Her last question was suspicious or was it? After all, I was supposed to have come alone. I described our location as best I could, and said we would take the next trolley in, or because it was now pulling away, perhaps the one after that. As for my friends, "They are wearing borrowed great-coats," I explained, "We took the wrong ones when we left the chalet. And what of our skis?"

"Just leave them on the trolley."

Our trip into Lyon was uneventful. Our biggest problem still being that of remaining upright and awake, though the unheated trolley car was much in our favor. We were sitting toward the back near where we'd first boarded and I noticed that all the other passengers did their best to avoid us. The greatcoats stolen from the Gestapo conveyed a very definite message.

The trolley halted twice for no particular reason. I gathered from the conductor's actions during the halts that they were occasioned by lapses in the delivery of electricity. The delays were unwelcome. Unchecked, I might nod off from fatigue at any moment and did all I could to stay awake, pinching my thighs, biting down on the soft flesh on the inside of my cheek.

At the second unscheduled stop, which occurred as we were nearing central Lyon, I noticed that two men who had just boarded the train had chosen to sit nearer to us than was necessary. The attempts of one of them to keep us under discreet observation were laughable. I took this as a positive sign. The members of the Resistance were more likely to be amateurs than employees of the Gestapo or the Milice.

Recognizing the bar where I'd once met with Mrs. A, I led the others off the trolley, motioning to Moyle to leave his skis behind. As we walked away, I saw that the two men who'd had their eyes on us had moved in quickly to retrieve them. "Waste not; want not," was all France's motto under the occupation.

From the sidewalk, I could see why the girl had elected not to meet us at the theater. This structure now was not much more than charred embers. Half-burned posts stuck up here and there about the deserted lot, and a half row of seats that had miraculously escaped total destruction stood by itself amid the ashes.

I saw the bar and motioned for Moyle and Wilson to go in and wait there for me. The girl was beside me in an instant. Her hairstyle had not changed, but her face was thinner and bore lines of fatigue. Worse, the bounce was almost gone from her step.

"Gestapo?" she asked.

"Killed before we took their coats. My friends are wearing RAF uniforms underneath."

"We must get them out of here. Quickly." I turned to go inside and she stopped me. "You're looking good," she said, and brushed her cheek against mine. The faintest scent of perfume stayed behind, like the last drops from an almost empty bottle.

I opened the door to the bar. Covered as the doors and windows were on the inside with steam, one could hardly see within. Fortunately, my fellow pilots had remained close to the entrance. They put down their drinks and Moyle reached for Reichmarks to pay for his. Wilson waved him off. The Gestapo did not pay for their liquor.

"Far too hot in there," Wilson said, "Moyle almost took off his coat."

"I did not," Moyle asserted before realizing he'd been had again.

"Wow!" was his next comment. I turned in the direction he was facing and saw that two other girls had joined my crop-headed friend. The newcomers, laden with lipstick, rouge, and some dreadful cheap perfume came across as professionals. They soon linked arms with the Flight Lieutenants and the six of us went on our way, though my friends and their escorts turned up a side street after we'd gone no more than a block.

"They will go to a safe house," my shorthaired companion, Suzanne, said, confiding her name. "We will go for a drink."

This new bar was not heated. Moisture did not condense on its windows. Which would explain why she felt no self-respecting police officer, agent provocateur, or informer would be hanging about there to listen to our conversation.

Suzanne was a good listener. And her breath held a delicate fragrance that I would be willing to live with day after day.

"Will your girlfriends expect to be paid?" I asked.

She laughed. "They can always use money, to pay for protection, if nothing else. But no, they are strictly volunteering their services for this occasion."

"I see," I said, though I really didn't have the slightest idea what she was talking about. Sitting side by side as we were at the bar, Suzanne came across as a good deal friskier and no less impulsive than when we'd first met five months before. I received frequent accidental touches on my arms and my thighs and heard her say, "I was so excited when I learned you would be returning to Lyon," not once, but twice. Both the touches and the statements were sure man pleasers.

"Perhaps, we should go somewhere," she said at last.

"The cinema," I suggested.

"Oh, no, we avoid all such places now. They were all locked in, you see. The railway workers, when the theater burned down. Some members of our group were there as were members from every resistance organization in the city. The fire broke out suddenly; no one yet knows its origin. Those inside rushed to the emergency exits and found them locked, all but the one they had entered by. Hundreds died in the flames or were trampled in the rush to escape.

"We do not go to the cinema."

I made no attempt to dissuade her. "We could rejoin my friends." I offered, missing the point of her original suggestion entirely.

"Impossible. We cannot go to such a place." She giggled. "You were right about their profession, but such is their residence, that it is the perfect place for ones dressed as your friends are to hide in. One cannot be out of uniform when one is not wearing any clothes."

"One of my friends may be religious." I was thinking of Moyle, although religion per se was not something we had ever discussed. Modest, bashful, restrained, even repressed, might have been better word choices.

"Perhaps he has already undergone a conversion." Again, she giggled. She looked at her watch. "Come. We will go to my apartment."

The streets of Lyon were dirtier still than those of its suburb. Some sand had been sprinkled on the main street, but when we turned the corner, the sidewalks were icy where they were not heaped with grayish snow.

Once up the stairs and inside her apartment, she hollered, "Adele." Hearing nothing, she took me by the hand and led me into what was obviously her bedroom. There she sat me on the bed and proceeded to unbutton my shirt. I might have told her that I, too, was modest, bashful, and restrained and, indeed, I did much prefer to initiate any lovemaking, but said nothing along those lines.

I did try to change the subject. "Mrs. A. is no longer here?"

She shook her head, "Mr. A. is gone as well. A vacation. They say I am in charge while they are away, but I do not want to be in charge." She continued to unbutton me as she spoke, finally pulling the shirt and undershirt up and over my head.

I set about trying to unbutton her blouse in return, but did not prove particularly skillful at the task. After a moment, she removed my hands from her front, saying she could not afford a rip, and replacement these days of such a garment would be impossible. She then proceeded to unbutton, unzip, and unstrap anything and everything that required such action on both our sets of clothing.

When she was nude and I was nude, she leaped into my lap and with the aid of one hand had soon settled herself in place. What happened next may well have been, no, was wonderful. But afterward—I only hope afterward and not during—no, it was afterward, I fell asleep.

I woke much later judging by the waning light, only to realize that I might well have fallen for the oldest trick in the book, the Mata Hari femme fatal who leads the innocent airman to slaughter. But no, I was still in her or Adele's apartment, still lying outstretched nude on her bed and extremely cold as a result. I put back on all my clothing and then wrapped myself in both a blanket and a wool shawl in an effort to fight off the fit of shivering that had overtaken me.

The money! My money belt was gone. The Reichmarks packed away in jacket and coat pockets were undoubtedly gone, also. No, the belt was on the floor; the Reichmarks, too, seemed to be all in place, though I would have to count to be sure. What a fool I had been, either way.

The front door opened and this time I heard her call, "Pierre," French for Peter. Arms laden with grocery bags, she peeked into the bedroom. Finding me wrapped in my blanket, she indicated I should join her in the kitchen. Still rubbing my arms to quell the shivering, I followed after.

"I will fix us something wonderful to eat," she said as she unpacked her grocery bags.

160

"Wait. I have forgotten your change. I had to borrow a little from you." Her voice dropped as she spoke the latter words.

I pushed the change back at her and ran into the bedroom to retrieve additional Reichmarks. "You'll need these to take care of the three of us. I don't know how many days we will be here. If there is extra, it goes to the Resistance."

"It will be three days, and I will require 5,000 more just for the two of us." she said in a practical tone, and tucked the offered bills away. "The prices you would not believe."

"And my friends?"

"They will dine courtesy of the house."

"The house?" I echoed.

"And of the Germans who patronize it. Do not worry," she added on seeing the look of horror on my face. "Their clientele is unlikely to wander from room to room. Your friends and their uniforms—not that they are still wearing them, are safer there than any place else in the city."

A major and invaluable difference between men and women is that following the act of love, while the man spent of sperm and energy will collapse in sleep, the woman enriched by the male's secretions and recharged by his energy is able to go out and do battle.

During the short period of her absence, this reluctant heroine of the resistance had learned where we airmen were to be sent and arranged for our transportation to get there. "Mr. and Mrs. A and Boubou are safe," Suzanne announced proudly. "The others sought to take the leadership from me but I discouraged them."

Of that meal that followed, let me say that in the six months that had elapsed since my last visit to Lyon, four under the Marshall, and two under direct German occupation, all pretension to the greatness of French cuisine had vanished.

The skill was there; the instinct that raises the French chef, including my Suzanne, above all others was present. The materials were not. The pate tasted little better than a hotdog; the one-egg soufflé with some oil of indeterminate origin replacing butter was little more than flour; the fish had died before it was caught; of the cheeses, one had the consistency of chalk, the other resembled the spray one can buy today in a can. The ersatz coffee, acorns in barley water, brought us both to the edge of tears. Only the pain d'épices, gingerbread, black market for sure, was to be savored down to the last crumbs that we licked from each other's lips.

As we climbed into bed, she explained the arrangements that had been made for our transportation. A long distance trucker would arrive from the South the next day. As soon as he had sold his produce, he would take the three of us with him on his return trip, dropping us near Annonay. From there, we would travel, again by truck, this time courtesy of the Resistance, to Yssingeaux. The long distance driver was a known friend of the Resistance but not an actual member.

Oh, and I was to hear news of my friends that Suzanne had forgotten to pass on till then.

Moyle had had his religious conversion—the fortunate fellow, though not so fortunate as I, and Wilson had hooked up with the madam. "And she is very selective," Suzanne assured me.

A snowfall confined us to the apartment for most of the next day. But as we'd still no sign of her missing house mate, this was not really a problem. We went out briefly, walked by the lake and later up the hill to watch the children as they made use of the downward slopping streets and stairways for their toboggans. These last, not much more than slats of wood.

161

The news that evening, brought to us by one of the women I'd not quite met the day before, was no less interesting but far more disturbing. A would-be-pimp had forced his way into Moyle's girl's room and Moyle had shot him point blank in the head. The pimp was no loss, but the blood spatter had created a mess that needed to be cleaned up. Moreover, the shot had disturbed the other patrons. Wilson had parted with a 5,000 franc gold piece to cover the bakeesh required by the Lyon police. How soon could we all leave?

Fortuitously, the long-distance lorry driver who was to take us down south had found his wares literally ripped from his hands by Lyon housewives desperate to put food on the table. Although he was unwilling to leave immediately as Lyon offered some extremely tasty things at bargain prices to pass away the night with, he did agree to take us the next day for a consideration. He was a regular patron, of course, of the very bordello where Wilson and Moyle were staying.

I found his request for additional payment disturbing. I'd seen Pierre Laval at work and knew that a man who buys and sells his honor on one day may well be available for sale to another customer on the day following.

Nonetheless, the following morning found us squeezed into the compartment behind the driver's seat, where the long distance driver or his assistant might sleep if necessary, ready to go south. The back of the truck carried only a few pieces of furniture that had been bartered for groceries, and any detailed inspection would be guaranteed to reveal our presence.

The first inspection, by German soldiers at the edge of town was only a cursory one; some money changed hands, and we breathed a sigh of relief when we were finally on the main road. The driver even suggested that one of us might come up and sit beside him.

We had all three taken brief turns when he warned us to return to the back. Surprise inspections had occurred along this section of the road. We did not like surprises and all three of us had our machine pistols in our hands when the truck started to slow.

Wilson, swifter than I, made sure by poking the barrel through the curtain that the driver knew the machine pistol was pointed at him. "You are to remain in your seat. If you try to step from the cab, you will die."

"But I am your friend."

Wilson's barrel did not waver. We stopped. Wilson translated the German for me later. The Gestapo were indeed expecting a delivery. But the driver explained (in French) that the delivery had been canceled that day.

How many Gestapo stood outside the truck? Would we have been able to kill them all before they killed us? The driver was trembling as we drove away from the road block, so that a mile later I took over from him. Wilson's pistol followed his every move as he shifted between the seats.

162

Chapter 15. The Three Hidden Planes

A second truck was waiting near the turn off to Annonay, its open rear piled high with furniture. I slowed as I drew near it, but did not stop, gesturing with my arm that the men in the truck were to follow. When our driver protested, grabbing at my arm, I did stop.

Things happened quickly. Wilson tossed me the machine pistol and brought his hunting knife up to the man's throat. Meanwhile, the driver of the waiting truck had come up to my window.

I signaled for the latter to wait, then watched as Wilson and Moyle dragged our own driver into the narrow space in back. When I thought he was out of earshot, I leaned out the window and asked quietly, "Can you direct me to Yssingeaux?"

The man began to babble and I hushed him. "Somewhere we can park along the way and leave this truck to be found?"

I believe he understood then, for he gave me a direction. I drove off, allowed him to pass me, and then pulled off the road where he did. We waited together, five minutes, ten. A second man, older than the one who had greeted us originally, emerged from their truck but remained silent. Still no one followed us into the clearing where we had parked. We were safe.

I embraced them both, gave them my name and summoned Wilson and Moyle. We exchanged introductions, then fitted ourselves as best we could into the back of their truck amid the furniture. Charles Dupuis, our new driver, and Maurice, his uncle and helper rearranged the furniture around us, and we drove away. Hopefully, our original driver was able to break free of his bonds and go on his way as well. If not, tant pis.

■■■

I have never in my life had such an unpleasant drive.

Oh, we trusted our driver, now. The tension that had existed before between the driver and us was gone. But our position in the back of the truck was cramped, the truck bed lacked shocks or springs, and the wood-burner that powered the vehicle yielded acid fumes for us to breathe. Oh, and the road that led over and across the mountains to Yssingeaux was paved only in sections, and even the paved portions were filled with potholes. We crept up long inclines; we shot down the other side seemingly without brakes to interfere with our downward passage.

Did I mention also that we froze? Not entirely, for the furniture acted as a partial windbreak.

Dusk slowly crept up upon us as we traveled the last few miles. Only a few moments later as judged by our position amid the stacks of unsold furniture, we had passed in and through the town of Yssingeaux and out into the countryside again.

We left the partially paved highway after a mile or so to find ourselves bouncing up and down once more on a truck frame ill-prepared for the transition.

"The old road," our driver shouted. The old road indeed, neglected for several decades as all traffic including the invader's vehicles traveled across the new one. When spring came, one would see grass encroaching on both sides, and even a few weeds rising among the ruts.

We turned again, traveled perhaps a soccer field's length across a somewhat smoother surface, and then the truck halted. Our hosts came around the cab and helped us to descend. Other men appeared rapidly out of the darkness. Perhaps fifteen men in all were present to greet us.

Our mustachioed driver led us proudly over to a cloth-covered shape about nine feet in height, followed by the others. When we were gathered around him fully attentive, though one could see that my two companions and I were still rubbing our arms and legs vainly trying to restore our circulation, he ripped off the cover and waited for our reaction.

A look of horror and dismay crossed over Wilson's face. And mine too, I suspect. A World War I biplane, a Spad III, was revealed in not quite all its former glory. Bird droppings spotted wings and fuselage. Wherever there were metal cables, we saw rust.

But the sour looks had to be removed from our faces and quickly, too. For it was evident that our hosts did not see what we saw, but were awaiting the compliments that their months of hard work beneath the noses of the enemy entitled them to.

Moyle, thankfully, was in pilot heaven looking like a kid who'd received exactly what he wanted for Christmas. "I've always wanted to fly one of these," he exclaimed in English. Quickly, I poked Wilson in the ribs lest he be tempted to reply.

"Thank you so much," I said to the men in French, "As you can see my partner is speechless."

"These are wonderful," Moyle said, first in English and then a second time in French. We all said, "Merci." several times.

Instantly, the resistance workers, all male, began to chatter among themselves. I think they had the impression they would soon be soaring aloft like birds following overnight flying lessons from the three British pilots. I would not have been surprised had they broken into song.

"Quiet!" I shouted in French. Actually, what I shouted was more along the lines of "Shut the fuck up."

"One, you must be quiet, tonight and always, as we cannot afford to attract the attention of the Boche.

"Two, we may be here one more night, we may be here a month. [It was to take three.] We cannot tell until we have inspected the planes in the daylight tomorrow.

"Three, if we are to be here for some time, we cannot risk having you all coming and going every day. One of you, and one only, may call upon us each day with the needed tools and such supplies as are necessary.

"Charles, would that be you?"

I turned to our mustached driver whom I'd assumed was the leader. He nodded. Some protests could be heard, but he cut these off.

Again, I signaled for quiet. "If Charles cannot come, he will appoint one of you to come in his place and provide them with a token by which they may be recognized. Capiche?" No dissent. We still had their full attention.

"From time to time, we may need additional assistance with the repairs. Charles will bring our needs to you. Again, our heart-felt thanks. Ours is a mission of great importance and your contribution to the war will not be forgotten." (Later, Wilson was to suggest that I might just have listened to one too many of Churchill's speeches.)

"Now, is there somewhere else we may go together and have a glass to celebrate?"

"Quiet." I said again to quell the ensuing uproar. We soon were back in our respective trucks and cars, this time riding upright in the passenger seats, and on our way to Charles' uncle's farm for a drink.

The next morning, Wilson, Moyle, and I set to work immediately to inspect the planes. Charles looked on for a while, but then had to leave for work.

Eight planes in all had been left parked on this abandoned airfield. The first one we uncovered was the single-wing Morane-Saulnier L, a tiny aircraft not much taller than

Wilson. Nineteen feet in length, capable of an incredible 90 miles per hour, at least for an hour or so, its canvas was ripped, its tail fins were broken.

To its right both in space and time, was the Spad VII, a biplane, a tad longer than the Morane-Saulnier and considerably faster in the air, though with no greater range. It appeared to be in immaculate condition, barring the need to remove some rust from its cables. Moyle loved it; of course, if he had flown in it, he'd have had to swim when his gas ran out over the Mediterranean.

The German-made Pfalz D.III was a great surprise. The largest plane on the field, it was 22 feet in length, stood more than 8 feet tall and had a 30-foot wingspan. Wilson, who seemed to know all there was to know about World War I aircraft, told us it wasn't much of a fighter, though "it could hold its own against barrage balloons." But it definitely had the range we needed. A gaping hole in its gas tank told us why it was no longer in the air. The undercarriage had crumpled on landing and its wings were barely off the snow-covered ground. We moved on.

Next came the prize—three Spad XIIIs in a row. Powered by 235 Hispano-Suiza 8 BEc 8-cylinder liquid-cooled inline V engines, 138 mile per hour maximum speed, 22,000 foot ceiling. Its larger gas tanks, along with its relatively high fuel efficiency (as far as World War I vintage biplanes went), meant it would definitely make the distance to Free France across the Mediterranean, much less to Foix on this side of the Pyrenees. "Dibs," I said, when I saw the first one. Wilson smiled. It would take me over a month to overhaul its engine and even then I would have to cannibalize parts from one of the other Spads.

The second Spad XIII looked great in front, but the damage became apparent as we walked back toward the tail. We marked it down as an organ donor and moved on. The third Spad XIII wasn't as clean looking as the first—much work would have to be done on the flap cables. Eventually, we would have to replace one of the aileron links with a cable taken from the second Spad XIII, but it would do. Still, without dibs from the others, the Spad was mine for the taking.

A Sopwith Camel attracted Moyle's attention. Indeed, dibs was on his lips, when Wilson noted that much like a real camel, this model often would turn and bite its rider. As the propeller went in one direction, the engine would try to turn the Sopwith in the other, resulting in the aircraft crashing on its starboard wingtip. Almost as many Sopwith camel pilots died in World War I from non-combat related causes as they did from enemy gunfire. I merely noted, aloud, that we might not have the tools to fix it.

Last to be exposed was a Nieuport 28, French-made but mostly flown by U.S. pilots. Didn't turn me on, but Wilson hollered "dibs" immediately. Surprisingly, though perhaps not—Wilson knew his planes, it turned out to require the least of all the aircraft to make it operational.

When Charles returned for us that evening to take us back to his uncle's farm where we were staying, we had a lengthy list of requirements: a hoist and pulley to aid in the removal of the engine, a set of wrenches, some oil—exceptionally clean oil, rags, something to scrape rust, and so forth.

"We cannot fly today?" No, we could not.

He confided that to provide the tools we required would literally put his small mechanic's shop out of business. "Is there another mechanic in the village?" Armand Peltier had a shop; he was one of the men we'd met the evening before. "Can you move in with him?" A Peltier and a Dupuis working together? Such had never happened before. "Were the Germans then to win as we could not fight as one?"

In the end, we had to speak directly with Peltier, but the problem was resolved, albeit in a rather stupid way, as the two men insisted on each providing us with tools from their respective shops. Each day thereafter, the two were forced to go back and forth between their separate locations several times to borrow, then return the tools they needed for their work. But then, a Peltier and a Dupuis had never worked together.

We slept well in the barn on the Dupuis property. The cold kept the smell of the cows at a minimum, while the warmth of their bovine bodies was welcome. Each evening, we tunneled our way into the straw in the overhead rack to sleep there like hotdogs in a bun, comfortably warm , though the latter was an illusion soon shattered if it were necessary to get up and pee.

The Dupuis shared breakfast and dinner with us and, as I provided them with Reichmarks, they were able to supplement their diets and ours with fresh pork from the village. Cheese we had in plenty and bread was baked fresh each day in long outside ovens. Rabbit would also put in an appearance whenever one foolishly let it itself be snared. Coffee? Well, coffee was a long forgotten dream.

Early on, I observed that the Dupuis barn could be glimpsed each day from the airfield, yet we were obliged to walk over a mile by road to get there. It was explained and quickly demonstrated to us, that any attempt at a shortcut would bog us down like Napoleon's retreat from Moscow, deep in the snow.

I had the happy idea of putting the plow to work over this distance to clear a path. But was soon discouraged, as it was obvious that each time a German plane flew overhead—a working airfield was located nearby, such a path would be immediately evident.

The not infrequent presence of German planes suggested a solution to a problem that was to vex us later, how to get aviation fuel for our aircraft. But I am getting ahead of my story. For the moment, all those nearby German planes represented was an inconvenience, a need to keep our repairs and ourselves undercover as much as possible.

We began day three by hoisting my engine from its cradle so that I could disassemble and clean and repair it when necessary. We were forced to halt almost immediately when I realized the oil I'd been provided simply wouldn't do. The exigencies of wartime had forced even the best garages—his was one such, Charles assured me—to use and reuse motor oil. A solution for cars perhaps, but unacceptable for the requirements of an aircraft even for cleaning purposes. A shame-faced Charles confessed that he had a secret store of virgin oil, and was browbeaten into turning it over to us. (Later on in Paive, I would make use of fresh olive oil for the same purpose.)

Meanwhile, we spent the balance of the day going over the fuselage of the three planes we'd selected. Apart from readily patched bullet holes, our main concern was with the correct functioning of the tail flaps and the ailerons. Wilson and Moyle began the hard work of replacing the defective cable on the otherwise unblemished Spad XIII, while I did what I could to patch bullet holes and remove rust from the still functioning cables on the other two planes.

On day four, I finally got started on my engine and on the evening of day four, Wilson ceased to sleep with us in the barn. The senior Dupuis were not man and wife as we'd first supposed, but brother and sister, Maurice being considerably older than his sibling, though neither was what I would call young. Still, the Dupuis sister had a good firm ass and naturally bright blond hair (or so I supposed) that she wore in German fashion in two curled buns, one on each side of her head. Wilson would share her room from that evening on and we did not begrudge him his pleasure.

We did kind of wish for similar pleasures of our own, at least I did, Moyle was less voluble about his needs, though on reflection either of us I'm sure would have benefited from intimate female company. During the day, one had ample work to keep the mind occupied, but at night one was left with one's thoughts and the sound of an occasional mooing cow.

It took me almost a month to disassemble, clean, and restore my engine to a satisfactory condition. We'd had too many days in which work was not possible because of blowing or falling snow. Moreover, the hours of daylight were few and seemed to fly by all too quickly. Night work was out of the question as a constant light in the forest would have attracted unwanted attention.

What to do on a snow day? Envy Wilson at work in the house? We talked to Charles. "Are there no widows who like to spend time with young men?"

Charles mentioned two sisters in town who earned their living along the lines I'd described. "Someone less professional, perhaps?" The men in the area, he observed, the ones we'd met that first evening and who would appear from time to time (despite my instructions) to watch us at work, were grateful for our presence, eager to help with labor, to provide food, or to risk their lives if necessary. But it would be best if we were to avoid contact with the local women.

Tant pis.

The time came in early March to test the engines. "Can you bring us some gasoline?" The looks of elation faded from the faces of the two Frenchmen that were helping us that day. "You must understand," Charles began, "it might be difficult." I saw Wilson reach for his knife, not a good sign, and Charles hastened to add, "we have some, yes."

"Combien," Wilson said, one of the few French words he knew. They looked puzzled at his request. Of course, no payment was required; they were all working to stop the Boche. I explained that we simply needed to know how much aviation fuel they had managed to obtain.

"Regular gasoline will not do?"

We shook our heads, no; now, even Moyle was looking concerned. (I worried about him. Lately, he had slipped into an almost trance-like state and would talk about Dorothy and his Dad and a great deal else that was far too distance and unattainable to bother thinking about.)

A short discussion ensued between the two Frenchmen. "Enough for three planes, if we need not fill the tanks."

"Bloody hell." Wilson said. He and Moyle looked at each other and I could tell I was about to hear two speeches on the order of, "It is a far, far better thing I do," or, from the more biblically minded Moyle, "greater love hath no man."

"We think we can get more," Charles said.

"How?" Wilson asked.

How else? They would steal the aviation fuel from the Germans.

These brave men would not share their women, but they would sacrifice their lives. A week later, the truck appeared well after dark, and the men unloaded a drum of aviation fuel. A living Armand Peltier was not among them. The Germans had shot him as he leapt aboard the truck. "Perhaps, we should have waited for a moonless night."

In retrospect, I wish I'd been told again by the air force that it would be hurry up and wait, that I could take several months, rather than several days to reach my destination. That whether I left immediately or waited a week for the new moon was a matter of indifference. But they never tell you that in the service. It's just, "hurry up, on the double," and only later, "wait."

Yes, we could have taken more time with our preparations. But how much longer could we have continued to camp out in the woods, spending our nights in the barn with the men sneaking food to us each day? Moyle's cough had gotten worse. We had no medicine, though a new one called penicillin, discovered by a British scientist, had just

167

come into use within the military and might well have cleared his cough up in no time.

Chapter 16. Flight to Foix—April 1943

The day before our scheduled departure was overcast. Good. One could only hope the cloud cover would last through the night and would extend almost but not quite to the southern border of France. The damp smell that always seemed to precede a snowfall was absent. Again, a positive sign.

Anticipating the worst, we had arranged for a guard to be thrown about the field. Our colleagues who had seen us through the last two and a half months of preparation were prepared to die if necessary to see that we did take off. They had already gone through terrible privations to ensure our success. Their deaths would merely be a final and inevitable gesture.

Away from the others, the three of us went over our flight plans. We would head due south toward the Cote d'Azure as Wilson had previously recommended. Just before the border, I would turn west and head across the Languedoc toward Foix staying just north of the Pyrénées throughout. If I were shot down before the turning point, Moyle would take my place. And if Moyle too were shot down, then it would be Wilson. Otherwise the two men would continue out across the water toward Free France.

We did not discuss, and were not prepared to discuss what obstacles might lay in wait for them out over the water—German and Italian shore batteries, German ships.

Over land, we felt reasonably safe, at least as long as the cloud cover continued. The Germans would have no reason to maintain radar surveillance in an area where no enemy was expected. The short-range radar at the nearby German airfield might pick up our departure. This was a risk we would just have to take.

The balance of the day we spent inspecting our own and each other's aircraft looking for possible flaws. Ideally, we then would have gone to the briefing officers' hut to look over weather maps, and to consider alternative routes. But, of course, we'd neither weather maps nor briefing officers.

A second shift of men appeared around four (five German time) bringing with them fresh but fake and lukewarm coffee. We corralled three and asked them to help move the planes out.

"But you do not leave till tomorrow."

"We need to run a check." I replied, lying gracefully. After which we wheeled the aircraft into place for takeoff, spoke quietly and individually to each of the three and had them stand by the propellers. They spun the props; we started the engines, and a moment later, we were rolling down the grass runway and off into the air.

Perhaps, none of the men on the ground was a traitor. Perhaps, no one had sold us out. I did not care to remain till the next morning to learn the truth. Besides, I would need to land in Foix while it was still dark.

Airborne, we rose at as steep an angle as our World War I vintage biplanes could tolerate while keeping one eye on the ground and one on our altimeters. My altimeter seemed reliable enough, at least within a thousand feet or so of ground level—after that, who knew? Our instrument panels lacked most of the modern gauges we'd come to depend on in our Hurricanes and even then, could we be really sure that they worked? Forget an air speed indicator.

Wilson would soon learn that his gas gauge was defective, though he would have no way of letting the rest of us know about it. We had no radios. We'd worked out a few hand signals—all useless in the dark. Our guns, for which we had almost no ammunition and which, in any event might or might not work, would be used for transmitting distress signals.

Other than that, our arrangements, based on our one reliable instrument, the watch—theirs air force issue, mine a gift from Giselle—called for a change in the lead position every ten minutes.

Moyle and I were flying Spad S.XIIIs with the 235-horse power Hispano-Suisa engine. These would get me to my destination and his to his, just, if we held our altitude to somewhere between 12,000 and 15,000 feet.

In his whale-tail Nieuport 28, Wilson would have to remain at 12,000 feet or below if he were to maintain speed. With all three of his gas tanks filled to the top, the Nieuport might just take him all the way. We'd already stripped the Vickers machine guns from his plane to keep its weight down and the fuel efficiency at a maximum.

The clouds ended at about 6,000 feet. It helped us to get above them that we had started at almost 3,000 feet, though we'd had some tricky maneuvering initially to clear the surrounding peaks of the Massif Centrale.

Wilson, who'd led us on departure, leveled off at about 12,000 feet (a guess, but that's what my altimeter read). Would a flight of Messerschersmitts launched from the nearby airfield follow? The answer was no, so we trudged along maintaining our speeds at about what I would later do in a ground-based Sunbeam Tiger sports car racing along between Vegas and Reno in the 1960's.

We went along without incident for some time, Puy Mary and Puy de Dome, the mountains of the Massif Centrale, now on our left but hidden beneath the cloud layer. I had only compass readings to rely on, but these seemed to be in agreement with those of both Wilson and Moyle, who had taken Wilson's place in the lead almost ten minutes before.

My turn to lead came, then Wilson's again. We had passed beyond the cloud layers that covered the Rhone-Alps region and could just glimpse the waters of the Gulf of Lion far ahead, the snow capped Pyrenees off to the southwest. I heard an engine sputter, though perhaps I'd heard nothing beyond a noise in my own head, all else drowned out by the constant drone of my engine.

We'd almost reached the coast, and it was time for me to make my turn. I could not afford to be seen out over the water. I accelerated ahead of the others, and then banked abruptly—the signal, then watched as Moyle continued forward. Wilson, going forward to the south also, appeared to be dropping in altitude.

We were separating rapidly now, but still I could see Wilson slipping down, down to what would be the coast of Spain where, ultimately, he would land on a narrow strip of beach.

From then on, of course, I had my own concerns, radio contact to be made with my hosts in Foix, flares to look for, and a landing to be made on a narrow plateau in the foothills of the Pyrenees.

170

Book IV. The Island June 6, 1944-Oct 31, 1945

Chapter 1. Foix

I have explained many times already how to go about getting established in a new location, whether or not one is a spy. First, find a place to live, then food, and finally a girl friend. Or, as was the case for me in Genève, simply reverse this order.

My hosts in Foix were a sour-faced old man and his equally sour-faced old wife. Impossible to believe, but they were Protestants, devout ones, in a land of Catholics.

The old man was possessed of a native intelligence that had been singularly lacking in Paul-Henri, my previous host in the Midi. A number of young men were on hand when I landed in Foix to help me hide my plane, a mixed bag of servicemen who'd evaded capture by the Germans: British, American, and even a few Frenchmen. That same evening they were sent on their way through the Pyrenees, where with luck and time, they might eventually reach Free France and the army de Gaulle was assembling across the Straits of Gibraltar. The result was that by the next day the farmer and his wife were the only local residents to be aware of the true nature of my arrival.

Oh, and they had a hired hand named Maarieta, some sort of niece or distant cousin. I've referred before to the "false hunger" used by the French to describe a woman whose thin boyish form is interrupted only by her unmistakable breasts. Maarieta 's was the true hunger that comes from short rations and a stingy aunt. Not that the aunt was that stingy when other than her family were concerned; this couple had taken on the responsibility of assisting men fleeing the Germans to escape through the Pyrenees into Spain. They fed the never ending series of escapees at a time when it was difficult enough to feed one's own family what with the demands placed by the Germans and the overly compliant and corrupt Vichy French. But somehow their niece was overlooked at feeding time. Not that the couple stuffed themselves; the old woman herself was little more than skin and bones, and while the old man was given large portions, not an extra ounce was discernable on his stringy frame.

No wonder at their thinness; the work on their farm was twice as hard as it had been at Paul-Henri's, the soil of Foix rocky and unyielding. Run a tractor—forget it, no fuel was to be had. I've already mentioned the wood-burning cars in the city of Lyon. In Foix, one used a skinny, half-starved horse or pushed the plow oneself.

Fortunately, though the old man looked to be far into his seventies, he was wiry and strong and fully capable of lifting a bale of hay by himself. Still, I could help out the girl and the elderly couple in various ways. I began by putting myself to work in the barnyard and field, working at first alongside the girl and then taking her place entirely. She was extremely shy and our work together was done in silence.

She looked 16 or 17 at most and I was surprised when she finally opened up to me to learn that she was actually 24. Malnutrition and the exigencies of the occupation had literally stripped her of her womanhood.

I determined to help them out financially by spending some of the monies the spymasters had provided me with. But spending a single one of the large denomination gold coins I'd been given either in Foix or in the surrounding neighborhood would have immediately revealed my presence.

The solution lay in a pilgrimage to Lourdes, disguised as a priest, a costume the old man was able to provide. The old woman looked at me skeptically once so dressed, yelled for the girl, and saw that the appropriate alterations were made to my vestments.

The old man also gave me a small (very small) quantity of olive oil to carry. "If it is necessary for you to give Extreme Unction, do so. All that is important is that the dying individual feel redeemed."

I liked that man and his brand of Christianity. I just wished I'd taken Latin instead of Science in high school.

I experienced no difficulty in getting a lift to the main highway, or in obtaining several further rides after that. The priest's robes did it all. Nor did I have to travel all the way to Lourdes, where I'd been sure that among the many pilgrims yet another gold coin would go unnoticed.

No, I found a long distance trucker who was pleased to announce that if the father drank, and what priest did not, he would be pleased to buy him a glass or two of wine at the next opportunity. As the driver had already had several glasses, it appeared that I might indeed have the opportunity to offer supreme unction. But who would administer the last rites to me were I to stay in his truck?

When I inquired as to the basis for his generosity, he announced that he had just been paid, finally, and waved a roll of large denomination notes in my face albeit notes in the debased Reichkredit currency. I offered to exchange a 5,000-franc gold coin for a mere 4,800 equivalent in Reichmarks. He said this would not be necessary; he would cheerfully give me full value (at the official exchange rate, of course). I said that for his trouble, surely 200 francs would be a modest enough reward. In the end, I gave him the coin and he gave me 4,900, the last 100 "for the Church."

We parted happily and I returned to the farm, stopping along the way to pick up a few items we did not normally have at the farm such as fresh veal and some local sausage. That evening, I saw that everyone at table, including the young cousin went fed.

That night, she joined me in bed. I suggested to her this was wrong—indeed, I felt it was wrong—she was only a child, not a child as Bébé was a child, but an undeveloped girl far from womanhood. It was then that I learned that she was 24, and that the old man and old woman were either deaf as advertised or extremely considerate.

Speaking of Bébé, I thought I'd seen her on the road, a much stouter, pregnant Bébé, and indeed I had I found on further investigation. She had never once thought to return home to her father but had remained in Saint Gaudens where she'd quickly seduced a mechanic who'd been courting her cousin and married him.

Bébé's cousin was stunning the old man informed me, much like his own wife had been when she was young, though taller, more elegant, and certainly better educated. "They all get the education these days, despite the Boche," he remarked.

I was soon asked to serve on the underground railway on which the elderly couple labored by which Jews (younger ones in their teens and twenties, for few individuals whether older or younger could handle the tough terrain), as well as RAF and other pilots were conveyed over the Pyrenees from occupied France to relative freedom in Andorra or Franco's Spain. My role was that of a route cleaner. Originally, I was intended only to be an observer, to spot places along the trail where the Milice (the French national police force who were all too eager to collaborate with the Nazis) might lie in wait. But though the old man was a pacifist, such being the nature of his religion, I was not, and I had brought my machine pistol with me, though it was soon to run out of ammunition.

The trail upward from Foix led not only through the Pyrenees but also through the seasons. One might start on the edge of summer amidst rich green vegetation, but as one gained in elevation, one made one's way through new spring growth, till finally there were

172

winter snows to contend with. As the months progressed, the grasses at the foot of the hills would turn brown, but there was always green somewhere in the mountains.

The limestone and dolomite canyons were filled with oaks, lime trees and Italian maples. One climbed through stands of beech into forests of Scotch pine and black pine. The stands grew thinner and thinner. Bare patches increased in frequency, though where there was sun in moderation, alpine flowers could be glimpsed through the snow, until in the highest passes, the final stage on an escapee's journey, there was no vegetation at all, only bare rock.

The Milice tended to take the easy road, parking themselves no more than a few feet off the lower levels of the trail behind some boulders, where in threes or fours they would engage in easy conversation till they spied their prey. If one were willing to crawl upward past their hiding place, then sideways across inhospitable terrain, sometimes through forest cover, more often across loose scree, one could eventually come down upon them and, with luck, fire a few quick decisive shots from only a few feet away.

The disappearances occasioned a few visits from the Milice to the farm and met with the old man's disapproval, but the bodies of the disappeared were at the bottom of ravines where few would care to venture, and so proof of foul play was lacking. Later, when the Gestapo moved their headquarters to Foix, we would be forced to move our entire operation westward to Saint Girons. More than one path had been etched through the Pyrenees and the Milice could not watch them all.

Chapter 2. The Trip to Pavie

Maarieta had filled out considerably with the additional food I'd afforded the family (that which we ourselves got to eat and did not get parceled out to our many visitors during their brief sojourn with us). Though she would never be much more than skin and bone, at least now the underlying form was feminine, with hips where hips should be, and the swell of breast. We no longer had to make love in the dark, nor did I feel the slightest shame in our lovemaking.

Her increase in weight and body fat uncovered another aspect of female physiology, one I surely would have been aware of had I continued to pursue medical studies at McGill. Her monthly cycles resumed and in no time at all, it seemed, she was pregnant.

As our small resistance group was centered on the small Protestant meeting hall at which my host conducted services, it soon became apparent that Maarieta and I were expected to marry.

And why not? My relationship with her was growing to be as permanent as any other I'd known. Still, I could not take life or marriage seriously, nor would I be permitted to as long as the war lasted. Some day soon, perhaps the very next week, perhaps not for several more months, my orders would come. I let Maarieta know this—it would have been cruel not to, but I kept it secret from her aunt and uncle.

Meanwhile, I had only to hurry and wait whilst the child grew inside my lover. All could be put off for another day. Or could it? In the past, any sort of contentment on my part had always been a prelude to renewed demands from Air Command.

Military types often refer to the "fog" of war, (though less so today what with twice daily satellite flybys) alluding to the fact that neither side can really be sure of where enemy units are located or in what number.

In my own case, I could not really be sure that Air Command knew where I was. Had I been sent to Foix because Pavie was no longer safe? Or because it was desired to strengthen the escape route there?

And why had I been given a second plane to fly to the Midi? Was the first plane now in enemy hands? Or was there a need for both planes? Did the needs concern me or was I just a delivery boy?

The answers to at least some of these questions lay in Pavie. I needed to return there, to see to what extent, if any, the original operation had been compromised. Was the Moraine-Saulnier 410 I'd parked there more than two years before still flyable? Had the various resistance groups followed through on their promises to secure a supply of aviation-grade fuel? If so, the MS 410's far greater speed and range made it preferable to the antique I'd arrived in at Foix.

I needed to answer all these questions, and to make whatever repairs and secure whatever fuel was necessary, and do it all without being caught by the Gestapo or the Milice.

But how to get to Pavie and remain there undercover?

The obvious solution was to adopt my priest role once again, put on my borrowed robes and head for Lourdes with a side trip to see my (fictional) cousin in Pavie. Barring the sudden appearance en route of someone who had a christening, wedding, or funeral that must be attended to that very day, my disguise should gain me the rides I need and shield me from suspicion.

And if someone did require spiritual aid, who said I had to be an affable priest?

174

Wouldn't a real one say, "And why haven't you consulted your own parish priest my child?," the response to which would probably be an excuse so palpably false that it could readily be rejected. No, the priest role it would be.

My first attempt to reach Pavie was killed by success. I wasn't all that far away from Paive, though there was still a short northward journey to complete, when a jeep zoomed by driven by a German soldier. It stopped and came back to pick me up. I saw then that the officer in the driver's seat had a young Frenchwoman, his girlfriend presumably, sitting beside him. Still, there was room for me in the back.

"I'm sure we can take you all the way to Lourdes. It's a little out of the way, but you know.

"O.K., with you honey?"

It was O.K with honey and the officer took the opportunity to tell me and his honey all about his German childhood and his admiration for the Church.

We shot by the turnoff for Pavie and I realized it was going to be a long day. A really long one if I could not extricate myself before we reached Lourdes.

We stopped sometime later so the officer might relieve himself, and when we were out of his hearing, the girl asked if I would hear her confession.

I considered, then rejected her request, telling her there were some things God could not forgive her for. After which I gave her the "see your own parish priest," routine. When we came near Lannemezan to the road that led to Lourdes, I was told—surprise, surprise, that a detour could not be made for me after all.

So late in the day, I had no choice to return to Foix, my mission incomplete. Months passed before I could again take the time for an attempt. What precipitated my renewed desire to view the plane was a little conversation I had with Paulette, the lady of the house.

I had been given something special to eat that morning, a pancake full of ripe sugar-laden berries, their natural sugars much sweeter than the white packaged granules that were now only distant memories. Our sugar rations were useless coupons in a book, for granulated sugar could no longer be found in any store.

And where had the berries Paulette fed me come from? A final jar of preserves taken from an almost empty shelf.

I started to get up when the others left to work in the field, but was waved down. "Eat, eat," the old man said and Maarieta, heavy-laden now in her eighth month but determined she would milk the one cow as always, urged me to stay, also. I stayed.

"You have decided to marry her?" the old woman asked. I nodded, my mouth full of pancake, the ripe juice of the berries dripping down my chin.

"Feeding her began again the interest in men," Paulette continued, seemingly voicing her thoughts aloud rather than speaking to me. "When she had been fed enough, then she could bear children." This tale from an old wife bore in it all the wisdom of modern medicine.

"Very well, Peter will marry the two of you." Peter was the old man's name, also. His marrying me meant a Protestant ceremony; I would not need to receive instruction or even, hopefully, to lie about my religion.

"But will we not need to post banns or sign a register?"

"You may use your false name for that. It is only important that we put your real name here, in this bible." And she showed me then the small volume that I would often see her reading from in those very few moments when she was neither cooking, doing chores, nor helping mend the clothing of another ongoing traveler.

"We will post your false name also in the large bible we keep in church. It is only important that we put your real name here where God can see it."

She stopped and stared at me for several moments as if analyzing the content of my character. "This will not bother you? Because of your religion."

I must have looked puzzled because she continued, saying, "You are Jewish, of course."

Correction. Only two other people who were not Jews ever recognized my heritage at first sight. A man from Xiang province in China and a woman from the foothills of the Pyrenees.

"I have seen too many Jews pass through here to believe that all Jews have hooked noses and a swarthy complexion, much less cloven hooves and a tail."

I laughed. She closed the book, then opened it again, looking directly at me. "Aren't you supposed to be helping Peter weed the barley field?"

I took one last bite of pancake and one last sip of rosehip tea, dipped my dishes in each of the pans and set them on the sink to dry. I turned to thank her, but was too late; she was deeply immersed in the book of Mark.

The next day, the wedding not being till Sunday, I set out for Pavie. This time determined that I would reach my destination and establish the safety of the plane. I got a lift to Pamiers, and then one to Toulouse, replacing my tale of a pilgrimage to Lourdes, with one of a sick aunt in Auch. Well short of Paive, I told the gentlemen who had given me a lift that I needed to walk and consult my breviary. Following which, I set out for my destination across the fields, acting solely on instinct and scraps of memory.

Dogs came out once to pursue me, but they too respected my robes. Incredibly, though it was well on toward evening, I did find the clearing that had once served as a landing field years before. It had not been maintained and would require at least one or two passes with a plow to be made usable again. The plane was still there beneath the trees, though, well camouflaged. And there were two relatively fresh-dug graves near by.

A chill went up my spine, not for any fear of death, but for the possibility that whoever dug those graves had either found the engine parts I'd buried or had covered them with fresh dirt so they were irretrievable. But memory and luck held. I used the trowel I'd brought with me to first excavate the parts then bury them again.

When I reemerged from the woods, a man was standing in the clearing. I recognized him instantly as a member of the Resistance group Paul-Henri had belonged to. Yet, if asked to describe him, I would probably begin by saying he had a far from memorable appearance. Slight of stature with a smooth-shaven round face. Thin brownish hair with some scalp showing once he removed his beret. I wasn't sure I remembered his name. Armand? No, that had been someone else.

His ideas, I recalled, had been equally unmemorable though he had defended them with the same ferocity that so characterized every other member of the group.

"Thank God, you are here Father. This ground needs to be consecrated."

I inclined my head as if listening, as indeed I was.

"Paul-Henri died here and Jacques Cuze. A misunderstanding."

A misunderstanding over what? The plane was here; the fuel drums were here. Also on the plus side, the two graves that had scared the hell out of me had not, after all, uncovered the hidden parts.

"You saw the plane?"

I nodded.

"Paul-Henri had vowed to defend it with his life. When he saw the communists were here, he thought they had come to steal it. He shot and killed Jacques before someone else shot him.

"But, of course, the communists had come only to deliver the gasoline they had promised the English flier. Stolen from the Germans." Armand, if that was his name, smiled.

"Will you bless this ground, father?"

I dropped to my knees, and indicated that he should drop to his knees, also. Making the sign of the cross, I began to pray in Hebrew, the only prayer I knew, a Baruch, that is, a thank-you, for the food we had received.

(What a waste—those two lives, yet how wonderful if it had meant the union of two groups both dedicated to the destruction of the Nazis.)

When we rose again, Armand had a pistol pointed at me. Had my failure to use Latin been that obvious?

"I'm sorry father. I know that to kill a priest is a mortal sin, but I have no choice." Armand's hand was shaking.

"I do not understand."

"This plane must remain secret."

"But what if I were not a priest but a Canadian pilot."

A look of joy spread across his face, not so much because I had confirmed his initial recognition as that he would now be spared having to commit a mortal sin.

We talked of our absent friends, with special mention of Paul-Henri. I said that I had gone off with François, not Bébé. We shook hands, hugged. He said there was now only a single resistance organization in the area, though of course, all the groups met separately as before. Tant pis.

Before I left, I also thought it would be well to provide him with the parable of the gold nuggets:

Once, a man much like Armand came across a cache of gold nuggets in the woods. Enough gold so that he could live in comfort all his life. He told his wife, of course, with whom he shared all secrets. She felt she should share the knowledge with her sister, after all there was so much gold. But when the man came back to the wood to replenish his supply, having spent the little he had taken to begin with, nothing of the gold remained. The sister had told her husband who had told his brother who had shared the news with his best friend, and so on.

And lest Armand still had not got the message, I finished by saying, "I do not exist. I was never here. But you must continue to guard the plane with your life until I do return."

A truly Christ-like admonition delivered by one of his earthly representatives.

Chapter 3. The Wedding

Peter's flock met each Sunday in a plain brown wooden structure that was painted once each year. No self-respecting Catholic would have ever gone inside it, but it was perfect for the more austere brand of Protestantism Peter's congregation practiced. The interior of the building held only a wood-burning stove, a pulpit, and several rows of benches. The one concession to the ceremony that was about to take place were the two pots of flowers placed just outside the open church doors, and the bouquet my bride-to-be held.

We knew our lines, the minister knew his. Indeed, Peter had been kind enough to provide me with a ring from the collection of mislaid items that our travelers had left behind.

To the usual Sunday congregation had been added the hired girl from a neighboring farm, whom Maarieta said was her best friend. Yes, the best friend was a Catholic. My best man was a Church of England RAF bombardier who would be shot by the Milice the next day as he traveled up the mountain path to Andorra.

We were some way into the ceremony—Peter had given a general discourse on marriage and its responsibilities and the responsibilities of the Christian life in general, when a visitor appeared at the church door.

One of the Church elders, who until then had been serving more as greeter than as doorkeeper, did not wish to let the man in. But Peter was more favorably disposed.

"Let him in. All are welcome here. He can bring only good luck to the wedding."

The visitor wore the vestments of a Catholic priest, a Jesuit. He was a tall man with a lean ascetic face, a man I ought to have recognized immediately had it not been for the glare of the sun on his face that contrasted so with the darkness of the meeting hall's interior.

Peter was wrong about his bring good luck. What Father Ignatius had brought with him was a new set of instructions from Air Command.

Chapter 4. The Mission—June 1944

The instructions passed on to me by Father Ignatius were exceptionally detailed, which meant one of two things: Either Air Command was now completely confident in the route by which agents were contacted in the field or they wanted those instructions to fall into enemy hands.

On an evening in June to be determined, I was to fly the length of France during late afternoon hours reporting on troop dispositions as I went.

The instructions provided for how the date was to be communicated to me—a Beethoven Symphony on British short wave, the course I was to follow—entirely over land following the Atlantic Coast of France from Lourdes to Cherbourg, and emerging near to, though not directly over, the Channel Islands. I'd also been provided with the codes I was to use in describing aircraft and troop dispositions, and the directions in which I was to make my transmissions.

Apparently, and unknown to me until then, the MS 410 had been fitted with a directional aerial. The MS L biplane I'd flown from Yssingeaux didn't even have a radio, which answered the question of which plane I was to fly.

I was to set the radio to a specific channel and upon receiving a specified signal, sent presumably by a ship or submarine lying offshore, was to transmit a list of all that I'd seen so far. A specific interest of Air Command seemed to be whether the German troops—nothing smaller than an army regiment, were still in fixed positions or were on the move.

Thereafter, I was to transmit every so many miles until I was out over the Channel. A little meter on my control panel, one I'd wondered about but hadn't really pursued the description of till then, would let me know if my transmissions were being aimed correctly.

I'll never know, of course, if my mission was really intended to fail, if, like so many others who followed a similar course a month or so before me, my flight was meant to convince the Germans that the Allied invasion of Western Europe might come from here, there, or everywhere.

The good news for me was that the Germans were not about to be fooled and my evening flight the length of France didn't receive that much attention. In fact, it was a U.S. air force plane that was to shoot me down. But I'm getting ahead of my story.

My wedding to Maarieta took place the last week in May which meant my flight and presumably my death—I didn't give much for my chances—would take place anytime between four and thirteen days later. Which gave the two of us at best a three-day honeymoon. As Peter and Paulette felt we'd already had honeymoon enough, this meant three more days of hard work. But at least we had the nights together, nights in which I could glory in the feel of my child kicking, either by placing my hands on Maarieta's abdomen or by having her lie behind me clasping me as best she could around my shoulders.

On the evening of May 30th, BBC overseas chose to play Beethoven's Fifth. As it turns out, this was an error; they were to have played his Fourth that evening but couldn't find the record immediately. By the time the correction was made the next day, I was already on the road headed for Paive.

Before I left, I had one more small problem to resolve. One of Peter's parishioners had taken photos of the wedding and appeared some days later with a picture of bride and groom standing before the congregation. I could not deny that the bride looked lovely but worried that if I were captured later and the photo was seen by the Gestapo that . . . But here, Peter cut me off.

"She will keep your picture in her room for the child to see. Your flight will be successful. And should the Gestapo come, surely your portrait is the least of the things they will find."

He may have been the bravest man I ever met. And Maarieta and Paulette the bravest women.

Chapter 5. The Flight

In its hiding place outside the town of Paive, the plane was still concealed beneath the trees. As on my last visit, the runway was overgrown and would have to be mowed. Paranoid as ever, I opened each canister of gasoline and smelled the contents. One held water, but the rest I was sure were high quality aviation fuel. (Unknown to me then, the quality of this gasoline stolen from the Germans wasn't quite as good as on the Allied side, but this hardly made any difference at the speeds I'd be traveling.)

I retrieved the hidden engine parts from where I'd buried them along with the needed tools, but by then the light was failing and I put off till morning their reinstallation. A few dabs of precious aviation fuel here and there on my face and body served to discourage flying insects and shortly afterward I was curled up and asleep.

The next morning I opened the engine and restored it to working order, though this fact remained to be tested. I needed someone to help me make the test; I also needed someone to plow clear the runway.

Strangely, Armand had not appeared. Clothing myself anew in the priest's vestments, though it would be far too hot in an hour to wear them comfortably, I set out for the nearest farm. This proved to be Paul-Henri's and, as expected, the house and barnyard were deserted. Continuing to walk along the road, I was soon offered a lift. "I'm looking for cousin Armand," I said and got only a puzzled look in reply. My bad. I should have learned the man's real name. "I need a plow," I said.

But, of course; the man had an errand to run that morning, would tomorrow be convenient?

I was staying with Paul-Henri, I said. Or, rather, I'd expected to stay with him and had to make do instead with a bed of straw in his barn. The man nodded his head in commiseration. A small plot of land existed adjoining Paul-Henri's for which one needed the plow.

"Where the plane is hidden?" the man asked.

Mon dieu, did everyone in the district know!

He would meet me there tomorrow.

The man was as good as his word, bringing with him his teenage son early the next day. The latter drove the tractor while the two of us stood and chatted and occasionally gave the boy unnecessary directions. The pair assisted me to fill the MS 410's gas tanks and stood by while I attempted to start the engine, succeeding only after some initial priming.

"You're not a priest, are you?" said the man.

I thought a smile was the best response. "Bon chance," he said and gave me a firm hug. I shook hands with the boy, and had them help me turn the plane, then push it back under the trees.

"You leave now?" the man asked.

"Tomorrow."

At five that day, I was in the air. The evening wind blowing down from the mountains would have made take-off difficult, but it had not yet begun to blow. Had I looked back toward Foix once airborne, I might have seen the Gestapo headquarters or, further in the direction of the Cote d'Azure, seven German infantry divisions, plus one of tanks. But along my route of travel there were few if any military installations. Indeed, there was only forest along the coast until I reached Bordeaux.

Seeing the many army vehicles that were parked in areas surrounding the city along with a very few landed planes I rose another 5,000 feet to be on the safe side.

Strangely, not once on my northward journey did I say to myself, this is the last time I shall fly over France and its patchwork of farms and rolling hills, the last and only time I shall pass the vineyards of the winemaking region. Nor would I share meals again with those who spoke only French, nor drink wine with very meal.

I was South of Royan over water when I received the first radio signal. My answering report, a dull one, mentioned shore batteries and the absence of any real concentration of troops.

South of Nantes along the coast, I spotted a heavy troop concentration and again within the peninsula from Nantes to Brest, Germans were everywhere. Little or no troop movement could be seen, perhaps all were at their evening meal, and I counted myself a fortunate lad for having traveled this far without incident.

I had passed across the water from Brest to the Cherbourg Peninsula when I began to notice activity in the skies. Movement on the ground, not the sky, was my assignment, and I continued to make careful observations in preparation for my next transmission. Still, a brief change in course would be required if I were to avoid contact.

The time came, the signal came though strong and clear, and I transmitted the new information successfully, though I had to keep altering course to avoid the flak. An air battle was in progress supported by firing from the ground. I did my best to identify the aircraft I saw; so many changes had taken place since I was last in the air. Perhaps, I'd have done better to think of myself as a participant rather than a spectator in the battle around me. For the next moment, some idiot Yank in a P-51, a model of plane I hadn't seen till then, blew a hole in my left wing just as I flew out over the Channel.

Chapter 6. Ditching the Plane

With my plane going down and the English coast between Worthing and Brighton in sight, my first choice would have been to parachute into the water as close to land as possible, but my parachute had long since been cut up and shared by the farm women of Paive to make into dresses. One could thank Paul-Henri for his generosity.

Ditching the plane in the water was out. I still had an outright gap in my memory from the last time I'd ditched at sea.

So though my damaged plane was making every effort to bank continually, I headed for a long stretch of beach. How hard could sand be? Quite hard, but it served to slow the aircraft which, had I not kept the nose pointing ever upward, would have pitched itself forward on the sand.

A crowd of people quickly gathered to assist me from the plane. No, I'd misread their intentions. No sooner was I on the ground, then one aimed a punch at me. "Lousy, murdering Jerry."

I let the punch glide by and watched as the lad with murderous intentions broke his hand and wrist against the hard surface of the plane. Still, there were a great many of them and not all could be avoided; gradually, my arms were twisted behind me. "We've got you now, lad."

I told them in Gascon French to go fuck themselves. Then, realizing my error, repeated the same phrase in English. "I'd of being safer among the Jerries," I said at last.

"What's he saying?" they asked in the same accents with which they'd greeted the Norman conquest.

"Talks funny."

"He's got no dog tags. Must be a spy."

"Are you a spy?"

"Yes." That shut them up.

"It's off to the police then for you, lad." an older man asserted himself.

"Air Command." I suggested.

"Let's shoot him here and now." This from the lad with the broken wrist. But they didn't shoot me, merely marched me off with a shotgun in my back till we reached the nearest police station.

"Flight Lieutenant Freygood, RCAF." I introduced myself.

"He's a spy," said one of my escort. "Told us so himself." "Has no dog tags."

The desk sergeant, wisely, thanked them all and escorted them from the building. After which he had me go through it all again.

"Could I go to the nearest airbase, please."

"Right, as if they have time for you today." So, off I went to the cells where I became part of a tour. Whenever a Bobby or his wife or his girlfriend came into the station they would be brought in to see me. Several tried out their high school German on me, but with no success. I tried hard to remember the 'eins, hein, drie' I'd learned one day while flying above the fog over Belgium but with no real assurance that I'd done so correctly.

Occasionally, I would ask for food, and eventually the jailer's wife brought me some. "You don't look like a Nazi, just a sweet young boy." I allowed that I was but had no choice except to do what I was told or have my entire family shot.

A day later I was picked up by the Army, interrogated, put in a cell, and the day after that escorted under guard to an airbase.

There I was told, that I might be right, I might be wrong, but that nobody really had time for me. And, yes, where were my dog tags?

I saw the men from MI5 before I saw anyone from Air Command or anyone of any influential rank whatever. "There's a ruddy war on, don't you know." Unknown to me, D day had come and gone; the Allies had landed on Omaha Beach and along the coast of Normandy. The longed for Allied invasion of Europe was on.

MI5 stuck me out in the country on a rather nice estate, asked me a series of questions, the same series several times in a row, gave me a nice comfortable room that I only had to share with one other person, and every so often would leap out at me and shout something in German. As my only response was to attempt to kill the person who shouted or to ignore him, they soon stopped this practice though the interrogations continued. The only person who did seem to believe me was my roommate. I'd swear he came straight from central casting for Prussian officers. He left the safe house before I did, shaking his head and saying, "Frygood, they'll never believe you; you only have the truth to fall back on."

But they did believe me, finally. A record of my enlistment, though not my last assignment, had been unearthed, and as all the particulars seemed to match, off I was sent to Air Command.

There I languished for another few weeks. "Group Leader Raffey is up to his ears, Sir. Don't you know there's a ruddy war on."

It seemed the Allied landing at Normandy hadn't put an immediate end to the war after all and we were to pursue the retreating Germans across France and Belgium and Germany itself for almost another year.

The Allies had landed on the Northern coast of France. Then what had my flight been about? Group Leader Raffey might have told me, but he was up to his ears at Sector Headquarters.

They put me in a cell for a bit, a very nice cell, but it was a cell. After which they had me escorted to a hotel each evening and back again in the morning, but the day soon came when they simply couldn't spare the men to escort me.

I asked if I might return to Northolt and my old squadron, but they had no orders concerning me. Someone did discover that I'd been promoted to Squadron Leader and I was handed insignia, but no uniform.

The question of my missing uniform did seem to spark an interest that my mere existence had not. I explained to the man sent to check on it that it had been left behind at Northolt three years before on my departure for the Midi. Wasn't that the second uniform I'd lost? This last question came from a second bureaucrat, a cost-conscious representative of the RCAF. I was to be the colonials' problem from now on, Air Command had decided.

Eventually, after yet another month had passed, they told me to take off for a bit. If there were orders they'd let me know. Whereupon, I was escorted down the steps of Air Command and out into central London.

I was free. I guess I must have felt the same way President Bush felt after been sworn into the Air National Guard when he was told he wouldn't actually have to report for service.

In my case, the elation would soon wear off. At that moment in time, I was more than glad to have shaken myself free of bureaucracy. I was out in the open air in a city where I had friends, Dorothy, Moyle, Wilson, and the Inspector. And where, come to think of it, one need not worry that at any moment the Milice or the Gestapo might penetrate my disguise.

The air was filled with sunshine, the morning neither hot nor cold. A fine day for lunch at the Club. I headed for the offices of the Metropolitan Police, Inspector Moyle, and news of my friends.

Chapter 7. The Missing Airman—July 1944

I was walking down the hallway in Metropolitan Police headquarters searching for Inspector Moyle's doorway when suddenly I was attacked. A furious woman was doing everything she could to reduce me to shreds with pounding fists and clawing nails. She probably would have succeeded had she not accompanied her attack with repeated screams of "bastard, you killed him."

The latter brought people running from the various offices and eventually they pulled her off me. I recognized Dorothy as my attacker at the same time Inspector Moyle recognized me as her victim. As the men and women who'd taken Dorothy aside had begun to glare in my direction, he led me into his office for a private chat.

"She thinks you're responsible for my son's death," the Inspector said. From his tone, I gathered that the Inspector wasn't altogether sure that I wasn't. I explained that the junior Moyle had been shot down over Belgium by the Germans but had succeeded in flying to safety in Switzerland. Inspector Moyle and Dorothy knew that but they also thought they knew that I'd lured him into occupied France where he'd been captured by the Gestapo and killed.

I explained that to the contrary I was sure he'd made it to Algeria and joined the Free French as a pilot. If he'd been killed since, it was as a hero fighting alongside de Gaulle.

A soft voice behind me in an opened doorway said, "you're sure." Turning, I explained to Dorothy that all I could really be sure of was seeing him fly out over the Mediterranean well clear of the shore batteries headed for freedom. This was my first opportunity to take a long careful look at her. She wore the same shapeless brown uniform, yet somehow her figure showed through; her face still shone as if newly scrubbed. Only her red hair, shaped into ringlets, seemed somehow different, redder or shorter. "You haven't changed," I said. "No rings, no babies."

"Babies. Oh, I expected to have plenty of babies by now. A loving husband who would come home each evening pleased to be with me. But that's what war did, that's what Hitler did. And now the man I love, the man I was to marry is gone and you say you had nothing to do with it."

"Wilson would know," I said.

"Flight Lieutenant Wilson was interned in Spain. He hasn't returned."

I sighed and began my story all over again from skiing through the Alps till I banked toward Foix and left the two of them to fly on South. "I was sure he had enough fuel."

"I hate London." Dorothy said from behind us, apropos of nothing. She looked at us defiantly.

"We'll find out what happened to Flying Officer Moyle, to Benjamin," the Inspector and I said more or less simultaneously.

"And give him back to me."

When the war is over, we both thought, but kept our mouths shut.

It took us several months to find out what had happened to the younger Moyle. Meanwhile, the Home Guard disbanded; Dorothy turned down a follow-on job with the Metropolitan police force and went back to live in the country with her father; I followed.

A half dozen government agencies, the RAF foremost among them, denied responsibility for Moyle Jr's whereabouts. Messages went forth from Her Majesty's Government to the reborn French Republic and to Franco's Spain with no response. I even got permission to go to Gibraltar, hitching a ride on an RAF transport. But I learned absolutely nothing there, though I was forced to undergo extensive interrogation as a result of my unscheduled landing on the Rock. The disposition of guns and troops in Gibraltar were among the most guarded of His Majesty's secrets.

The Inspector pursued his inquiries into his son's absence through police channels. These latter proved more reliable. Nobody in the French armed service wanted to admit his mistake. The story was this: As Moyle came in for a landing in Free French-held Algeria, riding on fumes, they'd shot him out of the air. Nothing personal. Very little in war was personal. "He did not respond to his radio."

His vintage aircraft had no radio. But it was too late to tell them that.

Chapter 8. The Courtship of Dorothy

I was not made for life in the English countryside, or for courting a girl who might or might not choose to see me on any given day. Dorothy was always unfailingly polite when I called upon her and would seldom turn down an invitation, but this would not prevent her from being fully occupied with preparing and serving tea to her father's elderly guests when I did arrive at the vicarage. I'd wait about for hours only to be told, "I won't be able to see you this afternoon."

Or, she might have decided to spend the afternoon on a walk through the countryside with one of her mates from her field hockey days, a girl with thick legs named Mildred, who wore heavy tweeds. Of course, I was more than welcome to come along and, however indifferent Dorothy might be to my presence, Mildred would be sure to track me down that very evening at my hotel, (or the next day if she'd not had a chance to check with Dorothy till then). An invitation to Mildred's for tea would follow; I'd meet Mommy and Daddy, and then we'd go for a short walk in which Mildred or Emily or Bessie would make it quite clear that all I had to do was spread my jacket on the ground for them to lie there with me.

Perhaps, this is a bit unfair, to lump them all together as there were profound differences among the young ladies most of which the young ladies themselves brought to my attention. Mildred, who I thought must have gone out of her way to find clothes that would emphasize her worst features, noted how poor Emily would select such drab garments. And Bessie, blessed with natural blond curls, ought do something about her hair.

Yes, hair, clothes, and bulk aside, I occasionally took advantage of their invitations, though I soon found myself having sex regularly with a blond schoolteacher in town, one who reminded me of Maarieta before she got pregnant. My schoolteacher was not a girl that a Flying Officer, much less a Squadron Leader, ought look at twice, but she had her own set of rooms and a landlady who was more than willing to act blind and deaf to the goings on in the floor above.

Not that everyone in the tiny Shropshire village didn't know about our affair, including Dorothy.

"But I want to marry you," I told the latter on several occasions, and but she only just smiled at me in reply.

The day came, finally, when a change in Dorothy's attitude occurred. Maybe it was the presence of the schoolteacher that made me seem more desirable to her, more likely the teacher's attentions had served to calm me down, making me seem less of a threat. Dorothy and I started to go for walks together free of the presence of some field hockey teammate of years gone by.

This didn't mean, and I know I ought to be ashamed of this, that I didn't occasionally take advantage of Mildred's hospitality and her bountiful figure so in contrast to that of my schoolteacher mistress or Dorothy herself for that matter. This sex on the side had to stop though when a pregnancy scare occurred accompanied by an exchange of cryptic notes, and during which Mommy and Daddy began to eye me strangely.

Anyway, on Dorothy's side began a series of sexual bargains which seemed almost silly as I was sure she'd gone all the way that one night with Moyle, while I could have full release any time I wanted with my flat-chested blond schoolteacher, or with Mildred, or with one or two others, their names long forgotten.

Dorothy told me, apparently after consult with her former teammates, that she would use her hand if I wanted. Would I like that? I was now permitted to put my own hand on her breast, though she persisted in keeping her bra firmly fastened the while. And I could slip my hand beneath the elastic waistband of her virgin-white panties, but only while she held on firmly to my wrist.

I got to know the Vicar, her father, rather better during this period, not as Freygood, young Moyle's comrade in arms, but as me. I sensed that I didn't quite do as far as he was concerned, but that I might be tolerated. "He's just panicking," Dorothy told me, "At the possibility of my going off to Canada, and leaving him to cope on his own.

"We'd have to be married first," she said, "It's the only way." Which was as close as she'd come to actually saying, "Yes."

Meanwhile, I'd grown tired of waiting for word from London. The war pressed forward, though for me it was only secondhand via the newspapers and the evening radio broadcasts. Our bombers and the Yank's made nightly raids on Germany. The German rank and file fought on, no longer as potential world conquerors, but in fear of their lives. The Gestapo would take them away if they didn't fight, to be tortured then sent to a concentration camp to take the place of the Jews, and Gypsies, Communists and other political dissidents who had preceded them. Deserters were shot on sight. Old men and small boys were pressed into service. For Hitler and his high command knew that the minute they let down their guard, we'd kill them all.

Throughout the summer, the Germans had been firing screaming unmanned missiles, nicknamed "doodlebugs," on London. Our best and only defense against them was to have a fighter plane shoot them out of the sky, and there was I, a fighter pilot, sitting on the sidelines. I began to make a nuisance of myself, calling on Air Command repeatedly and requesting a squadron to go with my squadron leader's insignia. I was given a medal instead and told to come back in a month or so.

In December, I got my squadron, thus avoiding having to make a final commitment (and marriage) by accepting one of the five invitations to spend Christmas I'd received, (four from members of Dorothy's old field hockey squad including Dorothy herself).

The job of squadron leader was not quite what I'd imagined it to be with me at the head of a huge flying V strung out on either side hurling ourselves fangs bared at the enemy. Mainly, it was paperwork and long motivating speeches while other men did the jobs of heroes.

I was also told in no uncertain terms that I need purchase two uniforms, one informal to replace the one "I'd lost" and the other formal that I might meet the demands of a squadron leader's rank interacting socially with the brass of my own and other services. No more borrowed uniforms for me.

A few questions to my fellow squadron leaders—all of whom eyed me strangely: where had this Freygood chap come from?—soon led me to a tailor, but the latter's questions concerning lapels, pocket closures, and other esoterica soon led to frantic phone calls from me to Shropshire. Eventually, it was the ill-dressed Mildred, rather than the more fashionable Dorothy, who came to my aid, leading me by the hand to the tailors, making all the necessary decisions for me, and acting exactly like the wife I'd hoped Dorothy would be.

She also was kind enough to spend the night—for once free of doodlebug—and again perform wifely services. Of course, most days, and many evenings too, I had a job. Less dangerous perhaps, but no less exhausting, than my duties had been hereto throughout my war.

My job was to motivate, mentor, and cajole pilots, mechanics, and supply officers, each group presenting their own range of difficulties.

When someone in my squadron, enlisted man or officer, looked depressed at having to spend Christmas in the air, I'd tell him to shoot down as many Luftwatte pilots as he could to ensure a merry Christmas for the folks at home. My speeches didn't work in every instance; occasionally the Jerries would shoot down one of my men before he could shoot down one of theirs, but, on balance, my squadron acquitted themselves well.

I had no trouble gaining respect with the pilots; my flight record, though it had been gained with the RAF, was soon common knowledge. A trip to the hangars in which I took over a repair from one of the men gained me respect there also. (Fortunately, I had chosen an older model of engine to work on.) But as for RAF supply sergeants, you'd have thought sometimes they were working for the enemy. The RCAF, it appeared, was to be supplied only as a last resort after all requests from the home services had been fulfilled. I was not without friends in that latter service, however, and one way or another, was able to keep my squadron up in the air.

As a squadron leader, I was now traveling in considerably more exalted company than I had as a mere Pilot Office. In particular, I'd reached a level where one could overhear a great deal of criticism that had nothing to do with the quality of food in the mess or the inadequacy of the intelligence. Air Vice Marshall "Butcher" Arthur Harris was a frequent target. Harris was the principal advocate of bombing civilian targets, something many of the men bawked at no matter that the Germans had been raining bombs down on our civilians for more than four years.

As far as I could see, the Air Vice Marshall's policy didn't concern fighter pilots one way or the other. We shot down planes and that New Year's Eve we shot them down by the dozens as Goering launched his last major air attack.

My squadron was flying a new breed of aircraft, P-51's made in America and designed for work at high altitudes. Yes, the same make of aircraft that had shot me down on my return to England. The P-51 had an incredible range; we didn't just fly into Germany, take a couple of shots at a Messerschmitt and come home anymore; we hung around. Four kills during a single mission might still be an once-in-a-lifetime experience, but more pilots were recording them. I got three kills on two occasions including New Year's Eve.

The P-51 could do almost 450 miles per hour at 30,000 feet and could come down at still greater speed from 40,000 feet—surprise, surprise—to launch attacks.

The German pilots who survived were the ones who turned around and went home without firing a shot or who simply stayed out of the way, hoping the lame excuses they'd offer when they landed would not be contradicted by anyone still alive.

190

Chapter 9. The Tribunal

We had a couple of pilots in our Wing who had chosen to avoid combat, including one from my own squadron. In mid-May, mere days after the last mission I was to fly in the war, I found myself sitting on a military tribunal.

For the past month or so, we'd seldom encountered a German fighter plane as we escorted our bombers into action. Our casualties, and there had been casualties, had resulted in the main from fire from ground-based anti-aircraft emplacements. As a result, we knew at the start of a mission that not all of us would return. But this shouldn't and couldn't matter. A war was on and an airman's job was to do as ordered.

Casualties no longer fazed me. Nor did the fear of death. I even got used to writing condolence letters. Of course, I now had a Flying Sergeant whose job it was to fill in the blanks on the master letter of regret I'd prepared months before.

I knew the Flying Sergeant's name, Thompson. I had a Thompson, a Tompkins, and a Tyler in my squadron. I didn't really know any of them well, though I might have spent an hour or so in a bar listening to one or two of them rant of an evening. A squadron's leader's job is to appear to be listening. We had our own concerns, to be shared only with other squadron leaders.

The problem was I no longer had a Wilson or a Moyle on my wing. Just men who came and went, got promoted to lead their own squadrons or died before I really got to know them.

Our tribunal had five cases to consider. A wing commander presided and another squadron leader served on the bench along with me.

First up, an airman had gone AWOL. At one time, we might just have patted him on the head and told him to get back up in the air. But we were no longer desperate for fliers so off he went to spend a year in prison before his dishonorable discharge.

We had an airman accused of rape. He offered to marry the girl, but apparently she hadn't been his girl to begin with. He was given a dishonorable discharge and turned over to the civilian authorities.

We had Jawoski, a Pole who'd come to England with his dad as a teenager after Poland fell and had joined the RAF as soon as he was of age. He'd refused to take orders from a Flying Sergeant Baron whom Jawoski said was a bit too Jewish for his liking.

Pre-empting the possibility that my comrades on the bench might want to give him only a slap on the wrist, I suggested to Jawoski that the bit about Sergeant Baron being a Jew was only an excuse, that he was really trying to avoid combat. "But I volunteered!" he said.

"Then chickened out after your first mission."

Along with the other two remaining defendants, Jawoski was given three years in a military prison.

The mission these three men had dodged the bullet on had required us to take on the last of the German fleet including any German merchant vessels still active in the Baltic. The war ships had their anti-aircraft batteries going full time. Plus, the German's last remaining fighters, hundreds of them, came rising up to meet us. We shot down over 100 of their planes to just 21 of ours. Still, twenty-four good men went down in that attack for none of our damaged planes made it home.

A squadron of rocket-firing Hawker Typhoons took care of the German fleet. And that was that for German activity in the Baltic Sea. Still, hundreds of men on both sides would die because the German High Command would not admit for another month that they'd lost the war.

This mission had been a first for me. Never before had I been in a situation where the man covering my tail had flaked out deliberately, though I'd come back alive from more than one mission to learn that the man covering me had crashed, had burned alive, had been forced to land in enemy territory. If the presiding officer of the tribunal had proposed death by a firing squad for those three deserters, I would have voted for that, too.

Chapter 10. Letter from Angelique

In July 1945, I received a letter from Angelique. Talk about a blast from the past. Visions of people I hadn't thought about in years came rushing back to me. That girl I was going to marry—what was her name? And her uncle, Mr. Jacoby, what had become of him? Had Inspector Moyle been able to help him? I'd totally forgotten to ask.

Angelique's good-looking mother and sister were mentioned in the letter; Wilson would surely go for the former. According to Angelique, after years of neglect, some Whitehall bureaucrat, a Major something, had landed on Guernsey and immediately begun to reward the guilty and punish the innocent. Angelique's mother stood accused of war profiteering, though she had struggled to keep her family fed and clothed and her store going during the war and had been able to supply many of the Islanders with provisions when they would have starved otherwise. A German friend of Angelique's, that same tall blond aviator I'd seen her with just before I left I'll bet, was going to be charged with war crimes, while his commandant who'd ordered him to do the bombings of civilians was about to be released.

Neither charge was without substance. Angelique's mother had made a deal with a German Quartermaster I recalled, and wasn't that oh-so-innocent aviator Angelique's new boyfriend. I was surprised he'd lasted that long. Now that the memory of her was fresh in my mind, I realized I still wanted her for myself.

As for the German spies whom Rebecca's uncle—that was the girl's name, Rebecca!—had uncovered, they were being appointed to the new governing council. What could I do to help?

About the spies, I might be able to do a great deal. If that is, I could somehow make contact with the security personnel who'd interviewed me so many years ago. And, of course, Mr. Jacoby could personally testify against them. Mr. Jacoby! I'd forgotten all about the dear old man, but I immediately began to correct this. Abandoning a date with Dorothy—the shoe was on the other foot now!—I took a train into London, and then a bus to his former address. The house he'd once lived in was a bombed-out ruin, indeed the entire block had been leveled to the ground, but perhaps Jacoby, Jacobson himself had escaped. I called the Inspector who immediately began to stammer apologies. Yes, I had asked him to look into the old man's internment. He'd meant to do so immediately, but there'd been such a pressure of work. By the time he had looked into it, the old man had been taken away.

Issak Jacobson had died in confinement, a chest cold that had turned into pneumonia, the principal fashion in which so many of the elderly inside internment camps and out had died during the war. The Inspector was very sorry. Yes, he'd heard the news about Dorothy and I—she'd called him, and was very pleased for both our sakes. He hoped he might have the opportunity to act as our host sometime before we left for Quebec.

Though the sun was shining, a rare thing in London that time of the year when rain and sun alternate turns, it was a very gloomy me who presented himself at RCAF Group Leader Raffey's office later that day.

"Just started to look for you," he said. "I was afraid that you'd already been sent home."

"They've totally forgotten about me," I replied, after which we got down to business, albeit not quite in the manner I'd anticipated.

"You've spent some time in the Channel Islands, Guernsey, I believe, and you did that fly by, dropped some morale-building leaflets, kept the Nazis guessing." I agreed that I had. "They're having some problems. Chap the British sent out is way beyond his depth. The whole thing is political. I don't think the Brits anticipated the antipathy the Islanders feel toward them. Do you know there was even some talk at Number 10 a year or so ago of interning Mosley himself there. And now the French are wondering if the Islands might do better to become part of the Republic. Which is where we come in."

I remained silent; this seemed the best course, given that I'd no idea where the conversation with Raffey was leading.

"We're neither British, whom the Islanders feel, not without cause, abandoned them, nor French, with whom the residents of Guernsey feel little or no attachment despite their proximity to the French mainland.

"We're Canadian. Neutrals. Which is pretty much going to be Canada's foreign policy from now on.

"And you my dear Freygood are Mad Harry, a symbol of freedom in Guernsey, beloved by all. We're even going to give you a medal." I sneered; I could tell the Group Leader has his tongue in cheek, but still. "We're going to give you several medals, look good on your uniform. And we're going to promote you to Acting Wing Commander so you'll outrank the Major. Then we're going to send you to Guernsey."

I liked the last part for the chance it offered to see Angelique and her family but was skeptical about the rest of it. The Group Leader wasn't through.

"Don't suppose you know anything that might give us some leverage over the man White Hall sent there."

Actually, I did. The Wing Commander got on the phone to MI5 immediately and, in their own sweet time they got back to him and confirmed everything I'd said about the German agents who'd been planted in the Islands before the war. My assignment as military governor of Guernsey for an indefinite transitional period was on.

The practical implementation of my appointment encountered some immediate difficulties.

"I'll need staff." I said.

"Not easy to come by. We're demobilizing in a highly unorganized fashion and we're never quite sure where anybody is. Most of the men you worked with in the past are with the RAF, anyway."

But Group Leader Raffey didn't blow me off, not completely. "I've got a man on my staff who might serve as your adjutant, Flying Officer Emil Pluffe, but he's near bloody useless as he fancies himself a séparatiste."

"A what?" The term was new to me and to most people then.

"Wants independence for Quebec. Masters in their own house. Expects to airlift in all supplies from outside Canada, I imagine. Fought for our side reluctantly, but bravely. Just turned a little crazy after the second time he got shot down."

"I know how he feels."

Group Leader Raffey smiled; he'd been shot down a time or two himself.

"Any other choices?" I asked.

"Not a lot. I've got a Flying Sergeant who is quite capable. But he doesn't speak French."

I shook my head. Guernsey French and Quebec French were too far apart for this to make much difference.

"Real problem is his name. He's Jewish. Name of Silversteen or stein. A lot of guilt about the Jews on Guernsey, they may not want him."

"We'll call him Silver, then."

The Group Leader nodded. A huge grin appeared beneath his bushy mustache. "Silver and The Lone Ranger, very appropriate."

"And I'll take Pluffe and whoever's left from their flight crews if I can."

"You'd best speak to Pluffe first."

He spoke into the intercom and shortly a block of a man in Flying Officer's uniform, morning shave already eclipsed by the shadow of a beard, appeared in the doorway and gave us both a snappy salute.

"Colonel. Lieutenant-Colonel." The son of a bitch was determined to speak French and call us by the titles the Frenchies used.

"Parle Anglais, s'il vous plait." I demanded in a tone that suggested indefinite confinement as an alternative

"Yes, Sir, Squadron Leader."

"We depart for Guernsey the day after tomorrow. And I've been told I'm now Acting Wing Commander." I looked to Raffey for confirmation of both the date and the appointment and received it. "Have your men ready to depart with us and arrange for a transport."

"They had hoped to return home."

"Plus tarde."

Pluffe smiled, saluted, and left the room.

I met Silverstein. He'd been a bombardier and a good one during the war, highly organized. I suspected the Group Leader was very reluctant to part with him. Silverstein got on the phone immediately in an attempt to round up what remained in England of his former crew. We would need at least eight men, I imagined and, extremely prescient, wanted at least four with training in firearms. Hopefully, the Guernseyites would prove as cooperative with me as they had with the Germans.

I telephoned Dorothy who was not in, telephoned the Inspector to suggest we have that dinner as quickly as possible, and telephoned Mildred to ask if she might want to come up to London that evening. She appeared to have the train schedules memorized, for she immediately replied that she could still make the 5:35 that evening. "Would I book a hotel room for her and Mommy?"

I wasn't crazy about Mommy coming along, but she told me Mommy liked to go to sleep early.

It was not difficult to see where her plan was going, but 'audace, audace, audace,' as Napoleon would say. Mommy, of course, would want to know why Mildred had come back to their room so late. Mildred would cry and confess all. Urgent phone calls would result. And I would be completely unavailable, thoroughly lost within Air Command's bureaucracy.

Chapter 12. First Day on the Island

The loss to active service of the aircraft Pluffe acquired for our transport to Guernsey would have little impact on the war effort. The Airspeed As.10 Oxford Mk V had already been through many years of previous service as a trainer and air ambulance. Now it served to carry our group of ten uncomfortably, save for our pilot, a former member of Pluffe's crew, and me in the copilot's seat. Pluffe, our navigator, had a window to look out of.

The crowd that waited to greet us by the recently enlarged Guernsey air terminal was far too large a turnout for an arriving official who rated at best a one-half gun salute. I could see a great many faces I almost thought I knew along with a great many others that were completely unfamiliar. All looked as if they'd been on short rations too long; in most of the men's cases, a decent haircut wouldn't have gone unnoticed either.

I sent Flying Officer Pluffe on ahead with the men to hold the crowd back and then stepped down myself with Flying Sergeant Silver coming around the aircraft to follow close at my heels.

The crowd moved forward jockeying for position, mouths all opening and closing simultaneously like baby birds in want of worms, "Please . . . " "I need to . . ." "You need to . . . ." I'd already spotted my Angelique in this crowd of supplicants, a somewhat thinner Angelique with a face drawn with care. Somehow, she succeeded in slipping through the crowd as well as past the circle of Pluffe's men. The next moment she was in my arms and we were kissing, a somewhat longer kiss than I think either one of us had expected. A flood of memories served to hold us together despite the crowd of observers and what seemed to me to be a wave of disapproval emanating from them.

I kept my arm around her while I shook the hands of the half dozen men who were more or less at the front of the crowd. These latter included Andrew, Angelique's boss, his ultra-blond head a sure identifying marker.

I was gesturing for the rest of the crowd to get back so that I might make a speech when a group of men in the brown uniforms of the British Army came charging through. These in turn gave way to their leader, the notorious Major Coffin, a limp-wristed chap with a long thin mustache of some indeterminate off-mustard color.

We shook hands. "I'm not quite sure why you're here . . .," he began.

"You put two German spies on the State Council," I whispered in his shell-like ear. He grimaced and then, not eager to discuss this topic in public, suggested we return to his office in the State building for a tête-à-tête. Holding on to Angelique's hand and waving to Andrew to follow me, I followed the Major.

Pluffe scurried up. "Put a guard on the plane?" he suggested.

"One man, then follow along. "

The Major was not expecting the crowd that tried to push into his office. "I thought you and I could just talk alone."

"We'll need Andrew. And . . ." I turned to Andrew, "What happened to that military man that used to be on the council?"

"Sir Abraham. He's at home, a bit under the weather."

I indicated that I would try to see Sir Abraham tomorrow, going to his house if necessary if he were still too ill to come to see me.

Andrew looked surprised; apparently, consulting the local authorities was not something the Major often did.

"Where's the German officer in charge?" I asked the Major.

"In jail, of course; he'll be off to the War Crimes Tribunal shortly."

"Not hardly. Send your men to bring him here."

"I don't have to do what you tell me." The Major pointed to his collar.

I pointed to my Wing Commander insignia by way of reply. One of his men, an Army Captain by the look of it, volunteered to get the German. I think this was the moment at which the Major realized the sharks were now circling the water and he'd best worry about staying above the surface.

"Get Dr. Bosch at once, Captain Grimes," he ordered.

To my surprise, the kraut that hosted the garden party years ago stepped forward and tried to take my hand. "Douglas Moodly," he said, "Guernsey State Council."

"You are Kurt von Schneed, a German spy," I countered. Looking about, I saw the same kindly Bobby who'd talked with me or, rather, Mad Harry, years before, still in full uniform but, like most Islanders, a great deal thinner and more care ridden. "Take this man into custody," I ordered. "Put him in a cell by himself if you can."

"Yes, Sir," the policeman replied. And his face lit up. "Come on von Sauerkraut."

Andrew was at my side in an instant. "That might not be too good an idea. Sergeant Gaudien has been accused of being a collaborator."

"And is he?"

"Of course not. If he didn't do what the Germans asked him, they'd have shot him and got someone else."

Andrew's reply suggested a thousand other questions to which I needed immediate answers. As the Major continued to beckon me into his office and out of the hallway, I waved Andrew in as well and indicated that everyone else apart from the Major and I should stay outside.

The latter included a protesting Angelique. "Stay here on the bench," I ordered—I was getting kind of good at ordering people about, "But don't go away; I'll need you." The velvet fist in the iron glove.

Pluffe was already seated at the Major's desk. A jerk of my thumb signaled he ought wait outside with the others. "And send Flying Sergeant Silver in."

The Major offered a series of polite nothings while we waited for Dr. Bosch to be retrieved from his jail cell ending with, "I'd be happy to take you on a tour of German's gun emplacements if you like, or their underground shelters. Quite extensive."

"Not really my cup of tea. I mean the sort of thing you army boys get up to. Like to see the German's planes though. Those ones on the field?"

"Those are all pretty unflyable or so I understand. Anything that could fly was long since sent back to Germany or shot down by you boys while it was in the air."

"We did our best." After which, I turned my back on the man and began to leaf through the briefing papers Group Leader Raffey had provided one more time.

Dr. Bosch—the Germans titled their attorneys Doctor, was not in uniform as I expected. Apparently, he had served as the civilian liaison to the people of Guernsey. "Rather pleasant on the whole," Andrew said, though I could tell that Andrew was not all that pleased with him.

To me, Bosch was merely a funny little man who would be more at home behind a desk than issuing orders, but he did have a certain presence.

"How many rapes occurred under your command?" I began.

The question did not faze him. "I would have to get the exact numbers from my assistant. And in any event, that would fall under the province of the military."

I said nothing, but waited and let the seconds pass.

"Five. Three were from women who had failed to receive an expected payment. An enlisted man was found guilty and put in prison until *he* released him." Bosch indicated the Major. "The last was an officer. He was broken in rank and sent to the Eastern Front."

I looked to Andrew for confirmation. He nodded.

"Killings of civilians?"

"Mainly looters. Islanders who tried to steal weapons from us. We caught three spies. One of them and several persons who had hidden the man in their homes were sent to prison in France. One was shot. One was already ill and died of fever."

I looked to Andrew a second time. "I was one of the men sent to prison. Dr Bosch was kind enough to intercede on my behalf; I know I could have been shot."

So Andrew liked Bosch or at least was grateful to him, but I could tell that he despised the man at the same time.

The Major, quiet until that moment, spoke up. "I think you ought to know about Dr. Bosch and Andrew's wife."

I looked at Dr. Bosch who hardly seemed my notion of a Casanova. He clicked his heels. "We wish your permission to be married."

A soap opera. I would have to talk to Angelique to sort it all out. I made a mental note to have Silver set up an appointment with Mrs. Andrew and then turned back to Bosch.

"Married? Regardless if you are sent to prison or executed for your crimes?"

"Regardless."

I looked at Andrew. "She wishes to divorce me."

Enough of this farce. Back to Bosch.

"Are there any war criminals under your command?"

He merely looked helpless. The Major said, "You really need to send for the Inselkommndant General von Schmettow."

"Send for him then!" I was losing, no, I had lost patience. 'Wait, I'll see him here first thing tomorrow." Silver scribbled down the order while I turned back to Bosch.

"How many Jews were on the Island?"

"We were told none by the Island authorities."

"We really didn't think there were any," said Andrew.

"And how many are alive now?" Neither man replied.

"The Jewish problem was entirely the province of the SS." Bosch said. "My job was merely to pass on the directives to the Island authorities. Neither my men nor I willingly participated in the roundup of Jews from this Island."

"The Jewish problem?" I echoed.

"The problem that so obsessed our Führer that he wasted valuable time, materiels and men on it, materiels and men that might have gone into the proper fighting of the war."

"You think you might have won?"

"Yes. But too many mistakes were made. The obsession with the Jews was only one of them. We were not yet ready for war. And as for our fighting men, too many of them were trapped on this Island, on holiday, building fortifications for a landing that never came, when we might have been of service to our fatherland.

"Understand, Commander, that I am proud of the behavior of our men. We behaved honorably and fairly."

The Major was sneering openly. It took an effort not to join him.

I asked the Major where the SS officers were. He looked embarrassed. "Most are in custody, but I'm afraid the senior officer got away."

"Off the Island?"

"Impossible."

"Pluffe!" I hollered. When he appeared at the doorway, I stepped past him and asked

Angelique to bring me a map. "Pluffe, take some men and search the home of the man I just had arrested. Search the houses next to his, also. Detain everyone in all three households and bring them here."

This thinking on my feet ought to stop but I felt, perhaps unnecessarily, that I was running out of time. "Is that policeman back yet?" He was and I realized I no longer needed the map. I thanked Angelique anyway, who looked pleased to have been needed, and sent Police Sergeant Gaudien off with Pluffe. He was to show the Flying Officer where the spies' houses were and then set guards on them.

"Are there frogmen available?" I asked no one in particular.

"They should be leaving with me tomorrow morning," the Major answered.

"I need them now." The three frogmen were summoned; they'd been at work in the St. Peters Port harbor to see if the Germans had left any surprises. I gave their leader the map and showed him the three houses I wanted examined below water level.

"Can you bring submarines in there?" the pink-cheeked midshipman asked, "Doesn't show on the map." I assured him one could, that this was precisely how I'd gotten off the Island.

Both Andrew and Dr. Bosch looked amazed. "Then Bert could have escaped anytime?" Andrew asked.

"He'd have needed access to a radio transmitter, of course, and you did your best to round all those up and turn them over to the Nazis." Andrew's face crumpled as if something had given way inside. Apparently, he had given the order to do just that.

It was not my job to cheer him up. It was my job to restore justice to the Island and then—ah, that was the real question: After the war, then what? What would life hold for me? A full time air force career? Not hardly. Back to McGill and a physics degree? Perhaps.

Andrew and Dr. Bosch were sent away to their respective dwellings: Bosch's was a jail cell, Andrew, no less isolated, half of the house he still occupied with his wife. The Major was given his chance to brief me at last.

He confessed that he had acted, perhaps a bit hastily, on the information provided him by Moodly/von Schneed, but in all honesty if one looked at the letters he'd received from the Islanders, most anonymous, virtually every person on Guernsey appeared to be guilty of something.

More than a hundred of those letters were in the stack he handed me, 154 to be precise. "So and so had been sleeping with enemy soldiers, letting down our boys at the front." Someone else had concealed valuable rations, stolen articles from one of the unoccupied houses, betrayed hidden radios and curfew violators to the German authorities. Still, with some 20,000 survivors left on Guernsey, it appeared that more than a few hesitated to throw the first stone.

I had ambition then. I planned to sort it all out.

Pluffe returned after an hour or so with a significant haul that included von Schneed's wife, his butler (my old friend, the waiter), his maid, neighbor number one's wife, her maid and their gardener (another old friend I owed a good kicking).

Police Sergeant Gaudien, he was now an Inspector, I informed him, had left guards on the remaining two houses just in case either of the householders should turn up.

The piece de resistance, obtained after smashing in a few doors, was Colonel Max Reinhardt of the SS. Surely, the Colonel must have a cyanide capsule, why hadn't he taken it already? He soon made the answer to this question obvious. We British (Canadians too) were a weak effeminate race incapable of following through. Tant Pis. I lined the spies up in the hallway including the Colonel and told them they would all be shot in the morning.

The only interesting protest came from Neighbor Number One's maid, who assured me in very bad English that she was a communist and had been placed in the German's household to spy on the lot of them.

Pluffe also conveyed a message from the frogmen. An underwater submarine landing had been detected at House Number 2 that could readily be used to slip men and materiels in and out. The professed communist said this was precisely how Neighbors One and Two had escaped.

Bored by the lot, I sent them off under Gaudein's and several airmen's care to the Island jail.

Just as Silver was going off as well to see what he could rustle up in the way of dinner, Angelique appeared with a sumptuous repast. She laid the plates and cutlery out on the desk, then pulled up a chair beside mine. Apparently, it was also her intention to feed me, forkful by forkful. She was putting on the full court press and with Dorothy still back in England I planned to take complete advantage of it. After all, I'd survived the best a field hockey squad had to throw at me. "Find us a hotel room, will you lass."

"You can stay with us."

"A hotel room, I think. I'm supposed to be dispassionate."

A troubling aspect of the letters I'd leafed though that afternoon was how many of them mentioned Angelique and her family. Her sister Madeline was a jerrybag. Angelique herself was a jerrybag and a collaborator. (A jerrybag? What was a jerrybag?) Her mother was a collaborator and a war profiteer. Apparently more discreet than her children, the mother's affair with the German Quartermaster had never come out in the open.

After downing the last of the cider I'd been brought, I went over the next day's schedule with Silver. Appointment followed appointment; there would be no more long walks in the country for me. Leaving Silver and Pluffe to continue sorting the letters of indictment into categories, I went off to the hotel with Angelique for the rest and recreation I so richly deserved.

Chapter 13. Sorting Good from Evil

A pounding on the door woke me at a completely inopportune time. I unwrapped myself from Angelique—whatever her feelings might be for her German aviator, she seemed to have every bit as intense feelings for me, and trotted across the floor in bare feet to answer the knocks.

Silver's old tail gunner, a chap named Ross from Kitchner, Ontario, had been sent to alert me. "They're loading the prisoners down in the harbor." The who, what and how of that declaration were soon answered, partly en route and partly once we reached the quay.

Transport had been laid on for the German prisoners, most aimed for POW camps in England, plus some who would be off for trial in France as war criminals. A small number of the prisoners had already been loaded on board ship, but most still waited under guard on the pier. I immediately ordered a halt to the loading and asked that the prisoners already loaded be taken off again.

"Can't do that, Sir," said the ship's first officer. T'was the Royal Navy versus Air Command all over again. No, the commander of the vessel, a Lieutenant Commander and thus equal in rank to me, informed me it was not that at all, it was really a question of the wishes of the Royal Navy versus those of the Colonial Forces. An airplane passed overhead at that moment, a Blenheim Trainer. Who'd have believed they were still in existence.

While the Commander, I, and the Major who joined us shortly all argued, the plane landed, its pilot exited and asked for transportation to the State House.

The Commander's position was that he would leave within the hour whether all the prisoners were on board or no. I asked him if he would at least take the Major then as well, but he failed to see the humor in it. Meanwhile, the pilot of the recently landed aircraft had reached the State House, asked for me, and been directed down to the harbor by a number of townsmen who were headed in that direction.

My airmen had lined up, rifles at the ready, squared off against an equally determined group of squids from her Majesty's Navy, when the pilot finally reached us.

"I'll be dammed. Roughy!" said the pleased Lieutenant Commander.

"Pumpkin," responded Flight Lieutenant Wilson newly arrived from Spain via Gibraltar, Plymouth, and London.

A naval Lieutenant thought of laughing, thought better of it, and wiped all traces of a smile from his face.

"Wing Commander Freygood," Roughy (Roughy?) said, "Looks as if you've had an awfully good war." A great many handshakes, shoulder slapping, and, yes, hugs followed all around.

"You know this mad man?" the Commander asked Wilson.

"Mad Harry? Known him for years. Taught him to fly, watched him go down over France, helped him through a nasty business in the Alps, and let him lead me back to the fight. Would have succeeded too, but for a clogged fuel line."

The Commander then supposed he could have the prisoners unloaded after all and might even wait around for a bit while I sorted things out, Wilson (aka Roughy) at my side.

"Separate the officers and the men," was my first order concerning the German prisoners and while it was being carried out, I asked Wilson about the Blenheim. Everything else by way of available aircraft had a military function and was either in or on its way to the Far East. In fact, Wilson himself was headed in that direction as soon as he'd had a chance to say hello to me.

I began with the larger group of German enlisted and noncoms. "Do any of you wish to remain on the Island?" Twenty-four men stepped forward. The reason for staying in each case was the same; they were engaged to local women. I explained that they would be permitted to stay, subject to approval from the local authorities.

"Now, are there any officers or members of the SS in this group?"

Most of the men looked puzzled, but one said that, yes, one of the men in an enlisted man's uniform was an officer.

I had the man fetched out and informed him and the group around us that he would be shot the next morning as a spy. "Anyone else who is not in the correct uniform may choose to leave at this moment without penalty." There were no takers. A voice lost within the crowd of German prisoners said, "He's not," and a man was shoved to the ground.

Looking about me, I saw that the former Inselkommndant Lt. General Rudolph Graf von Schmettow was on hand as I'd requested the previous day. "Perhaps, the Lt. General would be kind enough to tell me if the individual in question is a member of the SS."

The Lt. General declined, citing the Geneva Convention. I asked then if it were common for German officers to remove their insignia when capture was imminent. Perhaps it was the accompanying smile of contempt that did it for the Lt. General for he immediately confirmed that the man was Gestapo and in improper uniform. Shortly afterward, four members either of the SS or the German officers' corps were separated from the group of enlisted and marched off. I planned to shoot them the next morning with the rest of the spies.

Wilson said he was impressed.

I asked the Major if he had identified any of the remaining enlisted men as war criminals and he said he wasn't sure. Andrew was summoned and, I was pleased to see, brought Sir Abraham with him stumping along on a cane.

"We've met before?" Sir Abraham asked puzzled. Andrew assured him that he had, "But this officer had more hair."

"Ah. Mad Harry."

I asked if the pair could identify any of the German soldiers as war criminals, that is, men there had been complaints about. Curiously, the majority of complaints had arisen near the end of the war, when the German soldiers had started competing with the Islanders for the small amount of food remaining. Andrew and Sir Abraham stood by the gangway as the men filed past, and occasionally one soldier or another would be pointed out and then pulled aside by the Major's men. As soon as we could get the necessary paper work together, off the offenders would go to France for trial.

Which left the upper rank German officers to be dealt with. The lower echelon officers, Leutnants, Oberleutnants, Untersturmfuhers, and Obersturmfuhers were given essentially the same choices as the enlisted men. Again, I asked if there were any who wanted to stay on the Island. Two men, including Angelique's pilot, requested permission to stay. I again said fine, subject to approval from the local authorities.

The other officers were sent back to confinement to be dealt with another day. Perhaps, I'd just send the lot to France and let the War Crimes tribunal sort it out.

Andrew's soon-to-be-ex-wife, my nine a.m. appointment ,was waiting for me back at the office. She was a short blond woman, neither slim nor stout; I'd term her correctly dressed, rather than "smart" or elegant, something rather difficult to accomplish when one's only really new clothes would have to have been purchased four or five years ago before the war.

I apologized for the delay, but she said she hadn't really been waiting but had come down to the harbor with many of the other islanders to view the spectacle. "I saw you separating the sheep from the goats."

"And did I do a good job?"

"Rather an outstanding one for someone so new to the Island, though they tell me you were here before. I've got to confess I was surprised to find that the Moodlys and the Turners were really German spies. I'd never suspected. Then again, if I may plead my own case, I never really liked them either. They thought too much of themselves."

"And Dr. Bosch?" I thought it about time we got into more serious business.

"His is a different sort of problem. He's strong in contrast to my husband, though both are fair men in their dealings with others, extremely fair, but Franz is a bit of snob.

"A Baron so-and-so holds, held an equivalent position in the German civil administration on Jersey and let Baron say this or Baron say that and Franz will have to imitate him."

"You say he's a fair man."

"Franz is not a Nazi, he's too much of a snob for that, but he does believe that the German nobility is superior to all others, that Prussians are superior to Bavarians, Austrians, and any other type of German, and that Germans are superior to everyone else."

"And the inferior races are to be eliminated."

"No! He believes that they are to be ruled over. He read every one of the eight stupid Nazi decrees concerning the Jews to Andrew, read them aloud because it was his duty, and my stupid soon-to-be ex husband decided that he must enforce them.

"'Ignore the decrees,' I would shout at him. ' Dr. Bosch doesn't care!' But not Andrew, he had the integrity of all the Islanders to protect. 'If we do this, then we have no integrity' I would shout, but he would not listen."

"You wish to marry Dr. Bosch?"

"I do."

"He may be declared a war criminal."

"Not by you, I hope, not with your jerrybag fiancée."

Wilson who'd been sitting by, more or less impassive till then, suddenly looked up startled. I was startled, too. What was a jerrybag?

"Who's your friend?" she asked as if she had a perfect right to ask me all the questions she wished.

"Flight Lieutenant Wilson, a well-decorated war hero."

"I thank you Flight Lieutenant for coming to our Island's rescue." Was she serious? Was she sarcastic? With the absolute control she had over both tone and facial expression one simply couldn't tell.

After she left, Wilson told me that he admired her, "even though," he added with a grin, "She obviously is a jerrybag."

There was that term again. What was a jerrybag? I wasn't going to give Wilson the satisfaction of asking.

I brought Wilson with me that night to dinner with Angelique's family. But first, I had him help me make a phone call.

"Would you by any chance know someone, a Pumpkin, a Rutabaga, or some other vegetable in the Provost's office?"

He allowed that he might but he wasn't sure what a rutabaga was. I explained that it was a type of turnip used in Cornish pasties before I realized that his might not have been a serious question.

We got Darwin on the line at last—"Darwin?," a primitive beast. "And what does

Roughy stand for?" A teacher who was a bit of a brown noser had once referred to Wilson as a "mere ruffian."

"I thought it meant you were a terror at Rugby or something."

"That, too."

I asked Darwin if a German who'd landed on Guernsey before the war but used a fake British passport in the process would be considered a spy. Very definitely. And his household esquires, also on fake passports? Spies as well. And could spies be shot without trial? If under military jurisdiction.

Better and better. I went on to inquire about officers posing as enlisted men and Gestapo in fake uniforms or out of uniform entirely. All were spies, not covered under the Geneva Convention. I thanked Darwin and off Wilson and I went to dine.

Dinner offered several surprises.

The clothes Angelique and her mother wore were not at all typical of those worn by the rest of the women of Guernsey, some of whom had been darning and mending the same two or three dresses since the start of the occupation. Just how had Angelique and her mother succeeded in acquiring the latest Paris styles, along with lipstick and stockings?

Wilson, judging by his past performance, ought to have been putting the make on Angelique's mother; instead, he spent the evening listening intently to Angelique's younger sister Madeline as she prattled on about one topic after the other.

In sharp contrast to her elders, Madeline was dressed like the schoolgirl she'd been four years earlier. A bit dowdy and a bit out of place; she was older now and ought dress accordingly, I thought. I didn't realize then that she was trying to live down her totally undeserved reputation as a girl who slept with German soldiers. A Jerrybag! At last I understood the term. Her reputation had begun the night before Mad Harry left the Island when she'd flirted with the German soldiers guarding the wharf to distract them from their duties while her sister pilfered the equipment I needed.

As I later confided to Wilson, aside from Madeline's prattle, the Martel family's dinner time conversation made me nervous. It appeared to concern Angelique's forthcoming marriage—to me! All right, it wasn't that surprising. I had spent the previous night with Angelique in my arms and planned to do so again after supper. But marriage?

'You've been in fear of marriage before," Wilson observed, "Marie in France, Giselle in Switzerland. Why should you be so panicked about it now? And for that matter, aren't you engaged to some girl back in England, Moyle's former fiancée? What happened to Moyle by the way?"

The very question I'd been avoiding. But I took the time to explain how Moyle's Spad XIII and mine had both taken us to our desired destinations, unlike Wilson's Nieuport. Then the bastard Free French had shot Moyle down when he didn't respond on his non-existent radio.

Wilson had landed safely on a beach in Northern Spain, albeit on fumes. There, the widow of a Spanish Republican soldier had taken him in. After a week or so, he had come back to the beach to make the necessary repairs, hoping to be on his way south again, only to find his plane had been taken away. His explanation for the further delay in returning was that he had wanted to rest for a while, to let his heart slow down.

"You were . . . ?"

"Afraid. Sure. Just because I'm not one of you Mediterranean types who display every emotion, doesn't mean I don't have those feelings.

"Don't ever play poker by the way, Freygood, or Hearts. No way will you be able to 'shoot the moon.'"

205

He was way off base there. I do play Hearts and I've shot the moon successfully a half dozen times, well, twice anyway.

"The entire three months we were in Yssingeaux, I wondered when, not if, any of those bozos would give us away. Had they told their girlfriends, their wives, their second cousin once removed? Is that car we hear down the road coming for us? Will it be the Milice or the Gestapo?

"It drove me crazy trying to make sure those old planes stayed undercover while we worked on them. I'd straighten up, hit a tree branch, and get a shovelful of snow down my collar. Maybe the Germans flying overhead would make out the silhouettes of the planes beneath the trees. Maybe they wouldn't.

"That last flight over France . . . I know you're the world's premier mechanic, Freygood, but I'd of given my left testicle to have that Nieuport gone over by my regular pit crew.

"We hadn't even made it to the Spanish border, when I could tell I was out of fuel. Never mind what the gauge said. None of the gauges were accurate. Was the gas tank leaking? Or was it the fuel line? Did it get clogged by some crap that was already in the tank?"

"We could have used a test flight," I acknowledged.

Wilson smiled. At least I think he smiled, he may have grimaced instead.

"Or the gasoline was bad," we said together. This time I was sure he smiled.

"The other reason I laid low in Spain for a month or two, was that for the first time in months, I was warm. Do you have any idea how cold it is at 12,000 feet in an open biplane?

"You slept out in the barn those three months, tucked away in straw, warm as, what did you say, a sausage roll?"

A hotdog in a bun, I thought, but let it go.

"While I slept in a house where they let the fire burn down at night. By morning my ass was an icicle."

"Hey, you had a heater in bed with you."

"And I stayed snuggled next to her. That still left my ass out in the cold.

"Whether I was on the ground or in the air, I froze as the wind went whistling through my pants. The entire time we were in France, I was warm for exactly six hours, when we stole those coats from the Gestapo. Warm, you cannot believe it."

"Then what happened?" I asked, trying to bring him up quickly to the present day.

"I thought I ought to get back into the war, tried to reach Gibraltar, and got turned in to the Spanish authorities. Found our later they were the ones who'd taken the plane. They'd have ignored me indefinitely if I'd just stayed where I was and kept my mouth shut."

Chapter 14. The Courtship of Peter

Some days seem longer than others. Perhaps, it's because one has nothing to do that day, and wakes in a jaded frame of mind knowing that one will be trapped from morning to night with houseguests one really doesn't care for. Or worse, the guests and the entertainment they provide are gone, the weather is bad, and if you don't make up a series of chores, you don't know how you'll make it through the day.

At my age, a nap can be a good way to kill time, though sometimes those naps can be scary because I start remembering.

The worst days are those where you know in advance how long the day is going to be, how much you need to do, how many miles you'll need to walk before you can rest again. At Dunkirk and during the Battle of Britain, mission followed mission, and one day ran into the next, indistinguishable from the days before and after.

But this day in Guernsey would be the longest of all. Shoot spies in morning and arrange for burial. Sort and read mail, more than a hundred letters, hold meetings with Andrew, Sir Abraham, and the Major now almost desperate to leave the Island, leave time for at least three unplanned emergencies, have dinner with the Martel's while Angelique and her mother remain in unflagging pursuit of sex and marriage, and so on and so on.

Angelique had spent the previous night with me, though I could tell the moment I'd announced that her pilot would remain on the Island pending a decision by the local authorities that she also felt strongly about him. I had the impression that Angelique kept sex and love in two different compartments. Maybe she was a little like me.

When we woke together that morning, we did not have sex. The sheer pressure of the work that lay ahead of me that day had me intimidated.

First, the spies.

Bertrand Russell once wrote that you ought never tell a child, "I'll kill you," for either you must follow through or lose that child's respect. Having obtained the full if informal backing of the Provost's office in London, I had the spies, 12 in number lined up the next morning along the harbor front, the largest open area in Guernsey, and a mixture of airman and army personnel lined up with rifles facing them. Having spread the word that the Islanders were welcome to bring wagons to bear the spies' corpses away and shovels to bury them, we had a surprisingly large turnout.

Andrew, of course, urged me to reconsider, and even Silver wondered if this course of action would really be advisable. "You want to kiss and make up to the Nazis, Silverstein," I whispered in his ear, after which he chose to lead the firing squad into position.

The professed communist was still back in her jail cell, von Schneed had already killed himself with a cyanide capsule, but the officers and Gestapo who had posed as enlisted men, SS Colonel Reinhardt, and von Schneed's remaining attendants were all there.

The shots rang out on my command; ten of the prisoners crumpled to the ground. I stepped forward with my pistol to finish off the remaining two. But before I could do so, one of the gunners fired again and killed his woman. He was ticked off properly and immediately by Pluffe, his ranking officer, for violating protocol. Both Flying Officer Pluffe and Army Captain Klein then observed that it was their task and not mine to finish off the injured officer, that God-dammed Gestapo Colonel.

I flipped a coin and Captain Klein had the pleasure. After which the townsmen were invited to take the bodies away. This led to a problem that Inspector Guadien, thankfully, leaped into the breach to solve. Some of the men though the bodies ought simply be dumped in the harbor. Others felt they deserved burial, albeit in unmarked graves. The decision was made to bury the women and any German men who had actually attended local services or currently wore crosses about their necks. The rest were dumped in the sea along with the offal from that morning's catch.

Aside from cries of "now what about the jerrybags!" it appeared that almost everyone in town was satisfied.

The next thing on my agenda was a sit-down discussion with Sir Abraham in my office. He still looked a bit ashen; the effect of his recent illness on top of the long years of occupation had been hard on him, as it had on all of the elderly. He'd seemed a bit shaky when we stood together outside earlier that morning; I hoped he would last somewhat longer sitting down inside. I needed him.

"The principal concerns of the islanders appear to be jerrybags, looters, informers, and war profiteers." I waved a handful of the letters at him.

Sir Abraham's immediate and rather sensible response was that, "We also need to concern ourselves with jobs, and a steady food supply." I liked the sound of that 'we.' "As for jerrybags, I'd rather hoped we could forgive and forget. Looters? We've already punished the ones we caught. Collaborators? Punishment will depend on the extent of their collaboration. Some betrayals are unforgivable. As for war profiteers, I'm afraid your prospective mother-in-law is near the top of the list. And, uh, absent other redeeming qualities . . . .." He let his voice trail off without finishing the sentence.

"Perhaps, just a fine on excessive profits." I suggested.

"That may not quite cover it. But, uh, we could restrict the exchange of Reichmarks." A policy that would later be implemented, then reneged on after my departure.

I decided to sound Sir Abraham out on my plans for addressing the various topics via citizen committees or some sort of Grand Jury.

"Sounds a bit like Robespierre's 'Comite de salut public.'"

I grinned. The thought had crossed my mind. "A couple of questions about this morning. The woman in the crowd who fainted?"

"Von Schneed's mistress."

"He had a mistress and a wife, was allowed to keep his home, ate well throughout the occupation and never once did you suspect he was a German?"

Sir Abraham did not meet my eye. "Well, he did have a number of German officials sharing his home. We all did. Those of us with sufficiently large houses."

"One more question. Do you remember a well-dressed man with a supercilious grin who seemed to sneer at everything I said?"

"Von Djin? I hadn't thought you'd noticed him."

"We pilots, the ones who are still living, have no choice but to notice everything. The plane coming at you from just outside your field of vision is the one that will shoot you down. My big fear, and I hope I'm not showing it, is of all these people being so close to me at once. I rely on my men to hold them back just as I did in the air, although everything here is on a much smaller scale, crammed into a village square instead of spread out across the sky."

Sir Abraham reached for his pipe, looked at it hungrily, then tucked it away. "Pity. Now there's tobacco available and I'm still not allowed to smoke it.

"The man who interests you, Von Djin is one of ours, a newcomer by some standards. He's only been on Guernsey twenty years, my family's been here four hundred. A Dutchman, not a German, he was in construction before the war, and he kept on working during the war, working for the Germans, their Organisation Todt, supervising the construction of all these damned fortifications. He's still wealthy, if wealth can be measured in Reichmarks."

"A collaborator."

"Yes and no. A lot of people on this island survived because of the work he gave them. Because of this he knows there is no way you can touch him. You notice he didn't protest the killings this morning. For him the Germans were just another customer."

A knock on the door announced the arrival of Canon Robbins, a local C of E cleric whom I recalled looking on at that morning's activities. He hated to interrupt; perhaps I was busy? Yes, I was busy, but as long as he was there, what were his thoughts?

His thoughts, not unexpectedly, were of mercy tempered with long terms of imprisonment for those who'd informed on their neighbors, particularly those who'd informed on their neighbor's radio which he and his wife had been wont to listen to in the evening before bed.

I thanked him. He thanked me. Sir Abraham had taken out his pipe again. He packed it with tobacco this time, but he only looked at it for a bit, and then put it away.

"But the real reason I've come," the Canon said, "is to fix a time for the wedding rehearsal." Even Flying Sergeant Silver who'd more or less gone to sleep at his desk perked up his ears at that remark.

I came awake as well; I just wasn't ready for that question. "Uh, tomorrow, day after, later this week?"

The topic of marriage came up again at dinner at the Martel's that evening. An unexpected guest at the table was a four-year old boy with deep dark brown eyes that leaped out at you from under long dark eyelashes. Add in his curls of dark brown hair and you had the image of me at the same age holding on to my own grandfather's hand in a sepia and white photograph. The boy prattled on incessantly, which I'd been told I was prone to do at that age, also. I recalled once having been offered and failing to receive a penny for five minutes of silence from a guest at a party my parents were holding.

The full-court press was still on by the Martels, with much talk of flowers and gowns and Canon Robbins whom I'd met earlier that day. Wilson was no help whatever. He seemed much taken with the child, all right, my child, and he and Madeline both remarked on how important children could be in a relationship.

After supper, Angelique said she had some business to take care of but would be back almost immediately. Marcie, Angelique's mother said that with Angelique gone perhaps then she and I might have a chat, and without being asked Madeline said that she and Wilson would be happy to entertain young Phillip whilst we chatted.

Marcie ushered me into her inner sanctum, a bedroom decorated with dozens of knickknacks, wall hangings, and antique furniture. Clearly, not all the excess profits from her wartime activities would show up on her books.

Marci had been an attractive woman five years before and she was attractive still, taller than Angelique and with a fuller bust characterized by the slight slope down to the nipple, all of which gradually went on display while she sat at her dressing table before the mirror and unbuttoned her white lace blouse. Innocent enough had I been able to tear myself away from her reflection.

She asked me if I would fetch two hangers for her from her closet. She removed and hung up her blouse on one, then slipped off her skirt and hung it on the other, after which she slipped past my wood-like figure and hung both articles of clothing in her closet.

She came back to me then, put both hands on my shoulders and looked me full in the eye while she held me there in front of her—she was a tall woman. "I remember you telling me I looked attractive that day we first met, and I thought, this crazy man thinks I look attractive. My husband had been away for almost a year then; we didn't know he'd already died in combat. For the first time in months, I thought, I'm a woman, not just some kind of machine to keep the family going. In a way, you know, you were responsible, for my affair with the Quartermaster."

She turned—God knows I hadn't moved—so her back was to me and asked me to unsnap her bra. When she turned once more I was completely lost.

Later, on comparing the encounter with my experiences in occupied France, I found myself agreeing with Baron von Aufsess, the Head of Civil Affairs in the Feldkommandantur for Jersey, who wrote, "The Englishwoman is astoundingly simple, effortless and swift in her lovemaking. While the French woman involves herself totally in the game, which she likes to be conducted along intellectual lines, for the Englishwoman it is a surprisingly straightforward physical matter."

Afterward, Marcie smoked a cigarette she'd procured from who knows where and pointed out that one of the advantages of marrying her daughter would be that I would have access to her whenever I liked. Clearly, she hoped for the wedding to proceed as scheduled. Angelique's marriage to the German aviator would tarnish the family name forever. A marriage to me would spell redemption, as well as allowing the mother, given my current position as both judge and jury on the Island, to keep all the profits she'd accumulated during the war.

I remember I stammered something foolish in reply like, "what if Angelique found out?" and Marcie told me not to worry, she'd get me started up again before I went back to the hotel.

I also recall asking "what about the child?" and that instead of giving me the reply I wanted, Marcie said, "I almost forgot. Can you come back in the morning? We've got to talk her out." All of which meant nothing to me then, nothing whatever.

Chapter 15. The Girl in the Basement

In late 1942, when Rebecca was already preoccupied with raising our first child, the late Gestapo Colonel Reinhardt forced her to have sex with him, the alternative being immediate deportation to a concentration camp. Rebecca and I never actually discussed this directly, then or later.

When he left, she fled to the Martels who hid her in the cellar of their store for several weeks. Their home was searched several times, the Colonel heading up the search party, but her hiding place remained undiscovered.

Finally, the Martels were able to transfer her to one of the abandoned homes in the far reaches of the island, where she and the child could at least come outside occasionally when they were sure no one else was in the neighborhood.

Inevitably, she was betrayed, by a woman eager for a favor from the Germans of a job for her husband. Fortunately, the Martels and their friends were able to move Rebecca and Phillip to yet a third location in time.

When the ship from England arrived finally bringing news of the war's end, Marcie and Angelique went out to retrieve the two of them, but it took almost a month before Rebecca was willing to budge. Even then, on spotting a German uniform as they entered the town, really just a stream of marching men on their way to their temporary prison, she had insisted on going into the cellar and had yet to be coaxed forth.

It took only a few seconds after I'd entered the cellar in full uniform for her to burst from hiding, throw her arms about me and begin to cry.

I think at that moment Marci came to a full conscious realization of what she and I had known all along: I was not going to marry Angelique; I would marry the woman who clung to me so fiercely and to whom I clung in return.

"She's Jewish, you know," said Marcie, and lit a cigarette, something I had only seen her do once before. "Then, you must be Jewish, too.

"I'll be damned. Jewish men are incredibly sexy." A remark that Rebecca may or may not have overheard; she was still gripping me in a fierce hug.

"We'll never forget what you've done for us," I said to Marcie, "Never."

"Thank you." For she knew then, I never would abandon the family that had helped my Rebecca, and the letters that accused her and her family—"profiteer," "jerrybag," would be ignored.

When Rebecca and I emerged shortly thereafter from the Martel's, and I moved her and my son into my hotel room, the citizens of Guernsey must have realized then that there would be retribution for acts of betrayal and that significant changes were about to take place.

You could see it in their glances and sometimes in their conversations.

The next time we met, Sir Abraham said, "She's Jewish you know. But then you must have known that and you must be ..." He paused reflecting. "I almost said, 'You must be Jewish, too,' as if I believed that a Jew would somehow look and act different from the rest of us. Leave it to the Nazis to contaminate us all with their lies."

"I hadn't intended to ... we didn't think there were any," said Andrew referring to the Jews who'd lived on Guernsey as he once again stammered an apology.

"But there were, there were," Rebecca said.

Thirty-five Jews had been in residence on Guernsey when the order from England to evacuate came. Some had been there for generations. Some, like Rebecca's uncle had arrived during the 1930's, refugees from Nazi persecution. And some like Rebecca herself and an English girl who had come to learn animal husbandry in preparation for a further migration to Palestine were relatively recent arrivals.

Less than a dozen Jews were left when the Germans arrived, either having failed to heed the warnings or having failed to understand them given the ambiguous nature in which Andrew and his colleagues on the Governing Council chose to pass them on to the Islanders. Perhaps, like the would-be-Zionist, as well as Andrew and most of the Islanders, they'd not really believed that England would abandon them.

Rebecca was the only one remaining, and perhaps the only one alive. The others had been taken away. My future wife owed her life to a very few brave individuals. I would never forget or cease to honor the Martels; I would never forget the others if I could find them.

I would stick to my plan. First, would come public meetings to determine what crimes were to be punished. Next, the yet-to-be-formed *Comité de salut public* would determine what the punishments would be. Last, would come the trials.

And, in parallel we would have public hearings on which if any of the POW's including Angelique's boyfriend would be permitted to stay.

Our first public meeting, held at Cobo, a location on the island remote from St Peter Port went relatively smoothly. At issue was whether women who had consorted with German soldiers, the so-called "jerrybags," should be subject to prosecution as collaborators.

We'd promised that everyone would be allowed three minutes to express his or her views, but I didn't exactly stick to my promise. The instant the name of some offending jerrybag came up, I would interrupt to let the speaker know we weren't trying individuals, we merely wanted to know if such actions should be punished. This went far to eliminating cases in which two (or more) women had consorted with the same man. While there were a few older women who continued to insist on punishment, the majority held for live and let live.

One woman wouldn't let it alone. "What about the troop carriers?" she demanded. I looked around me, puzzled. An airman whispered to the man next to him who, beckoned forward by Flying Officer Pluffe, whispered to Pluffe who whispered to me.

Apparently she was referring to girls who had given birth to or were carrying German soldiers' babies. "Would you have their fathers take them with them to the prison camps." I replied.

"As if they knew who the fathers were."

Laughter broke out , at my expense, so I quickly changed the subject. "Are there any other concerns you'd like me to deal with?"

We heard the familiar refrains, looters, stolen property (by Germans, escaped slave laborers, and fellow islanders), informers, collaborators, and missing children. I wasn't quite sure I understood this last.

A meeting in St Peter Port itself yielded similar results and I began to feel pretty confident that we were getting things under control. The subject of "troop carriers" came up again; this time from the opposite point of view. An indignant grandmother wanted to know how a German soldier would be able to support his child if he was sent to a POW camp.

After the meeting as always, a few individuals wanted to continue the discussion on a one-to-one basis with me. While Pluffe and Silver handled the initial contacts, I noticed one middle-aged man hanging about toward the back of the crowd whose face I thought I recognized. He seemed reluctant to push himself forward. Probably we would not have met at all that evening had his wife not been there behind him to more or less urge him on.

I thought I recognized her also, so I resolved their domestic dilemma by stepping forward to greet them. "I'm sorry," I said as he took my outstretched hand, "I recognize your face, but I've forgotten your name."

"He's Robert Le Tournelle," the woman said and he echoed his name at the same time she told me, "And I'm Estelle."

"I'm afraid . . ." I began.

"You stayed with us when you first got to the Island."

"You were totally out of it," Le Tournelle added.

We had a small crowd gathered around us now and when Le Tournelle said, "I need your help." I immediately replied, "You've got it." This was the man who had pulled me out of the water when I'd crashed after Dunkirk; she was the woman who'd seen that I was fed and had clothes to wear.

"We're trying to find our children."

I looked blank.

"We got separated from them on the boats going to England. They took all the children on one of the boats; we got sent home."

"Where are they now?" I asked, and this it seems was the question. Other people, residents mainly of the farms deep in the Island's interior pressed forward with the same question. They'd been separated from their kids during the evacuation and now they wanted them back.

This delay in returning the children made no sense to me. Why hadn't the British authorities already done so? "I'll look into it," I said, though I knew as I said it that this was a pretty lame thing to say. "I will phone London tomorrow. And I'll talk to the Bailiff and Sir Abraham. I'll do everything I can to get your children returned to you."

Which would prove to be a promise easier to make than to keep.

213

Chapter 16. Phone Call from England

I met that day with Victor Carey, the Bailiff of Guernsey during the occupation, Andrew, Angelique (who appeared capable of remembering details the others weren't), and Sir Abraham.

The answers I received were far from satisfying. Carey said he'd explored the topic of the missing children with the Major. "That was it? You explored! Found a sacred white elephant with an immense ruby on its forehead did you? You'll call London today and demand satisfaction."

Carey looked back at me coolly.

"Or you'll go to France in chains as a War Criminal to be tried with the other Germans."

They made calls to London afterward; of course they did. It was then that Group Leader Raffey telephoned.

"You executed a dozen men!" Group Leader Raffey's voice leaped out of the telephone and filled the room.

"Yes, Sir."

"Including a Walter Mooley?"

"His real name was Kurt Von Schneed. You remember the man MI5 told us about."

"And his wife Millicent?"

"Trudy Von Schneed. She also was using a fake British passport. Their two servants hadn't bothered to use fake names, but their passports weren't real either."

Raffey didn't say anything for several moments and I could tell he was writing all this down.

"And the other men?"

"Out of uniform. Officers trying to pass as enlisted men. A Gestapo Colonel in civilian clothes."

"You don't think the shootings were a bit harsh?"

"After the years I spent underground in France?"

Again there was a pause. The anger was gone from the Group Leader's voice now and replaced by a certain weariness. "Expect to do any more shootings?"

"I think we have the Islanders' attention now. And they've got someone different to blame than those they've been blaming up till now."

"Who were?"

"Themselves and the Brits."

That evening's public meeting did not go at all well. We had a new topic, "punishment for collaborators," and it had gotten a bit out of hand.

First of all, more people wanted to get into the discussion than we could fit into the hall. The founders of the State of Guernsey had not envisioned that the general public rather than an elect few might wish a voice in government. The result was that the State Building in St Peter Port did not contain a meeting room suitable for large public gatherings. We were forced to meet in the nearby Anglican Church and that, too, had a limited capacity.

There were also a number of individuals who did not believe in the first-come, first-served equalitarian principle my men at the door had been directed to permit entrance by.

One individual, a member of the former Governing Council, pushed himself and his wife toward the front of the queue where he quickly got into an altercation with the men standing there. Inspector Gaudien tried to moderate, was told to "eff off," put the distinguished former member in a restraining hold and started to lead him out of the building.

"I was going to let him go on the steps, tell him to try another day."

But Mrs. Big-Wig was so grossly offended by the policeman's actions that she began to pound him with her fists. Within seconds, both Mr. and Mrs. Big-Wig had been led off to the jail.

The good news was that all this took place outside the hall out of earshot and I only found out about it after the meeting was over.

The question the meeting itself need consider was, "what was collaboration and how should it be punished?"

One older woman persisted in wanting to put fraternizing with the enemy in this classification and she was quickly shouted down.

I produced a list Dr. Bosch kindly had provided and said I had the names of those who had betrayed for money.

"What about after torture?" came a voice from the crowd, and I repeated that all I was talking about were those who'd betrayed their fellow islanders for a few pieces of silver.

"What about those of us who worked on the airfield?" came the question.

The expansion and improvement of the airfield had kept a lot of Guernsey men employed, put money in their pockets, and food on the table for them and their families. The airfield had provided employment when there were no other jobs to be had. It all made sense to me. But Wilson completely lost it. He'd been sitting in one of the side pews with Angelique's sister Madeline whom, one couldn't help noticing, appeared to be his now constant companion. All of a sudden Wilson was on his feet in full uniform, his medals, that he usually kept well hidden, rattling as he stood up.

"You bastards put the bombers in the air which attacked us night after night. The guns that shot at Wing Commander Freygood and I came from the planes you launched. You ought to be bloody ashamed. You came dammed close to losing us the war."

Canon Russell who shared the podium with Sir Abraham and I cringed at the language.

"And where were you when we needed you?" came shouts from the audience. "The war ended a year ago and it took you this long to get here?"

"We bloody starved; we're still starving. Tell me how to feed my kids." This last from a woman.

"What took you so long, Wing Commander?"

I took this to be a rhetorical question. Wilson was on his feet shouting, "He was in occupied France," but no one heard him.

I started to cry. Bloody stupid, uh. I'd let my wife-to-be stay here prey to the Nazis while I went about my business.

Someone in the audience said, "crying over that effing jerrybag," but others who knew better, for good news as well as bad traveled fast on the Island, said, "No, the Jewess."

Sergeant Silver stood up to help me but I waved him down.

"Thank you Flying Sergeant Silverstein," I said. "That's right, Silverstein, not Silver. We're all in this together. Everyone. I'm setting up a civilian jury. I want volunteers. We'll want one representative from every trade union. Yes, the unions are back, this is no bloody fascist state here, and I want one representative from every church on the Island and not just the minister."

"Spread the word. Select your representatives. Our first meeting will be Monday in the State Building. We'll also need someone from the hospital and . . . and we'll let you know." I finished weakly.

Then I was out of breath, worn down, prepared like virtually everyone else in the meeting hall, save those still waiting for the return of their loved ones, to go home to wife and child.

Chapter 17. Sending for the Rabbi

The following day was a day for decisions. The first was an easy one to make. Though perhaps a surprising one given that the Rebecca that I saw before me was not the one I'd fallen in love with. This one with her clothes off was like a deflated balloon, ribs showing, bags where breasts used to be. Yet her face when she spoke to me or watched me surreptitiously from the corner of her eye as I dressed or undressed or merely sat at the hotel desk fiddling with the endless paperwork was totally animated and alive.

"Will you marry me?" I asked her. "Yes," she shouted.

"And how do you want to get married?" After all, I'd a wedding rehearsal in the nearby Anglican Church already scheduled and a priest on tap. She looked at me incredulously, "By a rabbi."

Getting us to a rabbi or a rabbi to us was not that simple to arrange. I was stuck on the Island for the foreseeable future. Long distance calls were difficult to arrange—never mind that St. Peter's Port was far closer to London than the phone calls I'd made from Camp Borden had traveled to reach my home in Montreal.

Besides, whom could we call? Rebecca knew of no one, nor did I.

Flying Sergeant Silverstein was put to work and in record time had tracked down a distant relative, a Rabbi Frankel whose family had lived in England for more than three hundred years, though his Conservative congregation dated back a mere forty. His synagogue was being rebuilt, Frankel told me; it too had suffered bomb damage in the raids on London.

Yes, he'd be happy to come to Guernsey. How wonderful there'd been a survivor of the Nazi pogrom on the Island and one who'd escaped from Germany as well. The news of the camps and the ovens was already well known among the Jews of England though less well so among the general population, the last including me. "I didn't know," I stammered. And, "No, I did not want to see the photographs."

How was he to get there?

I would get back to him. I'd another telephone call to make first.

"Group Leader, would you be able to come to my wedding?"

"Who are you marrying this time?" Group Leader Raffey had a not-so-rare primitive sense of humor. I explained that this marriage would be performed by a rabbi and would be officially recorded at the Guernsey State House.

"Yes," he said, agreeing to bring the Rabbi with him as well. "I should be happy to attend at least one of your weddings." He just couldn't let the joke go.

The remainder of that day's meetings was equally successful, on balance. In one room, I had myself, Flying Officer Pluffe, Sir Abraham, Canon Robbins, Father Guillard, Justice Tabel, Dr. Wadland, the chief surgeon at the local hospital, Andrew, Andrew's newly-ex-wife, and Estelle Le Tournelle. The latter confessed she felt out of place in such august company. I explained that as far as I was concerned all citizens were equal and only collaborators need be excluded from our midst.

At issue was how we were to restore the island to normalcy. I had reason to believe that the Canadian government would be willing to supply whatever seed farmers required and that I expected a shipment of food shortly. I suggested a program of deficit spending on public works projects was in order. And I also proposed that the Island confiscate the properties of the late German spies.

A surprising lack of unanimity resulted though not quite so bad as in the discussions among the Trotskyites of Paive. Islanders did not accept charity. Deficit spending was not the Island way. And, finally, a way must be found to give the Islanders jobs and put food on the table. On that there was agreement.

Both Andrew and the Canon expressed some concern about the recent appearance on the Island of boats conveying prospective investors. Families were being invited to sell long-held estates. The money wasn't quite enough, but what other choice did they have. I proposed that the State of Guernsey refuse to register all such sales for the moment and this proposal at least was adopted. The question also was raised as to where the other former members of the Governing Council were. On their way to hell, I suggested.

"We'll meet again," I said.

Chapter 18. The Weddings

For the second time that month, a Blenheim trainer landed on the Guernsey airfield. Group Leader Raffey stepped out first, and then helped down the Rabbi who'd brought several wrapped bundles with him as well as a suitcase.

The Rabbi was not what I expected. No ear locks, no skullcap, and no long patriarchal beard though he did have a short, neatly trimmed one. He also wore a business suit and a tie.

"Who built this airfield?" the Group Leader asked, interrupting my thoughts and inserting me into his. He was seeing what Wilson has seen, the launching pad for all those bombing raids on England.

I thought now was a good time to introduce Rebecca who'd come with me to the airport to greet the two of them.

"So this is the girl," the Group Leader said, "That explains everything," and he gave me a wink. "I am truly honored to be your best man."

Rebecca blushed while I stammered that while I would be honored to have him as my best man, we were rather hoping that he might stand in for the bride's father along with Sir Abraham. "She has no living family."

The Rabbi said, "The Nazis?"

She nodded.

"And the Brits," I added, thinking of Mr. Jacobson.

By this time we were walking toward the automobile, four abreast, Rebecca and I between the other two, Rebecca holding my hand.

The Rabbi leaned across, "You are a conservative Jew?"

"Secular," I replied and gave a little wave of my hand.

"Secular?" Group Leader Raffey inquired.

"It's all the rage among modern Jews." the Rabbi answered, " It means you devote nothing of your daily life to either religion or God, but with births, marriages, and deaths, you show up at the synagogue looking for the rabbi."

Raffey laughed, "My brand of Presbyterian is pretty much the same." He turned to Rebecca, "You know the man you are marrying is a hero?"

"He's my hero. I knew that the instant I met him, even when he was mad."

"He had the gift of prophesy?" inquired the Rabbi.

"He told the Island authorities where the German planes and submarines would land."

"And as with all prophets, no one listened." we finished together.

Sir Abraham was waiting for us along with Wilson and the entire Martel family at the small room in the State building we'd be using for our marriage. Wilson was drafted to help the rabbi set up the marriage canopy, Sir Abraham excused himself briefly, and the Martels went off with Rebecca to help her dress, which left the Group Leader and I alone.

"I can see why you are marrying her," he said. "I suspect you made the right choice, though there are a number of English girls who thought you were going to marry them, and the French Government has submitted certain claims regarding women you allegedly married or impregnated there. Do you remember a Marie from Arras?"

I remembered Marie from Arras, as well as Francois from Quillon and Maarieta from Foix on whose behalf the French Government also had submitted requests for payments.

"I was rather hoping you'd settle down with that Canadian girl you met in Switzerland, what was her name, Giselle something. She could definitely be a problem in the future.

"Which reminds me, the Canadian consul in Switzerland is hopping mad that you helped your best man, Flight Lieutenant Wilson, and the other one, Flight Lieutenant Moyle to escape the country, 'thereby jeopardizing German-Swiss as well as Swiss-Canadian relations' was I believe the phrase he used.

"He also said something about an unsolved killing."

"Which he requested."

"Ah. A gun for hire. And here I was worrying all these years about the privations you must have suffered while hiding underground from the Gestapo and the Vichy Authorities."

The bride came back into the room accompanied by her entourage. A more beautiful bride in a more beautiful dress has not existed since the world began. Sir Abraham, Group Leader Raffey, the Martels, and at least a dozen Islanders we'd not expected appeared then to support the bride. While Wilson, Pluffe, Silver, all the remaining airmen, and Robert Le Tournelle came to support me. Even the just-arrived-from-England Robert Jr., stood by quietly, slightly in awe of all the uniforms, as Rebecca and I stepped beneath the canopy and exchanged vows.

I crushed the wine glass and was married then forever.

That same afternoon, we learned the true purpose of the wedding rehearsals in the Anglican Church that had continued even in my absence. Madeline and Wilson stood side by side before the minister. I, the best man, carried the ring.

I don't know which was the bigger surprise, Wilson getting married or Madeline, the girl he married. I suppose for Wilson as for me, the time had come. Edward VIII had married and given up his throne to marry the girl he loved. Why not Wilson, the ersatz Prince of Wales?

Madeline getting married was an entirely different matter. She was like my kid sister, not that I'd had a kid sister. Shouldn't she be dating or going to proms? Living that final piece of her childhood that had been swallowed up by the war? All around me I saw lives that had been destroyed by the German occupation of the island. Yet, somehow she'd come out of it more or less the same innocent girl who'd gone in. Mother Marcie, I salute you.

Did Wilson know what a prize he was getting? He knew, I was sure of it. Still, I wondered how he knew. That very first evening we'd had dinner together at the Martels, he'd sat listening to Madeline talk—talk that had seemed mere babbling to me, and known immediately that she was the sort of girl you married and took home to your family. Just as I had known that Rebecca was the woman I would marry and take home to mine.

The crowd at their wedding was smaller than it had been at mine and Rebecca's that morning; the Martels would never be popular on Guernsey again. Thankfully, we did have Sir Abraham, Group Leader Raffey, and the Rabbi in attendance to make the hall look less barren.

Afterward, Raffey and I had one last conversation before he flew back to England taking the Rabbi with him. "Do you anticipate any problems?" he asked, I knew he meant in regard to Rebecca.

"In Canada?"

"No, not in Canada. You people have pretty much your own society there. I mean here on Guernsey. Because Rebecca is Jewish, will people treat you differently?"

I thought about his question, thought about it for several years in fact. I don't remember what I said to him then, but what I would say to him now is, "Probably not. Hiding Rebecca from the Germans represented one of the truly decent things the Islanders did during the occupation, one of the truly decent things they could be proud of."

Chapter 19. *Comite de salut public*

When the representatives of some fifty organizations and church groups had gathered in the hall that had once hosted the Island's governing council (and would shortly thereafter once again), a number of them asked where Victor, Andrew, John, and some of the other principal wartime authorities were.

"Not invited and you may wish to consider whether they should ever be permitted to hold public office again."

After which I hauled out a black board on which I'd already written some of the issues I'd hoped we'd discuss. It soon became obvious though that a group this large was too unwieldy to discuss anything. At Angelique's suggestion, we decided to break up into smaller groups. Each group would prepare a position paper on a specific topic, which would, in turn, be brought to the larger committee for the authority to move on the issues raised.

This proposal, too, met with some resentment, followed by grumbling over specific assignments. But I persevered, arranged for swaps among truly aggrieved parties, and soon everyone was off to spend the balance of the morning in some group or another.

When enough groups had drifted back, I called a halt to all of them and we voted on the proposals that had been prepared. The first of these, a proposal bound to displease she who-would-have-been my mother-in-law was that the State would buy all Reichmarks on a sliding scale—full value below a certain level and only a reduced percentage thereafter. As the British Government would redeem all Reichmarks at full value, Guernsey would now have some money to begin paying its employees.

Many opposed this proposal—I had the impression there were some who would oppose anything that had not been done before—but the 'ayes' had it. Even then a few die-hards said, well O.K, but that nothing should really be done until the new council was in place.

While I was incredibly ignorant on the subject of economics, I trusted that any solution arrived at by a cross-section of the Islanders would probably be better than a remedy imposed from above and announced to the contrary that the implementation of this proposal would take place immediately. The incoming council, the date of its election still to be determined, could carry on with this proposal or modify it as they chose. "You are in charge," I told the committee.

I'd hoped this would inspire them. Unfortunately, rather than proceed immediately to solve the balance of the Island's problems, the majority of those in attendance then begged off for a dozen or so practical reasons and we adjourned our 'Comite de salut public,' as Sir Abraham had jokingly termed it for a further three days.

These intervening days too were filled with activity. First, the truly sad part, Rebecca and I and our son went down with the remaining Martels to the airport to say goodbye to Wilson and his new wife. A simple navy blue dress with a white collar and a red ribbon tied at the neck showed off Madeline's dark black hair to advantage and made her look more mature, the ideal match for the blue uniformed RAF officer who stood relaxed and smiling next to her. Wilson had recognized her potential from the beginning, seen what none of the rest of us had.

He'd confided to me earlier that he hoped to land a desk job in London and forgo going on active service in the Far East. "I want children," he said, "Sounds weird?"

Something had changed him, maybe the realization that he would have a wife and child who depended on him. Admittedly, the desperate urgency that had possessed us while the battle raged over the control of Europe was gone. Their plane took off, Wilson at the controls, became a tiny speck in the sky and the Freygoods and the Martels went off to their separate dwellings.

Next, each of the Germans who had asked to remain on the Island was given an individual public hearing. These went well for the most part. A sponsor, normally the German soldier's fiancée, would be on hand, and not once did we hear a counter complaint that so and so had been guilty of brutality. Angelique's pilot was granted permission to stay. The people of Guernsey may have hated Angelique for being with him, but they had nothing against the man himself.

Her mother wasn't quite so charitable. The greater the distance between Angelique's German and herself, the better for the grocery. Fortunately, I could give the newly-weds my hotel room to tide them over till they found their own place as Rebecca and my family had already taken up residence over the jewelry store.

The one problem that did arise concerned a young girl not yet of age whose mother refused to allow the marriage to proceed. This would not have been a problem, had not a second girl, also a minor in legal terms, spoken up from the audience to say that if that were the case, she'd like to marry him. When the mother of girl number one learned that Chantelle Brisson, the mother of girl number two was willing to give her approval, she quickly reversed course. No Brisson was going to get the best of her.

The young enlisted man in question would have gone free to roam the streets of Guernsey that very day had he not hesitated visibly in choosing between the two young women. Off he went to the POW camp to both girls' shouts of frustration and both mothers' relief.

Eighteen marriages were recorded in the State records the next day.

When we reconvened the Committee, several individuals simply didn't bother to show up. Their loss. The reduced committee was able to reach some quick decisions, though, again, it proved necessary to remind everyone that we weren't looking into individual cases but developing guidelines.

As far as informers for money went, we had Bosch's records in hand to help determine the level of guilt. The committee determined to publish the names of those who had been spur-of-the-moment one-time informers, and to provide prison terms for multiple offenders. Thus, someone might, in a single jealous impulse, have sent someone else off to death in a concentration camp yet evade punishment themselves, while another individual who'd made a steady living by seeing his neighbors punished for minor offenses would be sent off to jail for nine months.

Once again, I was glad I'd deferred these punishments to a citizen's committee. Justice is an elusive concept. Though I longed to deal out harsher sentences to those who'd betrayed their Jewish neighbors, I let the committee's decisions stand.

As far as looters went, we established a grace period in which articles might be returned, no questions asked, either to the neighbors from which they'd been stolen or to the police station.

It was then I discovered the true scope of the problem.

Rebecca had already confided that over half of the stock of Jacob's jewelry had disappeared, the remainder having been rescued and held for her by the Martel's. A great many pieces had been among the possessions of the late SS Col. Reinhardt; these were soon recovered from the household of the late von Schneeds. More were turned in during the grace period but still there were many pieces perhaps purchased by German soldiers with the now worthless Reichmarks that were gone forever.

Some vacant homes had been literally ripped apart and their doors and furniture used for firewood. Could someone be punished for wanting to stay warm and alive? The decision was made to rebuild these houses at State expense.

But our biggest problem as I soon learned both from Andrew and from Dr. Bosch's records was that several members of the Guernsey police force had been among those arrested for looting. They had stolen from German stores—fine, good for them. But they also had stolen from the island shops.

Pluffe, Silverstein, and I chose to conduct a separate interrogation of the policemen involved, Inspector Gaudien among them. They'd already served brief prison terms while the Germans were in power, but we decided that, regardless, those who had stolen food from the shops could no longer serve as members of the police force.

The numbers of the guilty were growing. The numbers of those without sin eligible to sit in judgment on the remainder were becoming smaller.

Chapter 20. Carpet Baggers

During the month of September 1945, and continuing to a greater extent a trend begun in August, the Isle of Guernsey began to be visited by large sailing yachts that could hold four to six people comfortably, yet be sailed by only one. Their owners and crew would anchor in the harbor as they had before the war, and spend a day or more wandering about the town and the Island.

The word came back that these new arrivals were eager to buy land and houses and had the pounds in hand to pay for them. Of course, all contracts had to be filed with the State and the appropriate transfer fees paid.

"But if Islanders sell their land and their house, where will they live?" No real answer existed to this question, for I knew that what must seem like a lot of money to any Islander at that instant would soon prove inadequate if they tried to buy similar lodgings and agricultural land in England.

"Do you want to move to Canada?" I'd ask them, for land was cheaper there, but I got only blank looks in reply.

Quite a backlog of documents had accumulated at the State House when I, Marcie really, had the happy idea that the State ought charge a hefty fee to the prospective purchaser. I suspected they'd probably pay it, but that didn't solve the real problem. Where would an Islander who sold his birthright for a mess of pottage be able to go?

"What if we charge a fee equal to the sale price to investigate the character of the prospective purchaser?"

The committee quickly approved such a fee though not without some scattered objections.

"What if I want to sell land to my brother, or buy it from him?"

"You and your brother are citizen of Guernsey. We don't need to investigate either one of you."

Holding up these sales proved to be a good idea for both seller and purchaser. Almost at once it became obvious that those who were most eager to sell their land were those who didn't actually own it. Perhaps it did belong to their family once but the deed had never actually been transferred from father to son or from a war casualty to his living relatives. Nor was it obvious that the true heir was son A rather than son B or son-in-law C.

Of course, we held off on notifying the prospective purchaser of such entanglements, and the consequent lawsuits that would surely go on for ages. They'd only have tried to buy another piece of land in the interim.

Many of the men who came ashore, like the carpetbaggers after the American Civil War, were there to buy up as much of the land as they could at bargain prices. We began to pass zoning laws restricting the sale of farmable land.

"You can't do that," Charlie the Weasel told us. Charlie—who knows today what his real name was, was a member of the Committee and, alas, an unshakeable one as he was one of those joiners who knows everyone's name and is always ready to buy them a drink. He was of English, rather than French descent, as could be easily seen when he smiled and his fangs and gums, both in desperate need of repair, became visible.

The Weasel, I knew, was in the pay of another Charlie, Charlie the Agent, one of the first yachtsmen to arrive on the Island. We called him Charlie the Agent because we were pretty sure he wasn't spending his own money. We thought he might represent a consortium of rich Englishmen but we weren't completely sure of that either. He had a British passport but he spoke with a German Swiss accent. Yes, he'd been born near Zurich. So, for all we knew he represented a set of rich Nazis on the run with the wealth they'd stolen before and during the war.

Charlie the Agent was smart and I'd never pretend to be smarter. But I knew something he didn't know I knew and certainly something Charlie the Weasel didn't know at all. Charlie the Agent had more than one source of inside information. And one of those sources was Marcie. "Accept all the bribes you can," I'd encouraged her, "Just let me know what they're bribing you to do."

We soon discovered that what Charlie was after was view property, like the rocky hillside that I'd climbed long ago to get my first view of the St. Peter Port Harbor. He was buying up the house and barn as well just because the owners expected to sell their land that way.

So we passed another ordinance forbidding the sale of farmland but permitting the sale of those portions "which are unsuitable for agriculture except for grazing."

The first day the change was brought up for discussion, the Weasel fought it tooth and nail. But that evening, I told Marcie about his opposition, and she told the Agent who laid into the Weasel who said the next day at the meeting that he'd thought it over and it really was a good idea.

Chapter 21. The Corvette Arrives

A high point of the Beggar's Opera, at least in the version due to Bertolt Brecht and Kurt Weil, is the song of Jenny the Chambermaid. Her dream is that someday an immense pirate ship will sail into the harbor with ten large sails and fifty cannon. The pirates will swarm all over the harbor and up through the town rounding up the citizenry and bringing them to the public square for judgment. And who is the judge to be? Pirate Jenny, once a lowly barmaid.

The news Silverstein brought to my hotel room was of the arrival of the corvette HMCS Lachute. Like all corvettes, it was small, 208 feet long, with a single smokestack and, apart from a 4-inch gun, carrying not much more armament than a Hurricane. Still it looked awfully impressive to me, especially with the big Canadian flag flying from its mast.

"What's it mean?" Rebecca asked, and Phillip looked up at me inquiringly. "We may be going home." But not quite yet.

Not very many Islanders had come down to the pier, which was a pity as in addition to its regular crew, the corvette bore a shipment of children, the children of Guernsey returned to their parents. Some were immaculately dressed, though in shirts and pants perhaps a size or two too small. Some wore hand me downs in want of darning, or clothes a size too large intended for someone much older.

Not all had returned of course. Some had refused; the ones who'd been very young when they were evacuated to England did not want to leave their foster families, Emily Le Tournelle among them. Some were still lost in the bureaucratic muddle and it would years if ever before they were reunited with their families. And some had died, casualties of war, though these were few. A similar percentage whose families had gone with them to England had perished together in German air raids.

The kids milled about on the Quay while we waited for their families to be notified and make their painful way from the Island's far reaches. Among the latter were Emily Le Tournelle parents, a much quieter and more mature Robert Jr. by their side. I could only offer them my sympathy and tell them to keep writing to Emily until she came.

For once the hapless Andrew was of some use as he did a great deal toward uniting children and parents, seemingly having an inventory of the entire Island's population in his head.

After the children left the ship, came a company of Canadian soldiers led by none other than Captain Howard Finestone. Finestone, whom I called 'Finestone' rather than 'Howie' or 'Rutabaga,' just as he called me 'Freygood,' rather than 'Pete' or 'Pumkin,' and I had ridden the trolley together to school for three years. He'd been a grade behind me but had entered the service just out of high school.

He'd started life as a mere private, so his captaincy testified both to his abilities and to the latent anti-Semitism in the service that had kept him from major's rank.

As the first order of business he handed me two envelopes, one for me and one for Flying Officer Pluffe. The one to me was addressed to Squadron Leader Good, which was a message in itself. Both were sealed, so I guess I would have to wait for Pluffe to tell me what his said.

Mine directed me to arrange as quickly as feasible for the election of a Guernsey State Council, if possible before the 31st of October, less than a month away. As of that date I was to return with my family via the Corvette HMCS Lachute to Halifax, and then by train to Montreal and Chateauguay to await further orders.

Pluffe had come down to the wharf by that time, but before opening his instructions he drew me aside for a private conversation. "I want to apologize," he began.

"Apology accepted."

"No, you do not understand. When we first arrived on the Island and you started ordering people about, much of what you did made no sense to me. But the more I learned about these people, the more right your actions seem.

"I met this girl, this woman, Denise Le Tissier. We speak French, her and me, though sometimes we need the English to be understood. She seems a nice girl; then I find she sleeps with the Boche. This I cannot forgive."

"And if there was no war and she had slept with a Guernsey farmer?" For city boys like Pluffe and I, "farmer" had been an insult to describe an uncouth person. No longer an insult for me, of course; I knew the vast knowledge, the endurance farming took.

He grunted by way of reply and ripped open his orders. He was to proceed immediately by plane with all the remaining airmen, first to Shannon, then to Rejecovick, Gander, Goosebay, and Trois-Rivieres.

Pluffe's face held a mixture of emotions. He wanted to go home. He wanted to see this Guernsey girl again. He was also disappointed. He would be discharged with the rank of Flying Officer not Flight Lieutenant as he had hoped.

The same orders noted that Silverstein would retire with the rank of Master Aircrew and insignia were provided; apparently this was to be Silverstein's reward for putting up with me. His promotion called for a round of whiskey at Silverstein's expense had there been any drinkable on the Island. Smiles returned when Captain Finestone revealed there could be definite advantages to the other branches of the service, producing a bottle of the finest Seagram's had on offer.

Unfortunately, both Pluffe and Silverstein were obliged to abstain beyond a mere taste. They'd a bomber to navigate and pilot home. Which left Howard and I to return to my office to finish the bottle.

My orders had called for him and the Army Company he commanded to report to me. "For a month," he said, "And then my orders are to put you on board that ship whether or not you want to go."

"They're not happy?"

"Not a bit. The Brits will come in after you've left and everyone can live on memories of what a rotten guy you were."

"I'll drink to that," I said, and we did.

Chapter 22. The First Elections

The preparations for those first elections gave me an excuse to take Phillip and Rebecca along with me in the jeep the corvette had brought and tour the Island.

Howard Finestone and his company were left behind in St. Peter Port to do the dirty work, calling on accused as well as previously-convicted looters to search their houses for still missing items, particularly jewelry taken from Jacobson's store. The searches were usually straightforward and limited to bureau drawers and jewelry boxes; no ripping up floor boards or tapping on walls for hidden panels, though a few well-to-do individuals were asked to open their safes. Despite this, cries of "Nazis," were common, Finestone told me, particularly if stolen items were found and the culprits, sometimes both man and wife were hauled off to jail. But the cries weren't aimed at me; from now on I was Squadron Leader Nice Guy.

From the heights above Roquaine Bay one could occasionally see transatlantic steamers making their way between Halifax and Plymouth or Plymouth and the Mediterranean. One could sometimes see planes also, our planes, and I would point them out to young Phillip, though the mere sound of their engines made Rebecca shudder.

Down on the coast, Phillip and I would run out across the rocks uncovered by the tides, gulls, sandpipers, and godwits our companions in the hunt, and pry abalone that the Brits call "ormers" loose from the rock, at least until we realized that Rebecca had no intention of cooking them.

I love crab, lobster, and shrimp, as well as abalone all of which were plentiful on the island now that the fishing boats were allowed to go out again, but none of which Rebecca would touch. Shellfish are on the prohibited list for Jews as far as she is concerned. We ate a lot of fish though, usually whatever was most recommended from the day's catch.

I fought and lost the battle to get her to prepare conger eel soup, but she prepared and we ate the cabbage soup, carrot pudding, and parsnip pottage that she prepares to this day, I mean until she died.

The sparrow pie which she and many other Islanders ate throughout the occupation, I found a bit off-putting. I tried it once though and once, at Rebecca's request, I helped to strip the feathers from a snared sparrow, but the result hardly seemed to warrant the effort.

Rebecca would often refuse to sit down at table until both Phillip and I had been offered second helpings, a practice I soon put a stop to. "The war is over. We need not worry ever again about where our next meal will come from." Whereupon, she would nod her head, eat a few bites, then wrap the rest of the food up carefully to be eaten the next day.

Regardless, she began to put on weight again. The roses returned to her cheeks, the flesh to her breast and buttocks. Once, I even saw her halt before a mirror content with what she saw there. When we had tea with the Martels one afternoon, she wore a blue dress she'd made with fabric newly arrived in the Guernsey stores, and I saw again that while Angelique and Marcie were both attractive, Marcie strikingly so, Rebecca was beautiful.

Our Island rambles continued. We visited places Mad Harry had failed to map, places that offered lovers comfort, rather than spots to land marines or drop brigades of paratroops.

Once, though Rebecca held my hand the entire time and fussed when Phillip ran ahead, we made our way out along the ancient stone causeway that linked the island of

Lihou and the L'Eree headland to visit the ruins of an ancient priory. Nothing to see really, just incomplete portions of weathered stonewalls that hinted at where buildings once stood. Our timing wasn't perfect, and we stepped in the occasional pool of water on our return, pausing on the headland to watch the entire causeway vanish beneath the waters of the returning tide.

On the plus side, Rebecca's shoes were ruined and I was finally able to persuade her to let me buy her a new pair. She hadn't fully accepted that the occupation was over, that she could have new shoes and a new dress and eat three meals each day without fearing for a knock on the door.

What I liked best about these trips was the chance to drop in on some farmer that I might or might not have met before, shake hands with him and his family and talk about the crop prospects for the year to come. My days as a farmer in the Languedoc would always be part of me.

I did know something about raising tomatoes and suggested they might consider putting in peppers and eggplants as well, though there was some skepticism about the latter. I knew pigs and they knew pigs, but the mere mention of goats seemed to make them nervous.

Amazingly, quite a few cows in prime condition could still be found on the Island, often in better health than their owners. Requisitioned by the Germans for food, somehow they'd successfully been hidden away or passed on from farm to farm a step ahead of the requisitioning trucks, informers for once intimidated, the life of a Guernsey cow being placed several rungs above that of a Jew.

We could always count on a cup of tea and a slice of apple pie or bread with apple butter from the farmer's wife before we left. And the farmer and I would usually have shared a cup of cider before we returned to the house.

An unwelcome vision on these trips was Charlie the Agent and others like him. A lot of money was being spent on this election and not on billboards and radio ads, the Canadian way. Of course, I'd a company of soldiers I could display if threats and coercion were ever used in place of greed as a motivating factor.

The election was boiling down pretty much to a contest between the wealthy representatives of the few wealthy families on the island (the good old boys) and my peoples' candidates. Women were running for office for the first time, Andrew's ex-wife at the head of the pack though they'd had the vote for years. I'd have thought these women's chances good, except too many farm wives looked over to their newly returned husbands before expressing an opinion.

If I'd known then what I know today, I'd have told my candidates to go driving through their parishes shaking hands and kissing babies. Even if I had, the problem was that most of my candidates like Estelle Le Tournelle already felt guilty about the time they were spending away from home and farm, Estelle especially, as she was obliged to write almost daily to her still absent younger daughter. The latter, barely out of toddler's clothes when she'd been sent away, identified so strongly with England and her adopted family that it would take another year before she would return home 'just for a visit'.

Anyway, what I knew how to do was to fly a plane and lead a squadron shooting at other planes while avoiding being shot at ourselves. Politics that called for more than a simple order to "move that plane" or "form two lines" were beyond me.

Chapter 23. Potter's Field

When Ruthie, our youngest daughter, was no more than two or three, a frog joined her one morning in our back yard wading pool. I was outside watching her bathe, wondering how she and the newcomer would get along, when Rebecca came out of the house. No sooner did she spy the two of them bathing together, then she screamed, scaring the child, though fortunately without imparting Ruthie with a lifelong fear of amphibians.

I'm glad it was I and not Rebecca who was with Phillip when we came upon a "nice doggie" toying with a bone on one of our wanderings near the north shore of Guernsey. The tibia, half in and half out of the ground, was clearly human. I brought Phillip back to his mother—the dog had barred his teeth at Phillip and though my son assured me he was not scared, thankfully, he was willing to leave. After which a closer inspection of the area revealed parts of several bodies in a mass grave, partly earth, partly concrete close to one of the Germans' observation towers.

When I brought up the subject with Andrew later, he said that the towers were really like icebergs, only a small part on the surface with the balance consisting of sleeping quarters for the men and storage for ammunition well under ground.

I told him I wasn't interested in the damn towers, I wanted to know who was buried there. Andrew looked embarrassed—he was always looking embarrassed, and said that the Germans had brought in laborers from outside the Islands to help them build the towers and gun emplacements.

"What do you mean, 'from outside the Island?'"

The workers had come from the various countries the Germans had invaded, civilian prisoners mainly from Eastern Europe that they turned into slaves. "They didn't speak English," Andrew hastened to explain as if somehow this made a difference. "They weren't well treated."

I could see that. If I'd had the power, I would have brought back the Germans I'd sent off so blithely to the POW camps from which they'd eventually be sent home unpunished, and sent the ones responsible for beating and starving the slave laborers to be tried as War criminals instead. But, I didn't have the power, of course. What I could and did do was send a message to London, telling what I'd found and suggesting they send someone out to do a more thorough investigation. For every generation must remind the next that we were once slaves in Egypt.

Looking back, I wonder what finally made the difference, what led to my abrupt removal from the Island? It wasn't the fuss I made about the slave laborers; I hadn't complained about them when the order to depart came through.

Was it my shooting the German agents including a well-liked party host and his wife? Or my pestering London for news of the missing children? Or my trying to change the status quo on Guernsey, treating all men equally rather than favoring the well to do?

As Mr. Jacobson had predicted, Churchill suffered a humiliating defeat in Britain's first post-war election and Labor was now in power there. Was England's old guard determined that Guernsey would remain unchanged? How I wished Wilson had remained close by to advise me.

Chapter 24. We Depart

It rained the day we left the island. Now that I think about it, it had been raining on and off since I returned to Guernsey. The difference was that until mid-October the rain had dropped from scattered clouds, sometimes lightly, sometimes intense, but always moving on to rain somewhere else across the Channel or in France. Now the rain clouds filled the sky to the northwest, bank after bank, and one knew that when the first storm clouds had drifted by, there would soon be another set to take their place.

Each storm was followed by an influx of birds, swept up from the mainland and driven to land on Guernsey. Hundreds of song thrushes, blackbirds and redwings, to say nothing of ring ouzels, finches and winter buntings.

I overheard one of the ship's officers reassuring Rebecca that morning. We'd be out of the rain by the end of the day, he said. He pointed first northwest to where the clouds were and then west by south in the direction of our passage. Phillip, running back and forth along the deck, threatening at any moment to fall overboard, could not have cared less whether it rained or not. A war ship offered endless possibilities for play. (A month later, he would be both captivated and repulsed by his first encounter with snow.)

The elections on Guernsey had not gone at all as I'd hoped. The tally had been the very opposite of England's own post-war experience. Angelique was soundly defeated. Her many contributions to the rebuilding of the Island's economy eclipsed by her unforgivable marriage to a German aviator. The former Mrs. Ambrose, not yet Mrs. Bosch, received a similar dismissal. Even Estelle Le Tournelle whom I'd thought extremely popular was defeated. No women were to be elected to the State Council that year.

Elsewhere on the Island, virtually all the people's candidates, as I termed them, went down to defeat. The final composition of the Island's governing council (the States of Deliberation) was virtually the same as it had been before the war. Oh, a man might have been replaced by his brother or his son, particularly if I'd refused the former permission to run, but if family names were a measure, the council's composition had remained unchanged. It was if the Islanders were saying in no uncertain terms we want things to be just the same as they were before the Germans came; let us forget all the nonsense that went on between then and now.

I ought not to have been surprised when the corvette HMCS Lachute pulled out of the harbor that morning bearing me and Rebecca and our child to see, as I did, the regular packet boat from England resuming its daily voyages.

One minor change, I suppose; Jews no longer resided on Guernsey. The last ones departed along with me. "I don't want to go back," Rebecca said, and I think she meant go back to all of it, to Europe, to all we'd experienced in space and time. She held my hand as tightly as Phillip held hers, but one day, I knew, Phillip would let go.

Most of the contents of Jacobson's Jewelry, later to become Jacob and Son on St. Catherine Street in Montreal, went with us as well. The Martels had turned over all they'd sequestered and what had not been returned to us piece by piece during the amnesty, Finestone's troops uncovered during their raids. In so far as possible, the rich and the poor on Guernsey would resume the roles they'd had before the war. And a woman's place would be in the home—nurses and spinster schoolteachers excepted, of course.

Afterward

When I started to type up my father's reminiscences, I wrote them down more or less as he dictated them, excluding the frequent pauses while he would try to remember a name or a location. Even then, I'd say, "Oh just give the person any old name, Dad," which would work for awhile, but then, when we were on some completely different topic, he would suddenly remember what the person's real name had been or what clothes they'd actually been wearing and nothing would do but that I should go back and make the correction.

Apart from those occasional lapses, his recollections followed in more or less chronological order, much as I've set them down here. The stories of his flight school training seemed pretty realistic to me and along with the descriptions of his first sexual experiences were very much along the lines of what I thought I would have or had, in fact, experienced.

With the second part of the first book and his descriptions of air combat I began to have my doubts. Could one man really have had all those adventures or was he combining the reminiscences of a half dozen cronies no longer alive to holler plagiarism?

Still, if one kept track of the days he was in combat and the number of combat missions he went on each day particularly during the virtually non-stop action of the Battle of Britain and the Evacuation from Dunkirk, then his stories did seem plausible.

But what about all the alley catting he claimed to have done back in the pre-birth-control pill days when women were ultra careful with their bodies. How many brothers and sisters did I actually have?

"I was told," he said, "that the French authorities did submit claims to the RCAF." And what about the British authorities? Given all the English girls he'd claimed to have had sex with, surely at least one of those encounters must have given rise to a sibling of mine.

"You could ask the RCAF," he said. I did ask, asked the Canadian Uniform Armed Services command, anyway, but by the time they wrote back that I'd need my father's approval to supply the information, my father was dead.

I did locate one sibling though, yet another sister, right here in Montreal, Giselle's first born. And maybe her third, too, because I found out from my half-sister, though not from Dad, that he'd been seeing Giselle from time to time all the while he was married to my mother and Giselle was married to . . . , well, whoever she was married to.

One fact, I'm sure of: I was born in the Channel Islands during the German occupation. And now I come to the real weakness in his accounts. It's in the final book when my Dad returns to the Isle of Guernsey. It's all lies.

My Dad was never the military governor of Guernsey. The British kept all Commonwealth personnel clear of the Channel Isles for fear they'd report back how bad things had been for the Islanders after the British chose to neglect them for strategic reasons till a year after D-Day.

Victor Carey, Guernsey's wartime Bailiff wasn't barred from ever participating in their government again—he was knighted! Knighted by the British for his collaboration with the enemy during wartime.

The man Dad says was a spy—he wasn't shot, he continued to serve on the Island's governing council for many years. None of the men and women who turned informer for financial gain, and there were over a hundred of them on Guernsey alone, ever went to prison. The Jew an Islander sent to a concentration camp would die, while the Islander and his or her family would get an extra meal or two and could spend the rest of their life satisfied that they'd complied with the wartime Guernsey Governing Council's order to cooperate with the Germans.

When I confronted my father with the truth—this was just two weeks before he died, he said that Commonwealth military personnel might have been officially banned from Guernsey, but that hadn't kept him from hitching a lift there in a Blenheim trainer with the newly-returned Wilson.

"But why did you lie about the rest of what happened on the Island after the war?"

"Because for four years, the woman I've loved for virtually all my life was left at the mercy of those sons-of-bitches on Guernsey and there was/is absolutely nothing I could/can do about it. During those four years, I went where the Service told me to go and I did what they told me to do, powerless to change things.

"Two of those years, I spent in France embedded in the civilian population waiting for an assignment, waking each night to hear the sound of a floor board creaking or a dog barking, wondering are they coming for me, killing from time to time not out of a sense of power but of helplessness.

"And afterward, they just wanted me, another damned foreigner from a former British colony, married now to a Jewess, to go home and get out of their way."

And he cried.

For more fine books like the one you've just read, go to http://zanybooks.com

www.ingramcontent.com/pod-product-compliance
Lightning Source LLC
Chambersburg PA
CBHW080901020726
47502CB00008B/2305